PLEASE NOTE

This is a work of fiction. All incidents and dialogue, and all characters with the exception of some well-known figures, are products of the author's imagination and are not to be construed as real. Where real-life persons appear, the situations, incidents, and dialogues concerning those persons are entirely fictional and are not intended to depict actual events or to change the entirely fictitious nature of the work. In all other respects, any resemblance to persons living or dead is purely coincidental.

MURDER *of an* HONOURABLE MAN

A crime thriller

PETER REDFORD

Murder of an Honourable Man
Published by The Conrad Press Ltd. in the United Kingdom 2025

Tel: +44(0)1227 472 874
www.theconradpress.com
info@theconradpress.com

ISBN 978-1-917673-22-8

Typesetting and Cover Design by: James Sadlier, jamessadlier@me.com
The Conrad Press logo was designed by Maria Priestley.

Printed and bound in Great Britain by Clays Ltd, Elcograf S.p.A

*Three can keep
a secret, if two of
them are dead.*

BENJAMIN FRANKLIN

CHAPTER
ONE

Brendan Slack was an honest man. That was why he had to be killed.

He had declined a hefty bribe. Although the word 'bribe' hadn't actually been used, that's what it had been. An attempt at blackmail had failed miserably. They had quickly realised he didn't care who knew he was gay.

They knew that even Brendan in his naivety would spot a blatant threat. If he reported it to the police and they investigated, well, that would be disastrous. They would be likely to uncover a multitude of illegal activities and that could not be permitted to happen.

It had left them with no other choice. There was no alternative that any of them could see. But they had to decide, and quickly, who was going to do it.

None had actually baulked at the idea. During their lives they had all arranged at one time or another to have people killed. Each knew someone who would carry out their bidding for money. Obviously they wouldn't do it themselves. That was the advantage of being rich. Everyone had a price, except of course, Brendan Slack.

His killer had arrived in the UK on Wednesday and booked into the same hotel as Brendan, using a false name and paying a cash deposit. Wendy, the receptionist, could not stop her gaze being consistently drawn to the nasty scar adorning the American's right cheek. Just as he wanted.

That night he ate in the hotel's dining room at the same time as Brendan. The waiter couldn't help noticing the small round clump of white hair in the otherwise black mop of the American. When Brendan left to return to his room, he was oblivious to the man following him and watching which room he entered.

The next morning as Brendan told the cabbie his destination, the rather plump American man using the name Mike was standing right next to him polishing his tortoiseshell spectacles. Mike was about five feet eight inches tall and wearing a brown tweed suit and a woollen dark blue tie. Mike heard Brendan say, 'Parham House please.' Mike had never heard of the place nor knew where it was but wasn't concerned. He knew Brendan would be away all day, and that was what mattered. As the taxi left and drove up the hill and out of Arundel, Mike put his glasses on and went back inside the hotel.

He was a professional and wanted to know everything about his target. Collecting his tiny electric picklock which, to the untrained eye, looked like the base of an electric toothbrush, he went to Brendan's room. Selecting a small thin metal tool from within its base, he slipped it into the holder on the top and pressed an unobtrusive button.

Then he slowly pushed the metal tool into the room's old fashioned door locking mechanism. Within thirty seconds he was inside the room. Nothing as modern as a key card entry system in a hotel renowned for its old-fashioned charm and character.

His search was swift and he quickly found a typewritten itinerary that confirmed Brendan was expected at Arundel

Castle on the Friday; the time he was expected and who he had to ask for. No need to write it down. Mike had an exceptional memory for details. It had often saved his life in the past.

Then he found Brendan's cheap, archaic, blue and silver Nokia mobile phone next to his journal on the desk. Why hadn't he taken it with him? Unusual to say the least. Why have a mobile if one isn't going to carry it? Mike put the thought out of his head. He absently turned it on and was mildly surprised when it burst into life without needing a password.

There were no numbers recorded in the phone's address book and the email function hadn't been set up. No texts were noted or documented. The phone's log showed a couple of dozen calls made to just a few different numbers.

Nothing outwardly exceptional. Mike opened up an app from his own phone and tapped in the numbers from Brendan's phone. There was a few seconds' delay. Then the destinations were all displayed alongside the relevant phone number.

One number for the National Gallery, one for the Victoria and Albert Museum, two different numbers for the British Museum, one number for an Oxford University college, one number for a Dr O'Donnell and numbers for two different London male escort agencies. Mike smiled at the last numbers and then did something very uncharacteristic of him: he accidentally cleared the numbers from his app.

Cursing himself, he glanced at the Rolex on his left wrist. He decided that he didn't need to put the numbers back on but reflected that he could simply take the phone the following day once he'd dealt with Brendan.

He turned the little Nokia phone off and put it back exactly in the same place as he had found it. He skimmed through the last couple of pages of Brendan's journal and knew he would have to take that as well.

Leaving the room, he walked out of the hotel and then the 200 yards or so to the visitors' entrance in Mill Road to the grounds of Arundel Castle. He paid cash and walked up the long winding drive and over the drawbridge to the pedestrians' entrance of the castle itself.

Sally, an Australian voluntary worker, was stationed at the door. She had given him a quick resumé about what was considered of interest and where it could be found within the castle.

Mike listened politely before casually asking her, 'Are there any Holbeins in the castle?' She didn't know for sure and checked a small booklet before directing him to a corridor on the first floor, not far from the restaurant.

Mike had stood for less than a minute in front of one of Holbein's lesser-known works. As far as he was concerned, it was just an old painting. It was the portrait of some long-forgotten baron. He'd never heard of Holbein and what he was looking at didn't impress him one bit.

He'd moved about in the corridor. He had walked the twenty-five yards to the end of the corridor, where it stopped abruptly. Stone steps led upwards and curled away from sight. The steps were protected by a red and white decorative rope slung loosely between two keenly polished aluminium stands. A notice clipped to the rope's centre rocked gently and indicated, *Private*.

There were numerous pieces of antique furniture set against the walls as well as four suits of armour on plinths. Mike couldn't see any obvious CCTV cameras, which surprised him. He sat on a large wooden chair which had a notice to one side of it saying, 'Please do not touch'. It was only a few feet from the Holbein. He scanned the corridor. There was definitely no camera. He concluded that the castle was so secure that there was no need.

Then he saw something unexpected. Tucked high above the stairs, as they rose and began to twist from sight, was a small motion detector. It was practically invisible as it was the same colour as the stone brickwork and blended in beautifully. Mike considered it. Not as efficient as CCTV and normally used to operate a burglar alarm. Its main benefit is that it doesn't need to be monitored. Perhaps there was no actual human, night-time security at the castle. Interesting.

No one else walked along the corridor whilst he was there. Most visitors headed for the keep and the spectacular views it afforded across miles of open Sussex countryside and distant glimpses of the English Channel. Others visited the stately rooms on show to see how the nobility lived in long past days.

A scatterbrained old lady, wobbling about with the aid of a walking stick much too big for her, exited the restaurant and turned left. She quickly realised she was going the wrong way. Retracing her steps, she muttered and tutted to herself.

Had she continued, she would have found the corridor turned ninety degrees left within ten yards of the restaurant and another ninety degrees to the right after a further eight yards.

Mike knew how he was going to do it.

CHAPTER
TWO

B rendan got back to the hotel just after 5pm. He had a shower and went downstairs to the dining room. The service was efficient and he was back in his room by seven. Plenty of time to write up his journal and make a phone call. He sat at the small desk and after nearly an hour had completed his day's record.

He rarely used his little mobile and didn't bother turning it on for days at a time. It burst into life and he dialled a number from memory. He'd called it five or six times before but didn't know how to save it to the phone's address book. It was easier for him to commit the number to memory than learn how the cheap phone worked.

A woman answered in a whispered voice, 'Hi Brendan. I can't speak too loudly in case they hear. I don't want to frighten them off.'

'I understand. How many of them are there?'

'Looks like just the two and the adults.'

'Do you want me to call tomorrow?'

'Yes. I'll be leaving here tomorrow morning and will be at the loch by nine o'clock. Can you call me after then?'

'All right. Have a good night.'

'Should be good. No one knows where they are at the moment so I think they are safe.'

'Speak to you in the morning, bye,' and they both hung up.

Violet was an environmentalist and determined to save the

planet from the plague of humans that were, according to her, destined to destroy it. She was currently sitting in a hide in a forest in Scotland attempting to protect the two osprey eggs in a nest from illegal collectors she regarded as abominations.

On Friday morning Brendan was enjoying an early breakfast. There was no need for a taxi today. He was in a jovial mood. It was a beautiful, sunny summer's day with blue sky untainted by cloud. He'd been in Arundel for four days and not once set foot in the town itself. Time to change that. He checked the small map that Wendy had given him.

He could have a slow amble around the town browsing the shop windows and a stroll by the river along the tow path to The Black Rabbit pub. Then a walk back along the quiet road past the Arundel Wetland Centre and a coffee in the café next to Swanbourne Lake. He'd still be at the castle by 11am.

Mike missed Brendan at breakfast but wasn't unduly worried. He knew where he was going and what time he was expected. He'd be in position in the corridor in plenty of time to see him arrive. It was a fine day and the American had never been around a British castle, or any other castle for that matter. The volunteer had enthused about the view from the keep and he decided to climb to the top. By the time he got there he was puffing heavily and cursing loudly. His padding was slipping slightly and made the climb harder. The spectacular view quickly captivated him and he spent a long time scouring the landscape.

When Brendan reached the Wetland Centre, he checked his watch. An apt place to phone his long-lost sister. Pulling his mobile phone from a pocket he dialled Violet's number.

'Hi Brendan. How are you?'

'I'm good. You'll never guess where I am calling you from?'

Violet had already come to realise that Brendan was quite naïve and had very few social graces. Most people she knew would have asked how she was. It was something that Brendan didn't always bother with and could cause those that didn't know him to sometimes take offence. She let it slip.

'Tell me, Brendan,' she asked trying not to sound irritated.

'Arundel Wetland Centre. Well, I'm actually outside but it's a place that I think you would like.' Violet laughed but Brendan didn't understand why. Then remembering where she had been all night, 'Did anyone steal the eggs?' Violet laughed again. Brendan was utterly confused.

Chiding him slightly, she sighed as she said, 'Brendan. I've been up all night and I'm going for a shower and then I am going to bed. I'll see you in a couple of weeks in Poblado. Was it something urgent you wanted to say?'

Brendan paused. He was going to tell her a long tale. He decided the full story could wait. Just the salient point.

Violet tried to sound interested, 'You can tell me all about it in a couple of weeks.'

Brendan was happy. 'Yes. I'm looking forward to seeing you again.'

Violet was desperate for sleep. She knew she had to be slightly rude to end the call. 'Me too. We have a lot to talk about. I'll see you soon. Goodnight Brendan.' The connection broke as Violet turned off her phone. She didn't want to be disturbed further.

Brendan hadn't bothered with his journal or the little computer tablet and its carrying bag as he could walk straight back to his hotel room after his visit to the castle and write up his report. He'd left both the journal and tablet sitting on the top of a desk in his room. The bag would have been an unnecessary burden as he walked around Arundel and along the river's tow path. He hadn't even bothered with a jacket as the weather was so nice, so whatever he would need was stuffed into his trouser pockets.

His cheap phone was forced back into an overcrowded pocket as he started walking. Few tourists had got as far as this and Brendan enjoyed the solitude of the walk. The elderly, overweight lady behind the counter at the café at Swanbourne Lake called him 'dear' several times which would have earned her a rebuke if the wrong person heard. Brendan was oblivious and was happy to buy a small packet of seeds from her to feed the ducks and swans.

He walked unhurriedly towards the water's edge and was immediately surrounded by hungry wildfowl. It was as if they all knew he had food. With coffee in one hand and the seed in the other he had no chance. Wings were flapping and feathers were flying. The paper bag was pecked viciously and quickly split, dropping all the contents onto the floor. The birds were all fighting and Brendan was standing right in the middle of them.

A large swan ambled out of the lake towards the commotion at Brendan's feet. The smaller birds grabbed what they could and got out of the way. The swan pecked at some seed and then saw the corner of a white handkerchief slightly proud of a trouser pocket. It snatched the corner in its beak and pulled. The mobile phone was yanked out of the pocket in the folds of the handkerchief and seized upon by a black-headed goose.

The bird turned tail and started to waddle back the few yards towards the water with Brendan's little phone secure in its beak. Brendan tried to run the few steps after the bird and his phone. Startled at being chased, the goose took to the air flying towards an island in the middle of the lake. It couldn't hang onto the phone and fly at the same time. Brendan watched in horror as his phone dropped from the sky into the lake's slightly deeper water.

There was nothing he could do. He knew the phone was gone. The water would probably destroy it before he could recover it. He resigned himself to buying a new one when he was back in London. The birds around him had demolished all the seed and were circling a young girl who had a bag and was screaming in fear. Her parents were convulsed with laughter at her plight and making no effort to rescue her.

Eddie Small, the man running the rowing boats for hire, saw an opportunity to make some quick cash. He'd seen the phone fall and called out to Brendan. 'If you want mate, you can hire a boat and row out there. You never know, you might find it. The lake isn't very deep and you can see the bottom quiet clearly.'

'No thanks. It was only a cheap thing. I don't think it's worth looking for.'

'Suit yourself,' and Eddie went back to tying up his boats and getting ready for the late morning's customers.

Brendan had to get to the castle entrance to meet a housekeeper who was to take him to the corridor accommodating the Holbein. He set off quickly to walk the half mile or so. At the ticket booth he identified himself and was asked to get into an electric buggy. As soon as he was seated, Graham, the driver, whisked him up the winding approach road to the castle's pedestrian entrance. Sally was waiting impatiently. She had unrelated matters on her mind.

'Mr Slack. Please follow me. I'm afraid there's been a problem with some plumbing and the housekeeper is tucked up. I'll take you to where you want to go. If you need anything while you are here the housekeeper is in the restaurant and will be able to assist you.' She paused as Brendan nodded his thanks to Graham.

Then she swiftly rattled on, 'The duke will be back later, he's supervising the preparations at the cricket ground. The Australians are in the country and they always like to play their first game at the castle's own ground. It's an amazing setting and probably the most picturesque cricket pitch in the country. I'm sure you would enjoy the preparations if you wanted to go along to see them later.'

Brendan could not comprehend the intricacies of cricket and had never ever seen a whole game. 'I'm Irish. I don't understand cricket.'

Sally, a proud Australian, looked aghast. 'Oh dear. I'm so sorry.'

Brendan didn't understand whether the volunteer was sorry he didn't appreciate cricket or that he was Irish. He decided not to ask.

Sally swiftly left him once they arrived in the corridor. She had quickly assessed they had nothing in common and saw no reason to hang around. The cricket ground was calling and she wanted to see the team that were due to thrash the English.

Brendan was soon standing before the Holbein. He

wasn't impressed. It was a portrait of a baron according to the blurb on the plaque next to the painting. The first thing that Brendan thought was the man had not paid enough. It looked like he was in a room with little light. It was a lot darker than Holbein's normal portraits and the baron looked decidedly bored.

The painting had not been considered sufficiently important to be displayed in the British Museum or the National Gallery. Therefore it had been stored securely in a crate for decades in the basement of the British Museum before the Duke of Norfolk had somehow got to hear of it. He had immediately asked to have it on loan as the image was of an ancestor. The museum was probably glad that someone wanted it and readily agreed.

The tubby little American with the nasty scar on his cheek was wearing a one-piece white coverall, apparently cleaning a suit of armour about five yards away from Brendan. A canvas bag next to him sat atop an antique, highly polished, wooden side table and contained several screwdrivers and a wrench. He'd already undone the security bolt holding the vicious looking mace attached to the armour and had put it on the floor. Sally, the volunteer who had led Brendan to the corridor, had seen him before but because of his appearance hadn't recognised him and ignored him believing him to be an authorised employee at the castle.

Mike spoke to Brendan in an American drawl, 'Sorry about this but I might be making a bit of noise. I hope you don't mind?'

Brendan was already concentrating on the picture and hardly heard and replied absently, 'No. Not at all.'

Mike was moving about quickly up and down the length of the corridor and Brendan disregarded him. Then he picked up the mace in his latex gloved hands. It was as heavy as it looked. Only about two feet long with a rounded end covered in small metal lumps. He wondered for a few seconds how a knight on horseback could lift and wield it successfully in battle.

Brendan was totally absorbed with the painting. He held his magnifying glass about six inches from it and was leaning forward examining the brush work. Mike lifted the mace and using both hands brought it down heavily on the back of Brendan's head. Brendan's skull was no match for the solidity of the mace. He died instantly.

Mike had dressed accordingly as he had expected a lot of blood, but there was hardly any. The mace had, with a dull thud, splintered Brendan's skull forcing shards of bone into his concave brain. There was a small amount of hair attached to the rounded end of the mace and a little blood upon it. Mike glanced at the mace and then looked down at Brendan who was lying in a heap on the floor below the Holbein. No point in checking, no one would have survived the blow. He was definitely dead.

Quickly giving the end of the mace a wipe with a damp towel stolen from the hotel, Mike reattached it to the suit of armour. He believed the police would take a while to work out how Brendan had died. It would probably allow him a bit more time to get out of the country. He needn't have worried. He would have plenty of time.

A rapid search of Brendan's pockets revealed nothing of interest. Mike slipped off his coveralls and stuffed them into his bag with his latex gloves. Within a further eight minutes he was walking past the restaurant on his way out of the castle back to the hotel.

He went straight to Brendan's room and picked up the tablet and journal. There was no trace of the little phone. He didn't care. He'd already checked it. A small niggle at the back of his mind caused him to wonder where it was. Returning to his own room, he put everything into his case with the few clothes he'd brought with him from the States and then booked out of the hotel. The taxi took him straight to Gatwick and two hours later he was on his way back to New York.

Brendan was on the floor in the corridor under the picture of the baron. He was found at 10pm by Robert Smythe whose job it was to secure the first floor of the castle for the night. The first uniformed police officer on the scene arrived and assessed the body. He called his sergeant who called a doctor who arrived promptly within thirty minutes and pronounced life extinct.

He briefly examined the lifeless body and told the police the back of Brendan's skull had been caved in. The night-duty CID were called. As soon as they saw the body they called out the forensic teams. Photographers arrived to record the details. By 11.45pm, the corridor became a major crime scene and a senior murder team detective was summoned.

CHAPTER
THREE

Mike had already landed in New York and had caught a cab to a café just next to Central Park within walking distance of his penthouse flat. As he sat drinking coffee he removed his heavy framed tortoiseshell glasses. He'd never needed glasses, especially ones that had plain glass in them.

They were destined for the dumpster at the back of the café with his blue coloured contact lenses and coveralls. He'd already dumped his bag of tools in a large wheelie bin at Gatwick. He picked casually at the blatant scar on his cheek with his fingernail. A small patch came away from his face and the scar was no more.

The small white spot to one side of his black hair was there to be remembered by anyone who had seen him in Arundel. As he'd landed in New York, he'd worn a trilby to cover it. He didn't want anyone in America to see it. It would be gone with the rest of his hair dye when he washed it away once he got home. His padding would be broken down and folded neatly before being put away in different drawers.

Mike took no chances. His disguise had exactly matched the photograph in his passport. Within a day he'd have naturally brown hair with slightly greying temples. His false passport would be concealed behind a panel under his sink. There was nothing left that could tie him to the trip or to the murder in the UK.

Except of course Brendan's journal and tablet computer. The customs officer at JFK, New York's premier airport, had seen both but automatically believed them to belong to Mike. He hadn't bothered to ask him about them. Mike would have lied anyway but hadn't needed to. They would soon be winging their way back across the Atlantic, with a recognised courier firm, to a large stately home in the Cotswolds. He hadn't even considered sending them whilst in the UK. The police could easily stumble across them in their enquiries. They'd never think of looking for them in a package from New York.

Everything had gone like clockwork. For just a few days' work he had been richly rewarded.

* * *

The temporary assistant curator answered his phone. He recognised the accented voice immediately.

'You may have already heard about the unfortunate death of Brendan Slack in Arundel. I'm sure you will forget what you discussed?'

The man had seen a brief news report on the late-night television about a murder in Arundel Castle. No name or other details were given. Now he knew who it was. He responded quickly. Too quickly, 'Yes. Yes. You know you can trust me. My lips are sealed.'

'I'll be in touch.'

The temporary curator believed he knew what would happen. A few pounds would be added to his bank account. Then he recollected: there was a little bit of menace in the voice he'd not heard before. Perhaps he'd just imagined it.

* * *

DI Alison Daines was at a birthday party in a large townhouse in Chichester with her boyfriend Simon when she received the call from DCI Groves. It was the excuse she needed to leave early. Being on call meant she couldn't have a good drink. Their friends were all seemingly getting slowly drunk as she remained diligently sober. Her green eyes were on fire. Her thin lips were pursed. It made her blushed cheek bones even more prominent. Her slightly turned up nose was starting to flare slightly with anger. She was a naturally pretty woman and Simon liked her even more when she was angry.

Someone had spilt a drink that nearly hit her new, sombre brown trouser suit. It was only her fast reactions that saved it. Simon had stopped her from assailing the culprit who was one of her closest friends. She was soon on her way to the castle. How Simon was going to get home didn't enter her mind, and she didn't actually care.

Sergeant Murray was having an early night. He'd only just got to sleep when his mobile phone started to dance across his bedside cabinet as it vibrated and started to blast out an innocuous ring tone. He'd thought he was safe. There had been no calls during the day. Now he was being summoned by his boss.

Reluctantly, he dragged his slightly overweight body to his bathroom for a swift wash. He glanced in the mirror above the sink. He hardly had any hair left. Should he shave his head and have done with it? He had assured his wife he'd never have a comb over.

His skin was starting to look a little saggy in places. Generally, he wasn't happy with what he was looking at. Age was surreptitiously creeping up on him and he wasn't impressed with what it was doing to his body. Only forty-six for goodness sake! He should be in his prime. Well, at least his mind was still firing on all cylinders. Looking away from the mirror for a towel, he made yet another promise to himself to try and get back in shape. How many times had he promised that before?

He dressed quickly in blue trousers and multi patterned shirt, and a brown leather flying jacket he'd had for decades. His wife kept reminding him that it looked a little tight. He didn't need her to tell him: he couldn't even do it up anymore. Claiming the zip was broken was his best excuse. Trainers were de rigueur. They were comfy and didn't make a sound which he'd always found extremely useful. He kissed his wife goodbye and ran to his car.

Daines and Murray arrived at the entrance to the castle grounds together. A uniformed officer waved them through and they drove towards the pedestrian entrance to the castle. Already a collection of different police vehicles, unmarked vans and cars were parked in a line. They abandoned their cars at the back of the queue and made their way on foot into the castle. Each carried a small bag containing a white one-piece forensic suit.

At the restaurant's entrance, they stopped and put their suits on and gave their names to a uniform officer who recorded them in an official book. Then they followed a designated path along the dog-legged corridor and saw the body of Brendan still on the floor. Groves called to them and they assembled at a safe area to the side of the Holbein.

Groves mumbled apologetically, 'Sorry about calling you out this late. I needed you both to see the body in situ. We'll set our office up tomorrow morning, but in the meantime, we'll have a quick scrum down in the restaurant. The doctor has said the back of this man's head has been caved in with what he believes was a single blow. The photographer has been and gone and now it's down to the forensic teams. They have nearly finished with the body and then it can go to the mortuary. It looks like it will take them at least a week to check out the whole corridor.'

Alison queried, 'Any idea who he is?'

'Something to do with the British Museum. He was here to examine that painting,' and Groves pointed to the Holbein. 'I think his name is Brendan Slack. We need to confirm that before tomorrow's meeting. The man who found him said he'd been at the castle since 11am. The morning volunteers who would have dealt with him then have all gone home so we'll have to track them down.'

Murray enquired, 'Any idea how long he's been dead?'

'That's the strange thing. The doctor reckoned he'd been dead a while before he was found. He even reasoned as much as ten hours. It'll be down to the pathologist to work that out. It's a bit weird that no one found him beforehand. Anyway, have a quick look round and I'll see you back in the restaurant.' Groves walked away, sticking rigidly between the markers placed by the forensic team.

Alison and Murray stood near the body of Brendan. Murray scanned the corridor as Alison spoke to Alf from the forensic team, whom she knew. 'What do you reckon, Alf?'

'It must have been something bloody heavy to do that much damage. Hardly any blood. He wouldn't have known much about it. Dead in an instant.'

Murray spoke up. 'Something like that?' and he pointed to the nearest suit of armour and the attached mace. The forensic officer gave it a casual glance.

'Yeah, that mace would have the desired effect. We'll obviously check it later. Trouble is, it's secured with a bolt so it's out of the picture as to being a primary object of interest.'

Murray scowled as he looked at the mace. There was a shadow being cast across it by the arc lights Alf and his team had set up. He was sure he could see a small smear in one of the indentations between the protrusions on the rounded end. Definitely not a shadow. 'Is that a smear? What could that be?'

Alf looked at it. Over the years, he'd learnt never to ignore a comment, no matter how stupid or irrelevant. He knew that a little thing could become hugely significant in the detection of a crime. With a bit of effort, he angled one of the powerful lights. He knew straight away. He was still going to confirm it. He called his colleague who had an ultraviolet 'black' light used to detect blood and other bodily fluids. Shining it onto the smear they both looked at each other dumbfounded. Without a doubt, a blood smear. 'Shit! How the hell has blood got up there on that?'

Alf's colleague looked closer. The arc light was aimed straight at the suit of armour. 'Look at that! The bolt. Is that a mark?'

All four focused on the hexagonal-headed heavy metal bolt holding the mace in place. A small scratch was clearly visible on one of its six sides. Murray was the first to speak. 'Hang on a minute. I'm getting confused. That mace is well secured. Could that blood have been on it for centuries? I presume the scratch could have been put on the bolt when it was fixed in place.'

Alf was the one to cautiously reply as if rhetorically. 'When it was put in place, it would have been cleaned and in pristine condition. No blood would have been on it because it would have been deemed a health risk. That is fresh. We'll examine it as a priority and confirm via DNA if it's the victim's. As to the mark on the bolt. Not sure. It's not got any dust on it. I don't believe any cleaner would have been that thorough. We'll be able to confirm either way if it has been turned recently once we can get it to the lab. Should it transpire that the mace was the murder weapon, it beggars the question, why would the murderer undo the bolt, use it, and then reattach it?'

The other three were all considering and pondering his main question. None were making any sense of it. It seemed totally illogical.

Alison spoke addressing all and no one, 'If that mace is the murder weapon, surely the perpetrator would have fled as soon as they had done the deed? They wouldn't hang around and spend time re-attaching it. The longer they are at the scene of the crime, the more chance they'd have of being caught. It just doesn't make sense.'

Murray was sanguine. 'Another problem I see. If our victim was standing roughly where he fell, and that mace was the murder weapon. Let's be honest, we have jumped to the conclusion it was, with very little reason. Our victim would have surely seen the murderer, either undoing the bolt and taking the mace down and then walking behind him or heard him coming up behind him lugging that heavy chunk of iron. Why didn't he run away? The killer would have struggled to keep up with him if he was carrying that mace in his hands.'

Alf had a beaming smile. He had something to prioritise.

'You two have something to start you off by the look of it. That'll keep Groves amused' and he chuckled. 'Meanwhile, I'll cut that bolt off as low down as I can and get it to the lab with the mace. A couple of days maximum and I'll have a result for you. Fresh or old blood: fresh or old scratch.' He walked away laughing and called to a couple of his outer team. 'Anyone remember who was the last person in the country to be killed by a knight's mace?' He chuckled to himself.

Alison and Murray sat at a table with Groves and told him what they had seen and discussed with Alf. He listened in astonishment. Indignantly, he asked, 'Are you two having a laugh?'

Murray didn't joke when death was being discussed, 'Straight up guv'nor. We're genuine.'

Groves stood up. He looked angrier than either had ever seen him before. 'I'll be back in five minutes, don't either of you move,' and he walked quickly out of the restaurant.

Five minutes later, he walked slowly back in and sat down heavily in a chair. 'This is ridiculous. Who undoes a mace from its mounting bolt, murders someone by hitting them over the head with it and then reattaches it?' He put his head in his hands and declared, 'Why me?'

CHAPTER
FOUR

As the police were initiating their work in the corridor, an elderly man was making a phone call.

'I'd like you to keep an eye on this. I don't want it getting out of hand. There's no problem at the moment, but anything could develop.'

'All right.'

'Use whatever resources you think necessary.'

*　*　*

Seven in the morning wasn't that early unless you had been up most of the previous night.

Groves, who was smartly suited and booted ready for the day ahead, strode into the murder team's office in Littlehampton Police Station. He was followed by Murray who was casually dressed in dark chinos, a thin pink short-sleeve shirt and his favourite trainers. Alison, who was last into the room, was wearing a different brown trouser suit to the previous evening and flat shoes. If she had to, she could run in them without hindrance. All three were blurry eyed.

Those seated made a half-hearted effort to rise to their feet knowing Groves would tell them, 'As you were.' He obliged. A youngish, handsome, well-groomed and nattily dressed officer handed Groves a set of photographs, ring-bound within blue card. The front card displayed the Sussex Police logo. In what

Groves considered a rather exuberant tone for the time of day, Jimmy fired, 'Morning guv'nor, Soon as we know the operation name, I'll update the front cover. Meanwhile, have a good shufty at these. Shows a dark corridor at Arundel Castle with the deceased on the deck. Looks really spooky. I'll get more copies run off once we know a bit more.' Jimmy sat back down next to a rather attractive scientist.

Jimmy's suit was hand made in a light grey wool with small blue flecks. A handkerchief was neatly folded and just proud of his top pocket. His shirt was white and his tie was a subdued colour with a slight pattern and very modern. Black shoes were highly polished and gleaming without a scuff mark anywhere. Wherever he went, people noticed him. Jimmy knew and loved it! The female scientist was one.

Groves flicked through the photographs. Because they'd been taken before the mace had come to provenance, it was just visible on a couple of long range shots along the corridor and on one of the photographs showing the suit of armour. Groves handed the album to Murray who passed it onto Alison. Jimmy was already making his play for the scientist he was seated next to.

Groves looked around the office. It was his usual team. He stood up and said, 'Late last night I was called to Arundel Castle where the lifeless body of a man was discovered. The force medical examiner was summoned by our uniform colleagues and he pronounced life extinct. He concluded quite swiftly and obviously that the deceased had met his end having been struck on the back of his head with a large, heavy, blunt object.' Groves paused and looked around the office.

All eyes were focused on him. 'Myself, DI Daines and

Sergeant Murray attended the scene. The forensic team finally finished with the body in situ at about five this morning. It's now at the mortuary awaiting a home office pathologist. The forensic examination of the whole corridor will take at least a week.'

Doreen, the typist, held out a small bottle of water. Groves took it with thanks and swigged half of it in one go.

He continued, 'To be honest, we haven't got a motive as to why this man was killed. All I can tell you at the current time is that his name is Brendan Slack and that he was viewing a painting, a Holbein, on behalf of the British Museum. He had apparently arrived at Arundel Castle at 11am yesterday, by appointment, and had been escorted to the corridor in question. He was found in front of the painting when the castle was being secured for the night at 10pm.'

DC Roland Fownes put his hand in the air and asked, 'Excuse me sir. That's nearly twelve hours. Surely someone would have found him before then?'

Groves concurred. 'That's what we thought Roland. The castle staff that we saw last night say it's not a corridor that's used much.'

Roland pointedly persisted, 'It's got a Holbein in it. One of this country's favourite artists for goodness sake. Surely some visitors might have wanted to see it?'

Groves answered him, 'That was what we asked last night. Apparently they don't publicise it at all well. It's not even shown in the castle guidebook. As you are showing some interest, how do you fancy dealing with the British Museum and finding out from them what this guy was up to?'

'My sort of enquiry sir. Leave that to me.'

'Thanks Roland. Team up with Lynne. Just keep Murray updated.' Then turning to face Jimmy, he said, 'Jimmy. Exhibits are down to you. Happy with that?'

'Certainly sir.' Then with a sly smile and a quick wink at Roland, 'My sort of thing.'

Roland got the joke and chuckled.

Groves continued in a mock chidingly manner, 'Just bear in mind Jimmy that our exhibits room isn't very large.'

Jimmy grinned. 'Point taken sir.' He could recall the first time, just three years previously, when he'd been appointed as an exhibits officer on a major enquiry. He seized so much that they had to use a hired container to store most of the items.

The phone rang and Doreen picked it up. Within a few seconds she hung up and said, 'Mr Groves. Headquarters have just assigned this enquiry an operational name. Stylus.'

Pens scribbled on pads.

Groves nodded his compliance before continuing, 'DS Murray will be our office manager and Doreen our typist. The office will be manned at the moment from 6am every morning until midnight. Morning briefings will be at 8am and evening ones at 5pm unless otherwise advised. Any questions so far?'

Officers were busy writing in their notebooks.

Groves finished the water and casually tossed the empty bottle into a wastepaper bin a few feet away. He was back firing on all cylinders. 'Right. Now I am going to tell you something that DS Murray and DI Daines discovered last night. I am struggling with it so please bear with me.' He started at the beginning when the smear of blood was discovered on the mace and continued on to the apparently newly scratched head of the restraining bolt.

Some of the officers had their mouths open at the end of his narrative. Hands were going up and Groves waved them all back down as he kept speaking. 'I know what you are all probably thinking. What killer would unbolt a mace from its secure restraint, hit someone over the head with it and then reattach it? It makes not a jot of sense. I can't explain it, so please don't ask me to try.'

Jimmy was quicker than most and saw what was needed. 'I'll sort out some more photos that will cover that possibility and liaise with the forensic teams. I'll have an update by this evening.'

Murray said, 'Thanks Jimmy. Keep me informed.'

Groves wound up the meeting. 'At the moment we have very little. Gathering background information will be the order of today. Murray will distribute your individual tasks and we'll reassemble at 5pm. Thank you everyone. Let's get going!'

Murray was besieged by twelve detectives and he was quickly assigning each one a task. Four uniform officers were deputed to attend Arundel Castle and secure a parking area for vehicles and to prevent unauthorised access to the corridor in question. A couple more were tasked with obtaining CCTV from around the town and two others were assigned specific enquiries. A few officers made short phone calls and then slowly drifted out of the office to complete their enquiries. Jimmy and the scientist left together. The first day of their new investigation was all about gathering information.

Groves and Alison were due to meet the Duke of Norfolk in his private quarters at 10am. There was very little they could tell him because they didn't know much. They were hoping he would be able to shed a little light on the matter.

At around eight o'clock, the office door seemed to be flung open rather aggressively, and the chief constable strode in. He was ram rod straight and looked taller than his six feet one. His fitness was unquestionable. His wife could attest to the fact he carried no excess weight. He was wearing full police uniform including a peaked flat cap. The badge upon it bore the Sussex Police name and insignia: a castellated tower surrounded by five martlets.

Those still in the office stood up. He didn't mince words and was well liked by all his officers. 'What on earth has happened Mr Groves? A murder in the castle? How is the duke?'

Groves was quick to reply, 'I am due to meet the duke at ten o'clock this morning sir. If you are free, would you like to attend?' Groves knew what his reply would be.

The chief constable had met the duke on many occasions and was not going to disappoint him by not turning up in person. 'Most certainly. We'll go in my car and you can brief me on the way. The duke must be devastated. Have you assigned a liaison officer to him?'

'Not yet sir. I was going to arrange that once I'd spoken to him.'

The chief constable's reply didn't surprise those that heard, 'No problem. I'll do it. The country's premier duke requires the services of a senior officer. A murder anywhere demands serious police efforts to bring the culprit to justice. I know Mr Groves, that your team are the best in Sussex. A lot will be on your shoulders. The press are already aware of the murder and I think we should keep them updated as best we can.'

Doreen handed him a cup of tea. 'As you like it sir.'

The chief constable looked appreciatively at the matching china cup and saucer before saying, 'Thank you Doreen. Good to see that standards are still maintained.' As he drank the tea, he walked about the office chatting to those still present.

Alison sidled up to Groves and whispered to him, 'I presume I'm not going with you now to the castle?'

Groves considered her question and said quietly to her, 'I'd like you there. I'll check with the chief and let you know.'

Not long before ten o'clock, Groves and the chief constable were seated in the rear of the chief's unmarked Jaguar and DI Daines was in the front passenger seat. The vehicle was parked close to the duke's private quarters. The driver was holding the door open for his boss. He didn't move.

Eventually the chief constable questioned, 'Inspector Daines. Are you sure?'

She nodded 'I can't say for certain that the mace was the murder weapon yet. It was several feet away from the body and according to the forensic team, too far to have been hit by any of the deceased's blood. Also, it was a smear as though it had been wiped with something. At the moment, we're in the hands of the scientists.'

The chief constable pondered everything he'd been told. Then quizzically he enquired, 'I don't understand a murderer spending any more time than they had to at the scene of their crime. Anyone could have walked into the corridor and caught them. The two questions I now have Mr Groves, are, what do we tell the duke and later the press?'

* * *

The woman was dressed as a staff nurse although she'd never worked in a hospital. She'd probably even struggle to put a plaster on a small graze. But that wasn't why she was there. Glancing towards the man in the bed, she cursed him.

Machines surrounded him and made occasional strange noises as their screens kept changing. Wires and tubes wended their way from them into his body. She knew, it was all his fault.

Her hands were rapid. The clothes that he'd been wearing when the stroke had struck had been hung tidily in the wardrobe. Nimbly, she searched all the pockets. She'd looked in the bedside locker. Just his wallet. No phone. Must be at the museum. She had to get it. And soon!

CHAPTER
FIVE

The duke lounged on a settee and considered what he'd been told. He had a large brandy in his hand. It was his second one since the police had left. The first time he'd drunk alcohol before lunch since he could remember. He'd been stunned by what he'd been told. It seemed so implausible. Even the police didn't seem too confident about it. The more he thought about it the more confused he became.

The chief constable had spoken to him after Groves and Alison had left the room. He exuded confidence that the police would quickly solve the mystery. Then the duke remembered whenever they had met before at official functions, he always seemed to exude confidence. Not always founded. What to do?

A thought came to him from the furthest recesses of his mind. Of course! The cricket!

* * *

The woman had discarded her nurse's uniform and was dressed as any normal tourist in her early thirties on a hot sunny day. Jeans, tee-shirt and trainers. Now she carried a guidebook which she kept glancing at. How close could she get without becoming obvious. A cup of tea in the castle's restaurant. Rumours would be rife in there. The police would be taking a break from their duties and chatting amongst themselves. That's where she needed to be.

* * *

In Scotland, a man was sitting in an upright leather swivel chair, with a rare malt whisky in a cut-glass tumbler. He always had a dram before lunch as he spent half an hour relaxing as he studied his collection. Today was different. His thoughts were elsewhere.

He considered what they should do about the temporary curator. They'd paid him handsomely in the past but it didn't ensure his loyalty if pressure was put upon him. Should an unfortunate accident befall him, it might alert the police to their activities. It was a situation that he would monitor closely.

* * *

Jimmy, at twenty-seven, was comparatively young for a detective on a major murder enquiry. He had learnt over the years how a well-tailored suit, modern shirt and tie and always smart leather shoes enhanced his performance as a genuine ladies' man. Always immaculately groomed. Lightly gelled hair cut in the most modern of styles. Clean shaven with smooth skin achieved by nightly moisturising. His tan was direct from the sun and numerous trips to where it was prevalent. He'd achieved a 'six-pack' when he was in his teens and worked hard with his personal trainer to keep in trim. His smile was infectious and his eyes twinkled when he was hunting his next conquest. He rarely failed.

He had gone to the castle to see the crime scene. There was little in the way of exhibits that he needed to seize. Most were already with the scientists. He was satisfied with who had what and when he would take possession of them. Since his first stint on a murder enquiry, when he was unsure of himself and took everything, he was now confident enough to select only relevant items.

Officers had established Brendan's identity and discovered he'd been staying at The Norfolk Arms hotel for a week. Jimmy strolled round from the castle to see how the forensic search of Brendan's room was progressing. It was an upmarket room which was providing the scientists with no useful information.

They had found fingerprints which they concluded were probably those of Brendan as they were all over the room. The cleaner had been questioned and the officers were aware she'd been in the room on Friday morning when she'd cleaned it. They were assuming her prints would also be present. It wouldn't take them long to verify their thoughts.

Jimmy was happy how the exhibits were being handled and dealt with. The photographer had been back to the castle and taken more photographs of the mace in situ and would update his albums. He'd been to The Norfolk Arms and photographed Brendan's room. The scientists and forensic officers were keeping Jimmy briefed as to progress. He'd have a full update for the evening's briefing.

* * *

Metropolitan police officers, in company with two Sussex detectives, briefly searched Brendan's home address in Thurloe Square in Chelsea. There was very little of note that they recorded. In his lounge they found a bookcase containing several shelves with journals in them completed by Brendan over the years. Checking just a few, they saw they were basically about art works Brendan had seen or had been studying and details of seminars or lectures he'd attended or given. They left them where they were. A pair of shoe boxes, one above the other with some papers in were keeping them upright and acting as a book end. The other end was flush with the wall.

The only item they seized as an exhibit was an old address book that was short on entries. It was clear to the searchers that Brendan spent little time there and apparently alone. A Metropolitan police photographer produced a video of the premises and a stills album of each room. Then the premises were secured pending consideration of a full forensic search.

* * *

All the first basic steps were being conducted with ruthless efficiency.

Came the evening meeting, Groves marched purposefully into the room. Progress was being made. He updated his team and then called on Murray for his assessment of the day's enquiries. Then Jimmy was called upon to explain how forensics were progressing. Everyone was positive.

Various officers updated their colleagues as to their own enquiries and questions were asked and answered. Many actions were still to be completed. Groves was scribbling in his murder book and Murray was making notes in his office book.

Officers were making their own notes and Doreen was easily keeping up with the typing.

Murray had created a rota for a fortnight as to who was to man the office until midnight. Officers checked for their names and noted their allotted day. Diaries were consulted and updated.

One young uniform officer, Nathan Ross, was having a little hitch with his allotted task. Not one that he considered worth sharing with others. He'd been deputed to ascertain all the details of the clients staying at The Norfolk Arms Hotel for the week that Brendan was there. One was proving a problem.

CHAPTER
SIX

The morning's briefing was short as nothing new of note had occurred overnight. Time was passing quickly, and officers were scurrying about. Some were collecting CCTV from various premises around Arundel as others were conducting interviews and taking statements.

Several white boards around the office walls were being updated with photographs and details of Brendan's antecedents, his backstory, as they became known. The analyst was going through all the statements and creating a chart linking every person and clarifying their alibis. Murray was shuffling papers into trays for further actions and Doreen was updating HOLMES and still had sufficient time to keep the office staff supplied with tea and coffee.

Nathan was a young uniformed PC waiting to join the CID when there was a vacancy. In the meantime he was attached to the murder squad just to get a bit of experience. Murray had allotted him the simplest of tasks which shouldn't have been a problem. So Nathan went back to The Norfolk Arms. Mainly to check he'd recorded all the details correctly.

At the reception desk, the uniformed attendant showed him the computerised register. Nathan checked his notes and saw he'd recorded the details correctly. He was perplexed and enquired sceptically, 'I can't find anything out about this American, Mike Caesar. He arrived on the Wednesday and left on the Friday.'

The receptionist, checking his screen said, 'Very unusual. Paid his deposit and final bill all in cash. He used his passport as verification as to his identity. Claimed to have come down from London. Apparently had been staying at the Ritz. Gave a home address in Garden State, New York. I'll print all this off for you. I never actually saw him, Wendy our other receptionist dealt with him. He ate in our restaurant so the staff there might remember him.'

Nathan quickly asked, 'When's Wendy going to be back?'

'About two-ish this afternoon. If you want, I'll get the restaurant team together now so you can have a quick chat. They'll all be clearing up after breakfast.'

'Yes please.'

Within a few minutes, Nathan had spoken to them all and discovered that Mike wore glasses, had a really nasty scar on his cheek and a small circular white tuft in his otherwise jet black hair. He also wore a wristwatch which looked to those that saw it as extremely tacky.

Clutching the several pages of printed paper from the receptionist, Nathan returned to the office. He knew what he would do before speaking to Wendy. Sitting at an unused computer, he tapped away at the keys using just his index fingers. Then he made a few phone calls. His problem was becoming bigger.

After lunch, Nathan returned to The Norfolk Arms and saw Wendy who was expecting him. She confirmed the description he already had. It took him no further. His phone calls and computer use were worrying him. Who to speak to without looking like an idiot?

Back in the office, he spoke unobtrusively to Murray.

'Excuse me sir. Can I have a word?'

Murray was always ready to chat to young officers and help them wherever possible. He'd been a trainer for many years, nurturing the young officers from Chichester Police Station. Many had climbed the promotions ladder or gone on to specialist roles. He'd always maintained contact with his charges. Now he was keeping a casual eye on Nathan.

'Please Nathan. I'm a sergeant not a sir. That comes when one reaches the dizzy heights of inspector. How can I help you?'

Nathan explained his problem. Murray listened intently and became worried. Then Nathan really brought pains to bear when he explained what he'd discovered. 'Well sergeant. I checked with the Ritz and they have never heard of this Mike Caesar. I checked the internet and various maps but can't find the address in New York. It just doesn't seem to exist. What should I do?'

Murray knew. 'Put everything down on a report and make sure Doreen types it up as a matter of urgency. But first, get hold of Jimmy and get back to the hotel. Find out which room this Mike fella was in and seal it off. We'll get a forensic team there and go over it with a fine-tooth comb. Well done Nathan. Now shift and get going.'

Nathan left the office at a slow jog as he phoned Jimmy. Murray knocked on Groves' door and walked straight in. Within minutes, Groves had been updated. He had a full description and a named suspect. Mike Caesar. The motive was the only fly in the ointment. Why would an American want to murder Brendan Slack?

The evening meeting was lively. Groves started it off

with Nathan's information. He followed it up with the announcement that a forensics team were already ensconced in the room that Mike had used. Enlarged copies of Mike's passport photograph were being created by specialists. However, the quality was poor as it was taken from a printout supplied by the hotel.

A computerised, coloured, identikit picture had been created with input from Wendy and the restaurant staff who all agreed it to be a fair likeness of Mike. Which technically it was when he'd been in Arundel. But no longer. The photofit image was already with the press and due to be published in the newspapers and shown on the television news programmes. Flyers were already being prepared for distribution around Arundel.

Other officers were reassigned tasks as Groves shifted the impetus of the enquiry towards Mike. A press conference was arranged for the following day. The first suspect was looking promising.

* * *

Someone had been talking a little too loudly. The woman heard every word. No problem so far. The police had their suspect.

CHAPTER
SEVEN

B y 10 o'clock, the sun was already high in the sky and the temperature in Littlehampton was swiftly approaching twenty-seven degrees. Both the chief constable and Groves agreed the press conference should take place outside the front of the police station.

It went well. The focus from the two Sussex officers was on tracing Mike Caesar. When asked by journalists to confirm how Brendan was murdered, both glossed over the details. They were only able to confirm he'd been hit on the back of the head with a heavy, blunt instrument. The chief constable was adamant that forensics and the post mortem would probably soon clarify the facts and a further press conference would be immediately called.

The TV crews and journalists were happy. They had found an old photograph of Brendan on the internet and were going to add it to their bulletins and copy for publication. Rumours were rife: some had even started spreading about Brendan being murdered by a knight in armour. Even being hit on the head with a medieval mace. No one would dare publicise that! They'd be laughed out of their jobs. Still, a murder in Arundel Castle was something out of the ordinary and each was desperate for more news.

*　*　*

Roland was wearing his favourite red cravat. He rarely wore ties. Always a colourful, casual jacket and smartish chinos. Once seen, never forgotten. A bit like Jimmy. Many people, if asked, could describe exactly what he wore but couldn't even say what colour hair he had. His age was somewhere in the mid-thirties, and he was constantly on a diet due to his slight paunch. Although well educated, he enjoyed learning about new subjects. He was happily married to a university professor, and their reading material was always eclectic and scattered around their house.

He and Lynne were meeting the supervisor, Nicholas Gulstrum, at the British Museum. He was temporarily responsible for all borrowed artworks. Nicholas enlightened them directly to the fact he had always considered Brendan a close friend and was devastated about his death. He confided to both officers that Brendan was gay and questioned whether it could have been a reason for his death.

As Roland recorded the fact, the supervisor explained that Brendan had no family. His parents in Ireland were both long dead and Brendan lived a solitary, lonely life with no long term partner and definitely no wife. His only real passion being art.

Lynne wrote the supervisor's statement as he dictated it. Nicholas clarified the reason why Brendan was at Arundel Castle. How he'd been called upon at short notice to replace Jake, an employee of the museum, who had suffered a severe stroke and was incapacitated and in a private ward at St Thomas' Hospital.

The supervisor visibly flinched as he thought about Jake. 'You don't suppose that Jake was the intended person to be killed. Oh my god! Poor Brendan. Do you think he could have been killed by mistake?' Roland pacified Nicholas and Lynne continued with the statement.

Nicholas explained that Brendan was checking the Holbein that had been lent to the Duke of Norfolk. He explained that each year, paintings on loan were checked to confirm they were still in good condition and secure. His thoughts kept drifting back to Brendan. He couldn't get the death of a close friend out of his mind. Roland gently brought him back each time to his statement. Nicholas' grief was mounting and facts were becoming inconsequential.

By the end of the statement, he had tears in his eyes. The death of his dear friend was pervading all his thoughts. People needed to be told. Academics throughout the world would mourn Brendan's death. He needed information. He asked Roland, 'Who will be arranging the funeral? When will it be? There will be lots of people who need to be told.'

Roland didn't know and promised to find out. The two officers had achieved what they needed to know. Background information about Brendan and the reason he was in Arundel Castle. They headed back to the office in time for the evening's briefing. Nicholas Gulstrum's pulse slowed down to its normal rhythm. He took several deep breaths.

* * *

The chief constable had gone to see the duke to tell him personally how the investigation was progressing. As he arrived, he was surprised to see a large purple Bentley car with blacked out windows and three aerials, leaving the grounds being followed by a black Range Rover, a large Jaguar saloon and an old Vauxhall saloon car. The Vauxhall was being driven by a woman and the front seat passenger looked vaguely familiar although the dappled light from some trees was casting shadows across the windscreen breaking up the view of the man's face.

The duke was pleased to see the chief constable and listened intently to his progress report. Then he made what the chief thought was an odd request. 'Could I have a copy of the photographs you have taken in the corridor? If you have a video from the corridor, could I please have a copy of that?'

The chief constable didn't want to give them to the duke because both the photographs and the video showed Brendan's lifeless body. 'To be honest Your Grace, they both show the poor deceased man's body. They aren't a pretty sight. Are you absolutely sure you would want to see them?'

The duke was adamant. 'Yes, I am. Obviously I would treat them with the utmost confidence and return them once I have viewed them. Since that dreadful incident, I haven't been brave enough to visit that corridor personally. I'd rather see it in pictures first instead of going there myself.'

The chief constable thought he understood. 'In that case, I'll arrange for copies to be brought to you.'

Both men chatted amicably for half an hour before the chief took his leave. The duke did not mention his previous visitors and the chief constable didn't presume to ask about the vehicles or their respective occupants. It wasn't his place. Once he'd left, the duke made a local phone call.

CHAPTER
EIGHT

Doreen looked at the elimination statement she'd picked out of her in-tray. She stared at the statement and scowled. It was a quick, simple statement taken by a detective to clarify the whereabouts of a person volunteering at the castle on the Friday. The person wasn't a suspect or considered as one. In fact, he'd been the assistant to the scorer during the cricket practice and had a cast iron alibi. It was the name and address that was troubling Doreen.

John Whiles with an address in Fulham, London. Frowning, she found her personal address book among the usual detritus in her handbag and flipped it open to W. The same address and phone number as recorded at the top of the statement. She cried out in frustration, 'What the hell is he doing here?' Several of the officers looked at her in surprise. They'd never seen her so animated.

Even louder. She couldn't stop herself. 'Assistant Scorer! Volunteer! Temporarily off work through injury!'

Murray asked her, 'Are you all right, Doreen.'

She suddenly realised she'd been rather voluble and drawn attention to herself. 'Sorry. I was thinking of something else,' and she set about typing up the short statement. Several eyes strayed occasionally in her direction, but she kept her head down and continued typing. Eventually people realised she was all right and ignored her.

Doreen handed the original statement to one of the designated office 'readers' who checked it for any further potential enquiries. None were considered. It clarified John Whiles' alibi as assistant scorer and named the actual scorer. His statement had also confirmed Whiles' alibi. The 'reader' recorded the facts on the computer and filed the statement. He'd never heard of John Whiles.

Doreen had casually watched the statement's progress into a file for storage. She knew what she was going to do.

The evening meeting was a long one. The press conference was gone through. Various messages had been received as a result of it and ensuing enquiries were detailed. Officers were deputed to conduct them as and when time allowed. None were considered of major importance.

One outstanding statement was causing some concern. Both Groves and Murray considered it of major importance. It was that of Sally, the volunteer who showed Brendan to the corridor and the Holbein. She was proving elusive. They deputed several officers to trace her. The address held at the castle for her had proved incorrect. Neither considered her as a likely suspect, but she was apparently the last person who saw Brendan alive. She would obviously become a major witness.

Murray was happy that numerous statements from volunteers and castle staff were completed which eliminated them from the enquiry. Forensics reports were awaited from both the corridor of the castle and the hotel rooms. It looked to everyone as though Mike was definitely the killer. The majority of CID officers had been delegated to find him.

When the floor was thrown open, the main topic of concern was the motive. Why was Brendan Slack murdered?

* * *

John Whiles was pondering the same question at his luxury flat off West Street in Chichester. Not his registered address in Fulham which he'd told the young officer who took his statement. He was sitting in a reclining chair with his left leg resting on a pouffe. His ankle was killing him. The X-ray had been inconclusive. The doctors couldn't say whether it was a very bad sprain or broken. So they'd wrapped it in plaster, just in case. Half-way up to his knee.

He swore to himself that he'd never use the stairs again at New Scotland Yard. He had been nearly at the ground floor when he had slipped and fell. Several people had rushed to help him and a couple had advised him to use the lifts in future. How he didn't respond other than politely shook even him. The back-hall inspector had deemed he should attend hospital. Now he was on the sick list for at least a month.

Carol, his long-time doctor girlfriend was looking after him. John believed it was the only good thing about the whole sorry episode. She'd made sure he was eating freshly cooked food as opposed to take-aways and sandwiches. She insisted on driving him to decent restaurants and wherever else he wanted to go.

She had driven him to Arundel Castle's cricket ground on that fateful Friday. Some swore it was the most beautiful cricket ground in the world. She couldn't confirm either way although John was adamant. As he had been busy assisting the official scorer clean and check the workings of the scoreboard, she sat on the grass in the warming sunshine reading a book.

When the duke had telephoned him, he wasn't really surprised. They'd actually spoken at the cricket. The duke had asked after his pot-leg and was amused at John's humorous recollection of his fall.

They agreed a time, and John was told to use the duke's private entrance. Far enough away from where all the police would be. That suited John down to the ground. He didn't want to encroach on their crime scene. Carol was to act as his chauffeur.

When Carol drove into the private parking area, a large Bentley, a Range Rover and a black Jaguar were already parked there. John knew exactly who the owner of the Bentley was due to its colour and he suspected who the occupant of the Jaguar was likely to be. Several smartly dressed men with overtly large jackets concealing assorted armaments, were talking amongst themselves and all stopped to watch the old Vauxhall approach. Some slid a hand inside their jacket and held butts of guns, just as a natural matter of caution.

As John struggled out of the car, an immaculately dressed man wearing 'tails' approached the old Vauxhall with a disapproving look. 'I'm Watson, the duke's butler. Would you please be kind enough to follow me? The duke is expecting you.' The men standing around all seemed to relax.

John hobbled painfully after the butler, assisted by Carol. When they approached a set of stairs, John became apprehensive and whispered to Carol, 'I'll never get up these.'

She whispered back, 'Don't be such a baby! It's got a handrail. You can hold onto me as well.'

They were shown into a large drawing room with numerous modern chairs and furniture. The duke rose from a settee as they entered and said, 'I'm sorry Mr Whiles, I forgot about your leg.'

The women occupying a sumptuous leather armchair pointedly looked down at his pot-leg and laughed out loudly.

John was struggling to regain his breath and composure after the exertion of climbing the stairs.

Carol said, 'I don't think it is as bad as he makes out. I've found men claim to suffer a lot more than women. They tend to use any excuse. Don't you agree minister?'

The Home Secretary, still chuckling, pronounced, 'I was told he'd just slipped on a wet step. About as bad as falling off a high heel. Looks like you really upset the doctors to make them put the plaster halfway up your leg,' and she burst out laughing again. Carol and the butler joined in the mirth.

The duke struggled to retain some decorum. However, a slow smile slid across his face. 'Please Mr Whiles, take a seat wherever you feel most comfortable.' John headed for an upright fireside type chair. He was the only one in the room who was not amused.

The duke, complying with protocol, introduced the minister and then said to her, 'This is Mr Whiles. I think we are both fully aware of his... shall we say, abilities.'

John wasn't sure what they considered his abilities to be.

The duke continued, 'Mr Whiles. You probably recognised the large Bentley in the parking area when you arrived. As the Earl Marshall it is my duty to keep certain people informed of anything that may bring that position into disrepute. I would be obliged if that remains strictly confidential.'

'That will remain confidential Your Grace.'

The conversation quickly turned to the matter in hand. Watson provided all with refreshments before withdrawing and joining the women's personal protection officer in the kitchen.

The minister addressed the duke, 'As a result of your approach to the Palace, I spoke to the Metropolitan police commissioner yesterday about your proposal Your Grace. He was adamant that as Mr Whiles was recorded as being unfit for duty he should not become involved. He declared that it would be inappropriate for a Scotland Yard detective to be foisted upon Sussex police without them requesting assistance. It appears that he is not Mr Whiles' biggest fan although he accepts he has extraordinary abilities.'

John thought, there's that word again: abilities.

The minister continued, 'Knowing Mr Whiles as I do, I don't believe it would prove a problem for him if he wanted to investigate this matter.' Then she looked directly at John, 'Am I correct?'

John said, 'I don't believe it would be too much of a hindrance. I have made a statement to the murder team. I expect one person to pick up on that fact. How she reacts will determine how I can conduct any enquiries. As long as I am able to claim to be one of Your Grace's representatives, I don't foresee too many obstacles.'

The meeting lasted a further thirty minutes as the duke outlined what he'd been told by the chief constable. The detail of the mace possibly being the murder weapon was news to John who mused to himself, 'Interesting.'

He considered the fact it had been reattached. Why? What did it achieve? He needed to see the photos and video from the scene and he knew how to get them. He needed to be kept abreast of any developments that the murder team discovered and he believed he knew how he could do that. Briefly, he explained how he expected the investigation would progress. It was agreed that he would keep the duke updated who in turn could update any other interested parties.

CHAPTER
NINE

Doreen waited until after the morning's meeting before making the phone call. John had kept his mobile close to hand and answered on the second ring.

'Hello Doreen. I wondered when you'd call.'

'Sometimes I really hate you. How did you know I'd call?'

'You couldn't resist once you checked it was me. Can I meet you later? I want to discuss something with you that would be better face to face than over the phone.'

Doreen thought for a few seconds, then said, 'All right. I know I'm going to regret it. I can't be seen talking to you in Littlehampton. How about the Bridge Café in Arundel? Say 5pm. All the officers will be at the evening meeting.'

'Thanks Doreen. I'll be there.' Then John couldn't refrain from some mild humour. 'Do you think you'll recognise me after all this time?'

'Unfortunately, yes. No one can ever forget you once you've crossed their path,' and she hung up smiling broadly.

She couldn't forget him. Black unkempt hair that a lot of people claimed unfairly came from a bottle and provided him with one of his pseudonyms, 'Black John'. Eyebrows that looked like grey steel wool and always seemed to need cutting as they hung way too low over his deep brown eyes. Eyes that seemed to twinkle one moment and then the next focus with such intensity that people became embarrassed by his stare. Doreen smiled to herself as she remembered his slightly crooked nose which he'd always claimed was from his sporting days long past.

His face used to confuse those who didn't know him. If he exerted himself, small scars would often appear and then disappear as he resumed his casual demeanour. Doreen had always wondered how he'd actually retained most of his teeth as he'd a fearsome reputation. She didn't know most of his top teeth were false and on a wide bridge.

Very few people actually used his true name but Doreen was one of them. Most of his acquaintances tended to use his other pseudonym, 'Oscar'. She couldn't bring herself to address him as such as his name was Whiles, not Wilde. She tended to be more formal addressing him often as Mr or DC Whiles.

Carol drove John's old Vauxhall to outside the Bridge Café where John struggled from the passenger seat. He hobbled into the café using a crutch and instantly saw Doreen sitting at a table. She always dressed the same when at work. White blouse, dark skirt and black court shoes, although today she had added a beige cardigan draped over her shoulders. She kept her slightly greying hair in a tight bun and seemed to shun the sun which caused her skin to have a strange pallor. Some lines adorned the sides of her brown eyes and a slight hint of rouge on her cheeks made her look older than she was. John had never come close to knowing her true age.

'Hi Doreen. It's good to see you again. How are you?'

'Mr Whiles. As I live and breathe. How on earth did you just happen to be so close to the scene of a murder?'

'Just lucky I suppose.'

Doreen looked at John's leg encased in plaster, 'Don't tell me, you were drunk and fell over.'

Indignantly, John whined, 'How can you say such a thing?

You know I'd never fall over. My balance is impeccable at all times. I slipped and fell down some stairs.'

Doreen burst out laughing. 'I suppose that's an elaborate excuse as to why you can't get to the counter and want me to buy you a coffee?'

'That would be really nice of you Doreen. No sugar.'

Doreen went to the counter and bought one coffee and a tea for herself and carried them back to the table. She said, 'All right. I'm listening. Tell me what you are up to?'

John explained what he'd been doing on the day of the murder and the fact he was now looking into it on behalf of the Duke of Norfolk. He didn't bother to mention that the Metropolitan police commissioner had stated he could not actively represent the police as he was on sick leave and it had nothing to do with the Met.

Then he put a proposition to her.

She sat quietly for a few minutes as she considered it. She contemplated the legality of it. She wasn't sure. She sipped her tea. She needed more time. She asked, as if rhetorically, 'Amazing how you know the Duke of Norfolk and the fact that he's asked you to be his eyes and ears in this matter.'

John sat passively and made no comment.

She sipped her tea again. Then again as if rhetorically she said, 'You always seem to have sufficient sway with the hierarchy of the police or even government ministers. Why haven't you spoken to them?' And then as an afterthought, 'Or have you?'

John remained quiet. His lips widened slightly and curled gently up as a slight smile crept across his face. A giveaway.

She read the sign. 'You have haven't you? Have they told you to keep out of this?' She glared at him. 'Well?'

John was succinct. 'It's nothing to do with the Met and the government cannot be seen to involve itself just because he's a duke.'

'Do they know what you are doing?'

'They probably have an inkling.'

'So if it all goes pear-shaped, they are not going to say, "Don't worry Doreen, we'll make sure you're all right."'

John looked imploringly at Doreen, 'Would I drop you in it Doreen? How long have you known me? ok, I may sail close to the wind but I've never dropped anyone in it.'

They spoke for a further ten minutes before each went their separate ways.

* * *

As John hobbled from the café, he was ostensibly oblivious to the woman watching him. She'd earlier identified Doreen by chance acting rather furtively leaving the office before the evening's obvious meeting. The woman had been curious. Strange. Surely she should have been at the meeting. It hadn't been a problem following her and now she'd stumbled across an unknown man. A man with a pot-leg. Who was he? Press? A friend, a lover? Why such a clandestine meeting?

The woman considered the meeting and was about to disregard it when she saw the pot-legged man getting into a car driven by a different woman. Her interest was aroused. What was it all about? Who was he? Can't be police with a pot-leg. Must be press. That's it. She's copping a bung for information. Something to remember in the future. Could be useful.

CHAPTER
TEN

The morning's briefings were getting shorter as the days rolled on. Forensic reports were nearly all completed. The ones about the room occupied by Mike at The Norfolk Arms revealed absolutely nothing. There were no fingerprints found at all. Not a trace of any DNA. The scientists had examined all the bedding and found nothing. They'd combed the carpet and got nothing. They'd even dismantled the toilet, sink and the shower to examine the U bends and found nothing. Not one single hair!

The conclusion all the scientists came to was that Mike sanitised the room each day he was in the hotel after the cleaner had been in. Then he wore latex gloves whenever he was in the room and slept in a one piece forensic overall. They didn't believe he used either the sink or the shower and probably not the toilet. All believed he had some advanced form of forensic training.

When they were asked how he could survive without using a toilet for two days, they explained he could have used the communal toilet just off the bar area. Any forensic evidence gathered from there could not be guaranteed to belong to Mike, so they hadn't bothered with it. Then they added, if need be, he could have used a bottle whilst in the room. Groves, nor any of his team, had ever heard of such a sanitised room.

An hour after the meeting, John saw the forensic reports. He'd already viewed the police video and seen the photographs of the crime scene courtesy, unwittingly, of the chief constable via the duke. He'd seen the photographs and video of Brendan's flat in Chelsea, South West London courtesy of a friend in the recently privatised photographic department in the Met.

Now he needed to see the photographs and video from within the rooms of Mike and Brendan at the Norfolk Arms Hotel. The duke couldn't really ask the chief constable for copies to view as he would have no logical reason to want to see them. He couldn't ask Doreen because it was not something she would have access to as the typist.

He needed a police officer on the murder team. There were several that he knew. John considered each of them in turn as he settled back in his chair, his pot-leg resting gently on a pouffe.

DCI Groves. He would probably record the fact and that could not be permitted to happen. The Met commissioner would go mad and stick him on a discipline charge. The Home Secretary would be put in an invidious position. The chief constable of Sussex would also show annoyance. Groves has access to everything though. Would he accept help if the investigation faltered? That may be too far in the future.

DS Murray. He's a stickler for following rules and doing everything by the book. Within reason. As the office manager, he would have access to all the forensic and police reports. Making copies of photos and videos would attract attention. If he believed something or someone could progress the investigation without doing anything illegal, he'd probably consider it.

DI Daines. She's very feisty. John smiled as he thought of the description her father had used to describe her once. She would be able to keep him abreast of progress made but may not be able to provide him with any specific items. In a fit of pique she would probably divulge his involvement. Although of course she owed him a lot as he helped save her life once.

Jimmy. He was the exhibits officer. Now he would have access to all the exhibits. Photos and videos. Although he wouldn't necessarily have access to any documents unless they were deemed to be an exhibit. Could he be trusted not to 'confidentially' tell one of his current girlfriends what he would be doing?

There were pros and cons for each of them. Which one should he approach? Is there anyone else he hasn't thought of? He had crucial questions already that he considered needed answering. And he had suggestions that the team might not have considered.

A glass of wine would help him decide. Without thinking, he lifted his leg off the pouffe ready to stand up to go to the wine chiller. The pain was excruciating!

He shouted, 'Carol. Help!'

She ran in from the kitchen where she'd been preparing lunch. Annoyed at the inconvenient distraction, she scolded him, 'What are you trying to do? Can't you just sit still. If you need anything just ask.'

'Could you get me a large glass of wine please? I need to think.'

Throughout lunch, John ate in absolute silence. Who could he approach? The one person he hadn't considered. He slowly came to a decision. He would have to engineer a chance contact. No problem there. It would help of course if he had something to offer. If he could pull it off, he'd be laughing.

CHAPTER
ELEVEN

At just after 10am, Doreen phoned John and updated him with the previous day's enquiries. The majority of which were rather mundane and of little consequence. He listened politely without comment. Then finally, she got to the item that she knew would whet his interest. 'Hetty Vendle is the middle-aged lady who runs the café at Swanbourne Lake. She saw an old picture of Brendan on the TV last night and recognised him from it. Alison and another detective ran round to her home address and took a statement from her. I typed it up this morning.'

John sat up a little straighter in his chair and queried, 'What's the rough gist of it?'

Doreen smiled. She didn't need the statement in front of her to update him. 'She runs the café at Swanbourne Lake. Apparently, she's good with faces but not dates. She recognised Brendan straight away from the old picture that was on the TV news last night. She is positive it was him although she can't remember what day it was. She just remembers him buying a coffee.'

John pronounced absently, 'He was in Arundel for a week. It needs to be narrowed down. How did he get to Swanbourne Lake? Why did he go there?'

Doreen asserted slightly aggressively, 'Hang on. I don't know. It's not in her statement. I'm sure Alison asked her.'

'Sorry Doreen. I'm not having a go at you. I'm just

intrigued. Is the team anywhere near finding Mike or coming up with a motive?'

Doreen settled back into her casual demeanour. She summarised the attitude of the office personnel, 'No. Mr Groves is getting a little disheartened although he's putting on a brave face. Forensics don't seem to be getting us anywhere other than confirming the murder weapon to be the mace attached to a suit of armour.'

John butted in, 'That is really strange.'

'Everything we know about Mike comes from the description and a photo obtained from the staff at The Norfolk Arms. The team are struggling to find the volunteer who showed Brendan to the corridor. It's a young Australian woman who gave a duff address. It's likely she used a duff name as well. Murray has checked her details which she gave the castle when she applied to be a volunteer and found they are all 'Micky Mouse'. The only genuine thing we have is a photograph which captured her at the pedestrian entrance to the castle when she met Brendan.'

John wanted to sound positive but struggled. He could only think to say, 'Slight progress then Doreen.'

'There's a couple of DCs trawling through the CCTV from the entrance to the castle grounds where punters pay to enter. You wouldn't believe how many people visit the castle during the day. They think they may have found Mike. The person has his head down and is wearing a hat. They have sent the image to be enhanced. Oh! He was carrying a small holdall which gave them a bit of a clue. Who visits a castle carrying a holdall?'

John apparently seemed to ignore the question. Something Doreen had said had tripped a thought. He couldn't quite put a finger on what it was. It would come to him later he was sure. Problem was, when? He put it out of his mind.

Now he was back in the present, grateful to Doreen for her trust and updates. He didn't want to cause her any angst. 'Thanks for the update Doreen. Can you give me a call tomorrow?'

'You're incorrigible!' and she hung up.

John looked out of the lounge windows. A superb summer's day with a few, high wispy clouds and some plane trails. He called out, 'Carol. How do you fancy lunch at the café at Swanbourne Lake?'

Indignantly she whinged, 'I've just started to prepare lunch!'

'Can't you put it on hold?'

'All right. Are you going to tell me why?'

'I'll tell you on the way. But first, I need a copy of the local paper.'

Carol parked the old Vauxhall practically opposite the large wrought iron gates guarding the entrance to Swanbourne Lake and Arundel Park. She helped John through the small pedestrian entrance and into the little café. There were already a few patrons sitting at tables in the restricted seating area reserved for the café's customers. John and Carol sat at an empty table and waited a few minutes before they were approached by the middle-aged, plump lady running the place.

Staring at John's plaster encased foot, she enquired sympathetically, 'Oh dear. That looks painful. Broken I'd wager.' Then returning to matters in hand, enquired, 'What can I get you?'

John tried to convey a painful expression, 'Extremely

painful. But not as bad as that poor chap,' and he indicated Brendan's picture on the front page of the local paper.

Hetty couldn't stop herself. Slightly conspiratorially, she revealed, 'I saw him you know. He was here and he actually bought a coffee from me.' She seemed to be miles away in thought as she looked towards the lake. Then, as though adding a rider, slowly uttered, 'And some bird seed I seem to recall. Strolled over there towards the lake,' and pointed to the lake's edge.

John asked directly, 'Did he meet anyone?'

Hetty was staring at the point where she'd last seen Brendan. Something was bothering her. She didn't seem to hear John's question. Then she remembered, exclaiming as though it was obvious, 'Of course. It was him. His phone.'

John was lost. 'Sorry. I'm not with you.'

Carol was exasperated. 'What about his phone?'

Hetty replied, 'One of the birds flew off with it.'

John and Carol just looked at each other. Then John asked quizzically, 'How could a bird fly off with it?'

'Oh, it was only a little thing. Not a smart phone. Now I remember. The bird dropped it in the lake.'

John was struggling with the thought, 'How did he get it back?'

Hetty had regained complete recall of the event. 'Oh, he didn't dear. It's still out there somewhere. I had other customers then but I think Eddie offered to help him get it back. I seem to remember he had an appointment and said not to bother. Would you like a menu?'

Both Carol and John asked in unison, 'Who's Eddie?'

As if it was common knowledge and obvious, she declared,

'The boatman. That's him over there,' and she pointed to the boatman who was busy hiring out the rowing boats. Other customers were arriving and Hetty needed to move on. She chivvied the pair along, 'Now, I can recommend the fish and chips. Fresh this morning.'

Carol could take no more. 'We'll both have them then please.'

Hetty rushed back inside the café.

John enquired casually, 'Can you row?'

Carol was not best pleased. 'How, may I ask, are we going to search the whole of this huge lake?'

John said, 'It's not very deep and you can see the bottom clearly. You row and I'll look.'

Carol was annoyed. 'That is the worst plan I have ever heard you come up with. Can't you get the police to come and do it?'

'I'll think about it. Let's eat first.' They ate in silence as Carol seemed to be sulking. At the end of the meal they went to see Eddie. He only had a few boats left. The lake was full of families and couples in rowing boats. Some were proficient rowers but the majority were weaving about all over the place and laughing at their utter incompetence.

John spoke to Eddie who didn't stop what he was doing. 'Just been talking to Hetty. She said you saw a bird drop a fella's phone in the lake the other day. Could you tell me roughly where it was? There's a tenner in it for you. I want to collect it.' When money was concerned, Eddie was interested and gave John his full attention. John handed him a ten-pound note.

Money spoke volumes to Eddie. He pocketed the cash and stood next to John and pointed to a boat house on the opposite side of the lake. 'See that building. Look at the right hand side of it and you see the tall fir that looks a bit brown?'

John said, 'Yeah. I see it.'

''Right. Look at the lake in line with it and you see the edge of the island?'

'Yeah.'

'About halfway between the two, say twenty yards from the bank. It dropped about there.' Eddie looked at John's pot-leg. 'You'll be useless rowing with that. My boy'll row you out if you want?'

Carol immediately took to the idea and forcefully declared, 'Pay the man. Get his boy to row you. I'm going back to the café,' and she marched off in a huff.

John said, 'Don't rob me. How much?'

Eddie yelled to his son, 'Eddie. Get your arse over here. Got a job for you.' Then he looked at John. 'Hire of the boat. Eddie junior's time and work. Twenty-five quid.'

'OK.'

'Cash up front.'

John dug out the cash from his wallet. 'You drive a hard bargain.' It went straight into Eddie's pocket.

'He should have got it when it hadn't had time to get too wet. It'll be soaked by now.'

John asked, 'Do you remember when it went in?'

'Let me think.' It didn't take him long, 'Yeah. It was a Friday morning. Didn't he tell you?'

'No. He hasn't been in a position to tell me the day.'

Eddie reiterated his statement, 'It was definitely a Friday morning. Must have been round about ten ish because I was by myself. Eddie junior has a lie in on a Friday. Idle git. Here he is.'

A spotty youth of about seventeen years of age ambled up to them. He was scruffily dressed and slovenly. 'Whatcha want pa?'

Eddie junior listened, said nothing and strolled over to a wooden cabin. John was bemused. Then he came back with a net on a pole.

By way of explanation, Eddie disclosed, 'Comes in useful this net. People are always dropping something in the lake. Clumsy sods. It probably earns us as much as the boats,' and he burst out laughing.

John struggled into a boat and then Eddie junior jumped in oblivious to its wild rocking about on the water. He didn't hang about. Within minutes he'd rowed to the right area. In a monosyllabic tone Eddie junior said, 'Here.'

John was looking over the side of the boat. Eddie junior looked over the other side. They could see the bottom of the lake clearly. Eddie junior rowed gently about in ever widening circles. Within minutes, John heard a grunt. 'There.' Eddie junior grabbed the net and fished out a small Nokia phone, covering John in sprayed water as he pulled it back onto the boat.

He dumped the net in the bottom of the boat and started rowing back to shore without another word. Eddie and Eddie junior helped John out of the boat and onto the jetty. A brief word to Eddie and another twenty-pound note changed hands.

Within thirty minutes of leaving the café John was back in it. Carol called to Hetty for a large ice cream for him. She asked, 'I was just thinking, how did you know her name was Hetty?'

'I thought you knew I was psychic,' and he licked his ice cream.

CHAPTER
TWELVE

A s John was 'fishing' at Swanbourne, the woman was reading the local paper's report on Brendan Slack's murder. The police had their suspect. She laughed at the photo fit image of the killer. She could see straight away that the man had used more trigger points than was necessary. Even so, she still knew who he really was.

*   *   *

Back at his flat, John scrutinised the phone. Neither he nor Eddie junior had touched it with their bare hands. When he'd picked it up from the bottom of the boat, he'd used the sleeve of his shirt pulled down over his hand. Now he didn't want to turn it on in case it did more damage. He knew very little about mobile phones. Somehow, he had to get it to the police without them knowing who was giving it to them. He cursed the Metropolitan police commissioner. The Home Secretary had no choice in her decision.

Eventually a plan came to him. It was as if God was smiling on him. Now he had something to trade.

He made a short telephone call.

Calling Carol back from the kitchen he asked, 'Can you take me to the castle please. I need to be there about 4pm.'

'Providing you take me to Blanc's for dinner tonight. Otherwise, you'll get no food at all this evening as I've not had time to do anything.'

'All right. You're on.'

'Great. I'll get the car to the front door. Make sure you use the lift,' and she sauntered out.

John collapsed onto the fireside chair facing the duke who was sitting on a sofa.

The duke enquired, 'What's this all about Mr Whiles?'

'Well Your Grace. I have recovered the mobile phone belonging to the victim. I need to give it to the police but as you are aware, I'm prohibited from taking any active part in the investigation. As the chief constable is due here shortly, I would like to give it to him.'

The duke was inquisitive, 'How on earth did you come across it?'

'To be honest Your Grace, I think it's best you don't know till I tell him. I haven't quite made my mind up as to what I am going to say.'

The duke looked reproachfully at him. 'You are a rather resourceful fellow Mr Whiles. It's a shame the Metropolitan police commissioner is a stickler for such petty protocols. However, I understand his logic. If he allows one person to break the rules, where would it stop?'

John didn't want to argue the point. Even he could see technically the commissioner was right. The noise of a car manoeuvring on the gravel outside in the parking area drew his attention. He recognised the vehicle. 'The chief constable is here.'

Within minutes, he entered the room. The duke, ever courteous rose and said, 'Thank you for coming at such short notice,' and inclined his head slightly. 'Perhaps you know Mr Whiles. He is acting as my representative while he is incapacitated. He's the deputy to the scorer at the cricket when he has free time.'

The chief constable smiled. 'I thought I recognised you the other day when I was coming up the drive. That looks like an uncomfortable leg.'

Before John could respond the duke said flippantly, 'Fell down the stairs at Scotland Yard.'

The chief constable burst out laughing. John couldn't understand why, when people heard how he'd sustained his injury, they burst out laughing.

The chief constable said, 'Interesting that whenever there is a serious crime committed in West Sussex you are somehow at the heart of it. I seem to remember you originally helped us out with a major enquiry working undercover. Then you turned up again assisting us on what we all thought was a cut and dried simple murder in Barnham. That ended up with two of the country's most prolific serial killers going to prison for life.'

The duke was surprised, 'I never knew that!'

The chief constable added thoughtfully, 'Mr Groves told me last year that you had some involvement with a couple of professional killers he was investigating. One of them caused rather a lot of trouble for me in Arundel itself. I seem to remember him telling me that the Home Secretary and foreign office were dragged into it.'

The duke looked at John. He now understood why the Home Secretary knew him so well.

The chief constable spoke to the duke. 'I've got a strange feeling that the message to come here was not entirely Your

Grace's idea.'

John said, 'I'm sorry for the subterfuge. Perhaps I should explain.'

The chief constable looked at John and smiled, 'I just know this is going to be good,' and he sat back in his chair, rested his elbows on the chair's arms, steepled his hands and placed them touching his chin.

John explained his situation. Why the commissioner had forcefully told him under no circumstances to get involved and the Home Secretary had concurred. The fact that even if Sussex had asked for help, he would not be the person sent as he was on sick leave.

The chief said, 'I thought I saw a government car the other day. I presume that was the Home Secretary.'

The duke clarified for the chief, 'After the murder, I spoke to my contact at the Palace, and they spoke to the Home Secretary. As I knew Mr Whiles I took the liberty of mentioning his name. However, as he has stated, the commissioner was adamant that the Metropolitan police should not become involved as it was entirely a matter for your force.'

The chief constable endorsed the claim. 'He is correct,' then looking at John's pot-leg added, 'You wouldn't be much use anyhow with your leg like that.'

The duke said, 'You might be slightly mistaken there. Mr Whiles is acting as my representative and has something that may be of use to you.'

John handed a small brown paper bag to the chief constable containing the small Nokia mobile phone. 'That is the mobile phone that belonged to Brendan Slack. It's been under water for at least a week. It was recovered by Eddie, the boatman from Swanbourne Lake. He gave it to me to give to you and he is willing to make a statement.'

The chief constable looked quizzically at John. 'Amazing! Were you just walking past, and he handed it to you?'

'No. I'd gone there for lunch and got chatting to him. Just lucky I suppose.'

The chief constable laughingly exclaimed, 'You do have a lot of luck if I remember. I presume you want your name kept out of this?'

'If that's at all possible, I'd be extremely grateful.'

'I'll see what I can do.' The chief paused before querying, 'As the duke's representative, did he by any chance show you the video of the scene and the photographs?'

John smiled as he responded, 'I was lucky enough to have been in the room when the video played.'

'And did you form any opinion?'

'As a matter of fact, a couple of things did spring to mind. I noticed on the video that as the cameraman started to film from the cafeteria, there were two silver-coloured upright stands placed to one side of the corridor with a limp red rope hanging from them. On the floor under them was a sign that I believed said, 'private'. I wondered who put them there? Perhaps they had ensured the killer had privacy when he committed the murder? Then, who moved them to the side of the corridor? Was it the castle's security man as he was locking up or the first police to arrive? Or even the killer as he left? If the latter, do they bear his fingerprints?'

The chief constable quickly said, 'I'll check as a matter of urgency. Several days have passed. I would hope they are still there and untouched. I can't say I'm hopeful.'

John declared, 'The murderer's description intrigues me. It beggars' belief that he has such a conveniently blatant scar on his cheek and a white spot in jet black hair. Glasses as well! Three things that draw the eye. Perhaps that was the object? Then nothing within his hotel room to even imply that he'd been in there. It has all the hallmarks of a professional.'

The chief asked questioningly of John, 'The description of the killer was in the press, but how did you know there has been nothing found in the killer's hotel room? That has not been publicised.'

'Some of the press seem to manage to get hold of information that is not common knowledge. For instance, a name for the killer is circulating amongst them. Mike Caesar. Apparently an American. Then they seem to believe the murder weapon is a mace. How and where they get their information has always amazed me.'

The chief constable didn't believe a word. 'Mr Whiles. You amaze me. How and exactly where you get your information is your concern. I would ask just one thing. If it has any bearing on this case, I would be obliged if you keep me informed. Should there be anything that I consider may be of use to you, I will pass it on. Do we have a deal?'

'Certainly.' Then, after a short pause while John cautiously adjusted his posture, 'One other thing that sprang to mind that I'm sure Mr Groves has probably considered. The victim arrived in Arundel on Monday. He was murdered on Friday. The alleged killer, Mike, arrived on Wednesday. What was the victim doing for the first four days of the week? The killer must have known he'd be in Arundel and where he was staying? Did something happen to promote his death?'

Both the duke and the chief constable said nothing. Each considered what John had said. After a full minute, the chief said sardonically, 'I don't know. I'll check that as well.'

John suddenly recalled his thought when he'd spoken to Doreen. It had come back to him. 'Something else crossed my mind. Did this Mike Caesar fellow suss out the corridor where the deed occurred. He had plenty of time, two days in fact. The CCTV at the entrance to the castle grounds would confirm if he did or not.'

The duke supposed, 'Interesting. It will be interesting to know.'

CHAPTER
THIRTEEN

At 5.30pm, the evening meeting was in full swing when the chief constable walked in. Chairs started to scrape before he uttered, 'As you were.'

Groves was surprised by his presence and stated, 'Good evening sir. We are just running through where we are and sorting out new lines of enquiry. If you would like, I'll pause the meeting and brief you as to the current situation?'

'No need, Mr Groves. I've been thinking and I'd like to run some thoughts past you and the team if it's all right with you?'

'Certainly, sir. Please continue.'

'Well first of all I'd like to give this to our exhibits officer. It's Brendan Slack's mobile phone. It was found in Swanbourne Lake by Eddie the boatman there. It hasn't been touched by him or turned on. He is willing to make a statement of how he came by it. If someone could visit him tomorrow to oblige? I'll obviously complete a statement of continuity.'

Murray, along with most of the officers present, was shocked. 'Certainly, sir.' Murray glanced at Jimmy. 'Jimmy, please sort the exhibit out and get it to the lab. We need every name and number in it ASAP.'

Jimmy was quick enough and took the paper bag with the phone in it. Within seconds, it was sealed in an exhibit bag. He knew exactly who he was going to get to check it.

The chief continued as if the phone was just a minor

exhibit. He mentioned the upright stands and within seconds Jimmy had placed a DVD into a computer and started the tape. After ten seconds the upright stands and the rope were visible. He paused the video. The chief enquired, 'Who put those there?'

There was silence. The chief continued. 'Mr Groves. They should not be there. They should be at the other end of the corridor just before the stairs to the private rooms above. Perhaps that is how our killer ensured he wasn't disturbed. Could his fingerprints be on them if he moved them aside as he left the scene? Forensics are nearly finished in the corridor. They may not have been examined as they were so far away.'

Groves quickly responded. 'Jimmy. Get over there now and find them. Take a SOCO with you. Go now.' Jimmy rushed from the room.

The chief constable went through Brendan's arrival on the Monday and Mike arriving on the Wednesday and the murder on the Friday. 'Have you considered why he was in Arundel four days prior to Friday? Could he have done something in the first four days that prompted his death? The killer seemed to know where he was staying and where he was going to be. Had the killer already checked out the castle? I seem to remember you saying the British Museum had booked the victim's accommodation. Why from the Monday? Does anyone know?'

Silence.

DC Fownes confirmed, 'I'll check why the British Museum booked him in for a week. When I spoke to them originally, I was mainly concerned with the victim's background and the Friday of the murder.'

The chief constable was visibly happy. 'Thank you. It may give us some guidance.' Then he looked at DCI Groves and said, 'Just a couple of things I thought of. I shan't delay you any further. Goodnight all,' and he left the room. Everyone watched him leave.

After a short passage of time, Groves recovered his composure. 'Well. That's a turn-up for the books. Roland, can you see if you can get a reply tonight? Can everyone hold pending the outcome.' Roland left the room to find a quiet office where he could speak to the museum's staff. Groves turned to Murray who was sitting next to him and whispered to him, 'I have a horrible feeling our chief has had a thought that he hasn't fully shared with us as to how he came by it.' Then for everyone's information, he called above the growing hubbub, 'Be prepared to work late tonight.'

Less than ten minutes passed and Roland walked back into the crowded office. 'I've spoken to the supervisor at the museum who sent Brendan to check all the paintings on loan to properties in the area and the accommodation manager. They told me that Brendan was visiting a different premises every day to check works of art that were on loan from the British Museum and the National Gallery. His job was to make sure that the art had not suffered any untoward damage during the year and that the security arrangements were still satisfactory. He was standing in for a member of staff who had been taken ill with a stroke. I have a printout of Brendan's full itinerary. Which property he should have visited on which days and the items he had to view.' He handed a sheet of paper to Groves.

Then he continued, 'They told me that at the week's

conclusion, Brendan was to complete a report on each individual painting. To assist him, they had lent him a small laptop computer with a template on it which he filled in nightly. He was to return it with the final report.'

Groves looked at the paper and then handed it to Murray. 'What do you reckon? Tonight might be too late for these places. Let's sort something out for the morning. We'll visit them all at the same time. I want statements from every one of them. If the chief is right, one of them may hold the key to this enquiry. Now I want to know, where the hell is the laptop? Anyone know?'

No one uttered a sound.

Groves added, 'We need to find it. If it was stolen by the killer, he must have had a reason to take it. I want the hotel visited again and the cleaners who went into Brendan's room interviewed again. Ask them if they saw a laptop. When Jimmy gets back, I want the photographs of Brendan's room checked just to make sure it wasn't somewhere in there and we have missed it. I'm sure Jimmy would have seized it if it had been there.'

A small, embarrassed titter of laughter rippled round the room from those who'd been on the first enquiry when Jimmy had seized everything. They knew he would not have missed it nowadays.

Murray cut across the end of the laughter, 'It looks like our victim visited four stately properties prior to his Friday visit to the castle which are normally all open to the public. I'll organise teams. I think two detectives and two uniform officers to each. Maybe allow the places to open and then go in at about 10am unannounced. Statements from everyone who spoke to or dealt with Brendan.'

Groves added slowly and meditatively, 'Hang on Murray. We are not art experts. We now know what Brendan looked at and why. We need someone with us who has some knowledge of art. How about seeing if the museums could give us a leg up with some of their experts?'

Alison, who had stayed relatively quiet piped up, 'We could always try the Arts and Antiques Squad up town in the Met. They are all detectives and have a grounding in art. They may be able to help.'

Murray looked at Groves and cocked his head. 'It's a thought. I can always give them a call and check out the lie of the land with them. It'll have to wait till tomorrow morning though. They'll all probably be at home by now.'

Groves was still considering the chief's information and absently concurred with Murray, 'Yes. Good idea.' He just couldn't stop thinking to himself, how did the chief come up with these ideas?

When the meeting drew to a close, Murray spoke quietly to Groves. 'Have you ever known the chief to be so insightful? How did he get that phone? He went to see the duke earlier. If these ideas of his come from the duke, we could do with him on the team!'

Groves had already considered the duke as the informant and disregarded it. 'The duke is a very clever man. We know he has seen the video and photos, so he could have noticed the rope barrier. Would he have known anything about Brendan's and the killer's movements during the week? Unlikely. The chief, another clever man, only ever seems to glance at the paperwork. Why would he have come to his conclusions?

Very useful admittedly. Has he been guided by something he's gleaned from our enquiry that I have missed?' Groves paused. 'Murray. Can I impose a thought?'

'Yes. Go on.'

'Can you do a swift check on HOLMES and see if anything jumps out that may have led him to his conclusions?'

'I'll get on with it now,' and he ambled back to his desk and fired up his computer. He checked all the completed actions recorded by the officers. Then he checked the enquiries still being conducted. He confirmed the locations of seized exhibits. Within the hour, he was staring at the list of statements taken. One name jumped straight out at him. He stared hard at it.

In an involuntarily loud voice he seemed to cry out, 'No! I don't believe it. It can't be!' He opened up the full statement. John Whiles. He read it. Less than a full page. Assistant scorer at the cricket. Then he read the notes. Alibi confirmed. Eliminated from the enquiry and as a suspect. No further action to be taken. Filed.

He stared at the address. Fulham, London. Then he glared at the occupation. Temporarily on sick leave. It didn't say from what job or employment. Murray knew. He didn't need to go any further. He rocked back in his chair with his hands interlinked behind his head and started to laugh.

CHAPTER
FOURTEEN

Jimmy struggled back to the office with the SOCO. They were carrying the upstands, rope and the sign that indicated *Private*. They put them straight into the exhibit store. The SOCO had found a palm print and five finger marks as though one of the upstands had been gripped. She professed that they were good impressions. It would only take a couple of hours to confirm if they were from anyone known to have a criminal record.

Robert Smythe had confirmed he'd not moved the upstands nor touched them. The cleaner responsible for the corridor confirmed she'd polished the upstands on the Monday as were her instructions and they were in situ at the end of the corridor by the stairs. The first officers to attend the scene swore they'd not touched or moved them.

Groves was desperate as he spoke to the SOCO, 'Please expedite the examination of the impressions. It could be the breakthrough we need.'

The SOCO knew she could possibly crack the case if she could only identify the killer's true identity via fingerprints. 'I'll have the result by tomorrow's meeting sir.'

Groves thanked her as Murray said, 'Can I have a quite word guv'nor?'

'Certainly. Come into my office.' When the door was shut, he enquired, 'Problem?' Murray handed him a sheet of paper which he looked at and immediately saw the name, John

Whiles written across the top. He looked up at Murray in astonishment. 'What on earth is this?'

'He was the assistant scorer at the cricket and he provided an alibi for the scorer who reciprocated with an alibi for him. Both their statements have been filed by the proof-reader who obviously does not know him. I've checked and he's off sick with a suspected broken ankle after falling down some stairs at Scotland Yard. As soon as I saw his name I thought it's got to come from him. He's somehow got to the chief.'

Groves read the short statement and the notes. 'I'm with you Murray. If you'll pardon the pun, it's got his fingerprints all over it. The question is, what the hell are we going to do about it? It appears that he is able to put good ideas into the chief's head. He must have recognised him. Sure as eggs are eggs Brendan's phone was probably recovered by him. How did he know where to look? Why didn't he come straight to us?'

'We are assuming he's the chief's informant. Do you think we should leave it as it is? I would presume that if he's giving the chief information, it'll probably be going the other way. I'm with you though, why didn't he come straight to one of us?'

'I hate being in the dark, Murray. Let's have a quiet meeting with him: lunch, say tomorrow and I'll pay. That is bound to ensure he'll turn up. Then we can see what he's got to say?'

'I'll sort it out,' and Murray strode purposely out of the room.

A short while later, Carol said to John, 'Where are they taking you?'

'Raymond Blanc's. Make a change for someone else to pay.'

'Why have they asked you now?'

'I think they've worked out that I spoke to the chief.'

'Are you going to tell them?'

John considered his reply. Thoughtfully, he answered, 'I will tell them why I can't be involved. Eddie junior will be saying he recovered the phone and passed it indirectly to the police so that will not be a problem. I'll see what they have to say.'

Carol responded, 'What if they don't want your help?'

'Then I'll continue as the duke's representative and hope I get information from the chief constable and Doreen.'

CHAPTER
FIFTEEN

The morning's briefing was in full swing by an exuberant DCI Groves. It was already approaching nine o'clock. He'd postponed the morning's visits to all the stately homes for the time being. Murray had been in touch with the Arts and Antiques Squad at Scotland Yard. He'd spoken to the reserve officer who'd passed him on to the D.I. The murder of Brendan Slack had already been noted by them as he'd acted on their behalf numerous times. They were only too willing to offer their assistance.

Roland and Lynne had been sent to obtain an additional statement from Nicholas Gulstrum at the British Museum covering Brendan's full weekly itinerary. Roland wasn't sure but thought he appeared a little more nervous than when they'd previously seen him. Nicholas confirmed he was still worried about when the funeral would be and if he'd have time to let everyone know. Roland couldn't tell him yet when it would be.

A statement was being arranged with Eddie on behalf of his illiterate son. The officer struggled to agree a time to take it with him. He concluded it was because neither were fans of the police and were being deliberately obstructive. Eventually a mutual time was agreed.

An officer had tracked down the volunteer, Sally, to a refuge for battered women in Brighton and arranged for her to return to the castle where she could make a statement.

The photographer had somehow enhanced the single frame of the man's face that they believed to be Mike Caesar as he entered the castle grounds with his trilby hat on. It was a good enough likeness to the computerised passport photograph that they already had but of a much better quality. The press would have copies of it ready for the lunch-time TV news.

The SOCO had been in touch and stated there was no record in any British data base of the fingerprints she had lifted from the upstand. Then she had suggested she send the fingerprints and palm print to the Americans as Mike spoke with an American accent and had given a false address in New York. The chief constable had authorised it. Groves was mildly hopeful.

Walter Hetherington, a specialist at Sussex Police HQ, had examined Brendan's phone and had managed to establish its number. There was no billing to any network as the phone had been loaded with twenty-five pounds when purchased. Walter concluded the phone could probably be classed as an expensive 'burner'. Being a highly qualified technician, he used a ladies hairdryer to dry the phone out.

Nicholas, the supervisor at the British Museum, had confirmed that Brendan used different phones as and when the money ran out on the one he was using. He claimed that Brendan would always let him know the new number. Then prudently added the rider: if he remembered! Wistfully, he concluded that trying to contact Brendan was often a nightmare. He preferred to write him a letter. It seemed to be the simplest method of contacting him.

Walter established there were only seven different numbers

called and he would be able to identify each recipient within the day. There had been just two incoming calls and he declared that would take a little longer.

One of the detectives viewing the CCTV gathered by the uniform officers had also seen a man he believed to be Mike walking towards the castle entrance. He was carrying a holdall. It showed the time as 10.16am. The CCTV at the entrance to the castle grounds had shown Mike arriving at 10.18am. The timing was right.

As the meeting concluded, the team set about their allotted tasks, sure everything was starting to fall into place.

John was already in Brasserie Blanc in Chichester, chatting to Maurice the head waiter, when Groves and Murray walked in. Maurice took their orders before leaving the three men. They were soon chatting as old friends do. A bottle of the restaurant's best white wine was helping. It wasn't until the first course arrived that Groves brought the conversation round to Brendan Slack's murder.

'Oscar. I see no point in beating about the bush. We noted you were at Arundel Castle's cricket pitch on the day Brendan Slack was murdered. The chief constable has recently come up with some interesting thoughts that have already born fruit. He was able to produce Slack's phone which had been languishing at the bottom of Swanbourne Lake. It's as though he's had an epiphany. Or of course, someone may have given him a large hint. What do you think?'

John had expected a question of this sort and was ready with his stock answer. 'I must tell you where I stand in this matter. As you probably know by now I am on sick leave from the Met having fallen down some stairs at Scotland Yard.'

Murray caustically responded, 'Careless.'

John ignored the gibe and continued, 'I often assist the official scorer at the first cricket match between the duke's eleven and the tourists and that's where I was when this poor bloke was killed.' He paused and took a mouthful of wine. 'Being on sick leave prevents me getting involved. I don't know if it's common knowledge, and I would hope this goes no further, but the duke spoke to his contact at the Palace and asked that I be attached to your team.'

Both Groves and Murray looked at each other curiously.

John continued, 'The Home Secretary was approached by the Palace and she spoke to the commissioner. He was adamant. I was on sick leave. I hadn't been requested by the Sussex chief constable. There was no way I would be permitted to join any team. If a request for assistance was made by Sussex for a detective, someone else would be sent who was not certified sick. He did not want to set a precedent. The Home Secretary had to agree. Therefore I am not to get involved in the investigation. Should my name appear in your murder book or on any official documents other than my statement, I'll be looking for new employment' He took another small mouthful of wine.

Groves and Murray could understand the commissioner's point of view. They understood that if he altered the rules for one person it would invariably lead to others. Both were advocates of the enforcement of rules. Sometimes!

Groves enquired sceptically, 'So you don't know anything about Slack's mobile in Swanbourne Lake or, for instance, whether a barrier in the corridor in question may have been moved?'

John held up his hand as he had a mouthful of food and didn't want to talk with his mouth full. It gave him a few seconds to think. Both men knew what he was doing.

'Well I think the chief has apparently surprised all of us with his insight. He was a detective in another constabulary before joining Sussex. I believe some time ago.'

Murray, ever more sarcastic, alleged, 'You're not going to answer are you?'

John's retort was swift, 'Would you?'

Murray considered his response. 'I suppose not. However, it does lead one to an inevitable conclusion.'

'In that case. Let's leave it there. But please. Do not put my name anywhere that could turn up later and cause me, the duke, the Palace, the Home Secretary, the chief constable or even the commissioner problems.'

Groves replied, 'OK Oscar. But should some startling apparition appear to you one night and give you a prediction, please share it.'

John smiled, 'I agree to that.'

The three men enjoyed the rest of their meal without any further reference to the vicious murder of Brendan Slack.

CHAPTER
SIXTEEN

G roves and Murray returned to the office in buoyant mood. Doreen placed a cup of tea in front of each of them and chidingly stated, 'That might help you sober up. Walter has been on the phone from his lab and has got something for the meeting, which you two are meant to be running in less than an hour.'

Murry was first to ask, 'What's he found?'

Something about one of the numbers on Brendan's phone. He is rather excited, and said he'll be here asap.'

Groves was indignant, 'We are not inebriated Doreen. We shared one bottle between the three of us.'

Doreen huffed as she walked off. She missed the reference to 'the three of us' not registering who the third person was likely to be.

As they were finishing their cups of tea, the clock ticked round to 5pm. Walter wasn't there although most of the murder team were. A few officers were engaged with enquiries that couldn't wait and had phoned in with apologies. Groves called the room to order. He stated that because he and Murray had been absent for most of the day, DI Daines was going to be conducting the meeting. No one queried where they had been or why.

Alison had acted as office manager in Murray's absence and was a capable officer. She had no trouble in bringing everyone up to date. She called on specific officers to give a resume of their enquiries and results. Groves busily wrote in his murder book.

The door was flung violently open as Walter burst in. All present turned to see who was causing the commotion. Walter was only just over five feet tall and looked like the image of Einstein by Andy Warhol.

'Sorry I'm late. The bus got held up at an accident.'

Several people burst out laughing but quickly stopped when Alison glared at them. She addressed Walter. 'Good evening Walter. Is there a reason you are here?'

'Oh yes. I had to come in person. This is amazing.'

Alison, still looking at him, enquired, 'Yes?'

'Mr Slack's phone. I checked all the numbers and found one that wasn't what it seemed.'

Alison liked Walter and was patient. 'Tell us what you have discovered?'

'Well. All bar one were easily identified as to academics and institutions and, em, male escort agencies. Then there was just the one.'

Alison queried, as if trying to elicit an answer from a reluctant child. 'Yes?'

'It's his sister.'

Groves was taken aback and stepped in. 'Walter. You are aware we established Brendan Slack had no living relatives. Why on earth do you think he has a sister?'

Excitedly, he cut across whatever else Groves was about to say. 'The last number. I traced it to a lady. I cross referenced her phone and found she had called Mr Slack's phone. Then I checked and found her social media accounts. She is an active environmentalist. Buried deep in her Twitter account, I found her email address. I, eh, got into the email.' He looked around worriedly. 'I didn't utilise official protocols to do it.'

Groves didn't seem to care. 'Go on Walter. What did you find?'

'This,' and he handed him a sheet of paper.

Groves looked at a photocopy of an email dated over a month earlier. It was from a Violet O'Donnell to a Janice Greer. It was a short message.

'Janice, amazing news. I've just found out I've got a brother! He's called Brendan Slack. I'll tell you all about it when I see you in Scotland next week. Love Violet.'

Groves looked shocked as he looked up at Walter. He handed the page to Murray who passed it on to Alison who read it aloud for the whole office. There was a general murmur that swept around the room. Everyone was considering what the information could entail.

Could she be the reason Brendan was killed? Could she have killed him? Could she know why he was killed? Where was she? Why hadn't she come forward to the police? Was she dead?

Jimmy was the first to recover his composure. 'Walter. I'll need Brendan's phone back as an exhibit as soon as you can please.' Then he enquired as to what probably everyone else was about to, 'Is O'Donnell's phone traceable? Can it be tracked?'

Walter had already tried. 'I've tried everything I can. I can't even find out if it's turned on or where it is. All I have is the number. It's on a contract with BT. She gave her address as the office of the bird sanctuary she works for when she took the contract out. The only thing I haven't tried is ringing it. I think that's something a police officer here should do.'

Alison agreed. 'That was the right thing to do. Thank you,

Walter.' She looked expectantly at Groves.

He quickly thought. Then said to Walter, 'I'll need a full statement from you straight away,' then addressing Alison, he asked, 'Could you please help Walter.' She nodded.

Walter usually had a simple pro forma statement that he completed after examining any phone. What he had discovered was going to be a lot more detailed. It had to be correct.

The office had quietened down. Groves took over from Alison. 'Well ladies and gentlemen. This has the potential to open a can of worms. Murray. I want this Violet O'Donnell traced and interviewed as a matter of urgency. In the meantime, if she proves elusive for whatever reason, I'd like Janice Greer located and spoken to. Find out what O'Donnell told her. See if she knows where we can get hold of O'Donnell. I'd like to crack on with this tonight before anyone goes home.'

Murray was already thinking on the same lines. 'No problem. We'll postpone any other enquiries tonight and concentrate on this.'

Groves opened the office up to any questions. 'Has anyone anything to add about these two women?' No one had. He continued after a few seconds. 'Unless there are any urgent questions arising from today's enquiries, I think this meeting should finish.' There were none. Any officer who was thinking of asking a question, put it on hold.

* * *

The woman was relaxing at home when the doorbell rang. She checked her watch. Dead on time. 'Hi. Come in.'

He didn't. He stood on her doorstep. 'What have you to tell me?' No beating about the bush.

She named the killer. 'If the police know what they are doing, they'll identify him shortly. But he's back in America. As to motive, it looks like they have no idea.'

'Set him up. Neutralize him. No loose ends.' The man didn't wait for or envisage a response. He expected her to comply with his instructions without question. He turned round and walked away.

She watched him cross the road and walk out of sight before she slammed the door closed. 'Bastard!' flew venomously from her mouth.

CHAPTER
SEVENTEEN

Lynne was late in her service to join the CID. She was in her early thirties but looked a little older. Her vibrant ginger hair had been allowed to grow long and was always well brushed. She relied a lot on makeup to cover blemishes on her face left from a nasty bout of shingles in her twenties. From a distance, one could not tell, closer, it was obvious. She had been a pretty young woman with bright blue eyes, but times had changed, and her eyes had lost their lustre and now she was considered rather plain.

As a uniform officer from Horsham, she had learnt her trade tolerating abuse from drunks and dealing swiftly with criminals. Her reputation had grown, and she was renowned for her wit and ability. She enjoyed uniform duties but was eventually persuaded to apply for the CID by her fireman husband. Now she was learning new skills.

Murray tasked her and Roland to try and trace Janice. The pair checked police indices without a trace. They moved on to social media sites and soon found her. Her Facebook site showed her to be an environmentalist who loved birds. She posted weekly about the charity she worked for. A rough location of where she was and what she was doing. Her favourite occupation appeared to be protecting wild birds' eggs from collectors.

As Roland was checking other sites, Lynne dug deeper into Janice's Facebook account. She read Janice's postings and links to other Facebook accounts going back several years. Lynne followed all the links before returning to the original account. It was a slow process, but Lynne was pedantic. She found nothing linking Janice to O'Donnell which she found rather strange. If they were friends, she concluded that there must be a connection somewhere, but there was nothing.

She sat back deep in thought. Walter had said he'd first found the information in O'Donnell's Twitter account. She couldn't understand why O'Donnell wasn't even shown as one of Janice's friends in Facebook. Looking about, she quickly cleared her computer screen. Then she opened O'Donnell's Twitter account.

She searched it for a reference to the email that Walter had found. It returned a negative result. Lynne scratched her head. She stood up and away from the computer. She mooched round the office stretching her back. Walter was reading his statement to make sure he'd included everything. She knew what she was going to do.

'Walter. Can you spare me a minute?'

'Yes. How can I help you?'

'Do you mind just looking at my computer for a moment?'

They both walked back to the computer terminal that Lynne had left open. 'You know you said you found O'Donnell's email in her Twitter account. Can you show me where it was?'

Walter sat down and said, 'Yeah. Give me a second,' and he started to search the Twitter account. Pensively, he mused quietly, 'Strange. I can't find it.' He started searching the inner workings of the computer. Lines of code were scrolling up the screen. Lynne stood behind him looking over his shoulders.

She had no idea what he was looking at.

Walter was worried. He turned to face her. Ashen faced he declared, 'Someone has altered the code. It's been deleted.'

Lynne called to Murray. He casually strolled the few yards from his desk to where they both were. 'What's the problem?'

Walter turned to face him. 'Someone has altered the code that the computer uses when it's being searched in Twitter. The email address for O'Donnell has been removed. It could only have been done by someone at the lab at police HQ.'

Murray queried, 'But you originally found O'Donnell's email in her Twitter account. What would deleting it from there achieve? You already have all its details.'

Walter stood up. 'I didn't tell anyone at HQ what I had found. Perhaps whoever deleted it didn't know and thought that would be the end of the matter. It would probably have meant we would never have found the email address for O'Donnell or even that message.'

Murray asked, 'Can you access O'Donnell's email from this terminal?'

Walter looked confused. 'Yes, why?'

Murray explained, 'If someone has tampered with the Twitter account, they could have possibly tampered with her email account.'

Walter sat back down and reset the computer so he could log in as though at his lab. He was shaking. He was starting to hit the keys on the keyboard a little harder. Lines of code were scrolling up the screen. He kept muttering to himself. Then he turned to face Murray and Lynne. 'It's gone! Her whole email account has gone!'

Murray said, 'Wait here,' and he rushed over to Jimmy.

'Jimmy. Where's that email that Walter brought us?'

Jimmy picked up a clear exhibit bag. 'Here. Why?'

'It may be our only copy. Can you run off a few copies please?'

Jimmy didn't understand the request but was happy to comply. 'Yeah. Certainly. Half a dozen do?'

'Great. Thanks. Can you bring one over for Lynne?'

'OK,' and Murray went back to Lynne and Walter.

'Can you both come with me and we'll go and see the boss? Something is amiss and we need to get to the bottom of it.'

Groves looked at Walter. 'Are you sure?'

An emphatic reply, 'Yes.'

Groves said, 'What would deleting her email account achieve? You could resurrect it. You have the facility to do that.'

Walter stopped him. 'I would only be able to resurrect it if I knew it existed. Whoever removed it from the Twitter account may have thought I hadn't found it. So, I wouldn't have even known where to look in the first place.'

Groves considered his reasoning. 'Logical. But why would anyone want to stop you finding anything? What would it achieve?'

Lynne stepped in. 'We wouldn't have known he had a sister.'

Groves concurred thoughtfully nodding his head. 'Yes. We need to find this O'Donnell woman and pretty smartish. She may be in danger. Come to think of it. The same may be true about Janice Greer.'

Walter had a trick up his sleeve.

CHAPTER
EIGHTEEN

Walter had got back to his office at gone 11pm the previous evening. There were a few officers still at their desks in other offices. He'd shut the door and sat still for a few minutes. No one came in. Getting up, he went to a small display shelf that had four trophies proudly on show that he'd been awarded in the past. He picked one up, an odd shaped one that appeared to be made of Lalique with a little clock in the middle of it. The inscription at the base stated, "Awarded for the best new covert clock inspired design," and it was dated 2011.

Walter turned it around to look at the back. There was a small housing holding an AAA battery and a small modern thumbnail USB. He gently removed the USB and placed the trophy back on the shelf. Sitting back behind his desk, he checked his door as he opened one of his desk drawers and took out a laptop. He turned it on before sliding the USB into a port. Within several seconds it opened and displayed the fact that it was a video recording running on a loop every seven days.

Pressing play, he rapidly sped the images to the time he left the office to go to the meeting. Then he slowed it down to three times normal speed. He didn't have to wait long. The image showed the majority of his office. Walter saw his office door open, and a tall man stroll in. He recognised him immediately as Clifford, one of the PCC's advisors who worked occasionally in an adjacent office. His last name however, eluded him.

Slowing the image to play at normal speed, Walter watched in growing anger and amazement as Clifford nonchalantly sat in his chair behind his desk and rifled through all the papers in his 'in' and 'out' trays. Walter looked in his 'out' tray for his report relating to Brendan's phone. It wasn't there.

His gaze returned to the video file. He watched as Clifford found his report and then he saw him patently turn on his desktop computer. Walter was furious. Using the report, Clifford manage to quickly find Walter's computerised file relating to Brendan's phone. Walter watched in sheer horror and amazement as Clifford calmly deleted the complete file and all his notes from the computer.

Clifford was rapid as he amended some of the programming of the computer. Walter knew that he would struggle to recover the files if at all. He swore loudly. He cursed the man. Then he watched as Clifford casually turned off his computer before having a look around his office. Folding the paper report and putting it in his pocket, he left the office.

Walter didn't know what to do. Should he approach the man? He didn't like any form of confrontation. Not a good idea. Should he approach the PCC? She may side with her advisor. Should he tell the deputy chief constable who was ultimately responsible for technical branches of the force. Would he be criticised for not having protected his computer with a strong password? Unlikely but possible. He needed advice.

He downloaded the complete video file to his laptop. Then

he composed an email. Attaching the file, he pressed send. She would know what to do. He felt better.

* * *

Groves, Murray and Doreen had arrived at the office before 7am. They sat together with their mugs of tea. All three knew they had to find at least one of the women as a matter of urgency.

Groves said to Murray, 'Unless there is anything that can't wait, I want the whole team tasked with this. I don't like the fact that someone at HQ was able to tamper with Walter's computer. I'm thinking of going to see the chief this morning at HQ to update him re progress of the case and I'll discuss it with him while I'm there. Have either of you any ideas?'

Doreen said, 'Before Walter left last night, he said something to me that I didn't quite understand. It was on the lines of "They don't know who they are dealing with," and that was it.'

Murray proffered quietly as though talking to himself, 'Walter was obviously upset last night. At one time, I noticed he was trembling. He was ashen faced for some time as well. But now I come to think of it, when Walter left the office he seemed in a belligerent mood. Although that is something I've never noticed Walter display before. He's normally a timid man.'

Groves said, 'He told me he won't be here for this morning's briefing. I'll pop in and see him when I'm at HQ. I don't want him to get despondent. Anyway. Let's sort out who's going to be doing what. I want one of these women found.'

The morning's briefing was lengthy. Groves put the visits

to the stately houses on hold for another day. More pressing matters had suddenly reared their heads. The previous day's disclosures were gone through meticulously blow-by-blow. Officers were appointed to their respective tasks. Some queried how they were going to trace the women. Others had ideas of their own. Some of the more tech savvy younger officers were to scrutinise computer web sites and were teamed up with others to check their findings.

At the conclusion, one young uniform officer enquired of Murray why such manpower was being used which had no apparent bearing on the original murder in Arundel Castle. Murray took him aside. 'One of these women is apparently the deceased man's sister. We need to know all about her. She may be in danger. She may be able to provide a motive for Brendan's murder. That is why.' The officer seemed satisfied.

* * *

Violet was abroad. She'd flown out on the Saturday so she could have a weekend to herself and get to know the village. Her phone was completely flat and she'd forgotten her charger. She seemed to recall someone on the internet stating that you should remove the battery if the phone was flat and one couldn't charge it straight away, so that's what she'd done. It was the usual rubbish some people put on the internet and was totally false.

The sun was high in the blue, cloudless sky and the temperature was climbing fast. Locals had been scurrying about conducting their business earlier in the morning when it was cooler. They knew how hot it could get. The sooner they were back in an air-conditioned room the happier they were. Tourists rarely moved much before 10.30am and were careless under the burning sun and some displayed painfully sunburnt bodies as a result.

Violet had already checked out the marina and decided which boats she was going to book with. Their advertising hoardings all seemed to promise that one would see whales and dolphins with a money back guarantee if one didn't. All the boatmen were bare chested and bronzed, and the sun didn't appear to trouble them. But she noticed they all seemed to protect their heads wearing floppy hats. She'd buy one soon.

* * *

The phone rang in Scotland at exactly 10am and the butler casually strolled from the library to the lounge and picked it up from its cradle. He didn't have time to acknowledge either his location or the phone number.

The butler recognised Gwendoline's obnoxiously whingeing voice. 'Is your Master available Campbell?' Campbell held himself in check. Master my arse! The pure arrogance of the woman.

In his smarmiest voice, he responded, 'I'll get him madam,' and he placed the phone on the table next to its cradle. He strolled at a leisurely pace back to the library and to one of the wooden panels between some bookcases. He knocked hard on the panel and shouted, 'The bitch is on the phone,' and then he strolled on down to the kitchen.

The panel slid to one side and a tall man, immaculately

dressed in a handmade tweed suit, expensive shirt and tie stepped out from it. His handmade shoes sank gently into the library's deep pile carpet. Muttering to himself, 'Bloody woman is starting to be a pain,' he ambled along to the phone.

Picking it up he put on a pleasant voice and said, 'Hello.'

As if speed was essential, she blurted straight out, 'My contact tells me they recovered the man's phone. They seem to believe he had a sister. My man tried to delete everything but may have been too late. I told you originally that one death always leads to others. Now I'm going to have to deal with her. When I can find her. This is turning into a real mess.'

The man calmly responded, 'You agreed originally that you would sort it out. Are you saying now that you can't?'

She hesitated. She wasn't going to admit to the arrogant idiot that she couldn't deal with it. 'No. Of course not. I thought I'd better let you know what's happening.'

He was blunt and pugnacious. 'I'll tell the others that you have everything in hand,' and after a few seconds, added sardonically, 'You have, haven't you?' She heard the menace in his voice.

She was unequivocal. 'Yes,' but she heard the slight tremble in her own voice. She was sure he wouldn't have noticed.

'Good. Keep me informed as to the sister,' and he hung up.

Gwendoline still had her phone to her ear. She'd heard the connection terminate when he hung up. Putting her own phone back on its cradle she said to herself, 'Ignorant sod.'

CHAPTER
NINETEEN

After the morning's meeting, the officers all set about their respective tasks. Alison sat at a computer and checked her emails. She read what Walter had written and her jaw slowly dropped. Looking around, no one was apparently paying her any attention. She started the video file running, speeding it to the respective time. Walter's email had been accurate and concise as to what was on the video file.

Alison looked about for Groves. She found him in his office. Within minutes he was sitting in front of the computer reading Walter's email to her. Then he viewed the video file. When he finished, he looked up. He swore. Loudly. Several times.

He sat still. He wanted to calm down but was struggling. Alison said nothing. Several minutes passed. His thoughts were racing. He considered his options and then made his decision.

'Forward a copy of this email to me and to Murray. I don't want this disappearing. Run a copy of it onto a USB and give it to Jimmy as an exhibit. Label it as something that is superfluous. When you've done that, I want a scrum down with you and Murray in my office. We need to know what we're going to do about this bastard.'

Alison added, 'What about Walter?'

Groves wasn't sure. Hesitantly, as though thinking aloud, 'You should phone him to let him know you are taking action. Nothing else for the time being. Tell him you'll keep him updated. Once Murray has seen this, we'll meet in my office.'

Once his office door was shut, Groves posed the obvious question, 'What are we going to do about this?'

Alison confirmed, 'I've spoken to Walter. He's coming over for tonight's briefing. Jimmy has a copy on a USB.'

Murray was incensed. 'This bastard should be nicked. He works for the PCC. He should be above reproach. The only thing then is what's he likely to tell us? Why did he do it? Did he do it for the PCC and if so, why? Or did he do it for someone else for a few bob? How can we be sure he'd tell us?'

Groves concurred. 'My attitude entirely. A dilemma.'

Alison was more thoughtful. And probably if the truth were known, a little more devious. 'Walter is incandescent with rage. I've a feeling he would take great joy in having a little part in sorting this man out. Maybe for instance he could get into this man's own IT and even maybe his phone.'

Groves considered the idea and liked it but didn't know the logistics of it. 'Who owns the IT the guy uses when he's working for the PCC?'

Murray knew. 'It's the property of the police authority.'

Groves was incandescent. Could they do it lawfully and get away with it? 'Let's do it, but properly. Let's get a search warrant for his HA and for his computer and phones.'

Murray was agreeable but cautious. 'If we are going to arrest him, we could seize all the gear without a warrant. Then the question arises, are you going to forewarn the chief? He might tell the PCC.'

Alison was shifting her position slightly. She was cautiously considering what Murray had said. 'If we just do it by way of a search warrant and he has done this for money, it may provoke some sort of reaction. If we forewarn the chief and he tells the

PCC, this man may get wind of what we intend to do and take some sort of remedial action.'

They sat silently for a couple of minutes as each considered different scenarios. Then Groves broke the silence. 'Right. Murray. Can you please establish this man's full details and home address? Alison. Once we have the details, I'd like you to apply for a search warrant. Obviously, we'll keep this under wraps. I'll put a team on standby.' He rocked back in his chair and scratched his head. Then, as though a rhetorical afterthought, enquired, 'What has this all got to do with the murder of Brendan Slack?'

* * *

The Scotsman was sipping the finest Scotch Whisky poured from a crystal decanter. He was seated in his specially adapted room. It was kept at a constant temperature and was only dimly illuminated by the picture lighting. Now he was considering what he'd been told. Brendan Slack had a sister. Would he have told her? He couldn't take a chance. She had to disappear. Could he trust that stupid woman to do it? She was becoming a liability. If the police got to her, would she roll over and spill the beans? He would have to speak to the others. To kill one of their own might frighten them into thinking they may be next. He'd need to put it in such a way that they would come to the inevitable conclusion without him suggesting it. But how?

* * *

Several officers were working on locating Caesar. The majority of the officers were busy trying to find the women. It hadn't taken them long to find Janice Greer's social media accounts. There was a lot of tittle-tattle about very little which didn't disclose much about her. Then an officer noticed a reference to her parents in Hull. Some searchers suddenly changed tack to checking local authorities in Hull. The department dealing with housing turned up trumps. They had only one person paying council tax by the name of Greer. Justin Greer.

Groves had been ready. His up to date copy of the Police Almanac gave details of everyone in police forces around the UK. Flipping it open to Humberside Police, he saw who he was going to phone. Within half an hour of Sussex police tracing Justin Greer, there were two detectives and a uniform officer from Humberside knocking on Mr Greer's front door.

Less than a further thirty minutes later, Groves knew that Janice was working for the RSPB in Ayrshire in Scotland, and he had her mobile telephone number and more importantly, the address of the hotel where she was staying. Soon, two detectives from Police Scotland were at the hotel. The receptionist pointed them to the restaurant. They found Janice Greer and three other women deep in conversation.

Once they had separated her from the group, they told her to expect an urgent phone call from Sussex police. Then they stayed close by which she thought rather strange. Janice casually checked her phone which had been on silent for several hours. There were three texts from her father. She started to panic.

Her mobile rang. Groves identified himself and began

to explain. Janice listened. She was shocked. He was talking about a murder. He was talking about her friend. One of the officers put a glass of water in front of her. She downed it. Groves mentioned the name. Brendan Slack. She nearly fainted. Her friend's recently discovered brother. She knew Violet had taken a fortnight off to spend time to get to know him. Oh. Poor Violet!

Groves hesitated. He needed answers and quickly. He finished his narration. 'I believe her life may be in danger. I need to find her as a matter of urgency. Do you know where she is?'

Janice was crying softly. 'She's gone to stay with him at his apartment in a place she called L.G. They were going to talk about their lives before they met. That's all she spoke about for the last few weeks. She was so excited. They'd both taken DNA tests and that's how they came to know about each other.' Janice wiped away some tears with the back of her hand. 'They only found each other a few months ago and she'd met him only a couple of times and now he's gone.' Groves could hear her sobbing.

He asked gently, 'Where's this L.G?'

She wracked her brain. 'I can't recall. I remember her saying the apartment was in a block called Poblado overlooking a marina.'

Groves was desperate. 'Poblado sounds Spanish. Does that ring any bells?'

Janice considered his reasoning. 'It's possible. I'm not sure.'

'Have you a phone number I can contact her on?'

'Yes,' and she relayed Violets mobile number. Groves knew it wasn't being answered.

He tried to speak as calmly as he could. His heart was pounding. 'Do you know of any reason why someone would want to hurt her?'

Janice burst out crying even louder. 'She's my friend. She wouldn't hurt anyone. Why would anyone want to hurt her?'

'I don't know just yet. It could be something Brendan told her, Janice. She may have told you and you don't realise it's significance. Please be careful. If you need any help, the policemen who are with you now will give you a gizmo that if you press it, they can get to you quickly.'

The call was terminated, and Janice sat with the two detectives. They tried to reassure her as best they could. She made a decision. She was going straight back to her parents in Hull.

CHAPTER
TWENTY

G roves called to everyone in the office. It was an impromptu meeting. He updated them all. The focus had shifted yet again. Find out what L.G. stood for and where Poblado was. Murray was deputed to ring Violet's mobile phone number every half hour, and Walter was to be tasked to try and locate the phone. The message was clear to everyone. They were slowly getting closer to locating Violet.

Murray had identified Clifford as Clifford Samsun with an address in Worthing. Alison was busy preparing papers she'd require to request a magistrate to consider granting a search warrant.

John was at home in Chichester when he got a call from Groves. They chatted for a while. He agreed that Violet had to be found urgently. At the conclusion of the call, he called to Carol for a glass of wine. Why had a member of the PCC's staff tried to obliterate any trace of her? He needed to think.

He sat with his eyes closed. Ten minutes passed. Then he remembered something. He scrabbled about for a copy of an email he'd printed off that Doreen had sent him. He read it and then looked at the small photographs that were attached to it. It might speed things up. John phoned Groves back who listened attentively. As soon as the call was ended, he yelled for Jimmy.

* * *

The Scotsman had been busy making phone calls. He'd

explained everything to them. They had all been aware of what had been planned for Brendan Slack and why. None had baulked at the idea. Gwendoline had agreed to complete the task. Now, the man was putting such a spin on how it was all going wrong, and that the police might actually find her. He implied that he was concerned. If she was arrested, would she name the members of the group? Were they all likely to be arrested? What were they to do?

* * *

Jimmy didn't linger. After a short chat with Groves, he had grabbed the keys for Brendan's house in Thurloe Square and had got Damien, a uniformed officer to drive him there. During the journey, Jimmy checked his laptop computer and found a copy of the email with the attached photographs. He knew what he was looking for. Why hadn't he spotted it before?

Damien stopped the car temporarily outside the house allowing Jimmy to jump out. He walked up a couple of steps to the front door and put the key into the lock. Within fifteen seconds of getting out of the car, he had stepped into the hallway. And then he heard it. A noise he recognised. It sounded like a kettle starting to boil. He knew that couldn't be right. The sound was coming from the room at the far end of the hall. It had to be the kitchen.

Jimmy walked along the hallway and was in the kitchen doorway when the gloved fist appeared in front of him for a split second. Then it collided with his face. His eyes watered as his nose broke. A dribble of blood slid down from a nostril to his mouth. Staggering badly, he lent on the wall for support but didn't fall down. Campbell was mildly surprised he remained standing. Normally, anyone he hit when he was wearing his special glove that had a built in knuckleduster was knocked to the floor unconscious.

He hit him again. Harder. Jimmy's cheek bone broke. This time, Jimmy's eyes closed, and he fell to the floor.

As the kettle finally boiled, Campbell poured the water into the prepared cup of coffee. No milk. He casually looked at Jimmy lying on the floor. Sent by that stupid woman I suppose in an effort to identify the sister. I get here from Scotland and she only gets her man here now. What an idiot. No wonder they all agreed she had to die. What to do about him?

Campbell hadn't expected anyone to be at the house and had been taking his time looking around. He'd read the last three months' worth of Brendan's journals. Five volumes. Every single word. He knew her name now and how they'd only met a couple of times. Whenever he had seen a reference to her on a page, he ripped it out. No point in leaving it for someone else to find.

He bent down and went unceremoniously through Jimmy's pockets and found his warrant card. It was a shock. Why were the police there? At first, he'd thought it was someone who'd been sent by the woman. Now he knew, he'd better get out. Fast. The backdoor. Can't risk the front door in case there were more police out there.

Damien had parked in a rare space the other side of Thurloe Square and was walking back to Brendan's house. He got to the front door and rang the bell. Scanning the other houses as he waited to be let in, he saw more CCTV in one London square than in the centre of Chichester and

Littlehampton combined.

Pushing open the letter box in the middle of the front door, he called, 'Come on Jimmy. Let me in.' No answer.

After about a minute, he called through the letter box again. 'Come on Jimmy. What's the holdup?' Then he bent down and looked through it and down the hall. Was that a leg he could see? He squatted slightly and held the letterbox flap open using a thumb on each side. Now he could see clearly. It was a leg protruding from a doorway. Was that Jimmy's leg?

Damien was anxious. 'Jimmy. Are you all right? Speak to me.' There was no reply. He pulled out his mobile phone and dialled 999. He wanted Metropolitan police backup and an ambulance.

He began to look to see if he could get in via any window. They were all secure. Should he try to break one? Then he heard a woman calling.

'Hey you. What do you think you're doing?' As he turned to face the street, he saw an immaculately dressed and coiffured woman glaring at him.

'I'm a police officer. Something has happened inside and I need to get in.'

She was not amused. 'Well I live next door, and someone has just climbed over the fence separating our gardens. They've broken part of it in the process and run off.'

A marked police car pulled up next to the front door and two uniform officers got out. Within minutes, one had climbed over the woman's fence and got into Brendan's house via the insecure back door. He found Jimmy on the floor with his warrant card close by. Opening the front door, the others entered. The paramedics were not far behind.

CHAPTER
TWENTY ONE

G roves listened intently before asking, 'How's Jimmy?'
Then when he put the phone down, couldn't stop
himself saying loudly, 'Fuck.'

He yelled to everyone in the office, then updated them all
with what Jimmy had managed to tell Damien. It had been
a struggle for Jimmy as one of his cheek bones was fractured.
That, as well as his broken nose, was preventing him talking
coherently. Groves concluded his narrative by telling them
Jimmy was conscious in a private wing of St Thomas's
Hospital and he'd be there for a day or two for observation
and any possible repair work to his face.

People looked shocked. Then the questions. Someone was
ahead of them. Who was it? Why? It seemed to confirm Violet
was in danger. What was it she knew? All set about their tasks
with renewed vigour.

Groves sat in his office. He telephoned the chief. It was not
a long call. The chief called his driver and told him where they
were going. As he sat in the back of his sleek black Jaguar as it
headed towards London, he started to make phone calls.

* * *

Campbell made a call. 'I've got everything. He'd put her
name in his diaries. Violet O'Donnell. And where they were due
to meet in an apartment he apparently owned in Tenerife.'

'Well done Campbell.' and after a perceptible pause, 'Come home. I miss you.'

'No! First things first. You know what I've got to do. I'm going to Tenerife.'

'Be careful. Do you think he told her?'

Campbell was ratty. 'How the hell should I know! We can't take a chance.'

The Scotsman practically pleaded, 'Will you come home then?'

Campbell was exasperated. 'Jesus Metcalf. You know I've got to sort out Gwendoline next. That might take a few days.'

Reluctantly he agreed. 'Ok.' Then the business side of him saw an opportunity. 'Make sure you find her collection. We'll be able to sell it on and make some cash on the side.'

'Money is starting to make you greedy.'

'Maybe, but I'm still cautious. So no clues to be left.'

'I know. Don't lecture. See you soon,' and they hung up. No point in telling him about the policeman. He'd only get more flustered.

* * *

John listened as Groves relayed what had happened. He liked Jimmy. Then he asked, 'Do we know if the person has taken anything?'

'No. The Met have agreed to leave a uniform PC at the address for security for twenty-four hours. I'll be going up there in a while to have a look around. Do you fancy a trip?'

'Yeah. I'll be outside Chichester police station in a few minutes. Can you pick me up there?'

'I'm on my way,' John yelled to Carol.

As Carol was leaving Chichester Police Station's visitors' car park, a marked traffic police car pulled up. In the front passenger seat was Murray and Groves was in the back. John struggled with his pot-leg and crutch into the seat behind the uniformed driver. The car took off and it wasn't dawdling. Occasionally, the driver blasted the two-tone horns when his speed dropped due to heavy afternoon traffic. They were at Thurloe Square within an hour.

All three detectives went up the steps to the front door which was slightly ajar. The Met uniformed officer was sitting on a kitchen chair that he'd put in the hall facing the door, and he was reading a book. Groves introduced himself and stated they were there to look round. They knew what they wanted to see. In the lounge they saw the shelves housing Brendan's journals.

The shoeboxes appeared to have been moved but not opened. Groves picked one up and put it on an occasional table. There were five of the journals already on it scattered about.

John questioned, 'These weren't on there when this room was originally photographed. Jimmy couldn't have put them there. The obvious conclusion is his attacker did. Has he discovered anything from them?'

Murray checked the journals. 'It looks like these are the last five Brendan wrote. At least a couple must cover the dates Brendan learned of his sister.'

John said, 'Let me have a look at the oldest. We'll never get fingerprints as Jimmy said the person who hit him was wearing gloves.' He slumped down into an armchair as

Murray passed him the oldest journal. Quickly, he started to skim the pages. Nothing of note. Details of art, lectures, and other non-related matters.

Groves and Murray began to go through the papers in the shoeboxes. They were crammed full. Lots of bills relating to the house and plenty of documents in Spanish. Neither could read Spanish, but they still checked each piece of paper.

John said to both, 'Nothing of note in this one. Murray. Could you please pass the next one? I can't quite reach it.'

Murray couldn't resist the jibe. Tugging his thinning hair and bowing, he said, 'Certainly my lord,' and he passed him the journal and bowed as he walked away backwards. They all laughed.

John began skimming the journal's entries. Then he saw it. A page had been ripped out. It was obvious. He read a few more pages skipping all the entries on art. Then another page was missing. 'I think I've found what the mystery individual was after. Unfortunately, it looks like he's taken the pages with him.' Both Groves and Murray looked at what John showed them.

Groves was troubled. 'We'll take the last five books then as exhibits and give them to the scientists. They should be able to see what Brendan wrote by enhancing the indentations on the following pages. Trouble is, it'll take a few days and I don't think we have that long.'

John looked towards one of the shoe boxes. Something caught his eye. Some way down below a lot of papers there was a little piece of red showing. 'What's that?' and he struggled to the table. Before the others could react, he delved in with a hand and pulled out a small red booklet. 'It's a Spanish bank book.'

He collapsed back into the chair he'd been sitting in to read the journals. 'It's from the Bank of Santander.' Opening it, he added, 'It's current. It's in Brendan's name and ... bingo. It's from a branch in Los Gigantes in Tenerife. L.G!'

Groves snatched it from him, 'Let me see.' He read what John had said. 'Brilliant. We're getting closer.'

He phoned the office and spoke to Doreen. 'Doreen, forget what you're doing, or going home. Los Gigantes in Tenerife. L.G. I need a large map of the island for when I get back. Find out if there's a place called Poblado. Anything you can,' and he hung up without any closing pleasantries.

He turned to the others, 'I want to go and see Jimmy while we're in London. I can't see that we'll gain anything extra from looking at anything else here. We'll take the five journals and all the papers etc in these shoeboxes back to Littlehampton. Come on. Let's go.'

When they arrived at St Thomas's Hospital, they soon located Jimmy in a private room. It was one the Met retained for their own officers should they need it urgently. Damien was fast asleep in an armchair and woke abruptly when Murray kicked his legs. It was only a quick visit to check on Jimmy's condition and Groves apologised that they had to leave so soon. Jimmy didn't really care. He wanted some peace and quiet.

He had been seen in Accident and Emergency and knew the full extent of his injuries thanks to a keen young doctor. Then he had been moved promptly to the private room. The chief had already been and kept him awake for a good fifteen minutes. Now he was praying under his breath that everyone would just leave him alone.

As they walked out of his room and into the corridor, John said, 'Hang on a minute. These are all the private rooms. Jake will be in one of them. While we are here, it wouldn't hurt to have a quick look at him. See what he had with him when he came in.'

Groves wasn't sure. 'He's out of it. Never likely going to recover. The hospital will let us know of any developments. We could see him then.'

John snorted. 'What I really mean is let's have a look and see what he has.'

Groves agreed and Murray went to the reception desk to see what room Jake was in.

A nurse accompanied them into Jake's room. 'I have to stay as he's in a coma. Hospital policy.'

John said, 'We want to check what he had with him when he was admitted.' Then a thought crossed his mind. 'Do you know who is responsible for paying his private fees?'

The nurse was sure. 'Yes. He is an employee of the British Museum. They are responsible for all his medical fees.'

Groves opened Jake's bedside locker and found his wallet. He swiftly went through its contents as the nurse kept her gaze on him. Nothing detrimental or of note. He put it back. There were some keys and pens but nothing else.

Murray opened the small wardrobe and found Jake's clothes all neatly hanging on a rail. He put his hand in every pocket. Nothing. He closed the door.

John, who had been propping up a wall, had watched him. Murray had missed something. He hobbled over to the wardrobe. 'Murray. Can I just look at something?' Murray wasn't offended and opened the door again. John couldn't bend down very easily with his pot-leg. He asked, 'Murray. Are there any socks in the shoes?'

Murray bent down and took Jakes shoes from the bottom of the wardrobe. One felt heavier than the other. There was a sock visible in the lighter shoe but not the heavier one. Dropping the lighter shoe back on the bottom of the wardrobe, Murray stuck his hand into the heavier shoe and pulled out a sock which appeared to have something inside it.

They were all watching as Murray took a mobile phone from the sock.

Groves looked in astonishment at John. 'How the hell did you spot that?'

John couldn't stop himself. 'It's a known fact. Hardly anyone checks shoes.' He didn't bother saying while he had been in a private ward recently waiting for his leg to be assessed, a nurse put his mobile in his shoe. She'd told him, "We get a few thefts from lockers. Normally they only take phones. So we put them in the patient's shoes. No one ever looks there!"

The nurse cut in. 'If you are going to take that phone, I must ask that you sign a form at reception to let them know.'

Groves was happy. He'd got a phone that might speed up part of his investigation. Another job for Walter. Would it divulge anyone else's name? Would it take him any further?

They stopped briefly at the reception before heading down to the car park.

Back in the car, Groves told the driver that speed was of the essence. He didn't need to be told twice. They were back at Littlehampton in less than forty-five minutes. Groves sought out Doreen who showed him a map of Tenerife that she'd stuck on the wall as it was too big for any of their white boards. He scanned the map. There it was, Los Gigantes.

'Talk to me Doreen. Have you found Poblado?'

'Of course I have. It's called Poblado Marinero,' and she pointed to a marked block that faced the enclosed marina. 'I can't get hold of anyone I can trust to tell me which apartment Brendan owned.'

Groves was on fire. He summoned a detective and handed him the five journals. 'I want you to go through these and see if you can get any address for Brendan's apartment in Poblado Marinero in Los Gigantes. Treat the journals gently. I want the scientists to check them out afterwards for indentations.'

He called out loudly to the officers that were still working in the office. 'Anyone here read Spanish?' He waited. No one.

Groves needed someone in Tenerife. He'd need authority. It would be for the chief constable to authorise. Would he tell the PCC? A risk. He could get round it. He snatched up a phone and called the chief. No problem. Authority for two to fly out. Back in the main office, he called Alison and Lynne.

Both women scurried home to find their passports and some clothes suitable for the climate. Murray booked the first flights available to Tenerife South. Mid-morning the following day from Gatwick. The flight would take roughly four hours. Then a taxi to L.G. Would it be quick enough?

There was only one hotel in the village. The price they demanded for a minimum five days' accommodation was astronomical and Murray told them so. He had no choice.

CHAPTER
TWENTY TWO

Campbell had been on Monday's last flight of the day from Heathrow to Tenerife. He had two night's accommodation booked in a hotel in Puerto Santiago. A village less than two miles from L.G. The flight had been tiring due to some brats crying during the flight keeping everyone awake. If he could have, he'd have killed them all. Who takes young kids on late night planes?

He'd arrived at the hotel in the early hours and decided to relax and recover with a lazy lunch and then deal with Violet during the evening. If all went well, he'd soon be flying back to England to kill Gwendoline. She'd be a totally different kettle of fish to deal with.

Brendan had advised Violet that he had to finish his work on Monday before he could fly out, so she wasn't at all worried he hadn't turned up as expected during the evening. A couple of days were neither here-nor-there. She'd been out as part of a group on a small boat whale watching with a handsome Spanish boatman. When all his other clients had left his boat, he offered her a private trip. She didn't refuse. Less than four miles out he stripped off under the baking sun. So did she. The boat rocked gently on the calm sea.

*   *   *

The woman strolled around Arundel. Her clothes,

although casual in appearance, were all designer items and her trainers were valued in the hundreds of pounds. She was five feet nine inches tall, extremely fit, statuesque and elegant. Her auburn hair was neatly coiffured by an expensive London stylist and her nails were immaculate. She fitted into the Arundel environs like a local.

A poster stuck in a shop window drew her attention. It was a kind of police wanted poster. It displayed a picture of Brendan Slack's murderer. But now he was actually named as Mike Caesar. She smiled, half right. The narrative explained brief circumstances of the murder and sought any information. She committed the telephone number of the police incident room to memory. She strolled on.

Time to head to Littlehampton.

* * *

Straight after the morning's meeting, Murray was seated in front of his computer with a Spanish interpreter alongside him. The shoeboxes were on his desk. As the interpreter stated what each item pertained to, Murray wrote a number in its top right corner in pencil. Then itemised it in an exhibit book. It was going to take him most of the day. He silently cursed Jimmy under his breath.

Alison and Lynne were in the air flying towards Tenerife South airport. They knew they were going to have to work fast to locate Violet. Each knew there were sixty apartments in Poblado Marinero split between six main blocks. Three blocks faced the marina with one, the main block, directly in the middle. That's where they were going to start.

Campbell knew the number. He'd found it whilst reading Brendan's journals. It was dead centre of the main block. It had the best, and most extensive view of the whole marina. The entrance door faced inwards and away from the marina and towards the building's main internal courtyard. Easily visible from various seats scattered about. Campbell knew that if you look as though you belong, no one will question you.

As the two detectives were in the taxi travelling to Los Gigantes, each got the same text from Murray. It was short and concise. The interpreter had discovered a set of legal papers showing Brendan Slack's Spanish property details. Murray forwarded the apartment number. Both women knew they were closing in fast on Violet.

They alighted from the taxi at the designated cab rank. Pulling a small trolley type case each, they entered the large internal courtyard. The case wheels clattered noisily as they were pulled uncaringly across the cobbled flooring.

Then they saw the number on a solid looking, wooden, ornate door. There was no letter box. Both seemed to walk quicker as they approached it. A pretty ceramic bell push was proudly prominent to the side of the door. Alison pressed it. Then waited. Nearly a full minute passed, and she was about to push it again, when the door swung silently open.

A perfectly tanned and beautiful woman in a white bikini stood before them. Aged in her early thirties and five feet eight inches tall with glossy short cut ginger hair. Her blue-grey eyes twinkled, implying an impish character. A pale lipstick was the only make up she'd used. When she spoke, she exaggerated her Irish accent.

Alison rummaged in her shoulder bag, and as she produced

her warrant card, explained, 'We're English police officers.' And then enquired immediately, 'Are you Violet O'Donnell?'

Violet was taken aback. 'Yes. How did you know?'

'We have been looking for you. I'm afraid we have some bad news. May we come in?' Alison could see Violet was hesitating. 'This apartment belongs to a gentleman called Brendan Slack. I believe you are expecting him?'

Violet acquiesced quietly and questionably, 'Yes?'

Alison wanted to clarify her own credentials and put Violet's mind at ease. 'We have already spoken to your friend Janice Greer who assisted us in finding you. For some reason, your mobile phone is turned off. So we have had no alternative but to fly out here personally to speak to you. Now, may we come in as what we need to talk about is private and confidential.'

Violet accepted the people at the door were who they claimed to be and seemed to know a lot about her. What was it they wanted to talk to her about? 'You'd better come in. Leave your cases in the hall.'

'Thank you,' and the two detectives followed Violet into the lounge that overlooked the marina.

Alison quickly broke the news to Violet that Brendan was dead. Violet's eyes moistened and she began to cry softly. The detectives sat in silence for several minutes allowing her to take in what she'd been told. Slowly, Violet began to regain her initial composure and dabbed her eyes with a tissue. Lynne offered to make her a cup of tea which she realised she now desperately needed.

'Please. The kitchen's down there,' and she waved a hand towards the hall. Within minutes, Lynne returned with three mugs of tea. Slowly, Violet began to feel better.

Alison gently queried of Violet if she was agreeable to answering some questions?

As Violet sipped her tea, several thoughts flew through her mind. She knew that British detectives wouldn't normally travel to a foreign country just to pass on a death message. They would arrange for the local police to tell the person. There had to be a lot more to it.

'Why have you come all this way? What haven't you told me?'

Alison replied cautiously, 'There is a lot more. Before I go into details, our main reason for coming here is to ensure your safety. We believe that you may be in danger. Would you consider moving to a hotel today at our expense? You'd be safer there.'

Violet looked at both detectives in turn. 'Are you serious? Who would want to harm me?'

Alison persisted, 'It's a long story.'

Violet was suddenly concerned about arrangements she'd made. They had to be cancelled. She was due to meet the boatman for afternoon drinks in a bar and would likely have been going back to his flat. Then later out for dinner. Not now. 'I 'm due to meet someone for drinks. I must let him know.'

Alison had picked up Violet mentioning a man. She considered what to do. Who he was and how they'd met. 'I'll come with you if I may when you meet him.'

'I've got a table booked at Charlie's restaurant up in the village this evening at 7pm. I don't have a number for it.' Then, after a short pause while she considered her options, she declared forcefully, 'I can't just leave here tonight. No! I shan't leave until tomorrow! The spare room here has single beds. You can stay there if you want.'

Alison could see a bit of logic in her response. 'We'll accept your offer and stay here tonight.'

As Violet went to put some clothes on, Alison told Lynne, 'I'll go with her. I'll phone you when we come back so don't answer the door to anyone. One of us will have to stay awake all night.'

CHAPTER
TWENTY THREE

Alison and Violet strolled alongside the marina and then up the hill towards the centre of the village. Campbell was bargaining with a boatman about hiring a small open type rowing boat with an outboard motor. He claimed he wanted it for some night-time fishing. The boatman was dubious but was won over by the wodge of euros that Campbell finally offered. Had he looked up, he'd probably have seen the two women walking past him.

When the two women reached the village's central square, Violet saw the boatman at a bar. She apologised to him and stated there had been a death in the family and she had to deal with it. He accepted the reason and left, alone. He knew the following day would probably see him find another single woman amongst the clientele who went whale watching with him on his boat.

Violet needed a drink and said so. They stopped at another bar, and she said, 'Earlier, you told me you wanted to ask me some questions. Now might be a good time.'

'We came across your details by a bit of luck. Very few people knew of your existence. How long have you known you were related to Brendan?'

Violet recalled reflectively, 'About five years ago, I bought a DNA test kit from an Irish firm on a whim. I'd heard about them from a friend. I spat into a tube and then posted it back to some obscure address on an industrial estate in Dublin. It cost me a pretty penny and then after a while they told me there hadn't been a trace. Janice chided me about wasting money. At the time, I thought she had been right.'

Violet paused as she sipped from her glass. 'Over time, I forgot all about it. Then I got a call out of the blue about three months ago. I thought it was a wind up at first. Some man with a voice that would make chocolate melt, telephoned me. He told me he worked for a firm that conducted DNA tests. It was a different firm to the one I'd used which made me think it might have been iffy. He said they'd taken over the firm I'd originally used. Then he said that I had a brother. Well you can imagine my shock.'

She took a large mouthful of wine. 'He told me his name. Brendan Slack. He even gave me a phone number for him.' She broke off and started to sob quietly for a couple of minutes as she thought of Brendan.

Alison deemed it prudent not to interrupt. She waited.

'I spoke to him a couple of times on the phone and I met him twice. My brother. Now you tell me he's dead. We were going to stay in his apartment for a fortnight and get to know each other,' and she started to cry again.

Alison said, 'So that explains why no one seemed to know about you.'

Through tears, Violet explained, 'I 'Googled' him and discovered so much about him. He was an art expert. He'd called me some time before I left England to tell me he might have been delayed in arriving here, so I hadn't worried. Now I've lost him.'

Alison checked her watch. It was approaching five-thirty. 'I'd like to go back to the apartment and make sure everything is all right for tonight.' She paid the bill and they strolled back in silence down the hill to the apartment. A quick call to Lynne and they went straight in.

Campbell had left the small boat moored as close to the entrance to the central block of Poblado as he could. Then he went for a quick pizza at one of the cafés close by. He knew he'd soon be back in Scotland where you were more likely to drown in the rain than be burnt to a crisp in the sun. He suddenly decided he preferred the rain.

Alison and Lynne went round the apartment and identified week spots in the security. They plotted how they should strengthen them. Violet stayed in her bedroom and slept for over half an hour. When she awoke, she was hungry having had a very light lunch. She had anticipated a late afternoon with the energetic boatman and never made love on a full stomach.

Now she told the two detectives she needed food and wanted to eat at Charlie's. She'd previously booked the table for two, having assumed the boatman would join her.

Alison and Violet left the apartment and walked back up the hill to the village's most popular restaurant. Lynne was happy with a sandwich which she'd make and eat later in front of the TV.

Campbell left the café and walked into the central courtyard of Poblado Marinero and sat on a stone seat with a clear view of the apartment. He watched the front door. No movement. Then he caught a glimpse of movement behind the net curtain covering the window to the side of the front door. It was the kitchen window. How could he do it? It was still daylight. He knew.

In the lounge, Lynne noticed Violet's handbag on top of a coffee table. She was about to phone Alison when the doorbell rang. Just the once. Forgetting security and believing it to be the women coming back for the bag, she opened the front door.

The gloved fist was the last thing she saw. As she dropped to the floor unconscious, her head hit the hall table knocking an ornamental glass dolphin off it. Glass shards flew across the tiled floor. Campbell stepped through the front door shutting it behind him.

So easy. He went into the first bedroom and pulled the duvet from the bed. Back in the hall, he wrapped it round Lynne tying it in place with the long strap of Violet's handbag. He had no trouble picking Lynne up from the floor and hoisting her over his shoulder. Then he left the apartment shutting the front door behind him. Less than ten minutes from ringing the doorbell.

He walked quickly towards the boat. Several people saw him. Some laughed thinking it was someone skylarking about. One who looked a little concerned appeared satisfied when Campbell shook his free hand by his mouth in a drinking motion indicated that she was drunk.

He lowered her into the boat and jumped in. The outboard fired on the third pull of the cord. Another ten minutes and he left the marina for the open sea between Tenerife and Las Palmas. Lynne didn't stir. Her ginger hair shone brightly in the last of the evening sun. Campbell saw it and thought to himself, Yep! Got to be Irish with hair that colour.

When there were no other craft about, he tied the boat's small anchor to her feet and the handbag strap around her hands. He lifted her onto the side of the boat and pushed her over into the sea. The anchor did its job and pulled her beneath the waves. She never regained consciousness. She drowned.

CHAPTER
TWENTY FOUR

They sat at a small table on the paved area outside the restaurant. Jason, the jovial host of Charlie's, was his usual self, keeping all his customers amused. He had quickly realised the two women did not want to be disturbed other than for their orders.

Alison decided the time was right to tell Violet what the police knew about the murder of her brother. She spoke for nearly half an hour. At times, she paused as Violet softly cried. The wine was consumed and then replenished as they slowly ate their food. Violet wasn't as hungry as she'd first thought.

Alison revealed the fact that someone had tried to destroy computer evidence of her existence. The police could only assume that someone might wish to do her harm. Then when a police officer had been assaulted at Brendan's London home, it advanced the theory she was being sought and was in imminent danger. Hence her and Lynne travelling to Tenerife.

The problem advanced by Alison was, why?

Violet picked at the last of her food. She had no idea. 'I've mainly spoken to Brendan by phone.' Then she smiled. 'I'd tell him I was busy in a hide somewhere and he'd rabbit on. I wasn't rude, but I told him a couple of times I couldn't talk. He never got the hint,' and she laughed. 'He was so wrapped up in his work. When we met, or spoke on the phone, he was so enthusiastic about what he was doing. He rarely asked what I was doing. I loved to listen to him,' and she laughed again before her eyes watered and she sobbed for a few seconds.

'He called me on a Friday morning about a fortnight ago. It must have been round about ten ish. You say he was killed on a Friday morning. I'd just got back to my hotel in Scotland after a night in a hide and I was knackered. I wanted a shower and my bed. All he wanted to talk about was some wetland in Arundel and a forged painting.' She laughed out loud attracting other diners' attention.

Alison enquired, 'A forged painting?'

'Yeah. A Turner I think. Yes. Definitely a Turner. I cut him off. I told him he could tell me all about it when he got here. Now I'll never talk to him again.' She finished the wine in her glass and watched the dying embers of the sun surrender to darkness.

Alison excused herself and walked a short way from the restaurant. She called the incident room at Littlehampton and passed on the information. Then for good measure, she texted Murray.

Campbell was in a taxi heading for Tenerife South airport. He sent a text. "Sister dead. On way to the Cotswolds."

After the meal, Alison and Violet left the restaurant and strolled down the hill back towards Poblado. En route, Alison rang Lynne's mobile number but got no reply. She tried several times. Still no reply. At the front door, she rang it again and could hear it ringing faintly inside the apartment.

Violet said, 'I've got a key,' and proffered it to Alison. She opened the front door and switched on the hall lights. The glass on the floor refracted different colours.

Alison called out, 'Lynne?' There was no answer. Where the hell was she? Now Alison was frightened. What had happened in the hall? Lynne would have cleared the glass up if she had knocked it off. Then she noticed a small smear of blood on the hall table. Urgently, she called out, 'Lynne.

Where are you?' She dialled Lynne's phone and found it ringing in the lounge by a chair. Why hadn't Lynne got it with her? Now she was really frightened.

She rang the office in Littlehampton. It went to answer phone. No time to lose. She rang Groves at home. He listened. He was worried. 'There's definitely no sign of her?'

'None guv'nor. Her phone's here and I've found her handbag by a bed. Strange thing, Violet's handbag is missing. She left it in the apartment when we went out to eat. I'm really worried. It's not like Lynne to wander off. I'm going to have to call the local police. What do I tell them?'

Groves thought quickly, 'You are ostensibly there to locate a possible witness in a murder investigation and get them back to the UK. I'll contact the British embassy and get someone to you as soon as I can. Things are going from bad to worse. Jimmy in hospital and now Lynne missing. Keep Violet safe.'

'One thing guv'nor. Might be nothing. Lynne looks a little like Violet because they both have ginger hair.'

He understood what she meant. 'Ok. Don't offer that to the locals.'

Groves was at home. He set about his tasks. The embassy in Madrid set about their task and contacted the consular officer in Tenerife. Alison contacted the local Guardia. Their night-time senior officer was contacted in Los Cristianos, who summoned his best detective from home who spoke fluent English. It was going to be a long night for a lot of people.

Groves called the chief constable. He had a lot to tell him and discuss. Then he called Murray. Officers were called from their homes to return to the office. Groves ignored all the speed limits as he scuttled back to the office. At midnight, he briefed his officers. They had the one extra clue as to why

Brendan may have been murdered and why Violet could possibly have been at risk.

The chief constable woke, and then told the PCC. She recorded the brief fact on a PCC computer that a woman police officer had gone missing in Tenerife and then went back to bed. Clifford Samsun awoke as the PCC laptop by his bed pinged that someone had posted a new report. Checking his bedside clock, he was surprised anyone would be working at such a late hour. He sat up in bed and read the one line his boss had just added. What the hell has happened out there?

Now he was wide awake. Then there was an almighty crash from downstairs. It sounded like wood splintering. Voices shouting. Noise of people running. Sounds of heavy feet on his stairs. His bedroom door flew open smashing against the wall. A man running straight towards him. People following behind him. Roland leapt towards him and accidentally headbutted him in the face. Then his arms were grabbed and wrenched behind his back and the feel of metal tightening around his wrists. Shit!

Roland told him from about two inches that he was nicked for corruption and then cautioned him, adding that he'd better pray that his new partner was found unhurt. Then Clifford was dragged brusquely from his bed wearing only his underpants. He wasn't even allowed to get dressed, nor even put on shoes. Down the stairs and into the back of a cold police van. Not even one of the many comfy and warm police cars abandoned at odd angles outside his house.

He was bounced about as the police van swung around bends and careered round junctions on its way to the custody suite at Chichester. He could hardly speak as the custody sergeant booked him in and then shut him in a cell. Huddling under a thin blue blanket, he cried.

CHAPTER
TWENTY FIVE

At his house, a team of officers were tearing it apart looking for anything incriminating. They'd recovered the PCC laptop from beside his bed and an additional personal laptop from his lounge. Hidden, taped to the underside of a drawer in the kitchen, they'd found a tablet computer. A small bag of cannabis and nearly a gram of cocaine. Enough to keep him locked up for a while.

Walter was summoned from his bed in Brighton. He'd hurriedly dressed and was driving his ancient 'Morris thousand' to Littlehampton. If he could find anything on the computers that would help, he was all for it. He'd teach that bastard to search his office and tamper with his work.

At four-thirty in the morning, the chief strode into the office. 'Did you get him Mr Groves?'

'Yes. He's at Chichester custody suite and Walter is in my office going through his laptops. It looks like he has a laptop from the PCC and his own personal laptop. The searchers found a tablet computer taped to the underside of a drawer with some drugs. Walter thinks there has to be something of note on the tablet, or he wouldn't have tried to hide it.'

The chief constable agreed. 'Good of Walter coming out at short notice in the middle of the night.'

Groves said, 'Once I told him who we had and what we had, I couldn't stop him.'

The chief constable smiled. 'I'm going to call the PCC

and tell her we've nicked one of her staff. Be interesting to see what she does.' Retrospectively, he said, 'Now you've got a PCC computer, you'll be able to see what is on it. Even if she demands it back, you can refuse as it's an exhibit. I hope Walter doesn't keep it charged up,' and he laughed. Then for good measure added, 'What a tangled web we weave.'

Someone handed him a cup of tea.

* * *

Campbell had got off the plane and found the car in the short term car park that had been left for him. The key was on top of the sun visor. He checked the boot. A long, thin, ornate wooden case that housed a rifle with telescopic sights, and a box of ammunition. A smaller, rectangular case that contained a Sig Sauer P226 automatic handgun with three magazines.

When he'd been in Tenerife, he'd had to use his false passport and credit card when he'd booked into the hotel. They didn't take cash. He didn't like it one bit. Cash was always simpler. The passport's picture of him was a passable likeness. You never knew who might come across it. It was bad enough that the airlines always seemed to scan the passports. It was always a risk. All his details were false and would take a searcher nowhere. Campbell wasn't a gambler.

As he drove away from the airport, he convinced himself that no one would ever trace him.

* * *

Walter strode out of Grove's office with the tablet in his hand. Everyone waited to see what he had to say. 'Mr Groves. May I have a word?'

Groves wanted everyone to hear. 'Tell me now Walter. The whole office is waiting on you.'

'Well. This tablet appears on first inspection to be used to communicate with just one person. There are emails to them and from them going back nearly two years. They are not regular. Mainly, if Clifford Samsun has something he deems of interest, he sends an email. He uses a completely different email account to any others I have found for him. If the person has a question, it seems to be answered by him on the next weekend. It leads one to think that Samsun only checks for incoming emails at weekends.' Walter smiled nervously as he looked around the office at all the faces focused upon him.

'I don't know if you are aware, but different PCCs often communicate with one another by email and pass on confidential information. He has had access to all this information from his official laptop. Some of which he has passed on via the tablet.'

A murmur went round the room. Someone passed him a mug of tea. Groves asked what everyone else wanted to know, 'Can you find out who the person he communicates with is?'

Walter smiled as he slurped his tea spilling some on the floor. He was loving the fact that he'd got Clifford Samsun. As if conspiratorially, he added, 'I took the liberty of using your computer Mr Groves. The person is called Gwendoline Hawthorne. She's a fifty-eight year old widowed woman and lives in a large manor house near Birdlip in the Cotswolds. According to my quick searches, she is extremely rich having inherited all her money from several deceased husbands. I have her full postal address. Would you like the post code?'

Groves didn't hesitate. 'Murray. We need a full team. At least eight detectives and four marked cars with drivers. Get them going now. Once they are within a quarter of an hour of the house, I'll contact the locals. I don't want anything leaking that we're on our way. Don't mess about. Knock once, then put the door in. Bring her back to Chichester.'

The chief constable checked the time. Approaching 6.15am. He phoned the PCC and updated her. She wasn't happy. He didn't care. Then he phoned John. He had a lot to tell him.

CHAPTER
TWENTY SIX

During the early hours, the usual two fishing boats that trawled between Tenerife, Las Palmas and La Gomera moved around. They followed their usual pattern. Each had 'fish finding' radar and 'bottom radar' to help. Trawling was only licensed during the hours of darkness so they didn't dally in one spot.

As they were conducting their final sweep of the night, one's net snagged. The men on the boat swore. They couldn't use the winch as it would probably destroy the net and cost them more than the night's catch was worth. They had to pull it up gently by hand, and one had to go overboard and try to untangle it. Slowly the net started to come up. The man dived into the sea. He kept to the side of the net. It was a dangerous job and he didn't want to get tangled up.

Then he saw the problem through the crystal clear water. An anchor rope caught around a body. He yelled up to his crew mates. They all swore. The police would want to speak to them all. No early breakfast and bed for them. Slowly they hauled it on board and untangled it from their net. It was a woman. Then they saw that the hands were tied by her handbag strap. The anchor rope was wrapped around her feet and tied. Each looked at the others. It was obvious to them. She'd been killed.

The skipper radioed the coastguard. The coastguard informed the police who told the Guardia. Their control room phoned the senior officer who was sitting in the apartment's lounge talking to Alison. He asked that the boat enter Los Gigantes marina and moor up, pending the body being recovered to the mortuary.

Turning to Alison, and speaking in English, he said, 'Would you please come with me. I would like you to see something.'

Violet said, 'Should I come too?'

'No. I don't think so. We will only be an hour at most. My officer will stay with you.' Then he got up, and with Alison walked out into the courtyard's early morning sunshine.

Alison enquired, 'What's this about?'

He said, 'A fishing boat has dragged up a body a few miles offshore. We very rarely have bodies found at sea. It seems a coincidence, the person is a woman. The skipper thinks she has been deliberately killed.'

Alison staggered. She couldn't believe it could be Lynne. What was he taking her to see? The body? Dead bodies didn't bother her as she'd seen so many during her service, but not one of her friends. She recovered her footing and they walked around the marina to the deep water mooring by the entrance. Then they waited patiently.

The trawler slowly entered the marina and hove to alongside the quay. An unmarked hearse drove around and stopped alongside it. The two attendants stepped onto the trawler with a stretcher. Then as they placed the corpse onto it, Alison saw the wet ginger hair. Tears flowed from her eyes. She had to be sure. She looked down into Lynne's lifeless face. She cried for less than a minute and then she was livid. She knew whoever had done this was going to suffer. She'd make sure of it.

The officer didn't need to ask. Alison's actions told him. They walked back in silence to the apartment. Alison had to tell Violet, who took it badly. Death was stalking her.

The doorbell rang and the Spanish officer sprang up with a drawn gun. He'd noted the hair of Violet and Lynne was the same colour although Violet's was short and Lynne's was long. It hadn't taken him any time at all to think that the murder could have been a mistaken identity. Caution at all times had kept him safe during his career.

Opening the door, he saw Vernon, a man he knew from the British consulate. Introductions were brief as he was brought up to speed and Alison confirmed the murdered woman was Lynne. She needed to brief the office before they heard from anyone else or from any news media. She excused herself, claiming to need a bit of air and stepped into the courtyard.

She called Groves on his mobile. It wasn't a long call. He composed a swift group text to all the officers. They would be a lot more circumspect when dealing with people if they had the knowledge that a police officer had been callously murdered. He'd brief the whole team fully at the next office meeting.

The chief sat down heavily. 'This is serious. She went out there to help solve a murder. Now she's become a victim. I don't care how you do it Mr Groves. Just find the bastard who's done this. I'm going to sort the PCC out. She's trying to protect a corrupt member of her staff. I reckon she must know he's bent.'

Groves thought for a second and said, 'Just a thought sir. Why don't you go and see the duke? He's got contacts in higher places than we have. He could protect your back if it comes to it. Remember, she could sack you and she has high political friends to protect her.'

The chief looked sternly at Groves. He was about to say something but thought better of it. Then, with a little forethought, 'You may have a point. I'll go and see Lynne's family first. I don't want them to be hounded by the press when they get wind of this. Murray. Can you sort out some accommodation for them?'

Murray nodded. He was too annoyed to talk.

Campbell had bought a sandwich from a small roadside service station and was walking back to his car when he heard a cacophony of sirens approaching. He stopped and watched the four marked police cars tearing past. Another punter who had stopped to watch, laughingly exclaimed, 'They won't sell any ice creams going that fast,' and he walked to his own car chuckling to himself.

When they were approximately fifteen minutes away, the lead car's passenger, Sergeant Greenthorne, updated Groves. It was his spur to begin to contact the local police station. The lethargic attitude when the phone was finally answered implied they seemed to be taking life very easy. The station sergeant on duty was eating his breakfast and with his mouth full at times, casually tried to explain that he knew Gwendoline Hawthorne very well and she was as honest as the day was long.

Groves wasn't concerned with what he thought about her. 'Sergeant, I'm telling you now as a courtesy. We are coming onto your manor. One police force to another.'

'Well thank you for the information. When do you think

you'll be here?' and he bit into his bacon sandwich.

In the background, Groves could hear the sound of several two-tone horns growing rapidly louder. 'I think that might be my officers just about to pass your station.'

The phone went dead. The sergeant dropped his bacon sandwich. He ran to his tunic hanging on the back of a door and searched the pockets for his mobile. He couldn't remember how to find the address book on the phone. Eventually he found it and searched for Gwendoline Hawthorne. Talking to himself, his sticky fingers misdialled. Swearing, he started again. It was way too late.

The four cars had swept up the mile long, meandering drive to the manor house's front door. The officers all decamped with a couple running all the way round to the back. An officer rang the large doorbell by pulling on an ornamental chain. No one could have opened it in time. Officers with several 'door boshers' were swinging in tandem at the lock. The door stood up to the onslaught for less than a minute. It finally gave way and the officers stormed in. Sergeant Greenthorne shook his head. Swinging the battering ram had temporarily affected his vision.

They searched the whole house. There was no one at home. But the bed was still warm and unmade. If she'd dressed and gone out, the bed would be cold. They searched the house again. She was in there somewhere. Greenthorne stood at the front door and looked around. Where was she? Then he remembered. When he ran in he thought a picture had moved but put it down to the exertion of swinging the 'door bosher'.

He went to the picture facing the front door in the centre

of the large entrance hall. It was nothing special, a horse standing still in a field. Was there a door here somewhere? Carefully, he tried to take the picture off the wall. It was secure. Other officers joined him. They were running their hands all over the wall. An officer tapped the wood panelling. It sounded the same all over. Was it hollow?

An officer lay on the floor and examined the panelling where it met the carpet. He prized the carpet back. The wood didn't appear to be attached to the floor. There was a minute gap. He took out a notebook and ripped out a page. He was able to slide it along under the panelling. But only for about three feet. Then the panelling was properly attached. It had to be a door. How to open it?

Sergeant Greenthorne made a decision. They'd break through using a battering ram and if he was wrong, he'd apologise at his disciplinary hearing. Two swings of the 'door bosher' and the wood panelling splintered as it broke. Through the small hole they saw her. Wearing a dressing gown and sitting in an upright chair.

With vigour, they battered the hole bigger. They could see the room was about ten feet square. Each of the three walls bore a single large painting in a guilt frame with a special picture light illuminating each one.

Greenthorne told her, 'We are police officers from Sussex. I am arresting you for conspiracy to murder and corruption.' Then he cautioned her.

Hawthorne was belligerent. 'I demand a phone call. I want my lawyer.'

Greenthorne was adamant, 'Certainly. When we get back to Chichester.'

'I'm not leaving here until I have my lawyer.'

Sergeant Greenthorne turned to two officers, 'Drag her out and put her in a car. If she can't be bothered to get dressed, so be it.'

Gwendoline looked shocked. 'Do you know who I am? I'm a friend of the PCC and the county's Lord Lieutenant. You'll do as I say.'

The two officers moved towards her with a set of handcuffs, via the battered, enlarged hole in the panelling. Each took hold of an arm and lifted her from the chair. They handcuffed her and marched her out to a car. She demanded the local police were involved. There was no way she was going to Sussex in her night attire. She was wrong.

Campbell was tucked in the undergrowth by the side of the drive about two hundred yards away with a monocular glued to an eye. He saw her being put into the car. There was no time to lose. He scampered back to his car as quickly and surreptitiously as he could, then he sent a short text.

The Scotsman swore. Now he knew they were in trouble. She had to be stopped from talking. Was it going to be too late?

CHAPTER
TWENTY SEVEN

The chief constable of Gloucestershire was soon on the phone to the chief constable of Sussex. As soon as he knew a police officer had been murdered, his attitude changed from mild belligerence to unparalleled support. He would deal with the local PCC and anyone else who tried to interfere.

Gwendoline wouldn't shut up as she sat in the back of the police car. She was going to complain to her political friends in the county. When no one seemed concerned, she started naming names, but that didn't help either. Then she started mentioning government ministers. It mystified her that no one seemed to care. As she moved about, the handcuffs dug into her wrists. That set her off even more. If the officers thought they could get away with it, they'd have taped her mouth shut. The driver and one detective were deemed sufficient to convey her back to Sussex.

The vehicle drove away from the house and travelled down the long winding drive. At the junction with the regular country road the driver stopped the car to check for traffic. That's what Campbell was waiting for. He'd set up the rifle and was in a comfy firing position. A single aimed shot from less than sixty yards. The bullet found its mark. It punched a small hole in the windscreen of the vehicle passing close by the drivers left ear. Then into Gwendoline's right eye and into her brain. Hardly losing any momentum, the bullet flew out of the back of her head leaving a larger exit hole. Bits of her brain, skull and blood were plastered over the rear of the car. She was dead in an instant. The bullet left the vehicle smashing the rear window and lodged in the trunk of a tree some fifty yards back along the drive.

The two officers were shocked. At first, they weren't sure exactly what had happened. A passing vehicle may have thrown up a stone that smashed a neat hole in the windscreen. Then they realised Gwendoline had shut up. They saw her head lolling back at an unusual angle. All the mess behind her. Both had seen the muzzle flash a millisecond before the hole appeared in the windscreen. They realised within a further millisecond it had been a bullet. Both ducked down in case there were more coming.

The detective fumbled for the car's radio handset. They had left their Airwave radio with the officer who'd remained with the searching party at the manor house. Now their car's fitted radio was tuned to the Sussex control room. They needed help. It was going to take a few minutes. Plenty of time for Campbell to jog unseen by them back to his concealed vehicle. Stashing the rifle back under the rear seats, he took the handgun out from under the driver's seat and tucked it into his waistband. No one was going to be a problem even if they found him.

The remaining officers, oblivious to what had happened, began a thorough search of the house. One took photographs on his phone of the three paintings and forwarded them to the office. Murray forwarded them to the Metropolitan Police's Arts and Antiques Squad who replied within minutes. They asked that no one touch them and was there room for a helicopter to land at the manor house?

When it was confirmed affirmatively by Greenthorne, they explained they'd be there by helicopter with an art expert in about an hour.

Greenthorne and his fellow officers heard the distant sound of two-tone horns. They didn't know about the incident at the end of the drive for eleven minutes. Sussex control room had called the incident room and spoken to Murray. He called Greenthorne.

Greenthorne knew he had to send someone to help. One car and three officers was all he could afford. He couldn't leave the house without an adequate number of officers to ensure its security. Everything was going wrong. He was running short of officers. He needed help.

All the Sussex officers knew the witness they were relying on was now dead. Murdered. It didn't take a genius to know she'd probably been killed to stop her from talking. But who by?

Groves updated the chief constable who was back on the phone to the chief constable of Gloucestershire. The IPCC was informed by both of the chief constables. They appeared happy with the way the investigation was to be handled. Although the murder had taken place in Gloucestershire, Sussex would assist the enquiry as it was all part of an ongoing investigation. Gloucestershire Constabulary would maintain a watching brief with several officers attached to Groves' team.

The helicopter landed practically ten minutes early, and four men got out. They walked briskly to the front door where Greenthorne waited. There were three Met detectives and a small man in a tweed suit wearing old-fashioned wire-rimmed glasses.

Introductions were swift. A DCI, a DI and a DC all from

the Arts and Antiques Squad. The small man, who was an art expert, and something to do with the National Gallery, was nervous and very anxious. He'd never been in a helicopter before and he didn't like the experience. Now he was on terra firma, he was delighted.

'Where are the paintings?'

Greenthorne said, 'If you'd like to follow me gentlemen, I'll show you.'

As they approached the small room which now had a larger opening, the expert saw the painting on the rear wall. 'Oh no! It can't be. He started to run into the room with the Met officers. He looked at the paintings on the side walls. 'No. They can't be. No. No.' He turned to one of the Met officers. 'My bag. It's in the helicopter.' The DC ran back out. The Sussex officers looked on with amusement.

Greenthorne asked the DCI, 'What's the problem?'

'You don't recognise these pictures?'

Greenthorne answered, 'No. Are they any good?'

The D.I. looked at him with incredulity. 'Good? If they are genuine, they are worth millions. They should all be hanging in galleries. One of them is a Gainsborough and the other two are early works by Bruegel the Elder. The reason we're interested is that there was a rumour from an informant some years ago that rich collectors were somehow stealing originals and replacing them with exceptionally good copies. Trouble was, we didn't know which ones were stolen or how they were doing it. To have checked every painting with an expert would have taken years. Gwendoline Hawthorne's name had been mentioned among many others at the time. We couldn't prove anything, so it was recorded and left on file. When your office sent the photos of the pictures to us earlier and mentioned her name, we were more than interested.'

The officer returned and handed the little man a black bag. He took out a small object that looked like a torch. When he turned it on, there was no light. A blue glow slowly grew at one end. The Sussex officers who could see it were puzzled. He stood close to the painting on the rear wall and pointed it at the signature. He was less than three inches from it. As the blue light shone from the 'torch' onto it, he held it steady for nearly a minute. Then the little man stepped back. He was shaking.

The DCI asked, 'Well?'

The little man ignored him. He stepped close to one of the other paintings and again pointed his blue light at the signature. He started muttering. 'No' over and over again. Then turning to the last picture he again shone his now shaking blue light at the signature.

Turning to Greenthorne, he said, 'Can I have a glass of water please?' An officer scampered off.

The DCI was anxious. 'Well?'

The little man stepped out of the room and sat down heavily on a chair. He was visibly shaking. 'I think all three are genuine. I need to get them back to London where I can confirm it for sure.'

A Sussex officer stepped into the hall and addressed Greenthorne. 'Sergeant. I've found these in the study,' and held out a journal, a laptop and a small tablet. 'This looks like the journals in the pictures from Brendan Slack's house.'

The little man heard the name. 'Brendan Slack? How do you know what was in his house?'

Greenthorne broke the news that he had been murdered. The little man was more shocked about Brendan than the discovery he'd just made regarding the paintings.

'He was an acquaintance of mine. We moved in the same circles. If you'd care to open that, I can tell you if it's Brendan's. I'd recognise his writing anywhere.'

The officer opened the journal. The little man looked at the writing. 'It's Brendan's,' and he drained the glass of water. Then he saw the small tablet with an indented motif on the case. Pointing at it, he said, 'That's from the British Museum. She shouldn't have that. It's confidential.'

Another officer held a piece of paper. 'We found this with the journals in an open package from a courier company in New York. I think it's best I read what this note says.'

Greenthorne didn't understand, but said, 'Yeah. Ok.'

The officer began to read the note loudly so everyone could hear. "This is what I recovered. Object achieved. Hope you are satisfied. Please place agreed funds in my usual account." Then after a short pause, he added, 'It's signed just MC.'

Greenthorne realised the relevance of the note. Especially the initialled signature. The DCI asked Greenthorne, 'Would you mind if I arranged for some of my officers to come here and search the place once you've finished? We would be more concerned with anything to do with art.'

'I can't see a problem, but as a matter of protocol, I think you should clarify everything with DCI Groves.'

'Yes. I understand. I'll do that.'

Back at Littlehampton, Groves had a lot on his mind. He had already assigned a couple of officers to interview Clifford Samsun. He'd politely declined Roland's offer to conduct it and assigned him to liaise with Alison and the Arts and Antiques Squad officers.

Greenthorne had kept Groves appraised by regular phone calls about the continuing search. He'd updated him on the art works. Not one was a Turner. Each was apparently worth a great deal of money, but no Turner. Groves was developing an urge to scratch his head. Alison had told him that Violet confirmed that Brendan said he'd discovered a forged Turner. Had she misheard?

When Greenthorne told him about the journal, laptop and tablet computer, Groves asked him to look quickly at the journals for the last week's entries. He waited expectantly with the phone pressed firmly against his ear. Greenthorne scoured the pages. He found what he was looking for.

'Guv'nor. I've got it. Monday's entry. Brendan has recorded he went to Parkland House and he examined a Turner which he believes is a forgery. He told the British museum but doesn't say who he spoke to.'

'Brilliant. We're getting there. Does he say which painting it is?'

'Yeah. Not any specific name. He just describes it and says why he thinks it's a forgery. Lots of scientific wording.'

'Don't bother telling me. Can you get one of the drivers to bring it back with the two computers. I'm sure Walter will be able to tie Gwendoline back to Clifford Samsun. Murray can sort out evidencing the journal. Things are definitely looking up.'

Greenthorne wasn't so sure, 'I don't get it guv'nor. If she had Brendan killed because he discovered a forged Turner, why hasn't she got the original? She's allegedly got three

154

other original paintings that should be in galleries around the country. Where's the Turner? Who has it? Was she killed to stop her telling us where it is? The person who shot her took a hell of a risk. Killing her while she's sitting handcuffed in a police car.'

Groves could see his point. He'd also tried to work out the answers to some of the questions without success. 'Lots of questions. No answers at the moment. Once you've wrapped everything up, we'll have a full office meeting and see what develops.'

Greenthorne agreed that the Met helicopter with the expert and the DCI should take the three paintings back to Battersea Heliport in London and then on to the National Gallery where more experts could confirm their probity.

Groves needed the journal, laptop, and tablet back at Littlehampton urgently. Greenthorne arranged to send one of the cars with just the driver back to Littlehampton with the three items. The two detectives originally from the vehicle were to remain at the manor house. Groves needed more detectives at Littlehampton.

Campbell was back in the undergrowth at the side of the drive. He watched the paintings being put into the helicopter. There was nothing he could do to stop it. The machine took off. He sent a quick text. Then he saw the journal being brought out of the house and put into a car. Could he get hold of it? Would it be worth the risk? Not now. Everything was going wrong. He texted again. The simple texted reply, 'Come home'. He had no real choice.

* * *

Alison was helping the authorities in Tenerife. It appeared to her that she would have to stay there for a few days. She was going to do whatever she could to bring Lynne's killer to justice, either in Spain or elsewhere. Violet was still her concern. She was probably no longer likely to be targeted, but she couldn't be sure. A phone call home to Simon was the answer.

* * *

The woman wasn't concerned. She heard the news on the car radio as she drove back to Littlehampton. Gwendoline was of no consequence. Dead, she wasn't a problem. Alive, well you never knew. She didn't care who'd done it. She had a bigger problem on her mind.

CHAPTER
TWENTY EIGHT

Unknown to the chief constable, Groves had made a call to John. It just clarified what he'd already been told by the chief. John sat in his chair thinking. Is this all about Brendan discovering a forged painting? Kill him and no one would be any the wiser? Surely there's more to it than that? John scratched his head.

Brendan had recorded discovering the forgery in his journal and the fact he'd informed the museum. Who? Probably said so on the tablet as well. That's why they had to be taken. How would the killer have known? Did Brendan tell someone other than Violet? Someone at Parkland? Possible. Someone who could have passed on the information for a backhander. Someone at the museum?

Where is the original Turner? Someone has it. Most likely Gwendoline's killer. Why kill her? Definitely to stop her talking. Did she have Brendan killed for someone else? Probably. Most likely the person who eventually killed her. Another collector of stolen art? How did they know about each other?

How did they discover his long-lost sister? Was it just from Samsun searching Walter's office? Why go after her? Did they think Brendan told her? Must do. It seems they didn't know what she looked like. Lynne found that out.

Clifford Samsun had made the serious mistake of being caught. That led police to Gwendoline Hawthorne. Is he going to become a possible target of the killer? She had three paintings in a hidden room. They must be the genuine articles. She hasn't got a Turner. Who's got that? It all comes back to the Turner.

He scratched his head again. Sod it. He thought better with a glass in his hand. He called to Carol who was making the bed, 'Carol. Any chance of a glass of wine please?'

She came in with a full wine glass. 'You're becoming an alcoholic.'

* * *

The chief had been to see the duke. He wanted to make sure he kept him updated. The police knew the identity of Brendan Slack's killer and where he was. Now the duke knew what the police were doing to put the man before an English court. He had a rudimentary knowledge of extradition procedures and knew they couldn't be rushed. Although the chief alluded to the fact that the enquiry had spread, he didn't elaborate. He had decided that he'd keep the information confidential for the time being.

* * *

Roland felt cheated. He would have got Samsun to talk. He was sure of it. No point in getting upset. Lynne was uppermost on his mind, and anything he could do to catch her killer was paramount. He needed to talk to Alison as a matter of urgency and find out everything that had happened from the moment they landed in Tenerife. Finding a quiet office he called her.

One thing he did well, and Alison knew, was investigate everything thoroughly including silly little things that some officers might overlook. If he couldn't get to Lynne's killer via Samsun, he would work it out by deductive work and logic.

He considered what was known. The police could prove that Mike Caesar was Brendan's killer. They had photos of him at the hotel and the castle, and fingerprints on the upstand. The Australian volunteer had identified him as the person in the corridor in the white coverall. They had tracked him to New York. The Americans had confirmed that the fingerprints had been identified as belonging to an ex-military policeman. Mike Calder.

Now the Americans were conducting their own enquiries as to his unexplained wealth and movements and they were watching him. He hadn't left the States. They knew the British would be seeking his extradition. If they could prove anything against him first, they'd rather he was locked up by them in America. Roland knew Mike hadn't killed his friend and partner.

He needed more help. Someone who might be able to ask questions and not be put off by people who don't want to answer. Alison was out of the game stuck temporarily in Tenerife still watching over Violet. Who could he call on? He needed a new partner. Someone pedantic who could get things done. Doreen was busy typing. Roland knew she was like him. Leave nothing unturned and then check it again. He decided to approach her when the office was quiet.

* * *

John was deciding who he was going to call on for some help. He'd phoned Simon who told him he was on his way to Tenerife. Perfectly understandable. His girlfriend and future wife was alone with a witness and an officer had been killed. Nothing would happen to her or Violet once he was there. His military training with the paras and then the SAS was second to none. And he was incredibly violent when he needed to be.

Rocky was an avid watcher of interesting news items from various outlets around the world. Terrorist activity intrigued him the most. If he believed he could help a Government in any way, he knew which person in which branch of their security service to contact. His address book had filled with their details over many years when he'd been employed by GCHQ.

The British Government had invested a lot of time and money training Rocky when he was starting out in the security services. They'd sent him to foreign countries to learn their tactics and methods which were often considered illegal in Britain. Armies at home and abroad taught him things that were definitely illegal in their own countries. The argument being that one couldn't always comply with the law when dealing with terrorists that were bent on causing multiple casualties. They had to be stopped in any way possible.

Known by most as Rocky, Richard Boulder was clever. Extremely clever. He had been the youngest person in the UK to achieve a degree in electronics. But he didn't stop there. A master's in engineering followed swiftly by a PhD in computer science.

He'd started as a junior employee with GCHQ and

had quickly worked his way up to become the head of his department. He should have been office bound, but he loved travel. That eventually became his downfall. He often went on precarious missions to far flung countries and was eventually shot in his left leg for his trouble. Now he walked with a limp due to a prosthetic lower leg.

GCHQ considered his impairment as grounds to part company with him. He had never worked out how a prosthetic leg affected his work. It was mainly his brain power that had ensured his meteoritic rise in the secret services. His enforced retirement had been a severe blow. But Rocky never held a grudge and would often 'subcontract' his services to his former colleagues.

John knew Rocky. He'd worked with him before. He knew his background well. He knew after he'd been shot, GCHQ had dispensed with his service and he'd wound up in a privately funded unit in Kent where many retired military personnel were employed. He knew he was completely trustworthy and not averse to bending rules, or actually breaking them. John made a phone call.

* * *

Put on a brown coat and you can practically walk anywhere in a museum unchallenged. Just like a nurse's uniform in a hospital. She carried a clip board. It added a little more credence to the disguise. There was the empty desk where Jake used to sit. Nothing on the desktop nor in the drawers. So where the hell was it?

CHAPTER
TWENTY NINE

Walter had readily agreed to stay on and wait for Gwendoline's laptop and tablet to arrive. Groves had told him he wanted to be able to associate Samsun with Gwendoline. It would be another nail in Samsun's coffin. Walter just wanted Samsun to be fully aware it was him who was hammering the nails home. No one messes with Walter and gets away with it.

As the clock drifted round to mid-afternoon, Groves called the chief constable and asked for more staff. He was surprised how quickly the chief agreed. The second murder team from Littlehampton was put at his disposal. They had all heard about the unusual murder at the castle and Lynne's brutal killing and were happy to assist in any way they could. Murray was soon dispatching them on assignments. Yet another car, this time with three detectives on board, was dispatched to Gloucestershire.

* * *

John called Alison's mobile. When she saw his name come up in the caller display, she forced a smile. She was awaiting Simon's arrival and knew she'd be safe when he got there. Now she saw John's name. They fought like cats and dogs, but really liked and respected each other. Suddenly, Alison saw John's fingerprints on parts of the murder enquiry at the castle.

She answered in her most polite of voices, 'Hello. Can I help you?'

John chortled, 'Yes you can.' Then more seriously said, 'I'm sorry to hear about Lynne. I didn't know her personally. Such a nasty way to die. From what I'm told, she could have been mistaken for Violet. Simon should be there soon and then you can rest easy for a while.'

Alison couldn't stop herself, 'How the hell do you know about Violet or Lynne? That's all confidential and part of a murder enquiry.'

John was unashamedly blasé, 'Yes. I know. I'll keep it to myself. What I wanted to ask you, have any local enquiries been done to trace the boat that the killer used to take Lynne out to sea? It was likely hired from someone on the quay. The killer wouldn't want to draw any attention to themself by stealing a boat. There are a few CCTV security cameras around the marina. I know someone who can tap into them if needed.'

Alison held the phone at arm's length and stared at it for several seconds. Then placing it back to her ear, said aggressively, 'I don't know. I'm just a witness as far as they are concerned. They don't tell me much.'

John needed an answer. 'I'm sorry Alison. I need to know if you can tell me a rough time. It's important. I should soon have access to a photograph of every person who flew out of Tenerife in the twenty-four hours after you got back to the flat from Charlie's. If I can marry one with someone hiring a boat, it will probably be the killer. Then I can get the person's name from their passport.'

Alison thought for a few seconds. She knew John had a lot of contacts that could do extraordinary things, including Simon. Many of them probably illegal, but they were only rumours. No proof. Well, perhaps she knew things that Simon had done that were definitely illegal, but that was different. He'd been protecting her.

She believed John probably wasn't always on the right side of the law. Again, no proof. He always seemed to have had the ability to think outside the box. Just the person to help her track down Lynne's killer. She welcomed his involvement. 'Listen John. When Simon gets here, I'll go out and make some enquires myself. We left for Charlie's about 6.30pm and Lynne was here then. If the killer did hire a boat, it must have been prior to that. We got back to the apartment at about ten o'clock.'

John was quiet as he considered what Alison had said. Then, as if speaking rhetorically, 'It wouldn't have been dark for long and the lighting around the marina is not switched off until 1am. So how did the killer get Lynne to the boat? It might be quicker to search for her on the CCTV cameras from 6.30pm. I'll get that started.' Then he said to her, 'I don't think either you or Violet are in danger at the moment. I suspect the killer probably thinks he's murdered Violet. It would probably help if the press got that impression.'

Alison saw the logic of implying it was someone other than Lynne who'd been killed and agreed about the CCTV. 'I'll see what I can find out and I'll call you.'

John added his now usual rider. 'Alison. For the sake of everyone, please do not tell anyone about me. For various reasons, I can't be involved in any part of the investigation regarding the Arundel murder or Lynne's death. Tell me you'll keep my contribution as confidential?'

Alison wasn't surprised and quickly formed an opinion. 'You seem extremely well informed, so you must be speaking to someone else.'

John snorted. 'I may be. Let's say someone keeps me updated. The murder of Lynne though is different. This is between us for the time being. Agreed?'

'Of course,' and she hung up. Now she knew she had the right person on her side. She didn't force or hide her beaming smile.

Rocky had already hacked into the marina's CCTV system and had downloaded all the video from it for the preceding two days to a stand-alone computer. There were only six cameras around the quay. They all played at the same time on a single split screen. When John called him, he was able to quickly find the images from 6.30pm. Then at ten to seven, he saw what he was looking for. He enlarged the camera's video to a single screen discarding the other five cameras.

He watched a man carrying a large object over his shoulder, which was nearly all wrapped up but just showing the top of a head, walk from the central block of Poblado to one of the jetties. What gave it away as a person, was the hair hanging down. Ginger. Rocky saw the bundle lowered indelicately into a small boat. Then the man jumped in after it, and within a couple of minutes, the boat left the jetty heading for the marina's entrance to the sea.

Rocky ran the images back and forth and ultimately managed to freeze a perfect frame of the man's face. He enhanced the image before saving a copy. Then it was a simple matter for him to hack into the airlines' manifests of passengers due to fly out of Tenerife within the following twenty-four hours. Each passenger had had their passport scanned by the relevant airline. He set a computer programme running which was able to search for similar images. As each potential image froze, he checked it and then set the programme running again.

Within two hours of John's call, Rocky was sending him an email which contained several attachments. The short video clip, the single image of the man's face and an image of a page of a passport.

John viewed the video. It was obvious to him that the man was carrying Lynne over his shoulder all wrapped up. The hair dangling down from the bundle was ginger. It had to be Lynne. He glared hard at the still image, committing it to memory. It was as good as a photograph for John. Then the single page of a passport. Rocky's email stated he'd lifted the image from the passenger manifest of EasyJet. It was that of a passenger on an evening flight back to London Gatwick. The picture was unquestionably of the same man. The name shown was Campbell MacTavish.

John considered it. It had to be a false name. No killer would use his real name. He looked at the date of birth. 23rd August 1979. It wasn't a usual false date that springs quickly to mind should someone ask. Could that be genuine? Whenever John had used an alias, he'd always used his correct first name. It was too easy to ignore a false name if someone called it out unexpectedly. Mike Caesar sprang to mind. He'd used his correct first name.

John called Rocky. The conversation was rather stilted. John explained his thoughts and then asked if there was anything that Rocky could do. There were no promises. It would be a long shot. The false passport, if that is what it was, had been issued by the Glasgow Passport Office. Hacking into it would not be a problem. If the passport had been posted to an address, it would solve a lot of problems. If it had been collected, it would cause even more problems. Both thought the latter was most likely.

Then John made a suggestion. Rocky wasn't sure. Even in his exalted position at GCHQ, he'd never even considered it before. He doubted if anyone had even tried to do it before. He'd need help. He knew who he wanted. Zena. They often worked together in the lab in Kent. John knew of her and was happy.

Rocky became thoughtful. Campbell MacTavish was obviously a Scottish name. The passport had been issued in Glasgow. A hitman would probably take a false name from the country of his birth. Also if the man had a patent Scottish accent, a name from anywhere other than Scotland may have caused risen eyebrows and be remembered. The one thing hitmen never wanted. Both Rocky and John agreed.

It would speed everything up. The population of Scotland was a mere six million compared to England's over sixty million. England was definitely out of the question. There were still no promises. Rocky ran through how he proposed doing it.

His first search would be the name Campbell MacTavish. He didn't hold out much hope of a direct hit. Any would have to be researched.

His second search would be for just Campbell as either a first or last name. Rocky believed there would be a lot. Then it became complicated. Next to each hit, Rocky would try the full date of birth, then just the year and then the date of 23rd.

A total of roughly thirty-six million searches in all. He couldn't even contemplate how long it would take. It all depended if he got a good hit and in what part of the search. Then there might be more than one hit. No guarantees. Every search would have to be completed to be sure. It really all depended on how well the Scottish civil servants had digitised their indices.

John was agitated. He couldn't work out how Rocky had come to the thirty-six million searches but knew that Rocky would do his best. Then he threw in a curveball. 'Rocky. Just another thought. You know what flight this guy was on. Is there any way you could check where he went when the plane landed at Gatwick?'

Rocky laughed. 'Ok John. Which one do you want me to start first?'

John laughed with him. 'You mean you can't do both together? I thought you were the best. Do I have to look elsewhere?'

'Cheeky sod! I'll do them together.'

'There! I knew you were the best.'

'I'll call if I get anything useful. Now leave me alone. I've work to do,' and Rocky hung up.

Zena was incredulous. She stared hard at Rocky. 'You're kidding.'

'No. I'll check the Scottish Passport Office in Glasgow, but don't hold out much hope. We need to get into the last census and the Electoral Role. Then we need to search each for anyone with a name of Campbell. First or last name. I would think there are going to be rather a lot. Probably in the thousands. Once we have them, we can search for dates of birth that marry up. Overall, I don't think it will take too long. Writing the code for the searches will probably take the longest time. Then of course we need to check what this guy does when he gets off the plane.'

Zena whispered to herself, is that all?

CHAPTER
THIRTY

The phone rang, waking John from a catnap. He answered even though the caller's identity was not disclosed. It was obvious to him who was calling. Rocky was exuberant. No greeting. 'You'll never guess.'

'Go on?'

'I thought I'd check the Glasgow Passport Office first. Definitely a false passport. The person applied in person for it with a 'Micky Mouse' birth certificate as ID. There was some sort of hold up and the guy was asked to return when it was ready.'

John didn't follow why Rocky was so pleased. They already believed it was a false passport. 'Well, that confirms our suspicions...'

Rocky butted in, 'John. He left a landline phone number to be called when the passport was ready for collection. What an idiot!'

'That's a great start Rocky!'

'Comes back to the Post Office in a place called Brig O'Turk. Somewhere in the Trossachs National Park. I thought I'd let you know straight away. We can't really call it in case they tip him the wink someone's trying to find him. It'll help with our searches though. I'll call you when I get anything else,' and the line went dead.

John sat back in his chair. The prospects were looking good. He drifted back to sleep.

Zena was casually watching lines of data on her computer screen scroll as it searched for anyone with the given name or last name of Campbell recorded in the Scottish Census. As it found them, it slotted their details into an Excel file. Nearly five thousand. Then she searched them all for a date of birth of 23rd August 1979. None. She searched again with just the name Campbell and the year 1979. Nearly nine hundred. They were gradually being whittled down.

She thought about the Post Office's location. Setting the computer to search for both the name, Campbell, and a part address, Brig O'Turk, she started the programme running. She sat back in her chair and stretched. Then she stood up and marched on the spot getting blood flowing back to her legs. She watched lines of data flying across her monitor so fast she couldn't make any of it out. It was looking for two details on the same file. Only about three or four million files to check.

Then the computer monitor froze and blipped. A single file was displayed. One name! Campbell MacIntyre at Castle Grevin, Brig O'Turk. She called to Rocky. 'It's got to be him.'

Rocky looked over her shoulder at the screen. The Census printout showed his occupation to be a butler. He agreed. It had to be him. How could they confirm it? They sat quietly considering their options. Everything pointed to him. They needed a photograph to confirm it. Where could they get one?

Zena broke the silence. 'Without going there and taking one, we're lost. Who do we know who could take one for us?'

Rocky didn't know. He swore. He could tell John who they thought Campbell MacTavish was but they couldn't actually prove it. Throughout his career, Rocky had always been able to fully complete any task. Now he could only point to a possible subject. He wasn't happy. He swore again.

Reluctantly, he phoned John. There was no point in beating about the bush. He told John what they had. John agreed it looked likely that Campbell was MacIntyre. But then John questioned why was he shown as a butler? Rocky was blunt to the point of rudeness, 'He isn't going to tell the Census he's a hit man is he?'

John conceded the point. Then in general conversation, rhetorically questioning himself, said, 'If the local police go there to make enquiries and he's not about, someone could warn him and he'll be off. That is of course if he still lives there. He could be anywhere.'

Rocky had an idea, 'call you back,' and he hung up. 'Zena, we need this guy's mobile phone number. He must have one. Everyone's got one nowadays. Specially if they travel abroad.' She knew immediately what he was thinking.

'Brilliant. What took us so long?' She started pounding keys. She soon found the answer on one of the major mobile phone company's databases that she'd hacked. A rolling, yearly contract signed by Campbell MacIntyre. It showed the type of phone he owned and the mobile number allocated to him. But better still, it showed his address as Castle Grevin, and the details of a direct debit used by him to pay the monthly bill. She'd got his bank details without even trying.

Now they were getting somewhere. Tapping in and out of secure private companies and governmental files with ease, she put the phone number in that she had found recorded for Campbell MacIntyre. She searched the phone's records against masts it had passed by. The phone had definitely been travelling. Recently in Tenerife and Gatwick. She couldn't constrain herself. 'We don't need a photo. He's dead to rights.'

Rocky was on the crest of a wave. He'd found Campbell MacIntyre's image leaving the airport and going to the short term car park. Secure CCTV was no challenge to either him or Zena. He recorded the event. Then, what he saw shocked him.

John was wide awake. He had to take action.

CHAPTER
THIRTY ONE

Now John was in a quandary. Who to tell and how much? If he tells Alison, could he trust her to keep his name out of it? Any of those he was liaising with in Littlehampton would have to name him as providing the information. The Spanish police could be the way forward. The killer has left Tenerife for the UK so the local police would probably be quite happy to pass it all back to the British. An anonymous email to them from Rocky. They would tell Alison who would pass it on in turn to the team in Littlehampton. No mention of John Whiles anywhere.

John called Rocky back. He agreed to send an anonymous email purporting to come from somewhere in Africa. The Spanish police would never be able to trace it. They may wonder how a person in Africa would know about a murder on Tenerife, but that would be all.

About an hour later John called Alison. All he asked her to do was call the investigating officer on the Island, ostensibly to confirm if she had permission to leave Tenerife with Violet. Then, as though in passing, ask how the investigation was progressing. Alison was no fool. She knew he had an ulterior motive and wanted to know what it was.

She asked, 'What are you up to? What do you expect him to tell me?'

'Maybe he'll tell you what you want to know. As soon as you've spoken to him, please ring me back,' and he hung up.

Alison looked at her phone. What the hell's he up to? She'd soon know. She dialled the investigating officer's number. 'Hello. It's Alison Daines. I was wondering if you still want me and Violet O'Donnell to stay on in Tenerife, or if we can go back to the UK?'

The officer was sitting behind his desk staring at his computer. He'd opened an anonymous email and had watched a video recording. It was obvious to him what he had seen. A man was carrying a large object over his shoulder. It was obviously an inert body and he could make out the top of a head covered in ginger hair. It was Lynne. He looked at the still image of the man and then compared it to the photograph in the passport of Campbell MacTavish. It was in his view the same person. Someone had given him Lynne's killer on a plate, but why?

He tried to see who had sent the email. It looked like someone in Angola had sent it. How did someone in Africa have access to the security camera at Los Gigantes or the details from EasyJet's passenger manifests? He had a couple of things to do straight away. Send his aid to Los Gigantes to obtain the original footage from the security camera and then to EasyJet at the airport for the original copy of Campbell MacTavish's passport. Now Alison Daines was speaking to him. A coincidence?

'Hello Miss Daines. About an hour ago, I would have said I want you to stay another day while my staff continue their enquiries. But within the last hour, I have received information that has, shall we say, possibly cracked the case. Do you know anything about that?'

She couldn't disguise her surprise, 'No, I don't. Can you

tell me please? What have you discovered?'

He believed everything in the email. What to tell her? The killer was apparently in the UK. His team would arrange an international arrest warrant. They would inform Vernon who would pass the information to the relevant authority in the UK. They would file everything they had pending its execution. He saw no harm in letting her know.

'Miss Daines. Both you and Miss O'Donnell are free to leave Tenerife at your leisure. As Lynne was part of your team, I shall forward an anonymous email and it's video attachment that I have recently received. It may put your mind at rest as to her fate. I will be finalising our enquiries pending the person's apprehension. I would presume once you have seen the email, you may make efforts to locate and apprehend the person yourself. If so, please be careful.'

Alison thought he was talking in riddles. Hesitantly, she queried, 'I'm not sure I understand what you are saying. I think I need to see the email. I shall keep in contact with you, and I'd be obliged if you let me know of any further developments?'

'I will. The email should be with you now. Goodbye.'

Alison viewed the email on a tablet. Within minutes she was in no doubt as to who Lynne's killer was. He was in the UK. An urgent phone call to Groves followed by the email. He'd get things started in tracing Campbell. Then she sat back on the settee and closed her eyes. The thought crossed her mind. How the hell did John know what he was going to say? She didn't care. She'd keep his name out of it.

* * *

Groves called Roland to his office. 'Sit down Roland. I know you were upset because I kept you away from Samsun.'

Roland was about to speak, but Groves held up his hand to silence him.

'I know that Lynne's murder has affected you more than anyone else. So now, I want you to concentrate on one aspect of the enquiry. I will tell Murray that you get, within reason, anything you ask for. But please, keep him or me informed.'

Roland was sulking slightly waiting to see what spurious task he was going to be saddled with. Groves spun his computer monitor around so Roland could see it. 'Please watch this short video Roland. It is very upsetting, and at the moment, only Alison and I have seen it.' He set the video clip playing.

Roland couldn't believe his eyes. He didn't need to see her face. It was Lynne. He'd know her anywhere. The flowing ginger hair. He just knew. Tears streamed down his cheeks which he wiped away with the back of his hand. One word flew bitterly from his mouth. 'Bastard.'

Groves didn't wait long. 'Have a look at this picture. It's of the man's face. It's been enhanced from the video,' and the full-frontal face of the man looking out at Roland filled the computer screen. 'Remember that face Roland. There's just one more picture I want to show you.'

Roland was seething. If he could have reached into the monitor, he'd have dragged the bastard out and happily beaten him to death.

Groves put the image of the passport on the screen. Roland just stared at it. There was the bastard's name. Campbell MacTavish. 'Roland. What I want you to do is find this man. I want him arrested and returned to Spain. He'll get a life term there which means life and is a lot longer than what he would get here. Can I rely on you?'

Roland spat out his words. 'I'll find him.'

'I'll forward the full email to you. There is one other thing Roland. Jimmy wants to come back to work but he's not fit for active duty. He would be willing to do office enquiries for you if you agree.' Roland agreed. He liked and trusted Jimmy. Between them they'd find Campbell. He didn't know that it was going to be a way for Groves to keep tabs on him.

Roland went back into the main office and was soon confidently searching police indices. It wouldn't take him long. His problem was he wasn't as competent as Rocky and Zena. He wouldn't even get close to Campbell. Without help.

* * *

Campbell was on his way back to Scotland. The rifle was wedged under the back seats of his car and the P226 handgun was tucked under the driver's seat. The cases for both the rifle and handgun were concealed in the undergrowth close to a mile from his shooting position. It was unlikely either case would be found for some time, if ever. He didn't care. Neither bore any of his fingerprints.

He was mulling over everything that he knew. They can't put the murder of Brendan Slack down to us. We didn't do it. That's down to Hawthorne and her American killer. They've got hold of her paintings. That might keep them happy. They might think she had him killed to stop him discovering the forgeries. That would be good for us. Wonder how they found Hawthorne? He swung the car out recklessly as he passed a bus.

The driver of the bus blasted his horn in anger at the stupid idiot who nearly collided with an oncoming car. Campbell was oblivious to how close he had come to a collision.

What can the police prove? Nothing. They could search Castle Grevin and not find a thing. The room is too well hidden. We would be in the clear. That copper in Thurloe Square never saw me. Shame I had to kill the sister in Tenerife. He rued the fact he'd had to use a passport, but quickly pushed the information from his mind.

All the others must have their special collections securely hidden. How would the police find any of them? They'll all be safe now Hawthorne is dead. No one saw me anywhere near her place. Once the rifle's hidden properly, I'm in the clear. He saw the speedometer was showing way above the prescribed limit and he slowed down. Don't get stopped for speeding.

Metcalf was thinking about his Turner. His pride and joy and the star of his special collection. It was with four other original paintings that should have been hanging in galleries around the UK. Only he and Campbell knew how to open the concealed door. Then he thought about Hawthorne's paintings. How did the police know about or open the concealed door in her manor house? Someone must have told them. Who knew? If the police ever got to him, they might start to look for a concealed door at Castle Grevin. He couldn't bet they wouldn't find it.

He pondered loudly to himself, 'It's time to disappear for a while. A long holiday where they can't touch us. The Lodge.'

* * *

Alison booked a flight for herself and Violet. Then she confirmed with Murray that transport would be waiting for her. She settled down and phoned John. 'I don't know how you did it, but thanks.'

John pretended to be confused. 'Sorry Alison. What do you mean?'

'I phoned the investigator as you suggested. He sent me a copy of an anonymous email which basically showed who killed Lynne. You knew who did it! Why didn't you tell me straight away?'

'I told you Alison. I can't get involved. Good to hear that the Spanish investigator passed that email to you. I presume that Groves and co now know and the fact the information came from him rules me out. I'm happy. You now have most of the information you needed.'

She considered John's last statement, 'most of the information' rather strange, but quickly dismissed the thought. Laughingly, she responded, 'You are the most aggravating person I know, after my father. I owe you. See you soon. Bye,' and she hung up.

John was smiling as he hung up. The first part of his plan had worked.

CHAPTER
THIRTY TWO

'Hi Doreen. Have you got a couple of minutes for a chat?'
Doreen looked about the office. A few people were
engaged on computers or speaking on phones. None were paying
her any attention. Murray, who had the closest desk to hers, was
not in the office. She couldn't hide her delight at hearing John's
voice. She knew him well enough to know he probably wouldn't
call unless he had something to say of note. 'Certainly. How can I
help you?' No way was she going to use his name.

'I'd like to run something past you. I presume you have
seen the passport page of Campbell MacTavish?'

Doreen kept her answer brisk. 'Yes.' Then a thought flew
through her mind, how does he know that already?

John continued without really waiting for her reply. 'You
may have noticed it was issued at Glasgow Passport Office and
they have apparently confirmed via email to Murray that the
person who applied for it did so in person and then collected
it. I understand that the email also confirms that the passport
office now know the information given was false.'

A clue, is he speaking to Murray as well as me? She
answered slowly, 'Yes,' as she pulled up a copy from HOLMES
onto her computer screen. It didn't occur to her to ask how
John had seen a copy of it. He would lie and she'd know it.
She just accepted from his questions, he had.

'I've been thinking. We know it is a false passport. Whenever
I have used an alias, I always use my correct first name. Most
people who use false details regularly tend to use their correct

given name. Mike Caesar is an example. Sometimes they make a mistake and divulge more than they might wish. Do you know if anyone from your enquiry has asked the Glasgow Passport Office for all the paperwork regarding Campbell MacTavish's application for his false passport?'

Doreen smiled. She got the message. There was something to be found. 'It's strange that you should say that. An officer has mentioned exactly that and we were about to call the Glasgow Passport Office.'

John's lips curved into a broad smile. He knew he could rely on Doreen. 'I'd better get off the phone then. I'd hate to delay you. Bye.' He knew the second part of his plan was as good as completed.

Doreen slammed her phone down as she looked about the office for Roland. Calling to him, she waved him over. Within seconds, she'd put forward her idea about the false passport and the possibility there may be something to be found within the fraudulent applicant's paperwork.

Roland saw the logic. It was worth checking. He'd come to an abrupt halt with his enquiries. He strolled over to an empty desk and picked up a phone.

Exactly twenty three minutes later, he was standing at the office's laser jet printer with Jimmy. Half a dozen sheets of paper were spewed out of it. Roland had discovered the phone number of Brig O'Turk's Post Office. He gathered all the papers together and called loudly across the din of the office to Doreen. 'Doreen. Result! He's somewhere near a place called Brig O'Turk.'

Doreen acknowledged the shout with a wave of her hand. How the hell did John know that? Staring straight at her monitor, a broad smile was etched across her face.

Roland shuffled the few pages into order as he walked back to stand next to her. He couldn't stop himself from saying, 'We know what the bastard calls himself, and now roughly where he lives. All thanks to you Doreen. That was inspired thinking. Whenever you want a drink, let me know,' and he went off in search of Groves.

One of the uniform officers who was in the office walked past Jimmy and casually remarked, 'I was born near there. Brig O'Turk.'

Jimmy was quick. Even though his face hurt, he called after him, 'Hey. Not so fast. You may be able to help. From what I've found out, it's smaller than a hamlet.'

The PC agreed, 'That's about right. Nothing to the place. Probably no more than a dozen houses scattered about. Beautiful place. My dad used to thatch roofs all round there.'

Jimmy had to ask. 'Do you know this man?' and handed him a copy of the enhanced photo.

He looked at it. Reluctantly he said, 'Sorry. No. I moved away when I went to uni. Don't know him. If you wanted work, you had to move away. It was desolate round there.'

Jimmy questioned with a pronounced lisp, 'Is that why you moved down here?'

He laughed. 'No. It's a lot warmer down here.'

'What did others around there do?'

The PC thought for a while. 'The majority did what I did to get away. Others worked on farms or for the nobs as gardeners or gofers.'

Jimmy hadn't heard the term before. 'Who are the nobs?'

The PC was contemptuous. 'The landowners. The rich bastards who own most of Scotland. They treat people like shit. Shoot everything that moves over or on a moor. I wouldn't lower myself to work for any of them.'

Jimmy decided not to pursue anything more with him. 'Thanks for your help,' and he bent to look at his papers. The PC walked away.

Roland looked at a map on a computer. Brig O'Turk was in the Trossachs National Park. It looked desolate. He searched for the local Post Office. It was marked on the map as closed. He searched the official Scottish Post Offices list and found out that it had closed for good and all enquiries had to go via Callander. Nearly seven miles away. He discussed with Jimmy what they should do.

They formulated a plan. It was a long shot. Jimmy went after the PC. He needed more information. When he got back to Roland, he seemed happy. They discussed who'd make the calls. Both agreed that Jimmy would probably be best as he was able to cajole people into disclosing probably more than they should. Even with a temporary speech impediment due to his injuries, he had the gift of the gab.

* * *

The car had left Castle Grevin at a sedate speed. There was no rush. No point in attracting unnecessary police attention for speeding. Being an old and immaculately kept silver Rolls Royce with a personalised index number attracted admiring looks from practically everyone. It was a long journey to Dover where they booked into a Premier Inn only because it had a secure car park. Normally, they wouldn't have been seen dead in one. They'd be crossing the channel the following morning and then a casual drive to the Swiss chalet. Safe.

THIRTY THREE

The woman was at home waiting. She was desperate to get to bed, but she waited. Exactly on time the doorbell rang. She opened the door. The old man was as arrogant as ever, 'What's happened?'

'His phone is missing. It's the only possible link. And then it's tenuous. I've searched his house, the hospital and museum. Gwendoline is dead. It'll take the police no further. The FBI are watching Calder. I have that in hand. Within a week, he'll be dead or in prison and then dead.'

'Keep me informed.' The door was pulled shut as he scurried off.

* * *

Simon had had a wasted trip. He'd met the two women at Tenerife airport. Just long enough time for a chat, a coffee and a sandwich before they had to board their flight. He managed to book a flight several hours later. Both women had been met when they'd landed at Gatwick by different officers. Violet had been taken to a safe house and Alison was taken to the office in Littlehampton.

The chief constable and Lynne's husband were waiting for her. It was a brief and slightly angry meeting. It was quickly understood by the chief that Alison wanted retribution and Lynne's husband was also after vengeance. The thought of forgiveness didn't enter either of their heads.

Trying to calm things down, the chief constable turned to the business of arranging Lynne's repatriation. He agreed that Sussex police would make all the arrangements in conjunction with Lynne's family. When he tried to discuss a funeral, Alison stepped in. The press had picked up the fact that Lynne was a police officer but they just thought she had been murdered whilst on holiday. It had barely covered a paragraph or two in some of the English press.

Now she put forward holding off the funeral for a couple of weeks and explained why it would help. She told Lynne's husband that she knew who her killer was. How all the British police forces had the killers picture and it was only a matter of time before he was caught. Alison expressed her opinion that he'd killed the wrong person and if he found that out, he'd go into hiding and make his arrest harder. Both the chief constable and Lynne's husband agreed.

Once back in the office, Alison updated Roland and Jimmy. All three were determined to catch Campbell anyway they could. They hadn't forgotten about Brendan but had left other officers to continue investigating other aspects of his murder.

John was thinking how he could pass on the information that Zena and Rocky had discovered. It had to be done quickly. The longer it took would potentially put people in harm's way. An email purporting to originate in Angola would end up as a piece of evidence and look dodgy to say the least. Especially as the email to the Spanish naming Campbell was on file. He needed to speak to Alison. Anyone else would struggle to keep his name out of it. Perhaps a casual phone call. Drop a hint. She'd act on it straight away.

He was picking up his mobile just as it rang. 'Hello.'

'Hi. Thought I'd give you a quick call to thank you.' It was Alison. A great result.

'No problem. Anything to help.'

'Do you fancy a quick drink?'

John and Carol were at the Chichester Festival Theatre buying some tickets for a forthcoming production. It was as good a place as any. 'I'm at the Café on the Park at the Festival Theatre. Do you know it?'

'Of course I do,' was the caustic reply.

'I'm there now. See you soon,' and he hung up grinning to himself.

His plans were coming to fruition. Alison didn't even have time to say yes or no. 'Ignorant sod.' She ran to her car and was at Chichester Festival Theatre twenty minutes later. John was the best part of a quarter of the way through a bottle of white wine.

She slumped into a chair next to him having run in from the car park. Carol was nowhere to be seen. John said, and meant it, 'Good to see you Alison,' and poured a large glass of wine for her.

'Sometimes Oscar, I could happily kill you.'

He smiled, 'It makes life worth living. Now what is it you want to talk about?'

'Thanks for what you did for Lynne. Now we know who we're looking for. It's going to be just a matter of time before we catch him.'

'I told you I can't get involved. Whoever passed the information to the Spanish did everyone a favour.'

'Thanks anyway.'

John put the third part of his plan into gear. 'I don't know if it will help in any way, but I heard a rumour that Campbell picked up a car from the short term car park about an hour after his plane landed. I believe he can be seen on CCTV. Maybe even an index plate. If that's correct, you could track him on ANPR. It's just a rumour so don't quote me. You'll have to check it all out for yourself.'

Alison glared hard at John for several seconds before breaking into a broad grin. 'You bastard. I really hate you sometimes.' She slurped the wine. Then lied, 'I was obviously going to check out all the CCTV around the airport. So any rumours are just that: rumours. I'll let you know if I find anything.'

'Thanks. I'd be interested to hear if you find anything of note.'

'Was that the only rumour you've heard?'

John laughed raucously. 'Fraid so.' Then, after a mouthful of warming white wine that made him grimace, proffered, 'Be careful Alison. He's a dangerous bastard.'

Alison couldn't stop herself. She leant over and kissed him on the cheek. 'Thanks John,' then after a short pause while he blushed, 'I still hate you.' She finished her wine and stood up. 'I can't stay any longer. Work calls,' and she ran back to her car.

John was still laughing when Carol rejoined him.

CHAPTER
THIRTY FOUR

Alison got back to the office and found Roland and Jimmy going through their collection of papers. She sat down next to them.

'I've had a thought. Campbell probably had a car at the airport. He was only in Tenerife for a maximum of three days, so any car would have probably been in the short term car park. I'm going up to the airport and I'll get all the CCTV. To save time, could you let the control room know I'm coming and get the CCTV downloaded ready for me?'

Jimmy smiled ecstatically. 'Brilliant deduction! If we can get an index plate, we can track his car on ANPRs.' Then he grabbed at his face. Smiling was not currently something he was happy doing. His cheek let him know it hadn't really begun to repair.

Alison gave the impression she was thinking. Cautiously she stated, 'Get the CCTV for a couple of hours after his plane landed. We don't want to have to search lots of hours' worth.'

'Ok. I'll sort that out.'

Alison practically skipped out to her car.

* * *

The laird was driving. Everyone in Brig O'Turk called him that. He wasn't really a laird. Somehow he had promoted the rumour in the past and it grew and then stuck. He was just obviously rich, flaunted the fact and lived in an old castle which allegedly was once owned by the Clan Campbell. His stationery all referred to him as The Laird of Brig O'Turk. One thing missing was a coat of arms. He'd have loved one but even he thought that a bit too ostentatious.

He liked to drive in Europe. Campbell preferred England. As soon as they had landed in Europe, they always had a quick stop in a quiet spot to prepare for their journey. The French autoroute South was practically void of vehicles. The Rolls may have been old but could cruise comfortably at 80 miles an hour. Unfortunately, it drank petrol.

They stopped at services just outside Reims and then again at Dijon where they topped up the tank. The laird had a comfort break at each but didn't deem to actually put the fuel into his own car. In Scotland it was always down to his garage man and now it fell to Campbell. Each time, as he strolled to the pay desk, he stripped a couple of fifty Euro notes from a large wodge. The French seemed to like it better than cards. Not that Campbell was stupid enough to use one. Cashiers always smiled as he handed the notes over.

They were soon approaching Geneva, crossing into Switzerland where they stopped again. As Campbell ambled imperturbably to the pay desk, the laird called after him, 'Get some chocolate.' He acknowledged he'd heard with a raised middle finger. The laird chuckled to himself. When Campbell got back into the car, he tossed a large bar of Swiss chocolate onto the laird's lap. He soon had the wrapper off and stuffed a load of chocolate into his mouth before he drove away from the pump.

They cruised back into France and around the South side

of Lake Geneva, and then back into Switzerland and away from the lake and up into the mountains. At the last garage before his chalet, the laird stepped out of the driver's seat and wandered into the small workshop. He was looking for his favourite Swiss mechanic. He always got him to check over the Rolls. He wanted to be sure it would start first time if he had to make a quick getaway.

The mechanic jumped into the back seat. Then they drove the last couple of miles to the chalet. As soon as they had unloaded their luggage, the mechanic was in the driver's seat heading back to his garage. He knew what he was going to do and he knew the laird would pay well with a handsome tip.

He quickly checked all the fluid levels, lights, and indicators. All good. Then he put the Rolls onto a rolling road and checked the brakes. Bit spongy. No real problem. He didn't bother with emission control. A polluting exhaust wouldn't make a ha'peth of difference in the mountains. In all the time he'd known the laird, he'd done nothing else mechanically, although his bills didn't seem to agree.

Lastly, he filled the car to the brim with petrol and got his apprentice to give the Rolls a refreshing wash and gloss. He knew the laird liked it topped up in case he had to leave quickly. No point of a quick getaway if he had to stop to put petrol into the car. The mechanic parked it under an awning. He'd take it back early the following day with his exorbitant bill.

When they had eventually arrived at the chalet, both men unloaded the car and were soon fast asleep in comfy armchairs. The journey had been gruelling.

*   *   *

Alison walked into the police control room at the airport. The air conditioning was on full pelt and she enjoyed the cooling breeze. Lighting was concealed and minimal. One wall was covered in computer monitors all playing live video feeds from around the airport. Several officers were answering emergency calls from passengers and retail outlets around the airport. Others were directing officers to potential flashpoints. On one side wall was an enlarged colour picture of Campbell. Everyone in the room could see it. A tear welled up in her eye.

The Inspector in charge was sitting behind his desk. He passed on his condolences. Nearly every police officer in Sussex knew what had occurred in Tenerife. If his officers could help, they would. Alison was more than grateful. He handed her five DVDs.

'These are all identical tapes of the short term car park. It'll save you time copying them. We confirmed the correct time of arrival of the EasyJet flight at its gate and estimated that the fastest time anyone from it could clear customs would have been thirty minutes. Then to reach the short term car park another fifteen minutes. To be honest, they'd have to run some of the way. Now we have downloaded the relevant hours. If you would like to have a quick look at one just to check the timings, we have a 'Super Viewer' working. He could view it with you.'

Alison readily agreed. The sooner she could identify the car Campbell was using the quicker she could get Jimmy or Roland to circulate it. 'I'd love to have a quick look if I may?'

The Inspector called to one of his officers. Then he showed Alison into a side office. She was putting a DVD into a stand-alone computer when the officer walked in.

'Hi. I'm Rav. The hierarchy seem to think I am good at identifying people. If you don't mind, I'll have a look at the tape with you.'

Alison jumped at the prospect. 'Yes please. You never know what you might see.'

The video began to play at normal speed. Rav was happy to view it at twice normal speed. Alison's eyes never left the monitor and she hardly blinked. The timer in the top right corner of the tape scrolled speedily on past forty minutes. Suddenly, Rav said, 'There!'

Alison hadn't seen what he had but stopped the video and rewound it ten minutes. Sitting bolt upright with anticipation, she set it running at normal speed. Now she saw him. Rav didn't need to tell her. The bastard was walking casually across the car park. Campbell was looking all around. It was obvious to her that he was looking for a car. So he hadn't left it there originally. If he had, he'd have gone straight to it. She made a mental note to check the CCTV at a later date to see who had left it there.

The pair of them sat silently as they watched Campbell suddenly look directly towards a Ford Focus. He made a bee line straight to it and opened the driver's door. Then he walked round to the rear and lifted the hatch. He picked up a small box and opened it. His head came up and he looked about. There were no other people close to him.

There was no mistaking what he did next. They were both shocked. Campbell took a handgun out of the box and then slid a magazine into the handle. He carried it back to the driver's door and seemed to place it somewhere close to it. The CCTV was only showing the rear of the vehicle clearly.

Rav said, 'Shit.'

Alison remembered a remark of John's earlier. "Be careful Alison. He's a dangerous bastard."

Campbell went back to the rear of the car and placed his hand on the hatch as though about to close it. He stopped and looked around. Still no one anywhere near him. Then he let go and leant into the rear of the car. The CCTV showed him opening a long box. He took out a rifle. Then quite openly he put a clip into the weapon and then replaced the rifle in the box.

Rav couldn't help himself. 'Shit! He's a fucking nutter. A rifle and a pistol. If a copper stops him...' and he paused thinking what might happen.

Alison wanted to be the person who stopped him. Under her breath she hissed, 'I'll kill the bastard.'

As Campbell slammed the hatch back down, Alison noted the index number. Jimmy needed to be updated. So did everyone else who was looking for him. Forewarned is forearmed. It's no longer a matter of finding him and arresting him. He was armed and dangerous. Under her breath she said, 'I owe you John.'

Rav heard but didn't understand.

Jimmy nearly fell off his chair. A stream of expletives tore down the phone. 'I'll update the PNC, Mr Groves, Murray and everyone else.' The pain in his cheek forgotten. 'Thank God you found that guv'nor. It might save someone's life. Get back here as soon as you can. I'll check out ANPRs.'

Alison sent a one word text to John. ' Thanks.'

Alison didn't hang about. She passed a marked police car that was cruising at the speed limit. Her warrant card being waved about out of the driver's window caused them to cancel their blue lights and siren.

She ran into the office. In the time it had taken her to get back, Jimmy had made a startling discovery. Now he was hard at work on a computer next to Doreen. His computer had a map on it with a route overlaid and marked in red. Both Groves and Murray were leaning over him looking at both their monitors. Roland was busy typing into the PNC on another computer. Groves was talking on an airwave radio to Greenthorne.

'Can you liaise with the Gloucestershire officers when you get back there. The car was less than six miles from the shooting position when it last hit an ANPR. It was there at the right time. Campbell had to be the shooter. The Arts and Antiques boys and girls from the Met are tearing her place to bits. Murray has briefed them.'

Alison could see the map. It wasn't of Gloucestershire but of Perthshire in Scotland. She butted in, 'What's happening?'

Murray said, 'The shit's hitting the fan. When you called Jimmy, he traced the car on ANPRs on a route back to Scotland via the Cotswolds. It looks like Campbell was Gwendoline's killer. His car was in the close area at the time she was killed. Then it's moved on to Scotland and the Trossachs National Park. We all know what's there: Brig O'Turk.'

Alison said, 'Oh shit.'

'We've sent Greenthorne and two detectives back to Gloucestershire to help out and Doreen and Roland are updating all the relevant indices. Looks like he may have used the rifle you saw.'

Someone called out that they were making tea and asked if anyone else wanted one. The orders flooded in from around the office. Groves and Doreen got their cups first to a chanted chorus of 'sniveller.'

Groves called the office to order. 'Right ladies and gentlemen, settle down, we have a problem.' Groves continued, 'Those who have recently joined us have had the opportunity to go through all the statements, reports and enquiries conducted. So, I sincerely hope you are all up to speed.' He sipped his tea.

'This enquiry started with the murder of Brendan Slack. We soon established that the killer was Mike Calder, an American. Since then, we have suffered a personal loss. That of Lynne. It appears that she was murdered by the man using the name Campbell MacTavish in the belief she was Violet. Now we believe that he has murdered Gwendoline Hawthorne. The deeper we delve into this enquiry we discover that it seems to revolve around a forged painting. We assume, thanks to Violet, the forgery is of a Turner. Gwendoline had three original masterpieces in a secret room that have the Met's Arts and Antiques Squad in raptures. One of their officers will be joining us later and will be able to keep us updated about the art world. Gwendoline didn't have the Turner. It looks like she was killed to stop her talking. It leads one to believe she may have known something about it.' He finished his tea.

He looked about the office at all the faces staring intently back at him.

One of the officers asked, 'I presume the forged Turner that Brendan noted in his journal was the one he looked at on the Monday at Parkland House. Are we going to recover it?'

Murray cut in before Groves could reply. 'If I may answer that Mr Groves. Yes we are. I will be taking a team to Parkland House very shortly. The art expert who was at Gwendoline's will be with us to confirm that their Turner is a fake.'

Groves was looking down at his notes. As if questioning himself, he mused, 'Something that is confusing me and the Arts and Antiques Squad, is how do they swap the original for the copy? Who paints the copy?' He looked up. Then in a more formal tone, questioned, 'Anyone got any ideas?'

The room was silent. No one had any idea.

CHAPTER
THIRTY FIVE

Another beautiful summer's day. Not a breath of wind. She was always amazed how the English whined and winged about the weather. She still hadn't bothered with anything over her tee shirt. When abroad, she always had a blouse. Even around the Mediterranean.

She was sitting outside Costa in Littlehampton reading the local paper. She noted the reports about the murder of Brendan Slack were getting shorter and fewer. The police knew the murderer was Mike Calder and that he was in America under the watchful eyes of the FBI. She'd dealt with that and was awaiting reading about it on the Washington Post's website.

Two officers carrying cups of coffee sat at the table next to her. They weren't talking loudly, but they were so close she couldn't help but overhear. They were gone in fifteen minutes. She learnt so much.

* * *

Carol had gone to work at the hospital. John was half asleep in his chair. The best part of a fruity, cheap red wine the night before had been the reason he was so sleepy. He'd considered the conundrum some time previously of how an original painting could be taken off a gallery wall and swapped for a copy without anyone noticing. He had considered the hypothesis several times when he'd thought about the forged Turner. It had crossed his mind again the day he heard that Gwendoline Hawthorne had three original paintings in her possession.

Questions were swirling around in the fog of his brain. The same ones kept creeping back. He had to get a plausible answer to each of them. How did Gwendoline know that she could get hold of the paintings? Did she get all three on the same day? Did she arrange for forgeries to be made? The three forgeries recovered from the galleries by experts from the British Museum had been hanging on walls for several years. They had been found to be exceptional paintings in their own right. Just not the originals. They can't be knocked up in a day. How did she know to get them made?

John was gradually formulating various answers, although he couldn't explain why. He had come to certain conclusions. He suspected that Gwendoline must have known a long time in advance that she would be able to swap the paintings. Therefore, she must have had the forgeries ready for that day. The chances of the pictures being removed from a gallery wall were highly unlikely. It was probable they'd be swapped when no one would see. Then a light bulb moment flitted through the mists of his mind.

He was fully awake as he snatched up his phone. He knew the man to ask. No time to go and see him. Four rings and it was answered by a woman. She wasn't going to disclose who was at the number called. 'Hello. Can I help you?'

'Yes. It's John Whiles. Can I speak to His Grace the Duke please.'

The woman hesitated. She was the duke's personal assistant

and had been in America when Brendan had met his gruesome end. She'd heard the name Whiles and was debating whether to grant his request. Placing her hand over the mouthpiece she queried of the duke, 'John Whiles?' He signalled her to accede to the request. She passed the phone to him.

'Mr Whiles. How are you? How's the foot?' and John heard a faint laugh in the background.

John didn't respond to the genuine enquiry. His agenda was much more pressing. 'Sorry to trouble you Your Grace. Just a quick question. Can you recall roughly how long it took from your initial request to the museum to the time the Holbein arrived at the castle?'

The duke thought for a few seconds. 'Mr Whiles, I can tell you exactly if you could give me a few minutes?'

'I would appreciate that,' and he decided to push his luck a little further. 'I don't suppose you recall who you dealt with at the museum?'

The duke chuckled to himself. He'd been right to get John on board. Why he needed to know baffled him. He knew John would probably not tell him even if he asked. 'Mr Whiles. As you have obviously deduced, I keep full records. I'll arrange for a complete copy to be emailed to you. It may save you some time.'

John was at his most courteous. Not snivelling. He would never do that, just being courteous. He liked the duke. He saw in him what he believed most of the aristocracy were missing. Charisma, intelligence, and wit. Also the ability to assess a situation quickly and take the most relevant course of action. 'That would be extremely useful Your Grace. Thank you.'

The duke had soon come to know John was always in an

apparent hurry. 'If that's all, I'll speak to you later. Goodbye,' and he hung up.

John laughed out loudly for nearly a minute. It was usually him that ended conversations abruptly. He'd been beaten at his own game.

He didn't have long to wait. The file was attached to an email from the duke's personal assistant. John scoured it. From the first enquiry by the duke to the time it arrived at Arundel Castle: just slightly more than eight months. John knew he had some of the answers. He checked the names. None jumped out at him as a suspect. The curator of the British Museum had been the duke's first point of contact. Several other members of the senior staff in different departments were consulted and their opinions sought and recorded as to the duke's suitability.

The painting had been seconded from the storeroom supervisor and had been checked over by the museum's art restorer. There had been a slight repair made. The frame had been touched up where it had been scratched whilst in store for so many years. The provenance of the painting was confirmed. Two experts endorsed it. An original Holbein.

The head of security had confirmed each time it was moved to a different department that it was kept securely. Then a senior member of the museum and a member of the security team visited the castle and approved security arrangements with the duke. The day it was to be delivered was finally agreed. A copy of the signed acceptance by the duke confirming he would adhere to the museums stipulations as to where he was going to display it was countersigned by several senior museum staff.

John was surprised to see that one condition was that the Duke of Norfolk had to insure it for just short of half a million pounds. Another condition John noted with interest, was to allow access once a year at an agreed time to a representative of the museum to check the condition and security of the painting. He muttered to himself, 'That did for poor old Brendan.'

A rueful smile crossed his face. A lot of the questions as to how Gwendoline came to have the three paintings seemed to be answered. If he was correct, it would also explain how the Turner was acquired.

He needed to talk to Groves. Urgently. He snatched up his mobile and called him.

'Hello Oscar. What can I do for you?'

'I need to see you.'

Groves heard the urgency in his voice. 'Where?'

'Luckes café in North Street, Chi. Thirty minutes.'

'Ok,' and he hung up.

John looked quizzically at his phone. It seemed everyone had reached the conclusion that idle chit chat or general pleasantries were a pointless waste of time when speaking to him. Now he was on the receiving end, he noticed it.

He found his crutch and set off to walk the half mile from his flat to the café. Within several hundred yards, he was starting to struggle. His foot was aching. When he got to the café, he was worn out and collapsed into a metal chair on the café's pavement area. A young waitress saw him and immediately took pity on him.

'Now you stay there my dear. Let me know what you want, and I'll fetch it for you.'

John was breathing heavily and wanted to object at being called 'my dear' but couldn't muster the energy. When Groves arrived, he'd just got a cup of coffee and was beginning to recover.

A quick greeting was perfunctory. John looked about for the young waitress and a brief glint of light from further down North Street reflecting from some glass caught his eye. He knew it wasn't right. As though searching for the waitress, he said to Groves, 'It looks like you'll have to go inside to order. Have you a piece of paper, I need to draw you a map.'

Groves was confused. He was aware that John like most officers, always carried a small notebook. Why hadn't he drawn the map already? What did a map have to do with the enquiry? Why did he want him to go inside the café? Why hadn't he brought some paper? He was about to speak when he saw John incline his head slightly and nod towards the door of the café. Something was amiss. He ripped a page out of his own small notebook and gave it to John. 'Will this do?'

'Perfectly. It'll take me only a few minutes.'

Groves took the hint and went inside the café. John didn't need long. He started to write. Five minutes later, Groves walked back to the table with a coffee and sat down. John passed him the paper and said, 'Does that make sense to you?'

Groves read what John had written. There was no map. He was shocked. 'Are you sure?'

'Yes. Without a doubt.'

Groves read it again. 'I need to show this to some of my team. We need to consider it. Let me jot down some notes.'

John leant back in his chair and looked casually along North Street as Grove feverishly wrote on another page of his notebook. A man and a woman were seated about fifty yards away near a cycle rack facing towards the café. John knew he hadn't been followed so somehow they had followed Groves. Or worse, they were already there waiting. That meant they had bugged Groves' phone. The problem he now had was, were they going to follow him? With a pot-leg, he had no way of easily evading them.

He asked Groves for another page from his notebook. He needed some help. Groves read the note. As though considering it, he stated, 'That map is very interesting. I need to think about that. Do you fancy another coffee? I'll pop inside and order them.' With that he was up and into the café.

This time he was nearly ten minutes. When he got back to the table, there was no coffee. They chatted for a couple more minutes and then John saw a large, marked police, personnel carrier slowly driving along the pedestrianised section of North Street. As it drew level with the two people by the cycle rack, Groves scratched the top of his head.

As the vehicle stopped, the two people stood up quickly and started to walk away from it. Several uniformed officers jumped out of the vehicle and followed them. The two started to run. The officers ran faster. Soon they were on their way to Chichester custody suite.

John said, 'Brilliant.'

* * *

The woman was sitting a couple of tables away reading her book and eating a sandwich. She'd tailed behind the two who were tracking Groves. It was easy following them. They weren't looking. They were more anxious about keeping up with Groves.

Now she was seriously concerned that the man with the pot-leg was meeting him. Her interest was aroused. Who was he? It was he who had obviously seen the two idiots when they initially arrived and tried to set up their devices. He was quick to spot them. Much too quick to be press. Must be careful when he's about.

* * *

Groves said, 'See you as agreed,' and got up and went to his car in the North car park. He sped back to Littlehampton. Running up the stairs to his office he bumped into one of the uniform officers.

'I need to speak to Walter. Please find him and ask him to come to my office. Urgently.' Then he slowed down and walked to his locker.

CHAPTER
THIRTY SIX

John got home and knew he hadn't been followed. His circuitous route had confirmed it. He'd seen that woman before. He wracked his brain. Where was it? It came to him. The café in Arundel when he met Doreen. Interesting. She didn't even try to follow him. In fact, she hadn't moved when either of them had gone their separate ways. Perhaps he was being hypersensitive. He put it out of his mind.

His leg was aching more than ever. Several pain killers from a large bottle in his kitchen helped. He slumped into his armchair and promptly fell asleep.

Carol got home after a long, hard day's work at the hospital. Not to her own house but John's flat. She woke him up. Before acknowledging her presence, he checked the time. Forty minutes to go.

He said, 'Hope you're peckish. Don't be too long because we are expected at the Earl of March.'

She glared at him. Her expected quiet night in was out! Why she ever bothered making plans with John escaped her. The only good thing was that she wouldn't have to cook. Then it occurred to her, this wasn't a social event. Unenthusiastically, she showered and dressed smartly. Carol expected she was going to be the gooseberry while the others talked shop. She cursed quietly as she brought the car to the front door so the invalid didn't have far to walk.

When she drove into the pub's car park, she saw Alison

getting out of her Ford Fiesta. All three ambled into the pub. Seated already, at a large round table, were Groves and Murray with their respective wives. Carol was pleasantly surprised. She knew both Groves and Murray but had never met their wives before. The evening, she concluded would be an interesting affair.

Drinks were ordered from the landlady who took it upon herself to look after the group. She knew who they were and didn't want them inhibited by unknown waiters visiting the table. John and the officers knew and trusted her to ignore anything she may overhear. It was an unspoken amicable understanding.

About ten minutes after they were all seated, Simon walked in and sat at the empty seat next to Alison. He greeted everyone. John enquired of him, 'Ok?'

Simon candidly answered, 'No problem, no tail.' All the officers relaxed. The meal became more of a social gathering. Carol was actually enjoying herself chatting to the wives. She'd quickly realised that they hadn't wanted to be there either. At the end of the meal, the mood changed.

Groves addressed the ladies at the table, 'Ladies. We need to discuss some aspects of our present enquiry. I fear you would be extremely bored. Our favourite landlady has a small comfy area with a sofa and a few sumptuous armchairs. She would love your company as she has decided to take a break.' Then as an afterthought he looked at Alison and, tongue in cheek, said, 'Not you Alison.'

She feigned indignation. 'Oh, all right.'

The wives and Carol were used to being side-lined and wandered off to the area which had been kept vacant. They settled down with the landlady for a pleasant drink and a chat.

Groves was the first to talk. He told them about receiving the phone call from John to meet him at Luckes café. The fact that John had spotted the two people watching them. Neither he nor John knew how long they had been there. They both considered whether Groves' phone was bugged or if there was some sort of tracking device.

Groves paused and looked about. Then he continued conspiratorially, 'I spoke to Walter and asked him to check my phone. It was clean. I can only conclude that I was followed from Littlehampton to the meet. But why?' He took a sip of wine. The others waited for him to continue without interruption. 'I arranged for the two people to be detained (using the personal phone of a member of staff) and they were taken to Chichester custody suite. They were searched and the woman was found to have a small, discreet, directional microphone that could pick up speech from a short distance away. Walter was in his element. He'd never seen one before.'

Alison had loads of questions. She bit her tongue. She glared at John who didn't know why. Groves hadn't finished. 'The man had a monocular which was probably what drew Oscar's attention when the sun reflected in its glass. Both claim to be private investigators. They refuse to say who they work for or what they were doing following me. They have a lawyer who has told them to say nothing. As neither has given an address, they are staying in custody. We can only keep them for a day and may have to let them go soon. Walter is going through their phones to see if we can get anything from them.'

Murray cut in, 'I've put a couple of officers onto them to see if they can glean anything useful. It doesn't look too hopeful.'

Alison was seething. She knew now that John was discussing the case with Groves and Murray as well as her. He hadn't told her! She had assumed he'd been kept up to date but didn't know by whom. From Groves' and Murray's attitude, it was clear to her that they knew he was talking to her too. She felt betrayed. She slipped into a mild sulk. She'd let him know how she felt when they were alone. The bastard!

Groves was oblivious to her attitude. Now he turned to John. 'We got a little waylaid earlier. You never actually told me why you wanted to see me? Would you care to elaborate?'

John took a large mouthful of red wine and savoured it. 'I would like to ask for your opinion on something that has occurred to me. I have been thinking of the three paintings that Gwendoline Hawthorne had, and the apparent forged Turner that is hanging in Parkland House. The British Museum and The National Gallery have, I believe, a simple system as to the loan of their paintings. Imagine I own a stately home. I get to hear about a painting that the museum owns and is in storage or is about to be removed from display and placed into storage. I would like to add it to my stately home's collection.'

Alison couldn't stop herself, 'Huh. No chance.'

John ignored her and continued, 'I first contact the curator of the museum. He or she records my interest and starts a file, both digital and paper. With other members of the museum's senior staff, they consider firstly whether I am a suitable candidate and secondly if my stately home is suitable to display the painting. The painting's provenance is confirmed and is examined by the museum's art experts and if need be, repaired. At all times as it passes through various departments, museum security officers monitor its progress and keep it secure. Everyone who sees it, or has any input about the painting, records the fact. While this is happening, a senior member of staff and a security officer visit my stately home.'

John paused and took another mouthful of wine. He had everyone's undivided attention. 'Now, they check out where I'm going to hang the picture and how secure it will be. Should they be happy with my arrangements, they insist I insure the painting while it is in my possession. They also insist that yearly, a member of the museum's staff visits and checks out that the painting is still in good condition and hanging where we agreed.'

Groves said, 'Brendan Slack.'

John answered, 'Precisely. If I agree to everything the museum asks, they will loan me the picture. They set a date for its delivery and when it arrives, I confirm it's the correct painting and sign an elaborate receipt. The painting then goes on my stately home wall. From my initial enquiry to the painting's delivery it can be anything from eight months to a year.'

Murray was the first to comment. Contemplatively he questioned, 'Can I say what I'm thinking. The time frame from request to delivery would be ample for any competent forger to complete a copy. The problem I envisage is, how would they know what painting has been sought? They would have to have information from within the museum.' He thought for a few seconds, 'Furthermore, a person who wants the original painting would have to be found. If no one wants it, it would be pointless to get a forgery.'

Groves considered another setback and was about to speak. But Alison was quicker. She faced John directly and addressed him rather aggressively, 'I have a problem with your narrative. I can see an inside agent at the museum could let someone know what paintings are being sought. That person would have to act as a broker. He, or even she, would have to know people dishonest enough to want the originals.'

John cut across her, 'Like Gwendoline?'

Alison reluctantly accepted the fact, 'Yeah. All right. People like Gwendoline. There can't be many.'

She frowned at him and in a slightly raised voice said again, 'Yeah.' She was desperate to have a good drink but held off. 'Ok then. We need an inside agent, a broker, a load of art thieves and a damn good forger. It's a lot of people to find.'

Groves piped up. 'We haven't considered how they swap the forgery for the original'.

John was ready. He believed he held the answer. 'One thing that I considered. Going back to my scenario, I said the painting would be delivered to me at my stately home. The museum places the painting in an unmarked security vehicle just like the ones that G4S and the like use to move enormous amounts of money. Neither museum has their own vehicle. So they have an agreement with a massive UK wide company. National Security Limited. Now comes the complicated bit.'

He paused and looked at his wine glass. He took a sip. What he was going to say was a little guesswork backed up with just a few facts.

'What if the person at the museum who arranged the transport was, as Alison put it, the inside agent. Could he or she ensure that a certain vehicle from the firm was going to be used. Perhaps, but extremely unlikely. NSL's protocols are that a request for a vehicle is made officially through normal channels. Then a contract is drawn up and at the allotted time and place a security vehicle turns up. NSL send who is available that day.'

He drank the last of his wine. He knew the next part of his narrative was the clincher. Casually he commented, 'What if NSL weren't approached but someone else was? NSL would have no knowledge or paperwork. So they couldn't raise any alarm. An unmarked security vehicle would arrive at the museum and the crew would present some form of identification. The painting would be placed in the vehicle. They would know from the inside agent where the painting was due to go. During the journey, they could swop the original painting for the forgery. On arrival, the recipient would assume they had the original.'

All those around the table were stunned. It seemed John had come up with the only logical explanation. He hadn't finished. He filled his glass. A large mouthful tasted so good.

'I took the liberty of arranging for some discreet enquiries to be made so I can't be sure they are correct. I believe the inside agent is Jake. I'm hoping the phone we recovered from his shoe will give us some more information about that. He is the person at the museum who normally keeps a record of which paintings are on loan and to whom. He is also responsible for arranging any painting's transportation. More importantly, he is the person who checks the pictures yearly in situ. So if he knows they are forgeries, he can dispel any doubts anyone should have. He has held this position at the museums for some fourteen years.' John paused as they took in what he was saying.

'Unfortunately, Jake had a stroke and is unlikely ever to recover. Brendan Slack stepped in for him at the last moment and quickly discovered a forgery. He was killed apparently as a result.' John stood up and raised his glass, 'Brendan Slack.' The others all rose and toasted the deceased man.

Once seated, John continued, 'You'll have to make your own enquiries as to what is correct or not. I would add that I believe the only small firm close to London that has an unmarked security vehicle is called Braithwaites and is based in Virginia Water in Surrey. They only have the one vehicle and three members of staff. They seem to rely on an answer machine. Convenient I would say,' and he forced a broad smile. Then, as if remembering a minor point, 'You never know, there might even be a saved still from either the museums CCTV or even the recipients CCTV attached to a file.'

He saw everyone's faces change to smiles. Even Alison's. They knew what he was saying. He held the silence for a few seconds to let the information sink in. Then he added, 'I tried to check the firm out. All I discovered was, the owner is an Italian, Leonardo Russo. An apt name I thought. Hardly a thing about him on the internet. I found that strange. Nothing about his family except they live in Italy.' John sat well back in his seat and quaffed his wine.

Then, as if to enforce the fact he didn't like the family or the firm, he added, 'I was surprised to see how much a security vehicle costs. A small firm would never be able to justify the expense.' He looked straight at Groves. 'What do you reckon? A starting point?'

Groves raised his glass to John.

CHAPTER
THIRTY SEVEN

The following morning's briefing was a longish affair. Gwendoline was discussed at length. A lot of the team had pinned their hopes on finding the Turner and then possibly revealing the motive for Brendan's murder. No trace of the Turner at her house and her blatant killing while seated in a police car seemed to drain their enthusiasm. The fact they had recovered three original paintings did not seem to appease them.

Groves tried to lift everyone's spirits. He struggled. He decided to put some of John's hypothesis into the meeting as his own, keeping John's name out of it. A few eyebrows lifted. They didn't understand fully why following the trail of a painting from its initial request to its alleged delivery to a gallery would help. But it was a starting point. Alison and Murray held their counsel.

When Groves suggested that Alison should pursue the enquiry, she readily agreed. She knew exactly what she needed to discover and quickly. It was decided she should follow the Gainsborough from the museum to where it should have been displayed. She knew that within three or four hours, she would be able to produce evidence of discovering details of Braithwaites as her own.

Groves needed more. He wasn't going to wait. He asked Murray to gather a team to visit Parkland house and seize the fake Turner and conduct enquiries. Whilst there, they could seize all the paperwork pertaining to it. He knew Murray would quickly find the details of Braithwaites vehicle if there was a still from any CCTV within their papers.

Then a thought occurred to him. He looked at Murray before adding, 'I don't know if they have CCTV at Parkland. If they do, see if you can get a copy for the day that Brendan was there. It might help.'

Groves was back on fire. He expected a lot of useful information very quickly. Then he knew where his investigation would lead. He scanned the room for his main interviewer. 'You getting anywhere with the two private investigators?'

The man looked downcast. 'Sorry boss. They are saying nothing. They know we'll have to release them soon and I can't do anything to stop that.'

Another officer spoke up, 'I've gone right through their correspondence and other possessions. Nothing of note. The monocular can be bought practically anywhere. The directional microphone and the small recorder come from a Swiss firm. It is individually numbered. They told me their equipment can be bought directly via them or from one outlet on Edgeware Road up in the smoke. The one we have, they told me, is from Edgeware Road.'

Groves wanted more. 'Right. I want you at Edgeware Road tout de suite. Find out who he sold this gear to, down to their shoe size. I don't want you getting a knock back from some stroppy shop keeper, so I'll see if I can get the Met to give you a leg up.'

The officer nodded to one of the dedicated drivers who acknowledged him. Nothing said, but a vehicle organised.

Groves was becoming happier and his mood was contagious. He looked around the room, 'Where's Walter?'

Doreen piped up, 'He's at HQ playing with all the phones and computers. He sends his apologies. He will be here as soon as he can.' Groves knew Walter was no slouch. No point in harassing him, he'd be at the office as soon as he had anything of note.

Murray went through all the completed enquiries relating to Brendan's murder. They all knew the true name of his killer, Mike Calder. They all knew where he was in America and that the FBI were currently watching him. Home office extradition papers had been completed and were being readied for service on the Americans. Everything was progressing at the usual snail's pace.

Then he discussed the assault on Jimmy. Who had been in Brendan's house and why? Jimmy was no help either way. He couldn't even confirm if it was a man or a woman that had hit him. No one knew, or believed they knew who it was. It had been concluded that the person was searching for information from Brendan's journals. The ripped-out pages confirmed as much.

Murray said with feeling, 'It's good to have you back Jimmy. We need a proper exhibits officer,' and then lightened the mood, 'I can't do everything!' A few unhelpful comments were whispered loudly from some members of the team.

Groves carried on, 'Thanks to Walter and his forensic chums at HQ, it appeared what the person was looking for was any reference to Violet O'Donnell.' He paused for several seconds as he chose his words carefully. 'The indents on the pages following those that had been ripped out from Brendan's journals all bore a reference to Violet.'

Groves lowered his voice and spoke with solemnity,

'Unfortunately, Alison and Lynne got to Violet but didn't have sufficient time to get her back to the UK. Lynne, as we all know was brutally murdered, possibly by mistake. We have been extremely grateful to the Spanish for their fast work in identifying her murderer.' He paused as Alison snuffled loudly.

Looking around the office, he confided, 'We believe that...,' he paused. 'No. We know. Campbell is Lynne's murderer. We will find him!' He looked pointedly at Roland.

Roland took his cue. 'You bet we will. We're getting closer. We reckon he's somewhere near a place called Brig O'Turk in the Trossachs National Park in Scotland. Jimmy and I will be updating information as we get it. I know everyone will check it out regularly.' He looked around as though daring anyone to contradict him.

As the meeting drew to a conclusion, Groves called to Alison. 'You know what we want. Three hours. Ok?'

'I'll have an evidence trail from start to finish.'

Groves smiled and gave her the thumbs up. It had been a good meeting. Everything was starting to fit into place. Then he saw Walter pushing his way through the team members trying to get to him. He called to his officers in an emphasised authoritative voice, 'Make way for Walter.'

'Mr Groves. You haven't released the two from custody yet?'

'No. Why?'

Walter let out a large sigh. 'Thank goodness. I need to get my breath back. I think I may have found what you want.'

Doreen, ever aware of people's feelings, offered to make him a cup of tea. He smiled broadly at her which she took as a yes. He undid his old, battered briefcase.

CHAPTER
THIRTY EIGHT

Walter handed five A4 sheets of paper to Groves. He looked at them. He saw lines of telephone numbers. Some were obviously mobile numbers. They meant absolutely nothing to him. He looked up at Walter who was smiling broadly. He was slurping his tea and spilling some on the floor. Groves shuffled the papers. They all had lists of telephone numbers shown and nothing else.

Groves was exasperated. 'Ok Walter. What the hell am I looking at?'

Walter seemed slightly put out that Groves hadn't seen it. It hadn't occurred to him that it had taken him nearly two hours and the use of several computerised systems. He put his mug down on the closest desk, spilling some of the contents.

He held out his hand for the sheets to be returned and put them in a set order. By now, a few of the officers who were still in the office laughed quietly at Walter's inability to hold a mug without spilling any of its contents. But they still waited to see what he'd discovered. Most of those that had left the office returned. The rumour that Walter may have found something spread rapidly.

He started to explain as though talking to a child. Handing a single sheet of paper to Groves. 'Mr Groves look, this shows all the phone calls to and from the man's phone in the last thirty days.' Then deciding to clarify his point further added, 'That's the man you have in custody.' Then he handed a second sheet to him. 'This is all the phone calls to and from the woman's phone. As you can see they are constantly calling, texting and talking to each other.' He picked up his mug and took a mouthful of tea as Groves tried to make sense of the two pages.

Walter gave him the third sheet. 'As you can see from this page, it's the phone calls made and received by Clifford Samsun in the last thirty days.' Groves couldn't see it but took Walter's word. Walter continued enthusiastically, 'The two in custody have both been called by Samsun.' He practically spat his name. 'They have both called his number as well. As you can see, I've only gone back a full month. I could go further back if you want.'

Groves hadn't the faintest idea of how Walter had linked the three people up from the lists of numbers on the three pages, but knew if Walter could see it, it could be proved. He knew if he had time, he'd also see it clearly. 'Well done Walter. It looks like we have the beginning of some sort of conspiracy.'

Walter was quick. 'There's more.' He handed a fourth page to Groves. Detectives were starting to crowd round. 'This is the last month's phone calls made and received by Gwendoline Hawthorne. As you can see, she made and received calls to the man.' He finished his tea and tried to put the mug down on the desk. He dropped it to the floor as people jumped away trying to avoid the sprayed remnants from it.

No one tried to retrieve it as Walter passed the fifth sheet to Groves. Walter seemed to stand taller. This was his pièce de résistance. He said nothing. Groves scanned it before wondering why. It meant nothing to him. Others tried to see it. Someone broke the silence and said, 'Come on Walter. Spill the beans.'

Walter was surprised no one realised what it was. 'Amongst Gwendoline Hawthorne's outgoing calls, I found this number. It's a Scottish number registered to a Metcalf Buchanan. As you can clearly see from this sheet of his last month's outgoing calls, he's called Hawthorne and the man who's in custody, and a man called Campbell MacIntyre.' He paused so those looking could see and understand what he was saying. Everyone picked up on the name Campbell.

A murmur ran around the office. Roland said in his ear, 'You bloody genius.'

Walter heard the compliment and nodded his thanks to Roland. He couldn't stop. He had more. He delved into his briefcase and produced a couple more pages of A4. Handing them to Groves, he added, 'I checked Metcalf Buchanan out and found he's known as the Laird of Castle Grevin. It's in Scotland. The Trossachs. Less than four miles from Brig O'Turk.'

Walter looked around happily. Every face was staring back at him. He made it abundantly clear. He wanted everyone to know. No misunderstanding. 'When I spoke to Jimmy earlier he mentioned a place called Brig O'Turk. Castle Grevin's address is Brig O'Turk!'

The office erupted. People were slapping him on the back and congratulating him. He'd linked about everyone up.

Groves thanked him profusely. Then cautiously asked him, 'Walter, I understand you have linked these people all up which could amount to a serious conspiracy. Would it be at all possible to establish who the owners of all these other phone numbers from Hawthorne's and Buchanan's phones are?'

Walter was taken aback. 'It'll take me a heck of a long time. But I can do it.'

Groves queried, 'If I allocate a couple of detectives to help you, would that speed it up?'

Walter was still in temporary shock at the thought. 'Four of us could probably do it in about four or five hours. I can't promise.'

'You'll have them. Can you start straight away?'

Walter was surprised at the response. With a team, it would be a lot quicker. 'Yes. We would need access to at least three computers, three phones and some peace and quiet.'

Groves pointed to four officers. 'Grab some computers and put them in my office. Walter, there are a couple of phones in the spare office next door, sooner this is done the better. Walter. We are all relying on you.' Then he turned to Murray. 'Get going Murray. I want a Turner to hang in the office!'

He looked round for Jimmy. He saw him the other side of the office chatting to a young female officer. He called out, 'Jimmy. You and Roland. Quiet word.'

Groves was brief. 'Shut the door Jimmy. This is between us for the time being. Roland, how do you fancy a few days in Scotland? Get up to this Brig O'Turk and have a good look round. I'll get you a pool car. It's a long way, but best to have a job car than fly and hire one. What do you say?'

'Fine by me sir. Anything I can do to find Lynne's killer. I'm your man.'

'Make sure you keep Jimmy updated and keep your phone on. I don't want any more funerals. Be careful.'

Roland was grateful for the trust Groves had put in him.

'No problem. I'll be careful.'

'Get going as soon as you can. I want your eyes and ears on the ground. Jimmy. Keep Roland updated.'

Now Groves searched for his interviewing team. He was relying on what Walter had told him. 'You heard what Walter has said. He can link them all up. I want those two who are in custody arrested for conspiracy to murder. See how they like that. Ask them a few questions and let them know about Hawthorne and how she was killed. Mention Campbell as the potential killer. It might loosen their tongues. Samsun can be arrested as well. I'm told by the custody sergeant that he does not like being in a cell. You could probably let him know how long a convicted murderer gets. The PCC might try to meddle. Let me know if she does. I've never nicked a PCC before.'

Groves couldn't stop smiling and called out, 'We're on the home straight people. Crack on!'

CHAPTER
THIRTY NINE

John was sitting in his comfy chair with his leg up, reading the daily paper that Carol had got him. He was waiting for news. Not from the paper but from one of his contacts at the police station. One had already updated him on the morning's briefing and what everyone was doing. Everything was progressing at pace.

Within a couple of hours, he got a swift call from Groves. He appreciated that enquiries were evolving quickly and Groves' update was very staccato. 'Alison's liaising with the Arts and Antiques squad. They have told her the Gainsborough Hawthorne had, belongs to the National Gallery. It was originally loaned to a large, university sponsored gallery in the heart of Oxford. The experts have established the one on display is a forgery. Local police have seized it.'

John asked, 'Who checked it yearly for the museum?'

'Hang on,' and John heard Groves yelling to someone. 'Got it. Jake.'

'Looks like the proof he could be the inside man at the museum.'

Groves agreed. 'I'll get that checked for all the paintings that Hawthorne had.'

John added, 'And don't forget the Turner at Parkland.'

'Good point. We've got full copies of all the paperwork re the Gainsborough and the two Bruegels from the museums. John. I've had a quick look. There is a still from the museum's

CCTV in each, showing the true picture being placed into the security vehicle. It is a stipulation for insurance purposes. The index number of the vehicle is as clear as a bell. The same one for all three paintings. PNC shows it belongs to Braithwaites.'

John knew it wouldn't take Groves and the team long to get the information. 'Great work.'

Groves ended the call. It was coming together. All the officers now knew the only time the painting was not secured by museum security officers was during transit. Logically, they'd concluded that was when the paintings were switched. No one would see into the back of the security vehicle. Museum staff would place the original painting into the vehicle. The driver and his assistant could stop anywhere en route and swop the paintings over. On arrival at their destination, the recipients would remove what they believed to be the painting they were expecting.

John knew Groves' next steps. His officers would discover that Braithwaites was a three man outfit. They'd question how a small firm could have afforded a large security vehicle. Then they would discover everything they could about the owner, Leonardo Russo. It would then result in a search of the offices of Braithwaites and the arrest of all three members of staff.

John anticipated that there would be something at the firm that would identify either the 'museum informant' who he now believed was Jake or the 'broker' or 'forger.' Just one could lead to the others. Then if the gods were smiling, he hoped that the police would discover who had the Turner. They owed it to Brendan.

Murray called Groves from Parkland House. 'Boss. I've got the fake Turner, and I've got the CCTV for the day Brendan was here. There's not that much paperwork. I'm told by the curator that the museum will have the majority of it. We have discovered something that I think is of interest.'

Groves was impatient, 'Go on?'

'The curator was off sick on the day Brendan was here. Just one day with a bout of the runs. He says he's never normally sick. He told us that there is a temporary assistant that stands in for him when he's not here. No one has seen the assistant for the last few days.'

Groves suspected what Murray was saying. 'What do you think Murray?'

'The obvious. Someone's done for him.'

'See what you can discover. We'll have to look into it.'

Murray had already started to make some enquiries to locate him. 'Ok boss. See you later,' and they both hung up.

Groves wasn't happy. Surely the assistant had just gone off somewhere. He didn't want another murder. He decided to hold off telling the chief. It would give Murray time to find him.

Doreen, Alison, Jimmy and Groves sat together in the main office. Walter and his little team were ensconced in Groves' office. He couldn't even get to his desk. They had all got mugs of tea. 'Well. It looks like we may have another murder. I can't see the chief giving us anymore staff. I just hope he authorises all the additional overtime!'

Doreen was contemplating how everything had seemed to snowball from the death of Brendan Slack. She couldn't help thinking that he was an honourable man who was well liked and respected by those who knew him. An unassuming expert in his field who was willing to pass on his knowledge by lecturing around the world. He was just helping out an old friend at the British Museum and died an untimely death as a result. Then she thought: why?

'Mr Groves. I know it's not my place, but I can't help thinking that Mr Slack would not have been at Arundel Castle if Jake had not had a stroke. Jake has worked at the museum for years and he has been the person confirming that the museums' paintings were kept securely and in good condition. It appears that he is definitely the inside man at the museums. What if he were completely dishonest? He would know which ones were or weren't forgeries. Could he be taking money to turn a blind eye whenever he looked at a fake? Do you think someone should make some enquires into his finances. It may be possible to tie up when he viewed a picture with a payment into his account. Then it may be possible to establish which paintings are forgeries.'

Jimmy said, 'Hang on,' and tapped at a computer keyboard. He pulled up the statement from the curator at the British Museum. Jake had had the stroke less than a fortnight before Brendan's death.

Groves read the relevant part of the statement. Pensively, he said, 'That's a good thought, Doreen. Jimmy. Can you do a little discreet digging into Jake's background. Bear in mind Jimmy that it looks like he's unlikely ever to recover. Show a little compassion.' Jimmy categorically needed to be reminded. Groves knew that Jake was the inside man at the museum, it was unlikely to get them much further. He considered passing the information to the Arts and Antiques Squad. They were the police experts in art. If anyone could work it out, it would be them.

Doreen answered a ringing phone. 'Murder Team, can

I help you?' She held it towards Groves who took it as she whispered, 'Greenthorne.'

'Sergeant Greenthorne. How are the interviews going with our two private eyes?'

'Good and bad boss. When we arrested the woman for conspiracy to murder, she fainted. The FME has seen her and given her some pills. He suggested we don't interview her for at least an hour.'

Groves queried, 'The man?'

'Different kettle of fish. When we arrested him, he was blasé. Said we were talking rubbish. Claimed at first that he had legal privilege and did not have to disclose any information. Then his brief told him that was incorrect. Once we had his address, we mentioned we were going to search his house and he was incandescent with rage. His brief put him on the straight and narrow. The murder of Brendan didn't seem to bother him. Denied even knowing who he was. He practically shat himself though when we told him how Gwendoline had been killed. He certainly knew her. From then on, he resigned himself to answering all our questions but claimed to know nothing about forgeries. When we asked why they were watching you, he said that's what he'd been paid to do. We have done one full interview.' Then before he could be questioned by Groves, he added as if of no consequence, 'Oh! He's named his employer.'

Groves smiled. 'Ok sergeant. You have my full, undivided attention. Who?'

Greenthorne paused a second longer for even more effect. 'Metcalf Buchanan. The Laird of Castle Grevin, at Brig O'Turk.'

Groves couldn't stop himself. A full list of expletives shot from his mouth.

Greenthorne laughed. 'I knew you'd be pleased.'

'Great work. Doreen will type the interview up as soon as you get back. See what he's got at his HA. I want evidence to put him on a charge sheet.'

They hung up as Groves asked, 'You all right to do a bit of overtime tonight Doreen? I'll get you a lift home.'

She had no objection.

Murray had sent a couple of uniform officers to the assistant curator's home address. He was hoping they'd find the man alive and kicking although he didn't hold out much hope. Unfortunately they did find him at his home and he was definitely kicking. He kicked one of the officers who hadn't expected it. Then he ran. Out of his house and straight across the road. Right in front of a large four-by-four. He didn't know much about it. He was flung into the air like a rag doll. Over the roof of the vehicle and onto the road behind. The following car couldn't stop and drove over him. One wheel hitting his head with a glancing blow. The officer called for an ambulance and local officers to deal with the carnage.

Murray listened in astonishment to the telephone report from one of the uniformed officers. It appeared that the sight of two policemen in full uniform had frightened the assistant curator sufficiently to run. Not the actions of an innocent man. Murray cursed the fact he'd only sent two officers. He updated Groves.

Groves was as shocked as Murray. Questions formed. Why did he run? Implies guilt. Did he know the Turner was a forgery? No one could ask him now. He was already in the care of the coroner's officer. The PM would be a formality.

The art expert from the British Museum who had accompanied the team to Parkland House had already confirmed the Turner that had been on display for several years was a forgery. A very good forgery at that. Now it was languishing in the boot of an unmarked police car on its way back to Littlehampton.

Jimmy knew where he was going to keep it. On the office wall. He didn't want it getting damaged in the exhibits store!

CHAPTER
FORTY

Murray and Groves sat together. 'What do you reckon Murray? Do you think the guy knew?'

Murray was adamant. 'He must have done. Why run if you're innocent.'

Groves wanted evidence. 'Perhaps he was scared of police. Some people are.'

'No. He knew it was a forgery. I bet Brendan told him when he recognised it was a fake. When he saw the uniform boys, he probably thought it had all come on top. Running was his only option.'

Groves needed hard evidence. 'See what you can find out Murray. I'm going to update the chief. I've a lot to tell him.'

He set off to go to his office before remembering Walter and his little team were still in there. He diverted to the car park. At least it was quiet. He clearly heard the chief go through his own selection of expletives.

When he walked back into the office, there was a buzz in the air. He asked worriedly of no one in particular, 'What's happened now?'

Doreen answered. 'Nathan has just had a result viewing the CCTV from Parkland. The relevant bit is only a few minutes long.'

Groves saw a small group of officers huddled around a computer with Nathan seated in front of it operating the keyboard. He walked over, 'What have you got Nathan?'

Nathan was happy. 'Sir. I've found Mr Slack examining the Turner for about twenty minutes. It looks like he calls to someone and a man moves into view. I'm told that the man is the assistant curator who got run over.'

Groves wasn't really that concerned but didn't want to dampen Nathan's enthusiasm. 'Well done Nathan. Run off a couple of copies and give the original to Jimmy.' Nathan replied slightly bewildered, 'No. That's not the thing sir. Can I show you?'

Groves had a lot on his mind but could afford a few minutes. 'What is it?'

Nathan set the CCTV to play. Groves watched what was probably the end of the chat between Brendan and the assistant curator. Then in the background apparently looking at other paintings in the room he saw the two private eyes. Now he was more than interested. They were obviously earwigging the conversation.

'Wow! Well done Nathan. Please play it till they move from view. I need to see all this.' The two were only on the CCTV for about three minutes. 'Nathan. Speak to Murray. I want to see if we can get a lip reader to see what Brendan said to the assistant curator.'

Groves needed to update Greenthorne. Didn't know Brendan eh! Lying bastard!

The evening meeting was put back to 10pm. Too many officers were tucked up dealing with urgent matters and were not available at five o'clock. Reports were being forwarded to the office by email, texts and occasionally, via land lines. Doreen was busy typing them up as soon as they came in. Alison was acting as office manager answering the phones and disseminating intelligence from one group of officers to another. As 10pm approached, the office slowly filled up.

Groves had finally got into his office when Walter and his team finished just before 9.30pm. He had a couple of calls to make. One to the chief and another to John. Then at 10pm exactly, he strode purposefully into the main office. Not one person made any effort to rise. They were nearly all exhausted. Chairs had appeared from other offices and some old, green, plastic garden chairs had been found and were being utilised. Those without chairs were seated on desks. No one was standing.

Groves looked around. Tired faces were staring back at him. 'Ladies and gentlemen, I'd like to thank you all for your hard work today. Some of the day's events have been challenging to say the least. To save time, I'll update you with some facts that you should all be aware of. Then I'll call on individuals to bring us up to date with their work. I've sent Roland to Scotland. He's wasted no time.

He has established already that the Laird of Castle Grevin, Metcalf Buchanan and his so called butler, Campbell MacIntyre are no longer there. Jimmy. Carry on.'

Jimmy was confident. He suffered as he spoke with a slight lisp. 'Roland called me. He's scouted around the castle area. The local shopkeeper has told him that the daily paper, bread and milk have all been cancelled. There's been no movement at all at the castle. It looks to Roland that the two have done a runner. Roland has found Campbell's car and he's established the laird has a Rolls with a personalised index. It's missing. All the details have been circulated. Now we wait.'

Groves was grateful for Jimmy's brevity. 'Thanks Jimmy.'

He nodded to Murray, 'DS Murray has been at Parkland. As you can see from the new adornment on one of our walls. Please bring us up to date with your visit.'

Murray started, 'As you all know we went to Parkland and recovered the forged Turner that is now hanging on our wall. We recovered all the paperwork that Parkland had, as well as the CCTV for the relevant date. It appears that the assistant curator, who was present when Brendan examined it, may have known it was a forgery. When two of our uniform lads went to check on him, he did a runner. Straight into a busy road where he got run over and killed.' Murray acknowledged the two officers with a swift nod.

Returning to his brief story, he continued, 'Nathan has viewed the CCTV and discovered that Brendan spoke to the assistant curator and was earwigged by none other than our two private eyes.' A few murmurs were heard as Murray wound up his day's work. 'We'll be getting a lip reader to see what was said.'

Groves needed Alison to add a supplement. 'DI Daines has conducted some enquiries about the Gainsborough that Gwendoline Hawthorne had. DI Daines...'

Alison took her cue. 'From all my enquiries, the only time any painting is out of sight, and not monitored by museum security officers, is when it is being transported from the museum to its destination. The normal firm used is NSL. Due to the stringent insurance conditions placed upon the museums, stills from the museum's CCTV are always attached to the file which confirms the painting has left their premises. It invariably shows the security vehicle from the rear, including the index plate.'

A loud murmur ran round the room. Groves called for quiet.

Alison continued unfazed, 'The Gainsborough was picked up from the museum by a vehicle owned by a small firm. Not NSL. PNC shows the vehicle is from a firm called Braithwaites based in Virginia Water. It's a three man band with a very expensive security vehicle. I have confirmed with the British Museum that the index plate of the vehicle that picked up the Turner was the same.'

There were woops of joy as the officers knew they were getting closer to the Turner and the reason for Brendan's murder. Groves gave them nearly half a minute before calling for order. He smiled as he added, 'Our officers together with Arts and Antiques Squad officers from the Met, will visit that business premises tomorrow and all three employees will be arrested. We'll be dealing with them tomorrow. Groves turned to Greenthorne. 'Your turn now sergeant.'

Greenthorne had a lot to add. He wanted to keep it brief. 'We have interviewed both private investigators. Both have confirmed they were employed by Metcalf Buchanan. Neither appeared to know who he is. Both showed genuine shock at Gwendoline's murder, although neither seemed to have any concern for Brendan. When we interviewed them for a second time, after Nathan's discovery, the man claimed he didn't know it was Brendan at Parkland. He claimed that he'd been employed to try and hear what was said when anyone went near the Turner. The woman said they'd been told the painting was to be examined by an expert. They were to report to Buchanan what was said. She claimed the man told Buchanan that the expert had discovered it was a forgery and had told the curator from Parkland House. I presumed that would have been the assistant curator. We shall do concluding interviews tomorrow and then I'll approach the CPS for conspiracy charges. We have both their mobile phones and laptops. In a nutshell Mr Groves, that's roughly where we are.'

'How are you doing with Samsun?'

Greenthorne chuckled. 'He threw his hands up in his first interview. Said he was approached a few years ago by Hawthorne when he was hard up and working for the Police Authority prior to it becoming the PCC. She gave him the tablet and often sent him drugs through the post. Each month a hundred pounds would be placed into his bank account. She knew that he could see a lot of what the PCCs in the South of England said to each other and wanted to know about anything of interest. Nothing really special about him. A bent official. The CPS have already authorised charges.'

Groves wanted both private investigators on charge sheets as well. 'Nice one sergeant.' He thought for a couple of seconds before asking, 'Jimmy. Did you get anywhere with Jake?'

Jimmy was on the ball, 'Oh yes. Jake has been a permanent employee of the British Museum for seventeen years. His main job is travelling around the country checking that all the paintings on loan are where they should be and in good condition. He was due to conduct the checks at properties here in West Sussex when he had his stroke. The museum asked Brendan to stand in for him and we all know what happened.' He paused for effect. 'The museum has confirmed that Jake would have been one of the first people to know when someone made a request for a painting. I've got a couple more enquiries to do tomorrow. That's all at the moment boss.'

'Thanks Jimmy.' Groves looked around and latched onto Walter. He looked shattered. 'Walter. You look worn out. How have you and your team done?'

Walter tried to perk up. 'We have finished. We have the details of just short of three hundred people. Names and addresses. We have the majority of their bank details, but we couldn't get all those from outside of the UK. We have a printout of the last six months of calls from each phone and have colour coded linked numbers. We were surprised how many there were.'

Groves was happy. 'That's really useful Walter. I'd like to go over it with you tomorrow. Thanks for all your work. I'll make sure you get a lift home tonight.'

Walter smiled. It was about all he could manage.

Groves addressed the floor. 'Normally I'd open up the floor now to any questions or comments. I think it's late enough. They can wait for the time being. The chief and I are extremely grateful for what you have all done. Tomorrow is going to be another busy day. Go home and get some rest and then please be back here for 7am tomorrow.

CHAPTER
FORTY ONE

Groves called John at six-thirty in the morning and gave him a brief update. When John offered to buy him lunch, he jumped at the chance. Come 7am and Groves was in the main office. The chief was already there chatting and laughing with the staff. He was offering his opinion on the Turner. Two members of the Arts and Antiques Squad were present and were trying to explain how to spot a forgery.

The morning's briefing was mainly to answer any questions or comments from the previous evening. There were a lot. The main concern was a search of Castle Grevin. It was discussed at length. ANPRs had tracked the laird's Rolls Royce to Dover and then no other sightings. Customs officials had confirmed it left the UK on a P&O ferry. There were two people in the vehicle. They would confirm the details of them later.

The whole office knew who they were without being told. Campbell MacIntyre was the one they all wanted. He was Lynne's murderer. He probably killed Gwendoline Hawthorne as well, but that was a secondary concern. Now they knew he'd fled the country. Where to? When would they search the castle?

Roland had been in touch with Jimmy. He had told him he'd been scouting around the castle. It was obvious that there was no one in the premises. He confided that he'd found a small, insecure window close to the back door. When Jimmy unconcernedly queried if he'd forced the window, or been inside, Roland was evasive and didn't actually confirm either way. If roles were reversed, Jimmy would have definitely broken the window and been inside. Within reason, anything to catch Lynne's killer.

Greenthorne answered a few questions about the private investigators. Groves listened intently. He didn't like them and wanted them dealt with swiftly. That would tuck up that part of the enquiry. They could join Samsun in court the following day.

Alison was deputed to lead the search of Braithwaites which was set for the following day. A warrant had already been issued and force would be used if required to enter the premises. Interviewers were ready as soon as the employees arrived at the Chichester custody suite.

The chief was the last to speak and was generally congratulatory. He confirmed that he had updated the duke on the main issue of Brendan Slack's murder and he went on to explain he was liaising with his counterpart in Gloucestershire and the IPCC. The enquiry to establish Gwendoline's killer had practically concluded that Campbell was her murderer. The evidence was mainly circumstantial but considered sufficient to seek his apprehension.

Then the chief became sanguine. 'Ladies and gentlemen. We have to consider what we know. It appears that Buchanan and Campbell have fled the country and our clutches. I'm sure Customs at Dover will confirm as such later today. We know Campbell killed our colleague and friend Lynne. Our Spanish counterparts have issued an international arrest warrant and have been very helpful. I don't want it to be left un-executed. However. It's a problem.'

He looked around the room. There were a lot of despondent faces staring back at him. 'I'm sorry to have to tell you this.' The silence in the room was deafening. Several seconds ticked by. 'There are still loose ends that need to be tied up. They all amount to nails in the killers' coffins. Please don't cut corners believing they are a waste of time. When they 'grip the rail', and they will, I don't want fancy lawyers getting them off because something wasn't done.'

Groves was worried for the same reason. He never gave up hope. The phone that Walter had identified as Buchanan's had not been used for several days and couldn't be located. It appeared that he'd abandoned it. His only way forward was to try and locate the Rolls. His worry was that if Buchanan knew to dump his phone, would he dump the Rolls?

Groves wrapped up the meeting. His brain was racing. He wanted everything watertight. Brendan's murder was solved and the paperwork was practically finished. Now he considered the two current, main sticking points. Why did Gwendoline apparently organise the killing if she didn't have the Turner? Did she do it as a favour, possibly for the laird? And where the hell was it? Castle Crevin had to be its present location.

Lynne's murder had been quickly solved by the Spanish and Campbell MacTavish had now been identified as Campbell MacIntyre. Groves and his team all believed she was killed in the mistaken belief she was Violet O'Donnell. The police in Gloucestershire had, in conjunction with Sussex officers, come to the conclusion that Campbell MacIntyre was also Gwendoline Hawthorne's murderer.

Groves had wanted everything linked up. His team had excelled. The major problem was three people had died violent deaths at the hands of two killers who remained free. It all seemed to revolve around the painting by Turner. The more he thought, the more confused he became.

* * *

Chuck Connors of the FBI wasn't overtly confused. He was seated behind his ornate desk which only had a telephone and a computer on it. Around the walls were certificates and photographs that meant a lot to him. He looked out of his window over the rooftops of New York, deep in thought. He had received a call from his watchers that Mike Calder was moving about his apartment early in the morning. It appeared that he was getting ready to leave. Chuck didn't know why.

His minions had read every letter addressed to Calder and listened to every phone call he'd made or received. One was eavesdropping as he walked around his apartment. They'd even seen his swollen bank account going back three years. There was nothing to suggest a reason that he should go out so early in the day. There were four agents in place ready to follow Calder anywhere in America. Chuck waited for an update. He soon got it.

Calder had left his apartment and gone to an underground garage a street away. In a space reserved for an apartment in the building above, he pulled a tarpaulin off a battered old Chevy vehicle and left it lying on the floor. The watchers saw he was wearing latex gloves. Calder looked around but didn't see anyone. He opened the trunk and looked inside. He seemed to smile as he shut it before getting into the driver's seat. Now he was reported leaving New York heading North. Roughly following the Hudson river.

Chuck called for a driver. He needed to catch up with his team and see where Calder was going. A large jeep and driver waited for him on the street outside the FBI building. Parked behind it was a hefty, black SUV containing four fully armed FBI agents all wearing body armour. Chuck wasn't taking any chances. He knew what Calder was capable of.

The vehicles left at speed. Multi-coloured lights flashing and sirens wailing. They were already twenty odd miles behind Calder and needed to catch up quickly. Within another twenty miles they were at the rear of the team. Chuck could see they were heading towards Albany. Calder wasn't speeding nor breaking any traffic laws. Chuck came to what he believed was the logical conclusion, Calder was working.

They arrived at Albany and followed Calder to a leafy suburb. Then in a wide road with a few parked cars, Calder pulled to the kerb and stopped. An agent walked, apparently unconcernedly by, as Calder sat still and watched him stride purposefully to a nearby house and knock on the door. He ignored him. The house Calder wanted was four further down the street. No one else was visible walking and no vehicles passed along the road. Perfect. As he'd been told. He needed to be closer. He pulled away from the kerb and drove to within thirty feet of the target's house and parked.

Calder went to the trunk and took out what appeared to be a tennis racket in a canvas holder. Then shutting the boot he walked to the target's house and knocked on the door. He began to open the zip of the racket holder. Chuck knew it wasn't going to contain a tennis racket. No one drives to Albany from New York which is at least 150 miles distance for a game of tennis. He yelled down his radio for his four man assault team to 'take him out.'

The huge vehicle careered into the road with screeching tyres. Calder turned to see what was making the noise just as the front door to the target's house opened. An elderly, white haired man saw the vehicle and Calder standing on his stoop with what looked like a tennis racket in his hand and a cover lying on the floor. He slammed his door shut before Calder could react. The heavy vehicle drove across the pavement and over the man's manicured front lawn leaving thick tyre tracks.

Calder dropped to the floor pulling his beloved Colt Custom 9 millimetre pistol from his waistband holster. Four heavily armoured FBI agents left the vehicle. Calder had no time to think what he was doing. He'd pulled the trigger just the once. It was enough. They open fired on him with assorted firearms. He didn't have a chance to surrender. He was dead in seconds.

Chuck walked up to the front door of the house and knocked. He called out, 'FBI. It's all under control out here.' The front door opened about two inches. No one was visible. He waved his ID through the gap and the door slowly opened.

The elderly man stood stock still and demanded, 'What the hell has just happened?'

Chuck kept it brief. 'We've followed this man from New York. He's a hired assassin. Do you know of any reason why anyone would want you dead?'

The man glared at Chuck. 'How long have you been in the FBI? You don't recognise me?'

'I'm sorry sir. I don't.'

'I'm Jackson Deacon. I'm preparing a bill for Congress that will make it easier for the courts to send drug dealers to prison for life. Some people, understandably, don't like the idea. Mainly the drug dealers. When that guy knocked on my door, I thought it was my security detail arriving an hour early to take me to Washington. It was a lapse, by me, in my own security. I didn't follow protocols. I should never have opened my front door. Anyway, how was he going to do me any harm with a tennis racket?'

Chuck had the item in his hands. He had already worked out what Calder was going to do. 'This is no ordinary tennis racket. You see those two small prongs on the top, they act as contacts. The handle is full of batteries and there is a small trigger device as a button. If he'd touched you with the prongs and activated the trigger, you'd have had a massive electric shock that would probably have killed you, giving the impression of a heart attack. He'd have had plenty of time to get away before anyone could do anything about it. Mr Deacon. I would suggest you enhance your security.'

Deacon stared at Calder lying on the floor covered in blood which had leaked from the numerous bullet wounds. He could only agree.

* * *

A day later, she read the report on the Washington Post's web site. Brief and concise. No real details. Nothing said about either a false passport or a pager hidden behind a panel under his sink. If they were ever found, she knew Mike would have deleted all the details of the hit from the pager. He was a professional after all. She smiled. Problem solved. Mike neutralised.

CHAPTER
FORTY TWO

At 1pm, Groves sat in Brasserie Blanc in Chichester with a cold beer, deep in thought. A slight commotion at the door brought him back to the present. John was being helped by Maurice, the head waiter towards the table. Several people were laughing at the exaggerated efforts of Maurice. John swore at him under his breath.

Groves genuinely smiled for the first time that day. As Maurice held John upright in front of a chair, two waiters were directed to keep moving it one way or another by no more than an inch or two. By the time Maurice allowed John to sit down, the whole restaurant was engulfed in laughter. John swore vengeance at Maurice as he feigned hurt. Groves couldn't stop laughing.

As the meal progressed, the two chatted about the case. Or rather Groves updated John and bounced various scenarios off him. The more they chatted, the more Groves realised how much there still was to do. Eventually, they were about to leave the restaurant when Groves got a text from Murray.

He said nothing and turned his phone to allow John to see the text.

John considered it. 'I suppose that saves the British taxpayer a few bob. Would have been nice if one of your team could have spoken to him first though. He might have confirmed why Hawthorne got him to kill Brendan. Live by the sword, die by the sword.'

Back at Littlehampton, Groves found Murray. 'What happened Murray?'

'I took a phone call from the lead guy at the FBI in New York. He said they'd followed Calder to Albany where he was obviously plotting to kill someone. They seemed to know he had some sort of an adapted weapon in his vehicle. When he was getting ready to use it, they pounced. The man at the FBI didn't seem too concerned that Calder fired a handgun at them. They retaliated and killed him.'

Groves swore. 'That suits them. An assassin caught by the FBI in America. Feather in their cap. They wouldn't have known anything about him without our initial input. All we know now is that he killed Brendan Slack, apparently at Hawthorne's instruction,' and he swore again.

One of the Met officers said, 'Excuse me sir. I might have a little good news. I'm not sure. I'll confirm it as soon as I can. We've been looking at the phone records of Metcalf Buchanan. My colleague believes he is on our files as a person of interest.'

Groves wasn't sure he understood what the officer was saying. 'I'm sorry? What does that mean?'

The officer wasn't used to the informality of the Sussex office at times. 'Sir. My colleague seems to think he is an art collector who was once suspected of dubious practices. Possibly buying paintings at well below their value, by threats or coercion, and then selling them on for a grossly inflated price. We'll confirm this within the hour.'

Groves was intrigued. It had already been confirmed by Walter that Hawthorne and Buchanan were known to contact each other by phone. They could have been talking about paintings. Were they both dealing in stolen artwork? He needed to search Castle Grevin. He was perking up. Could the Turner be there? A stroke of luck? He couldn't wish for more at the moment.

Turning to the officer, he asked, 'Could you please check your files asap?'

The officer scurried off to find his colleague.

Groves turned back to Murray, 'I'd like to hit that castle tomorrow. I reckon eight of us would be enough with the Scottish lads. We could take an art expert and an architect who could check out the internal spaces. If Gwendoline had a hidden room, perhaps there's one at Castle Grevin as well. I'm starting to feel more confident.'

Murray was hesitant. 'How are we going to get up there guv'nor? Drive or fly? Stay overnight?'

'Good point. Can you make a few enquiries about flying from Southampton and hiring some cars when we get there. I'll see what the chief thinks.'

CHAPTER
FORTY THREE

A couple of unmarked personnel carriers took the officers
and two civilians to Southampton Airport. They landed at
Glasgow Airport and were met by officers from Police Scotland
who had two marked personnel carriers. They didn't dawdle.
They were due at Castle Grevin in less than an hour to meet
more officers who were in possession of a search warrant.

The single track, private road leading up the hill to the
castle had tufts of grass growing in the middle and passed
through a small coppice. Twigs and even small branches lay
about on the unmaintained track. The vehicles navigated
carefully and swerved occasionally to miss the larger potholes.
Then they all saw the castle. A large, grey, stonework
pile perched atop a crag. Four turrets, one on each of the
building's corners, were adorned in the Scottish style of an
upside down cone. Even the bright sunlight didn't enhance its
austere appearance.

A couple of the officers shuddered. It hadn't helped when
one claimed Dracula had probably lived there in the past.

Over the arched front door was a stone canopy that made
the place look Gothic and even older than it was. A large
gravel area to one side was where vehicles were able to park
and manoeuvre ready to return down the track to modern
civilisation. To the other side of the castle was an open fronted
wooden garage capable of housing seven or eight vehicles. There
were three expensive looking cars towards the rear and a couple

of small runabouts in front of them. Right at the front was the vehicle used by Campbell. Next to it was a drip tray on the floor. It was obviously where a vehicle was normally parked.

Officers from Police Scotland, some in uniform, stood about in the parking area chatting. After brief introductions, they all moved to the front door. Several times one of them pushed the large copper button in the middle of an ornate circular bell housing. There was no answer. They didn't really expect one. A uniformed officer lent on the solid wooden door. The 'door bosher' would hardly put a dent in it. They needed something much more powerful.

A Scottish officer walked nonchalantly to a van and took out a heavy, metal extending calliper. Carrying it to the front door, he pressed the control button opening it slightly. Two officers held the arms either side of the door against the door jamb. The machine began whirring as it took the strain and started to force them apart. The door seemed to become moveable. It wobbled marginally as a couple of substantially strong metal hinges were broken. Two officers lent heavily on the thick wooden door. It didn't budge. The machine kept whirring. The last of the hinges broke but the door still remained upright and intact.

The officer left the callipers in place as he put the control unit on the floor. Another officer moved forward with a 'door bosher'. Several strikes close to the handle and the door fell inside the castle onto the tacky welcome mat.

All the officers stormed in.

A thorough search of the building confirmed the castle was not currently occupied. As the officers all gathered back in the entrance hall, the Sussex officers noted that Roland had surreptitiously joined them. None deemed it appropriate to question where he came from. Nor the fact he had a mobile phone that he claimed to have just found on a bedside cabinet in the master bedroom. Boniface, the sergeant from Sussex, raised his eyebrows.

Roland said, 'I bet this is the laird's. The one we were hoping to find.' Then he passed it to the dedicated exhibits officer. A few of the Sussex officers looked at each other as Roland continued, 'When I came downstairs, I walked through the library and I noticed there was a gap between some shelving. Gwendoline had a false door. Do you think it could be one as well?'

The architect said, 'I'll check it out,' and walked off. A couple of Sussex officers went with him. They had quickly come to the conclusion that Roland had been inside the castle for some time. If he thought there was a concealed door, he'd have probably found where it was already.

The architect walked round the library. He shone a handheld laser device from one wall to the opposite side of the room. Then checked the device's LED display. He kept shining the device at walls as he walked about. Then he went into a large lounge to one side and looked at the stone wall. His device blipped. He moved about and went into a corridor leading to some carpeted stairs. Standing still he stroked his chin. Then with the Sussex officers in tow, he worked his way to the rear of the building. He looked at the long, stark, stone wall. His device blipped again. He glanced into a couple of rooms. Then they returned to the library. He stared at the wood panelling. He went to the gap and started to tap the wood. He shook his head. It was solid.

One of the Sussex officers assumed there was no door. 'Well, it was worth a thought,' and turned to leave.

The architect quickly corrected him. 'I think there may be a concealed room, but I can't see where the entrance is or how to get into it. I'll confirm the room by taking some accurate measurements and draw a map. The officer who noticed this had a stroke of luck.'

They returned to the entrance hall and informed everyone what the architect suspected. Boniface spoke quietly to Roland. 'Any ideas how to get into it?'

Roland whispered to him, 'I'm sure the entrance is somewhere behind the panelling in the library, but I'm buggered if I can find it.'

The sergeant called to everyone, 'Let's all assemble in the library and see if we can find anything.'

Everyone stared at the wooden panelling. An officer lay on his belly and tried to slide a piece of paper between the floor and the bottom of the wood as he'd done at Hawthorne's. He couldn't. Others tapped it. There was no discernible difference in sound. Some tried to push the wood first one way and then another. It didn't budge.

One of the Scottish officers stared at the panelling. He looked it up and down. There was a very small black smudge of a mark on the ornate, white painted ceiling above it. Standing on a chair he reached up with a handkerchief. Grease. He put his hand on the top of the panelling by the ceiling for support. He felt something sticky on his hand. More grease. He ran his handkerchief along the top of the panelling where it joined the ceiling. It was covered in grease. It had to be a concealed runner. Now they roughly knew where the door was. But they still couldn't open it.

A Scottish officer in a cavalier manner, proffered, 'We need a heavy duty drill to punch a hole through that panelling and see if there's a stone wall behind it, or a room.'

Roland made an aside to one of his colleagues. 'There's a toolbox and some powerful tools in the shed at the rear of the garage.'

He took the hint and said rather too loudly, 'I think I saw a drill in the equipment shed at the back of the garage.' Then he set off at a jog.

Five minutes later, he returned with an industrial size electric hammer drill and some masonry bits. Not excessively powerful, but sufficient to drill a reasonable sized hole through concrete. Someone plugged it in, and it swiftly made a quarter inch hole in the ornate wood panelling. Then as the drill bore into the concrete behind, dust and debris flew out. The officer lent on the drill forcing it forward. And then the drill shot forward as the bit found fresh air. Boniface squinted as he looked through the hole. He couldn't see into the void. It was as black as the ace of spades.

Another hole was drilled. A mobile phone's torch was placed against the hole as the sergeant squinted through the first hole. Now he could see. A room. He tried to adjust his position. There was something on the wall. He called it out. They all asked in unison, 'A painting?' He wasn't sure.

Fresh eyes were placed against the hole. Someone said, 'What's that propped against the wall?' No one could say. They needed to get into the room.

Hands ran over the panelling, searching for some kind of way to open the door. They pushed and pulled at every slight indent or nobble on the wood. Nothing moved. Some crawled around the floor looking for any button or loose slab. Nothing. Books were moved from shelves and the walls behind checked for any switch. Nothing. The senior Scottish officer came to a decision. He would get a contractor from Callander to cut a large hole through to the room. A call to his control room got his idea going.

While they waited, they took it in turns to go to the village to get food. No one had brought any food with them. They had all eaten within an hour and a half and were either sitting about chatting or snatching a few minutes shut-eye. The exhibits officer was looking at the phone Roland had found. He turned it on. No password. He was always amazed how many people couldn't be bothered to set passwords. Had he thought about it, even he didn't bother.

He glanced at the touch screen. Lots of the usual icons from various firms. All with some sort of name below stating what they were. There was one with a small, indistinct icon. Below it was the word, 'My Pics.' He couldn't resist it. There might be a useful picture of the laird on it. He pressed the icon.

People jumped as the complete panelling, with the stone wall behind, slid noiselessly to one side out of sight behind the library shelving. The room was revealed. It was only slightly larger than the one at Hawthorne's. There were five paintings hanging on the walls. Two on each side and just one on the back wall. In the middle of the room was a leather, reclining, swivel seat with a small glass table attached. Just large enough for a whisky tumbler.

The Sussex officers were ecstatic. They recognised the one on the back wall immediately. It was identical to the one currently adorning a wall in their office at Littlehampton. The senior Scottish officer shouted that no one should go into the room until the art expert had had time to check everything. Nothing was to be touched. Propped up in a corner was a rifle.

The art expert went into the room. He triggered an automatic lighting and air conditioning system. The Turner was beautifully lit. He shone his little torch at the signature. Then moved to one side of the room. His torch glowed bluish. He crossed the room and shone his little torch at the other two paintings.

When he'd finished, he turned his torch off before sliding it back into its chamois leather holder and then into his pocket. Then he stood next to the chair and just stared at the Turner. Seconds passed. Then a minute. No one wanted to disturb him. The minute turned to four. Roland watched him. He broke the silence. 'Well. What do you think?'

The man couldn't take his eyes from the painting. 'It's the most beautiful painting I've ever seen.'

Roland persisted. 'Yes, but is it the original?'

Without turning, the expert answered, 'Undoubtedly.'

Someone asked, 'What about these others?'

It was as if a spell had been broken. The man turned to one side. Then, not quite disdainfully, he pointed at one painting. 'There's a Caravaggio,' and waving his hand, added, 'and a Titian.' Then pointing to the other wall said, 'There's a Degas and an early line drawing by Picasso. I am sure they are all originals. But ladies and gentlemen, that Turner is surely the jewel amongst them. You will never see a painting in such glory. No glass protecting it and lit to perfection. The brush strokes are clearly visible. The signature is a work of art in itself. You are seeing the painting as the artist intended. It is truly magnificent.' And then he placed a hand on the back of the chair for support, and just stood and stared at it.

The exhibits officer spoke to the SOCO. 'Is there any way to check these paintings for fingerprints without causing them any damage?'

'I can check with ultraviolet light to see if there are any marks, but to lift them without touching the painting is practically impossible. If there are any marks, I'll just photograph them. The gun won't be a problem.' He moved into the room.

The expert couldn't take his gaze from the Turner. Someone outside the room asked a colleague, 'Wonder how much this lot are worth?'

The expert heard. He answered without turning to see who'd asked. 'Several hundred million as a starting price. Maybe as much as half a billion pounds in total.' Officers looked at each other as if to enquire whether they'd heard correctly. The Scottish Inspector knew what had to be done.

He called his control room. Armed officers were summoned. The paintings had to be protected. The chief constable was informed. He called for a marked vehicle. He needed to get there quickly. His press officer was notified. It was a coup for his force and he wanted everyone to be told.

Sergeant Boniface called the Sussex office and spoke to Groves. He called the Sussex chief constable. Contact was made between the two chief constables. Murray called the British Museum. Art experts started enquiries. They established where the paintings should have been. Groves arranged for officers from various constabularies to visit galleries and stately homes and seize the forgeries and associated paperwork.

Alison and Jimmy had other matters on their minds. Where was the laird and more importantly, Campbell? Jimmy called Roland, 'Heard a little rumour that you might have had time to mooch about Castle Grevin. Have you found any clue as to where they might be going?'

Roland forced a laugh. 'I saw a load of papers in the study. Give me a little while. I'll call you back,' and he hung up.

CHAPTER
FORTY FOUR

Groves, Murray, Jimmy, and Alison were all hard at work with enquiries. Doreen was busy typing but still able to keep everyone in the office supplied with drinks. An occasional call came from Boniface keeping them all updated. The Scottish chief constable decided that the paintings should all be taken to the police HQ. He claimed it was for security, but in reality, he knew he could show the paintings off to the press more easily.

Roland made a call to Jimmy, 'I can't find much paperwork which is strange. It wouldn't surprise me if Metcalf and Campbell have got anything of note stashed away somewhere. A concealed wall safe or something similar. I saw an old empty envelope by the side of a bin which looked like it had missed when thrown away as rubbish addressed to Metcalf from the Northern Scottish Provincial Bank. Can you make some enquiries with them to see if he has an account? If he's got one, Campbell may well have one there to.'

Jimmy was struggling. His cheek was hurting more than previously. He was due to go to St Richard's Hospital for a check-up at the maxillofacial unit. He didn't want to miss it. 'I'll do my best. I'll call you if I get anything.'

He tapped the keys on his computer keyboard. The Bank's minimalistic opening web page was displayed. It only had four links that led to the details of its four branches. Nothing showing what facilities they offered. It was apparently only a small bank with all its branches around the Trossachs. Jimmy opened each link in turn and checked the address of the given branch. Then he returned to the one that was closest to Brig O' Turk.

He soon found the telephone number and dialled it. The manager wasn't willing to discuss clients and pointedly said so. When Jimmy asked who the police should contact, he quickly passed on the head office's unlisted phone number. He didn't want anything to do with the police and couldn't get Jimmy off the phone quick enough.

There was a head office in Stirling. Jimmy considered it. Strange. Feeble web site about its four branches but not a mention about its head office. Jimmy checked his watch. Time for a quick phone call. He called the number he'd been given.

A female voice with a strong lilting Scottish accent answered the phone on the second ring. 'Northern Scottish. How may I help you?' No mention that it was a bank.

Jimmy replied with a slight lisp, 'Hello. I was wondering, do you have a security department?'

'Who is calling please?'

'I am a police officer in Sussex,' and he suddenly realised the lady probably didn't know where that was. 'That's a county on the South Coast of England. I am engaged on a murder enquiry and was hoping you have a security department who may be able to help me.'

'I'll put you through to their extension. I can't promise an answer as they only work two days a week. I don't know if today is one of them.'

Truth be known, there was only the one security officer for the bank. Hamish MacKinnon, a retired police chief superintendent from Glasgow who had moved to the Trossachs National Park to enjoy his retirement. He had soon become bored playing golf every other day and jumped at the chance to work two days a week.

Jimmy heard some clicks on the phone and then heard a ringing tone. He rubbed his jaw. The phone continued to ring. After about a minute, Jimmy was about to hang up when the call was answered brusquely and abruptly. 'Yes?'

Jimmy identified himself and enquired, 'Would you be a security officer?

A man with as strong an accent as the original woman who answered the call, apologised for his abruptness. 'Sorry. I thought you were someone else. Perhaps I should tell you who I am, or more to the point, who I was.'

Jimmy heard the man shout to someone to close a door. 'My name is Hamish MacKinnon. I was a policeman in Glasgow before I retired. I am the only security officer that the bank employs. It makes a pleasant change to speak to a police officer as opposed to bank employees who think they are minor gods. Now, how can I help you?'

Jimmy briefly, very briefly, outlined the murders of Lynne and Hawthorne. Then he went on to explain that a man by the name of Campbell MacIntyre had been identified as the killer. Further, they had found Metcalf Buchanan, the self-proclaimed Laird of Brig O'Turk had a collection of stolen art works. Both lived at Castle Grevin. Now both had disappeared.

'We have just searched Castle Grevin and found a reference to Northern Scottish Provincial Bank. We believe they may have accounts with you. If at all possible, could you confirm either way and then I can arrange for Police Scotland to get a warrant to see their documentation.'

Hamish gave a little guffaw, 'No need for a warrant. Murder is murder. Specially that of a police officer. If we have anything on them, I'll forward it all by email. For your information, all our clients must have a minimum maintained account agreed by their branch manager. It's normally substantial. Very substantial. If you'd like to hang on, I'll fire up my computer.'

Jimmy could hear him tapping away on a keyboard. He checked his watch. He was going to be late for his appointment. Sod it. Lynne's murder took preference.

Hamish was soon speaking, 'We've got Metcalf Buchanan at Castle Grevin,' then a short pause. 'And Campbell MacIntyre. Same address. I'll send it all to you. There's a fair bit.'

Jimmy was in the process of thanking him for his assistance and was going to hang up when Hamish added slowly and thoughtfully, 'I appreciate you are more concerned with the murder of your colleague, and from what you have told me, the banking details of MacIntyre practically confirm his guilt. The reason I say this is, some time ago, I dealt with a man who I believed was a contract killer. He was a bus driver. A person who, like a butler, shouldn't be rich. His bank account was similar to this one. Large sporadic deposits always of five thousand pounds were put into his savings account. Each time, we believed it had been payment for a killing somewhere although we couldn't prove it. This account shows ten thousand pounds occasionally being deposited. Maybe it's something you might consider. Is he a hit man?'

Jimmy paused. Then cautiously replied, 'We'll look into

that. If need be, can we please call you again?'

The retired policeman laughed. 'Only on Mondays and Wednesdays. Other days, it's golf or futile meetings.'

Jimmy was appreciative. Whether what the bank held would assist the enquiry any further, Jimmy didn't know. He gave Hamish the office email details. Then thanking him in advance, terminated the call. He yelled to Damien, and they ran out to the car park. He needed a lift urgently. He'd check the email from Hamish later.

Doreen was the first to notice the email with several attached pages of Campbell's details which had landed in the office email's inbox. It was gold dust. His name and address adorned the top of each page. His actual bank account details with his account number were displayed. His current account held in excess of three hundred thousand pounds. Doreen whistled. 'Not bad for a butler.'

Then another email from Hamish. A couple more attached sheets showing details of Campbell's savings account. Another half a million. It showed sporadic deposits of ten thousand pounds. Hardly any withdrawals.

Doreen called to Murray. He looked at the emails and the attachments.

'How the hell does a butler accumulate all that money?'

There was a printout of a debit card's use with several sheets showing its rare use around the UK over the last six months. Mainly to just draw cash. The last transaction recorded being at Gatwick Airport for five hundred pounds and three hundred Euros. On the day before Lynne's murder. The evidence jumped out at them. Proof? Not exactly, just another nail in Campbell's coffin. If they could only find him!

Murray enquired mainly to himself, 'He must have used cash when he was in Tenerife.' He was wrong. Campbell's false credit card only had a few hundred pounds left on it. He was forced to use his real one to get a sizable wodge of cash. He hadn't liked it one bit!

Doreen was about to print everything off when another email arrived from Hamish. She sat still, glued to her monitor. Now it was all about Metcalf Buchanan. He spent freely from his current account that never dropped below a million. Murray pulled up a chair and sat next to her. He just said, 'Wow!'

Doreen asked, 'How much do you reckon he's got in savings before we look? I bet it's three million.'

Murray thought. Then advocated, 'I'll go for five million.'

Doreen opened the attachment. Murray saw it. He couldn't help himself, 'fucking hell.' Seven hundred and eighty five million. 'Where the hell has that lot come from?'

Doreen was dazed. She just couldn't imagine that sort of money.

* * *

Jimmy had got to the hospital a quarter of an hour after his appointed time. They were running slightly behind time and he was called into a consulting room within minutes of his arrival. Medical people began running their fingers over his face and discussing what they should do. They were holding X-rays of his cheek. None seemed to want to talk to him, just about him. Jimmy started panicking. They were talking about metal rods into his jaw.

'Would you open your mouth please,' came from a doctor.

Jimmy complied. 'I'm sorry perhaps you didn't realise I was talking to you. Can you please open your mouth?'

Jimmy stated indignantly, 'I did.'

Several of the medics tutted. One declared, 'It's worse than we thought.'

Jimmy was really starting to panic. He felt gloved fingers inside his mouth. He had thought he was well on the road to recovery. His speech had a slight lisp to it, but he'd assumed he was recovering. The pain killers he'd originally been prescribed were stopping nearly all the agony. Just the occasional twinge reminded him of his injury.

Then all the medics in the room seemed to stop talking. Several walked out. Only two left and a couple of attending nurses. Now was the moment of reckoning.

'Well. Your cheek bone is not healing as quickly as it should. There are two alternatives. We can put some titanium rods in, but they will leave a couple of nasty scars when they are removed, or you will have to stop talking and keep your mouth completely shut for a couple of weeks.' Then added, apologetically, 'Other than for fork mashed food, and drinks via a straw. Our nurses will fill you in as to what that means.'

Jimmy wasn't going to have scars on his face. He resigned himself to sitting at home with his mouth shut. Daytime TV was anathema. He couldn't bring himself to watch it. He'd have to read or listen to music. What a choice. He had entered the consulting room full of optimism and now it had all been dashed. He slumped dejectedly an inch or so down in his chair.

The medic didn't seem to notice and carried on regardless, 'Then you will have to do some oral exercises. Your nose evidently hasn't suffered any real, significant damage. What would you like to do?'

Jimmy didn't hesitate, he knew what he'd have to do, 'I'll keep my mouth shut.'

'That's the way I'd go if I was in your place.' He looked at one of the nurses, 'Amber, can you fill him in with what it will all entail?'

The nurse agreed and all the others left the room. Jimmy looked at Amber. She smiled at him. A really pleasant smile. Jimmy was smitten. He didn't understand his own emotions. She wasn't the prettiest woman he'd known by a long way. But he liked her immediately. Her blonde hair was tied in a pony tail and her makeup was minimal. Twinkling green eyes were her second best feature. He tried to snap out of it. He explained he had to contact his office and then he'd shut up for however long was needed.

She sat down directly in front of him and pulled a nail file from one of her pockets. Crossing her legs she started to file a nail. Jimmy saw her legs, which she knew were her best feature. Half way through the call to the office she exaggerated the nail file as though asking silently if he wanted his nails filed. He nodded and held out his left hand. She gently took it and started to file his nails. She knew what she was doing. She'd taken an instant liking to Jimmy. He didn't understand but his immediate thought was, the coming days might not be so bad after all.

* * *

Those in the office looked at the printouts. Groves was soon on the phone. First to the chief constable, then to DS

262

Boniface. He in turn updated the team at Castle Grevin. Then Groves made a call to John.

'We've got the Turner and four more paintings from a secret room at Castle Grevin. The expert has confirmed that they are the originals.' Then he gave John a quick rundown on what Hamish had produced about both Campbell and Metcalf. 'It appears they have fled the country. They've gone in a vintage Rolls with a personalised number. Crossed the channel from Dover and just disappeared. No sightings on the French autoroutes or their ANPR system which is weird.'

John cogitated and then submitted prudently, 'That is curious. Could you email me the details from the bank?'

'I'll get Doreen to do that. A rifle was in the room. If that comes back as the one used on Hawthorne, that'll be another nail in Campbell's coffin. We have enough to get warrants for the arrest of both. Trouble is, we haven't a clue where they are. Must go. Work to do. Speak soon,' and the line went dead.

John hobbled into the kitchen and poured himself a large glass of wine. Returning to the lounge, he sat in his favourite chair and lifted his foot delicately onto a pouffe. He sat with his eyes closed. Within minutes, Doreen had forwarded copies of Hamish's emails. Two mouthfuls of wine later, a simple idea came to him.

'Sorry to call you back so soon. I have a question. The Scotsman has given you details of both their true debit and credit cards. If they use them in Europe, the fact would be recorded at the Northern Provincial Bank. Most likely within an hour at the most. Has he been asked to let you know of any usage? As to the vehicle, the number plate has probably been changed. I'll look into that.'

Groves agreed. 'I'll sort that out with Hamish. Cheers Oscar,' and the line disconnected.

John sat with his phone held between his shoulder and head. He scanned the emails on his computer as he spoke, 'Hi Rocky. You busy?'

Rocky laughed, 'What are you after?'

John told him.

'I'll call you when I know.' The line dropped. John was reminded that people no longer bothered with pleasantries when talking to him on the phone.

CHAPTER
FORTY FIVE

R ocky and Zena were confident that they could locate the Rolls. They quickly hacked into the CCTV of the terminals at the Port of Calais and found the footage of the vehicle as it left the ferry. They weren't directly concerned about the occupants, just the vehicle. Both studied the video until it was clear in their minds.

Then they turned their attention to the French autoroute South: the logical route for any southbound vehicles which weren't interested in dawdling. Rocky checked the time stamp for when the vehicle left the ship. He estimated at least half an hour to reach the first set of toll booths.

Zena was soon looking at the toll booth's CCTV. It was playing at three times normal speed. The two sat back and watched the monitor. They soon saw what they wanted. An old style silver Rolls Royce was approaching the toll booths. Then the next camera's view showed the vehicle leaving the toll booths to continue south. She rewound the images and played them at normal speed.

Prominently displayed, in addition to the normal headlights on the front of the vehicle, were two small fog lights and a single large spot lamp as well as a silver stag as the radiator mascot. The side view was nothing unusual. But the rear of the vehicle confirmed it. A plate bearing an old RAC touring symbol was attached somehow to the back bumper. They had the vehicle. It was so easy. They noted the index number. It was no longer on Scottish index plates, but Swiss ones.

Rocky moved to a large computer. He tapped away at the keyboard. He checked where all the tolls were and soon located the Rolls heading away from the South of France and towards Geneva. There were few cameras similar to ANPR, but the new Swiss number plate gave him the route. All the way through France and into Switzerland. Rocky was about to close it and move onto the Swiss system, where he noticed a link. It appeared that the French and Swiss authorities had some form of bilateral agreement.

The system showed very few images of the Rolls as it progressed up into the mountains along the main road towards Gstaad. Then at the pretty little town of Ormont-Dessus, the road split. The only camera in the town was old and covered the junction and it was linked into the Swiss system. Rocky saw a clear image of the Rolls as it waited patiently for the lights to change as it left the town heading even higher into the mountains. He was surprised to see another image of it returning nearly thirty minutes later. Then nothing else for that day. No other sightings. Now they knew roughly the area where the vehicle was. More importantly, where Campbell and the laird were.

John grabbed for his phone and knocked it off the side table. He lifted his leg off the pouffe and looked on the floor for his still ringing phone. He kept calling, 'hold on,' as though the caller could somehow hear him. Finally, he picked it up and answered it.

Rocky told him what they had discovered. Now John knew they were getting closer to where the two criminals were. He knew that the Swiss were reluctant to extradite anyone but wasn't unduly concerned. He was thinking way outside the box. Nothing remotely legal. Not that he would act unlawfully. The people he might tell would be prepared to though!

When Rocky had hung up, John searched Google maps and located Ormont-Dessus. It was quite high in the Swiss Alps. He needed a bigger map. How would anyone get there unseen, search the area for the Rolls and then look for the laird and Campbell? If anything went wrong, how would they get away. John hobbled to a drawer and pulled out a selection of old maps and found one for the area. A cloth map. So old. Not even paper.

* * *

The woman was in Costa's in Littlehampton. She'd learnt quite quickly that officers from the murder team often stopped for a swift coffee before heading off to conduct their enquiries. Now she was considering her options. Gwendoline and her hired killer were dead. A result. The press had first reported the police recovering all her paintings and then had a field day with the laird's stolen paintings. She knew where both Cambell and Metcalf were. Both far from the reach of the British police. She'd deal with them later. By fluke the bent curator from Parkland had died in a traffic accident. It looked like a complete security failure. The police had obviously linked it all up somehow. From what she'd learnt from overheard conversations, probably by phone records. They had all known they were expected to use burner phones.

Serves them right!

Now she needed to know where Jake's phone was and what was on it? Anything that could tie the controller in or the transport system? She should have put a pillow over his face when she was in his hospital room. Hindsight. It probably won't matter in the long run. He's never going to recover.

Should she neutralise Braithwaites? It had taken the organisation a long time to set up and had cost a lot of money. Ok, they'd made over three hundred and thirty million as a result. They'd be well pissed off but still free and not adorning cell walls with photos of famous paintings. The controller would not be happy. If the police had Jake's phone, they may already know about the security firm. The only other weak link was the controller himself.

She cogitated. He isn't stupid. She'd already told him she couldn't find Jake's phone. He'd quickly realise she would consider him a weak link. Would he take some sort of action against her as a precautionary measure?

Bloody families. You can't trust any of them!

* * *

Doreen was due at her book club at 7pm. She would amble home, grab a sandwich and then catch the bus. Her mum, who used to nag her and expect her home at exactly the same time each night, had died peacefully in her sleep five months earlier. Now Doreen was a free agent. She could get home whenever she wanted and do whatever she wanted.

She left the office and strolled to Littlehampton bus

station. Her bus was already at its stand. As she boarded, she was barged gently from behind. Showing her season ticket to the driver she looked around. No one there. She walked halfway down the aisle before sitting down. Putting her large shoulder bag on her lap, she looked in to make sure she'd remembered to take her book from her desk.

There was a mobile phone in her bag. It wasn't hers. There was a crumpled envelope that wasn't hers either. She looked at the few people seated on the lower deck of the bus. None were paying her any attention. She picked up the unsealed envelope and opened it.

A short, typed sentence. 'Give this phone to the man with the broken leg.'

Doreen looked around again at the half dozen or so passengers. None seemed interested in what she was doing. One was reading a local paper. As Doreen looked back inside her bag, the woman casually watched her from over the top of the paper. She smiled. Doreen was shrewd. She didn't touch the phone and dropped both the letter and envelope back into her bag. Then she took her own mobile phone out of her handbag and called John.

'Hi. Didn't expect any call from you today.'

'I'd like to speak to Black John please. Is he there?'

John knew. Serious problem if Doreen called him that.

'Are you in trouble? Yes or no.'

Doreen paused, 'Not sure.'

'Where are you? Do you want me to call the police?'

'No.'

'Do I need to see you?'

Indefatigably, Doreen replied, 'Definitely.'

'Is someone listening?'

'Not sure.'

'You anywhere near Bognor?'

'Will be shortly.'

'Walk through the Arcade and go into the Regis Centre.'

'Yes'

'Carol will collect you from there.'

Doreen hung up as John called to Carol.

CHAPTER
FORTY SIX

C arol was speeding along the main road between Chichester and Bognor. John kept telling her, 'Go faster.' She was getting ratty. She dropped him off in the High Street and then parked at the back of the old Bognor Fire Station. Slowly she looked about. Walking around the edge of the car park she went into the Regis Centre. No sign of Doreen. She got a cup of coffee from a machine and sat down. No one had followed her in.

John sat outside Bonito lounge at the corner with London Road. A long green canvas banner attached to rods concreted into the pavement about three feet high marked the café's boundary with the footpath. It also hid his pot-leg and most of his torso from the gaze of any passerby. He had a clear view across the road to the entrance of the Arcade and along both London Road and the High Street.

Within minutes, he saw Doreen walk calmly into the entrance to the Arcade. He waited. John's gaze drifted casually around the area. No one had apparently followed her. He waited five more minutes. Then a woman he recognised strolled nonchalantly along the pedestrianised High Street and sat on one of the stone seats facing the Arcade. So he had been right. The woman who had been in the café in Arundel and later, Luckes. Slowly, he sank a little lower in his seat. He ordered a latte and watched her dispassionately.

His mobile vibrated on the tabletop and he answered it.

Carol was using her own phone. 'Got Doreen.'

'Take her to the car and wherever she needs to go.'

'Ok.'

Then as an amusing afterthought, he added, 'First. Get her to ring whatever number is programmed on the phone and see if it's picked up. If it is, get Doreen to say, "You'll get a cold bum sitting on that concrete seat. Would you like to join Mr Whiles outside Bonito Lounge." I've got eyes on the person I think gave it to her. I want to see what she does.'

'Ok,' and Carol hung up.

Minutes passed. The woman looked about indifferently and at one time seemed to stare directly in John's direction. Then she pulled out a mobile phone and put it to her ear. Within seconds she burst out laughing and stared straight at John.

Casually, she got up, put the phone back into her bag and strolled along the High Street and into the outside seating area of Bonito Lounge. John pulled a seat out for her from under the table. She laughed, 'I thought I recognised you. Clever of you to hide your broken leg behind this hoarding.'

'I thought it would be a lot easier talking face to face rather than on a phone. If you don't know, my name is John Whiles. Would you care to tell me yours?'

'Please call me Catherine.'

'From your accent, which you are desperately trying to hide, I'd have thought you could have come up with a name a bit more Italian.'

'Well, you are surprising. Not many people would spot that. I'll stick to Catherine if you don't mind.'

'In that case, how can I help you Catherine?'

'Maybe, I can help you. I have been following the police

investigation into the tragic murder of Brendan Slack as closely as possible. I am aware of the untimely deaths of both Gwendoline Hawthorne and her contract killer, Mike Calder. Also of the genuine works of art she kept in a secret room.' She paused for more effect before continuing, 'I am acutely aware of the vicious, and murderous Scottish killer, Campbell MacIntyre. And his sadistic employer, Metcalf Buchanan, the apparent Laird of Brig O'Turk and his hidden art collection. I understand both have left the country to evade capture.' She paused as the waiter took her order. 'But then you know all this already.'

John waited until the waiter was well out of earshot and expressed, 'I'm sure there won't be a problem. Metcalf Buchanan will probably return voluntarily to the UK and, well, we'll see what MacIntyre does.'

She looked him straight in the eye, paused and then smiled, 'I believe you may actually know where they are. Do the police?'

'Surely you can't expect me to tell you.'

'No,' and she paused again. 'Perhaps not.'

'Catherine. I don't want to dampen your enthusiasm for following a murder enquiry, but there is something troubling you. A lot has happened since Mr Slack was killed. I feel that you seem to know more about the art side of things. A thought did occur to me when I believed you to be of Italian heritage. Perhaps you are a talented artist yourself?'

Catherine burst out laughing but stopped abruptly. With a serious expression she said, 'That's an inspired guess. There is something that is troubling me. I feel that I may become a victim myself. I thought I'd approach you as you seem to know a lot of the investigating officers. I can protect myself but no one is invincible. I was considering giving you a leg up with how they came by their stolen art. Somehow, I think you probably know a lot more than the police.'

John smiled at her condescendingly. 'To be honest Catherine, I think the police may know a lot more than you think. If you are, shall we say, in any way involved, it may only be a matter of time before they come looking for you.'

Catherine sat warming her hands on the coffee cup. Neither spoke for a while. They each held their counsel. It was like a game of chess. Who was going to make the next move. John wasn't going to tell her anything about the investigation. Nor what he was planning. Catherine was debating the pros and cons of naming the controller. Could she trust John? From what she'd gleaned, she believed he was probably working to a different agenda than the murder team.

She stood up. 'Keep that phone I left you. I may call. I'll think about it. I can't afford anyone knowing that any information emanates from me.'

'That's all I could ask.'

Smiling at him, she added, 'I will say that Campbell is a very dangerous individual. Keep well clear of him.'

John laughed, 'I'd hide behind a mountain if he came near me.'

Looking squarely at him, she now knew. He'd as good as confirmed it. He knew. She strode off to find a taxi, leaving him to pay the bill for her coffee.

John summoned the waiter and ordered another coffee. He wasn't in a hurry. He looked about. Was she going to try and follow him? He wasn't sure. He phoned Carol. He'd walk, or more to the point, hobble through the Arcade and she could pick him up at the other end. No problem. Back to Chichester and a long meal in Blanc's. If anyone was watching, it would be a boring night. Simon would easily spot them.

Catherine was back in Littlehampton collecting her car, then she would have a slow drive back to Wimbledon. Would anyone be waiting for her? She checked her small Bond Stinger RS22 derringer. It stood no chance against a modern automatic, but it could surprise an assassin and kill.

The questions kept creeping back into her thoughts. Could she trust John Whiles? Would the controller find out? If he did, she'd definitely end up dead. At the moment she had a chance. What to do? Bloody families!

CHAPTER
FORTY SEVEN

John considered updating Groves but something kept stopping him. Catherine had to be a 'Micky Mouse' name. Why had she approached him? She'd seen him with both Doreen and Groves. He knew that. Her comment though implied she'd seen him with members of the murder team. More than just the two. Where? If she was telling the truth, he'd not seen her. Therefore, she wasn't to be underestimated. She had claimed she knew where Campbell and Metcalf were. If so, how? His little throw-away remark of hiding behind a mountain seemed to resonate with her. Yes. She knew where they were. How?

He was feeling a little bit tipsy after the meal in Blanc's and was in his cosy chair with his leg on the pouffe. Carol handed him a coffee. 'When are you due to have that cast taken off? It's occurred to me that it should be off by now.'

John was taken aback. He thought she was talking nonsense. 'What! The doctor who put it on said six weeks. He said I could have it taken off in St Richard's. It would be confirmed by email.'

'When did you last check your email?'

'I was going to do it now,' and he picked up his mobile. 'Oh!'

'Oh what?'

'It could have been off last week as long as the bone had healed. It apparently would have to be checked by X-ray. Oh.'

'Stop saying, oh.'

'An appointment had been made for me last Tuesday.'

Carol was fuming. 'This sums up why the NHS is having so many problems. People like you ignoring appointments. I'll sort a day out tomorrow and you will attend.'

John didn't want an argument. 'Right oh'

'Say oh one more time and you might not live long enough to have that cast off.'

* * *

Midnight, and the phone Catherine had given him burst into life. A short text. 'It wasn't me.' John slept on. Carol cursed the noise and turned over.

* * *

The morning's meeting was a short affair. Groves assembled and dispatched a team of four detectives and two forensic search officers. Alison was the lead officer. They were joined by four uniform officers in two personnel vehicle carriers. Enough spare room for three prisoners and anything they might find and seize. They were to meet a couple of detectives from the Met's Arts and Antiques Squad at Braithwaites. The interviewers were ready.

When they arrived, the large, electric shuttered door to the industrial garage was at its highest. The black unmarked security vehicle was parked in full view. No people were anywhere to be seen. Alison sent a couple of officers to find the back entrance before she led her troops in. She walked in at the front of them.

Where were the three people who should have been there? They checked the building. A set of stairs in one corner led to a small, glass fronted, first floor office. Alison went upstairs and into it. There was a desk against one of the walls and all the six drawers had been pulled unceremoniously open and were hanging down. They were all empty except for the remote control for the TV that was fixed to another wall. An old-fashioned answering machine was on top of the desk. It should have contained a small cassette tape that recorded the messages, but the compartment holder was sticking up and the tape was missing. There was no sign of any telephone. A kettle was lying on the floor having been knocked over. It was obvious to Alison the place had been well searched.

In the middle of the room was a metal wastepaper bin and inside it were the burnt remnants of a lot of papers. An officer with her bent down and pulled a small piece of paper out which wasn't quite destroyed. They could just make out that it was a heading. NSL Delivery Service. Alison knew the correct title should be NSL and nothing else. It wasn't right.

A sudden yell from downstairs caused them to run from the office. Alison called out, 'Who shouted?'

An officer was sitting on the garage floor at the back of the security vehicle with the rear door open in front of him. He was too shocked to speak. Alison and other officers ran to him and saw what he'd seen. Two men, lying together in the rear of the vehicle. It was blatantly obvious to everyone there that they were dead. Flies were already circulating around the bodies and landing on the men's faces and their softer areas. Blobs of blood were visible on the men's clothing. Some flies were crawling from under their clothes. It looked to Alison like there were bullet entry wounds. A couple of officers threw up at the stench. Others turned pale.

Alison swore. She felt slightly nauseous as the stench hit her. An urgent call to Groves from outside in the fresh air. Where was the third man? Was he the killer? Why was the shutter up? It invited the inquisitive.

Groves couldn't believe it. Two more corpses. He had no choice. He was going to have to leave it up to Alison to deal with for the time being. He needed to speak to the chief. It wasn't a long conversation. There were no more staff to help. He had to hand the enquiry over to a Surrey murder team. At least a lot would be done for them by the forensic officers.

Midday, he called John. A swift summary of what had happened. John listened. He knew they were covering their tracks, whoever they were. They'd worked out the police were closing in. They couldn't be sure that Braithwaites was safe. Better safe than sorry. Only two corpses.

John offered his thoughts. 'I bet the man missing is Leonardo Russo. I'm willing to place money on it that he's their killer and he has already legged it back to Italy.'

Groves had come to the same conclusion. 'I'm with you. Not much that can be done about it if that's the case. Yet another bloody extradition request and we'll probably get nowhere.'

When they'd hung up, Carol queried, 'What was that text last night?'

John didn't understand. He checked his phone. No text. 'What text?'

'That one in the middle of the night?'

Then it dawned on him. He went into the bedroom and

found the phone Catherine had got to him. In the readout on the screen, an icon showed an unread text. When he opened it, he was shocked. She knew at midnight about Braithwaites. Long before the police. How? She had to have been there. Why had she gone there? The clue was in the text.

CHAPTER
FORTY EIGHT

The chief strode into the office. He made a beeline for Groves. He wasn't angry. Just apparently getting fed up with the amount of murders that Brendan's death had sparked. 'What the hell is all this about? Brendan Slack is viciously murdered in Arundel Castle then all hell seems to break loose. I've been to see my counterpart in Surrey. One of their murder teams is going to take this part of the case on and will liaise with you.'

Groves could only tell him what he already knew. Then he put forward his idea. 'There were three people who worked at Braithwaites. The main person, Leonardo Russo is missing. It looks like he's the killer at the moment and may have legged it back home to his native Italy.'

Doreen handed a mug of tea to the chief. He looked at it in semi disgust. 'Doreen. Just because you are busy, there is no reason to lower standards. Where's the china cup?' He still held onto the mug and sat down.

Groves resumed, 'We have discovered one thing during the initial search and that was a charred piece of paper bearing the heading NSL Delivery Services. It confused us at first because the firm the museums use is just known as NSL. One of the team sussed it. When the art is placed into the Braithwaites security vehicle, besides a photo confirming it, the curator gets a signature from the crew of the vehicle. Then the file is completed and the final invoice is raised.'

The chief was enthralled. 'I'm with you so far.'

Groves kept going, 'The person who was due to get the original painting is billed by the museum. Then the museum pay the invoice provided by NSL Delivery Services. If there was no invoice the museum would likely smell a rat. They can't pay NSL, because that would also open a can of worms.'

The chief drank from the mug as he thought. 'I'm still with you,' and paused, 'Just.'

'It looks like Jake used to take the invoices to the museum's finance department. He probably arranged that if it was a genuine invoice, the finance administrator would pay NSL. If it was one of Braithwaites' invoices, they would pay NSL Delivery Services. Apparently they were using the same bank as NSL. So it appears that the finance department didn't notice the different bank account numbers.'

The chief had got it, 'I suppose that because it also had NSL on the invoice, they paid it straight away. Ironic when you think about it. The crooks get an original painting and are also paid delivery costs by the museum when they've nicked it. Clever.'

Alison walked back into the office. She was still looking a little pale. She practically collapsed onto a chair. Doreen passed her a mug of tea. She didn't care what it was in. She said as if in passing to Groves, 'The forensic people and the coroner think they have been dead a fair time. They were covered in flies and maggots. The stench was atrocious. They'd been confined in the back of the security van and the heat had built up in it. When the door was opened, it was horrendous.'

Groves enquired, 'Any idea who was missing?'

'The alleged owner, Russo. At a rough guess, he probably killed them to stop them talking. Destroyed all the paperwork

282

and took all the phone gear. If they had a computer, there was no sign of one. No CCTV either. The Surrey team have started already and are going to search all their houses. I bet they'll not find anything. It definitely looks like damage limitation on Russo's part.'

The chief looked aggrieved. Those in the office listened intently to him. 'Have we come to the end of the line? It certainly looks like it. Unless Walter can find out anything more then I fear we are snookered. At least you've solved Brendan Slack's murder. I can't say I'm too concerned about the death of his killer. You also know Hawthorne's and Lynne's murderer. The artwork you've recovered is worth astronomical amounts. Arrest warrants for MacIntyre and Metcalf Buchanan are good as completed. Overall Mr Groves, your team has excelled.'

Groves didn't agree. He wanted more. A lot more. Jake was definitely the inside man. Trouble was he was unlikely ever to recover and would never face a court. Braithwaites wasn't going to take them any further. Leonardo Russo had probably fled the country and he was now Surrey murder squad's problem. Groves wanted the broker and all the others who had benefited. But he saw the problem. How was he to find them? His remaining hope was Walter finding something on Jake's phone.

He knew the chief would want to close down the enquiry. Likely sooner rather than later. Groves needed more time. 'Guv'nor. There are a few things that need to be cleared up. Silly trivial things but they may take a little while. Can you give us another week?'

The chief stared at him. He couldn't understand why

Groves was asking. What had he got? Was it a hope Walter would turn something up? He thought about it. There were no other enquiries pending for the team. He could afford the time. 'All right Mr Groves. Just one week unless anything becomes pressing elsewhere. One proviso. No overtime unless authorised by me. Agreed?'

' Thank you sir.'

The chief left the office. He could see that Groves didn't want him there. He was heading to Arundel Castle. It was time the duke knew absolutely everything.

Groves called Alison and Murray into his office. 'I want a quick scrum down with Oscar. I'll call him. Where shall we meet?'

Alison couldn't resist a jibe, 'Carluccio's if I'm paying or Blanc's if he's paying.' Groves and Murray laughed.

An hour later, the three strode into Carluccio's and met John. Alison told him she preferred the cakes there. Whether or not he agreed was doubtful.

Groves updated John. 'I'm relying a lot on Walter to give us a leg up to finding the broker. I'm not too optimistic. Now you know where we are, have you any ideas?'

John thought for several minutes. He bit into his slice of cake. Creamy and rather nice. Shame the coffee was a bit rough. Should he mention Catherine? He considered her text. Was she going to sanitise Braithwaites but found the carnage? Possibly. He'd hold back. He needed to speak to her. He considered the burnt piece of paper. A thought slowly came to him. He had an idea.

Wiping the cream from his top lip, he offered, 'Nice cake.' He drank the rest of his coffee and grimaced.

'Here's an idea that I'm sure you may have thought of,' and smiled. 'I am intrigued by the NSL corundrum. Correct me if I'm wrong. Jake used to take the invoices to the finance department. That has been confirmed?'

Murray quizzically confirmed that it had been, 'Yes?'

'Good. The invoice would have to show the details of the painting and who it went to, so it could all be married up. The finance department then could be the key. They obviously must keep records. And I would assume they have them computerised although it wouldn't really matter. What if their records were searched, and each time NSL Delivery Service were paid instead of NSL, you'd know which paintings were stolen.'

Murray considered it. Jake had been employed for years. He knew just the person to search the records. 'Nathan is diligent, he wouldn't miss anything.'

Groves saw John's logic. 'That'll probably net us a fair few forgeries but not the genuine articles. I suppose it's a start.'

John hadn't finished. 'Every time a picture was sought, you need to check Jake's phone records from the first date it was requested until the final invoice was settled. We must assume that Jake would contact the broker to see if any of the people collecting this art wanted it. He would do this for every painting. Then the broker would confirm either way. The broker's phone number should then be able to be identified as each time it will be recorded as an outgoing call and then later as an incoming call. This would happen for every painting.'

The three officers looked at him in bewilderment. They slowly understood what he was saying.

Alison was the first to respond. 'Jesus John. Could you make it any more complicated? I think I understand. The same number should be called by Jake each time. Once we have that number, we have the broker.'

Murray saw a problem. 'What if Jake calls his Mum each time?'

Groves was ahead of him. 'Unlikely that he would call her each time someone sought to borrow a painting. I like it Oscar. I like it a lot. We could check Jake's home phone and mobile. If needed we could even check his office phone. Yep. I like it a lot.'

Alison happily paid the bill.

CHAPTER
FORTY NINE

G rove called an urgent office meeting. The majority of officers attended. He looked around the room. He explained what he wanted to do. Some officers saw the logic straight away. Others took a little longer as their colleagues explained it to them. He picked his officers carefully. He wanted Walter to be on standby from 8am the following day.

A car with a driver was to take two detectives to the British Museum and another car and driver was to convey two more to the National Gallery. They knew what was expected of them. The curator of each museum would be present to take them to the relevant finance departments.

Groves was amazed how many works of art were borrowed from the museums. He needed a result urgently. A day would be a long time out of his week's reprieve. Murray and Alison were to be points of contact in the office and Walter was arranging for Jake's phone records going back to when he took up his post. There were several hundred pages of them.

6am, the office was packed. Everyone knew what their respective roles were. The cars left for London and the museums. Officers fired up all the computers. They were ready.

At the museums, the officers were taken to the respective finance departments. Everything was computerised. It would speed up the searches. Within a few hours, they knew of the first hundred borrowed pictures. They identified all the relevant information. Dates first sought and when invoices were paid and to whom. Then what the painting was and where it should be. As one kept searching, the other updated a spreadsheet on their laptop. Whenever there was a pause, the spreadsheet was emailed to the office. Slowly, stolen art was discovered.

As the initial first days were categorised, Walter handed copies of Jake's mobile phone records to the officer deputed to search them. They had been designated a computer with another spreadsheet where the phone numbers were to be recorded. As one officer called out the number another recorded it.

The batches of information kept arriving by email. Soon, everyone in the office was busy. The first officers were given more to search as soon as they completed their previous consignment. It was well-nigh working like clockwork. As Groves and Murray had hoped.

Two civilian analysts kept linking all the spreadsheets. They could search all of them together quickly on a computer. Slowly the same number kept cropping up within a couple of days of each picture being requested.

One of the analysts called out to Groves. 'Guv'nor. We've searched the first two hundred of his outgoing mobile telephone calls and have got the same number each time.' Officers looked up from what they were doing. Some smiled, others laughed. They were getting there.

Groves called to Walter, 'Don't bother yet with any incoming calls. Let's concentrate on Jake's outgoing ones. Can you identify who that number belongs to?'

Walter was happy. 'I'm on it.'

As the day wore on, more and more details were recovered by the officers at the museums. Each time they forwarded their spreadsheets, they were rapidly disseminated to small, specialist groups in the Littlehampton office. At 3 o'clock Groves called a halt. Everyone stopped what they were doing. 'I'm satisfied we know the number of the broker. We'll call it a day. Get the guys back from London. Please just finish the job you're on now and then go home. Be back here tomorrow at 7am.

Groves went to his office and updated John. 'I think we've got the phone number of the broker. To be honest Oscar, I didn't think it would work out as planned. I would have expected Jake to have used a burner phone. I think they felt so secure they couldn't be bothered.'

'Remember, Gwendoline and Metcalf didn't seem to bother either. Perhaps they have spoken to the broker on their phones. Something you could check?'

'A good thought Oscar. I'll sort that tomorrow. Speak to you soon,' and he hung up.

Alison, Murray and Groves waited for the officers to get back from the museums. They discussed the following day and what was to be done. Walter had provided the details of the phone number. Alison remarked, 'Worth sticking a surveillance team on the address?'

Groves looked at Murray who had cocked his head to one side as he thought. He didn't take long. 'Considering what happened at Braithwaites, it's a good idea. Won't the chief have to authorise it?'

Groves agreed. 'Good idea. I'll update the chief and see what he has to say.' He went into his office.

The officers from the museums walked into the office. One asked, 'How did it all go today?'

Murray and Alison both knew the day's tally. Murray

made a slight nod and said to Alison, 'Down to you guv'nor.'

Without recourse to any notes she was able to tell them. 'Thanks to everyone and your good selves, we probably know of at least forty-five forgeries and where they are hanging. Trouble is, at the present time we don't know who has the originals. We have identified the person we believe to be the broker. It's a start.'

Groves returned to the main office and saw the officers. 'Thanks for your work today. We've had a great result.' He smiled as he looked at Alison, 'We have a team.'

The chief had laughed down the phone for nearly a minute. 'Is this one of those silly trivial little things that need clearing up? All right Mr Groves. Crack on and see what else you can discover. You've got your overtime back but don't go overboard.'

John had his leg on a pouffe when Carol took him a glass of wine. 'Why have you got your foot up? The cast is coming off tomorrow. There's nothing wrong with your leg. You'll get no sympathy from me.'

John feigned hurt. 'You never know. The X-ray may say otherwise.'

Carol walked back to the kitchen in a huff.

John picked up the phone from Catherine. He held it for nearly thirty minutes as he thought about calling her.

* * *

Catherine was thinking about calling him. What could she tell him? She knew that the controller must have authorised the sanitisation of Braithwaites. Telling her originally that she could utilise all facilities and then going over her head and saying nothing. It had obviously been done some days previously for the bodies to be in that condition. It had to have been little Leo. He was probably now home in Italy.

She thought long and hard about the different options. If the controller had wanted Braithwaites sanitised, she could have done it. Why didn't he ask me? Because he didn't want his darling little boy killed! He knew I'd kill all three - brother or not. Or, he doesn't trust me. He always preferred him over me. Would he have me killed? The bastard probably would. It might end up with one of us dead.

If he was the survivor, he was still the weak link. The police might trace him. Then use him as a stepping stone to carry on down the line of the organisation. That would never be allowed to happen. They'd deal with him. My death wouldn't be a problem for them.

Bloody families! Then a serious thought occurred to her. I need to carry a proper gun.

CHAPTER
FIFTY

By 7 o'clock in the morning, the surveillance teams had swapped over. The night duty team leader told Groves there had been lights on in the house during the previous evening and they'd seen movement behind curtains. They couldn't say if it was a male or a female. No one had entered or left the premises. Alison had already got a search warrant from a magistrate earlier in the morning.

Now the office was buzzing. The chief walked in. Chairs scraped across the floor. People stood up. He didn't seem to notice. Murray waved the officers to sit down again. 'What's happening today Mr Groves?'

Groves explained, 'I'm just sending the teams off to arrest the broker and search his premises in Wimbledon. They are to go in as soon as they arrive and arrest everyone in the house.'

The chief said, 'Right. After the killings at Braithwaites, no one is to take any chances. I've spoken to the Met and they will provide a firearms unit. Make sure you are behind them.' A lot of the officers saw his reasoning.

Groves looked at Greenthorne, 'Ok. Get going.' Six detectives walked hastily out to their vehicles. It was a very fast run from Littlehampton up to the plush suburb of Wimbledon. They were followed by a slower couple of vans. The two forensic officers in one and a photographer in the other.

The firearms officers were waiting for the detectives. They had already been briefed by Vince, the surveillance team leader. As soon as the officers from Littlehampton arrived, the firearms officers battered down the front door. There was the usual loud shouting from the first firearms officers through the door.

Then a dog tore along the hall and launched itself at the first officer's throat. It looked to the officer like the Hound of the Baskervilles. A hound from hell. It was actually a huge Bullmastiff. It knocked him off his feet. Its teeth were colossal. He could only just hold its head to prevent it getting its jaws around his neck. He yelled to his colleagues for help. The dog was gradually overpowering him.

Another officer struck the dog on the head with an extended metal baton. It didn't seem to deter the animal. It was starting to growl loudly and to slobber. The officer dropped his baton and drew his Glock sidearm. There was no alternative. He put the gun close to the side of the dog's head and pulled the trigger. The dog collapsed on top of the officer on the floor. Using all his remaining strength, he managed to push it off him then struggled back on to his feet.

There was a sudden, dull thud of something hitting the wall close to the head of the officer who'd shot the dog. He ducked down. Another slight crack of a silenced firearm. They were being shot at by someone from the other end of the hall. Three firearms officers drew weapons. One shouted down the hallway, 'Armed police. Lay down your weapon.' Two rapid cracks and one officer felt the impact of a bullet hitting his body armour right in the middle of his chest. He was lucky. It would only leave a bruise.

They couldn't see anyone. Then a hand appeared, holding a silenced handgun. It was fired in their general direction, not aimed, and then withdrawn from sight. They saw what they could do. All three holstered their firearms and drew their tasers. They waited. The hand appeared again with the gun and fired. The bullet hit the ceiling.

As the hand withdrew from sight, they rushed down the hall and at the end they saw an elderly man leaning on a wall for support. The first officer grabbed the silenced handgun and wrenched it from his grasp. He was led out of the house and handed to a Littlehampton detective. Then the search of the house began in earnest.

* * *

By 9am, John's cast had gone. He tentatively got off the trolley and took a few steps. The doctor looked at her watch. She'd done Carol a favour and slipped John into the day's list. John wobbled as he walked. Carol couldn't take it.

'For goodness sake John. There's nothing wrong with you. Stop pretending. Let's go because you are holding Dr Zabreschi up. She's got a busy morning.'

John wasn't sure and used his crutch. He felt better. Safe. By the time they had a coffee in the hospital café, John got off his chair and walked to the toilet. He forgot his crutch. When he walked back into the café, Carol glared at him and exclaimed rather too loudly for his liking, 'Malingerer!'

* * *

Catherine was looking out of her bedroom window. She'd seen the officers battering down her father's front door several houses down on the opposite side of the road. He would fight. He had no hope of winning, but he'd fight. With a bit of luck the police would kill him. When she watched him being led out of the house she started to worry. Would he tell them about her? What could he say? He asked me to monitor the police investigation of the murder of Brendan Slack. I've actually done nothing wrong. I might have been about to but I haven't done anything.

Then again, I did dress as a nurse and search Jake's gear. And I did put a disguise on and search his desk in the British Museum. He knows about that. Would the police be able to prove it though? Probably. They'd find me on CCTV. They'd charge me with something and I might get locked up. He knows I set Calder up. That could be a problem.

He's the controller. He's the one who organises which paintings are taken and by whom. There will be a lot of very frightened people. He'd try anything for a deal to keep out of prison. Would he name them? That would never be allowed to happen. The organisation would silence him. Then they might see me as a weak link. They'd have no compunction about killing me. Time for me to disappear.

Bloody families!

CHAPTER
FIFTY ONE

John listened to the update from Groves closely. He'd never heard the name before. Giuseppe Russo. A seventy-four year old Italian. No previous convictions in the UK. No one else in the house. What did he hope to achieve by shooting at armed police? He couldn't win. Questions were forming in John's mind. They'd have to wait. He had an appointment.

Carol was at work. John looked at the paintings on his dining room wall. One was an original that he was particularly fond of. An early picture by Jack Vettriano. He'd got it at a bargain price before Vettriano's pictures became unaffordable to everyone except millionaires. He could understand why someone could become fixated by a picture they were particularly taken with. But to steal it was definitely not on.

He heard the toot of a car horn signalling the arrival of his taxi. Climbing in he told the driver, 'Arundel please.' Before he could settle, the car took off at speed. The driver asking him whereabouts he wanted in Arundel. 'Butler's Restaurant.' It had been his choice.

Catherine arrived shortly after and sat down opposite him. She looked around the restaurant approvingly. 'I like your taste in restaurants. I hope the food is as good.'

'I'm surprised you never tried the place when you were here.'

She laughed freely. 'I was more concerned with understanding what had happened at the castle. I doubt that any police come in here. I'd have learnt nothing other than how amenable the place is.'

John smiled back. 'You'd be pleasantly surprised.'

She looked at him curiously. 'You're more local than me. You would know.' The waiter approached them. They ordered and John enquired of her what wine she preferred. 'Nothing thanks, I'm driving.' Then as the waiter left, she said, 'Good to see you have got rid of that plaster cast.'

'Yes. It was rather a hindrance. Now. What was it you wanted to discuss?'

'Something has happened this morning that concerns me.'

John exclaimed, 'Oh. That. I thought it might. The arrest of Giuseppe Russo. Because you are both Italian I came to the conclusion when you called that you are probably related. Daughter perhaps?'

She glared at him for several seconds. Then her face lit up in a warm smile. 'You are good. No wonder the police knock on your door. I was surprised initially that, although I never followed you or gave you any cause to remember me, you did. Exceptional. I don't think I've ever come across anyone like you before.'

John laughed, 'Thanks for the compliment. They are always welcome. It's a shame that I haven't met you before. I think we'd have got on famously.' He decided to speak frankly. 'The problem I have is that I do not believe you are quite as honest as me. For instance, I presume you knew within a few days who Brendan Slack's murderer was.'

'If we are being honest, it didn't take the police long to work out.'

John couldn't help himself, he laughed rather raucously.

'The police took a while to arrive at Hawthorne's door and Buchanan's Scottish pile.'

Now it was Catherine's turn to laugh. 'Yes. But let's be really honest. The paintings they had between them were absolutely beautiful.'

John nodded sagely. 'I have to admit I have only seen photographs of them. They are remarkable.'

Catherine considered what to say. She grasped the nettle and took a chance. 'I was fortunate enough to have seen them in the flesh as it were. Absolutely exquisite. Much better than by a photograph.'

John grinned. 'Have you seen many of the others?'

She innocently declared, 'What others?' Looking at him as though totally naïve.

'I think at the last count yesterday, the police had identified forty-five stolen paintings. They had to stop due to a time constraint. I'm sure when they start looking for more, they will find them rather quickly.'

Catherine was shocked and couldn't hide the fact. She picked up a breadstick. 'Wow. They have been busy.' She bit off the end and chewed it as she thought what to say. John waited. 'There are going to be a lot of terrified people John and they can all call on others to do their bidding, for the right amount of money. I believe what you are telling me. At a rough guess, I think there are nearly a hundred paintings in total that they have stolen. These people are ruthless. I don't care what happens to my father. He's as greedy as the rest of them. I am sure he will be dead within a few days. They won't allow him to talk. The police can't protect him.' She bit off another piece of the breadstick. How much more should she tell him?

John called the waiter over and ordered a large glass of Chateauneuf-du-Pape. He was in no hurry. He savoured the wine. 'I don't know how deep you are in this organisation Catherine. But it's unravelling quicker by the day. If it makes you feel better, I haven't mentioned you to anyone else. The logical assumption that I would make is, if your father were likely to be killed, where does that leave you?'

She looked at the ceiling. He's right. I have known it for a couple of days. She felt the larger gun in its holster in the small of her back. It was better than nothing. Fully loaded with fourteen rounds. A lot better than two. 'I'll give you one thing. My father only used his landline to speak to Jake. Then his mobile to speak to his clients. He kept the mobile hidden, taped to the underside of the dog's bowl. Feel free to pass that on.'

John was grateful. 'Thanks. I'll make sure you are not mentioned.' Then he stated what she already knew, 'You have a predicament. What are you going to do?'

She'd already decided. 'I'm going to disappear. Somewhere that they won't find me. I think you are in no danger except from Campbell. Just warn your contacts that the people with the artworks will not give in too easily.'

The waiter put the plates down in front of them. Catherine spoke after the first mouthful. 'Not bad.'

John queried of her, 'Did your brother kill the two in Braithwaites?'

She didn't bother trying to lie. 'Yes. And before you ask, I went there to sanitise the place. What I found was a complete shock to me. It had been orchestrated by my father.'

'I'd like to know another thing.' She saw his lips curl into a wicked smile. 'What's your real name?'

'Catherine Russo. My mother is English and insisted I have an English name. She's become the complete epitome of a matriarch. I love her for it. Such a strong woman. She was taking a law degree when she met my father. They were both basically crooks. At the time neither knew it. As she was accepted into the family, it was her who had all the ideas.

I learnt English from her and Italian from my father. He was a bastard who beat me with a cane if I did anything wrong. Girls were always treated like dirt in some mafia families until they were old enough to be fucked. Then it was different. It didn't matter to him who came after me or how old they were. My mother kept them off me. She soon had a reputation when she killed the son of another mafioso.'

She drank some water as memories of her childhood were recalled. It hadn't really been as bad as she professed. Her mother had seen her talent as an artist at an early age and made sure some renowned fraudsters of the time taught her. It was that which had saved her mother from mafia vengeance. A forged painting of his favourite artist by her daughter was presented as a peace offering. He couldn't tell it was a forgery and accepted it as genuine. What an idiot!

Back in the present, she smirked as she thought of Leonardo. 'My brother never once got beaten. Obnoxious little brat. He'd do anything for money.'

John had watched her closely as she spoke. A simple question sprung to mind. 'Why did you get chosen to look at Brendan Slack's murder instead of your brother?'

It was a question she'd already considered herself. Hesitantly she replied, 'I'm not completely sure. I obviously know all the players, but so does my brother. I think my father

300

rather saw the writing on the wall and that it would escalate. Then if need be, I would be eliminated. My father would protect his son in preference to me.'

John felt slightly sorry for her, 'Is that why you're going?'

'Yeah,' and she asked quite candidly, 'Is that all you want to know? A potted version of my family history.' She ate some food as John thought.

'Something else has occurred to me. Why did Hawthorne and Buchanan know about each other's stolen art? Surely, safety dictates that the fewer people who know, keeps it more secure.'

Catherine chortled, 'It's a good point. My father had sold each of them a few paintings. There was a bit of a bidding war going on as to who wanted a painting the most. A Turner. A total of five drove the price higher and higher. Buchanan wanted it the most and paid an absolute fortune for it. The five people just seemed to get together and form a sort of group.'

John was eating. He emptied his mouth before taking some wine. It was lovely. 'Would you be willing to tell me the three others?'

Catherine wouldn't even consider it. 'No. I'm sure the police will get there soon.'

'Fair enough. Is there anything I can do for you?'

Catherine was no angel. John wasn't sure but he thought he saw her eyes moisten. She kept her head down as she ate. Then looking up at him whispered, 'You are the only person I have ever met who has said that to me and meant it.'

CHAPTER
FIFTY TWO

John was at the theatre picking up some more tickets. It was costing him a fortune, but Carol was worth it. Groves strolled round to the Café on the Park and sat down next to John. He looked at his cast free leg and guffawed, 'About time.'

John didn't want to dally, 'Did you find the old guy's mobile phone?'

Groves wasn't happy. 'No it looks like he's ditched it. Walter could have had a field day with it.'

'Anyone still at the house?'

Groves wondered where the conversation was going. He wanted to get home and John had insisted on a meeting. Surely there was more to it? 'Yeah. I think they'll wrap it up in a while. There's nothing in the place of note.'

'I'm sure you've thought of it. Check out the underside of the dog bowl. It's a place I have found items before. A lot of police don't look there because it's dirty and smelly.'

Groves agreed thoughtfully, 'Yes. Dirty and smelly. I'll make sure they have checked it.'

John said, 'I have also heard a rumour that Braithwaites may have stolen anything up to a hundred paintings.'

Groves was shocked. 'A hundred paintings?'

'Yeah.'

'I'll get a couple of the teams back to the museums. I thought forty-five was a lot. Are you sure it is a good rumour?'

'Best sort.'

Both Groves and John had places to be. The conversation was stilted and swift. Groves could only ask, 'Any other rumours that might be useful?'

'The old man is the broker. His mobile will prove it. A lot of dangerous people will want him dead before he can tell you anything.'

'Seriously?'

'Yeah.'

'Any suggestions?'

John could only say, 'Take him somewhere else.'

'Where?'

'Sorry. I can't help you there. Alison or Murray may have ideas.'

Groves swore. Then said, 'Cheers Oscar. I owe you,' and ran back to his car. He rang an officer still at Wimbledon and told him where to look. Holding the line open he heard the officer swearing.

Withing two minutes he'd got his answer. 'An old smart phone boss. What made you think of that?'

'No one looks at dog bowls. They are dirty and smelly. Officers tend to overlook them. I'm sure you would have looked eventually.'

The office took the hint, 'I'd have got there in about another half an hour.'

Groves was happy. John's first rumour was correct. What about the rest? A hundred paintings. Giuseppe Russo's security. He muttered 'Shit.' He rang Alison.

'Hi Alison. I've had a nasty thought. What if some of these people who have the stolen paintings are like Metcalf and Campbell? They may try to stop the old man talking. Do you think we should try and find a quieter place to house him?'

Alison could understand Groves worrying. Where could they put him? 'Chichester is the safest at the moment boss. It's like Fort Knox. Even the lawyers often complain they can't get straight in to see their clients. I wouldn't go to Brighton. Too busy and people can't be watched all the time. Durrington is like Chi. Nothing would be gained by taking him there. I'll think about it and call you back.'

Groves thanked her. She was right. Chichester is safest. Just to make sure, he decided to call the custody suite and ensure that Giuseppe Russo was always accompanied by an officer when anyone spoke to him. Should he arrange for an armed officer to remain outside his cell? That's probably going over the top.

The phone rang. He waited. He knew they often didn't answer for a long while when they were busy. He put the phone on speaker in his car and started to drive home. It took him nearly half an hour. No one had picked up the phone. He wasn't unduly worried but was getting a little anxious. He should have detoured and stopped off there on the way home. Cursing, he hung up.

His mobile blipped to let him know he had a couple of messages on his answer phone. He cursed again. Sod's law. I hang on the phone that doesn't get answered and miss a couple of calls I probably want. He rang his answerphone. It was Alison. She sounded harassed, 'Call me boss. Urgent.' The second message was from her as well. 'Guv'nor. Call me urgently.'

Groves thought her voice sounded strange. She'd probably come up with a location to house Giuseppe. He went indoors.

He needed a drink. Once he'd got a cup of tea and sat down he called her. He could here sirens in the background. Alison lived to the North of Chichester. It was normally peaceful around the area she lived in.

'Thank goodness you've called. We're too late. Giuseppe has been shot dead.' Groves dropped his cup which smashed on the wooden floor.

'What! What's happened?'

'The custody officer called me just after you called. A woman claiming to be the old man's brief asked to see him. She had all the correct credentials so they let her in. She asked all the right questions and asked to speak to him in an interview room. The custody officer complied. As soon as Giuseppe sat down, she produced a small revolver and shot him twice. Once in the head and once in the heart. Guv'nor. She knew exactly where to shoot him. Then she took the custody officer hostage and pressed the fire alarm which got her out of the building. It's apparently all on CCTV including everything she said. I've just arrived. I've called Murray who's on way.'

Groves jumped up. The tea was running all over his lounge floor. He ignored it. 'I'm on way,' and hung up. His wife had stepped into the lounge on hearing the cup smash. Groves apologised to her, 'Sorry love, I've got to go,' and he ran from the room.

When he arrived, it was pandemonium. Cars at odd angles in the blocked road. Yards of blue and white police tape fluttering in the breeze. Men and women, mostly in uniform were dashing about. Groves abandoned his car half on the pavement. A siren was wailing in the distance and getting louder as it approached. He ran towards the custody suite and found Murray in the car park outside. He was trying to make sense out of all the chaos.

Groves called out to him, 'Murray. Where's Alison?'

'She's inside guv'nor. Trying to sort out what actually happened. You can go straight in. The doors were all unlocked automatically when the fire alarm was pressed.' Then under his breath muttered, 'Bloody health and safety!'

Groves ran into the building. A uniformed officer at the open front door recognised him and waved him straight through. He ran to the central desk. Alison was writing notes. Several uniform officers were around her. Groves rightly assumed they were all the custody personnel. A couple were obviously in shock.

She spotted Groves and called to him, 'Guv'nor, interview room three. No one's been in there since it happened. An officer is downloading all the CCTV. The FME has been called and the forensic teams are on way. So's the chief. I'm getting all the staff names and sorting out statements. Murray is arranging searches outside to see if anyone saw where the shooter went.'

Groves went along the corridor to the open door of interview room number three. He stared in. Guiseppe was sitting in his chair with his head flopped back. A black mark of a powder burn around a small hole in his temple was visible. Groves couldn't see any exit wound The bullet was lodged in his brain. It had to be a small calibre weapon. The hole through his clothing over the entry wound to his heart was hardly visible.

Groves went back to the central desk as the chief strode in.

Two officers were still in shock. The chief went to them and tried to offer words of comfort. It wasn't his strong point. At least he knew who could help. He'd arrange it later. He called to Groves, 'A quiet word please Mr Groves,' and he walked off to the inspector's office with Groves trailing behind him.

As soon as they were seated the chief queried, 'What do you know about this?'

Groves expected the question but didn't really have any cogent answer. 'Very little at the moment sir. It appears that the killer knew how the legal system in the custody suite works. Once the victim was in the room, she shot him and then took the custody officer hostage to get out of the building. Then she set off the outer fire alarm which automatically unlocks all secure doors. All of it is on CCTV which is currently being downloaded. Murray is trying to fathom out what happened outside once the shooter left. That really is all I know at the moment.'

The chief sat in the chair behind the desk. He stroked his chin. He adjusted his peaked hat. Then he spoke. 'Mr Groves. We have a problem. Every time you are about to make headway, something happens. This is the most blatant killing yet. As soon as you can, I want to see the CCTV. This is all to do with stolen paintings. These people are going to extraordinary lengths to protect themselves.'

'I'll get it set up and ready to be viewed in ten minutes.'

'I'll be outside. I'll make a quick statement to the press and I'll see you in the viewing room.' With that pronouncement, he got up and strode out.

Groves went back to the central desk. A sergeant was busy downloading the CCTV to a DVD. 'Sergeant. I need a copy set up to be viewed. Where's your viewing room?'

The sergeant was as good as finished and handed a DVD to Groves. 'Down the end of the corridor before the emergency exit door.' Groves walked off to find it. In the room he placed the DVD into a stand-alone unit. There were half a dozen chairs in the room. He needed both Alison and Murray to view it as well. It was easier to phone them.

When the chief walked in, he didn't hesitate. 'Turn it on. Let's see what this woman does.'

CHAPTER
FIFTY THREE

John heard the news from Carol. She'd been at work taking a break in the staff room and the radio was on. She heard the breaking news. A quick phone call to John elicited one word. Should he call one of the team to find out exactly what had happened. They would probably be rather tucked up. He decided to wait until one of them called him. In the meantime, he turned the TV on.

He was just in time to see the report by the chief. He heard the shooter was a woman. It surely wouldn't be Catherine? She'd warned him. You don't warn someone and then do the deed. You'd be asking to be caught. He needed to see a photo of the killer. Then he'd know either way.

* * *

The elderly woman was already en route to Heathrow. She'd booked an open ticket when she'd heard police were battering down Guiseppe's front door. There had been no time to organise a professional. She'd had to do it herself. She could only count on a small gun. It served its purpose.

* * *

They were seated in front of the computer as the CCTV unfolded. All were shocked to see the killer was an elderly woman. Probably in her seventies. Smartly dressed as most lawyers are. A slight accent at times, but not definitive enough to be recognisable. Carrying a small attaché case. She knew who to ask for and how the system worked.

Alison saw the mistake. The woman went out of her way not to touch anything. As the sergeant asked her for a signature on a form the woman dropped her case on the floor, leaning it against the footing of the central desk. She used her own pen. When she bent down to pick up her case, she struggled to stand back up. She placed a hand on the side panelling of the desk to assist her.

'Stop the tape!' Groves stopped it as Alison explained what she saw. He rewound it for less than a minute. They all noted it. 'I'll go and secure that section for fingerprints,' and she left the room.

Alison was back in minutes and Groves set the tape running. It was nothing remarkable from then on until they were in the interview room. Giuseppe sat down. The woman and the custody sergeant walked in. The viewers all noticed that Giuseppe looked at the woman and smiled. He knew her.

As she sat down she opened her case. She didn't identify herself.

Giuseppe said to her, 'I'm sorry it is you that has to do it.'

She smiled lovingly at him. 'We've had a good life together. I've always loved you. We'll meet again in heaven.' Her hand came out of the bag holding a small revolver. She leant forward and put the gun close to his temple and pulled the trigger. He made no effort to move. Then she placed the gun to his chest and pulled the trigger. He was dead.

The noise from the little gun had brought officers running.

She spun around and pointed the gun at the sergeant. Grabbing up her bag she demanded, 'I'm leaving now with you. If you want to live, I suggest you help me.' They left the room. As officers approached her, the sergeant told them to back off. She easily walked away from the building. She couldn't run at her age. None of the officers followed her. The tape stopped.

The chief wasn't sure. 'When they spoke, I got the idea they were partners. Did anyone else come to that conclusion?'

Alison had. Her eyes had moistened. The woman was a killer, but there was definite affection for the victim. She made sure he didn't suffer. Both Groves and Murray had picked it up as well. They all concurred.

As they returned to the central desk, the sergeant handed Groves a couple of spare copies of the CCTV.

* * *

The plane was in the air and soon to arrive back in Rome. Leonardo would be waiting, and they'd go to their large villa on the shores of Lake Como. All the artwork could be enjoyed at their leisure. Everything was an original. No one there knew who they were. Just two killers on the run.

* * *

Groves called John. 'Do you want to see the CCTV?'

'What's its main thrust?'

The killer was an elderly lady who appears to have been Giuseppe's wife or partner.'

John let his breath out. 'Really?'

'Next time I see you, I'll give you a copy to have a look at.'

'Interesting. I wonder what her role in the organisation is? He was the broker and she must have known that. Surely she's not an assassin?'

Groves would not rule it out completely. 'She appeared to know what she was doing.'

John forced a laugh and said, 'Elderly female assassins stalking the UK. No one is safe.'

Groves gave a slight guffaw. 'John. She walked out of the custody suite and no one followed her. We are trying to get Chichester's CCTV for the town. Then we might have a clue where she went or if someone picked her up.'

John couldn't get Catherine out of his mind. Would she have helped her mother after warning him? No. Doesn't make sense. 'Keep me informed please.'

'For your information, there was a mobile phone taped to the underside of the dog bowl. I'm hoping we will get a lot of names from it. Then its hunt the original art.'

'Brilliant. I'll speak to you tomorrow when things have calmed down.'

'Ok. Speak soon and thanks.' Groves terminated the call.

John sat still. Why the elderly killer? His wife? Why not a professional? No time to organise one? Very strange? I wonder if Catherine will answer her phone?

He rang the number. No connection. He rang it again. Still no connection. If he wanted to disappear, he'd destroy his mobile. She's probably done that. He pulled his old laptop out of a drawer. It had a flat battery. He plugged the lead in. It fired up. It asked him for a password. He took a while to remember.

Now he could see the screen a lot clearer than on his phone. He googled her name. Catherine Russo. Nothing. Linkedin. Nothing. He searched social media sites. Nothing. He searched for Guiseppe Russo. Nothing. The family didn't seem to exist.

Then he remembered Leonardo Russo. Occasional mentions in newspapers saying he was wanted by the police. Nothing else. Whatever had been on the internet had been wiped. He sat and stared at the screen.

Then a flicker in his brain. Could he search only as if in Italy. No idea. He called Rocky and asked the question. He said, 'Tell me the name. It might be a lot quicker than me trying to tell you how to do it.'

'Catherine Russo.'

John heard a keyboard tapping. Then Rocky said, 'Are you after the artist, Catherine Russo?'

'That could be her. Any location for her?'

'Yes. She died about a hundred and fifty years ago. Buried in Perugia with the rest of her family in a crypt. A mediocre artist by all accounts. Often accused of being a better forger than artist. Parents were apparently high up in the mafia.'

John let out a sigh. 'Rocky. Was her Father Guiseppe?'

Seconds later, 'Good guess John.'

'I don't know the Mother's name. Does it say?

'Hang on. Yep. Francesca. She was believed to have been English. Does that help?'

'I suppose they had a son called Leonardo?'

'John. Why am I looking if you know most of this?'

'Thanks Rocky. I only started to get it as you spoke.'

He chatted about the Kent unit that Rocky worked at and

eventually hung up.

John called Groves. 'Hi Oscar. What can I do for you?'

'I've had an epiphany. I think your killer's name is Francesca Russo. Just don't ask how I know and make sure you find it some other way. Keep my name out of it.'

'Cheers John. Any idea how I could find it out?'

'Search the internet as though you are in Italy. Look for Guiseppe Russo. He died about a hundred and fifty years ago. His wife was probably English and called Francesca. They had a son called Leonardo Russo. That's two killers and a broker. Their daughter Catherine was allegedly a good forger of paintings.'

'Bloody hell Oscar. When you have a thought, it lights a fair few candles. I'll sort it out with the techies.'

'Speak soon,' and John hung up smiling ruefully. He had no choice but to mention Catherine.

CHAPTER
FIFTY FOUR

The following day's meeting was rather chaotic. The chief was already in the office well before 7am. As officers slowly gathered, he met them and passed on his thanks for all their work. They took their seats and waited for Groves. Alison and Murray were busy collating their notes of the previous day's events.

Walter was late, as usual. He'd been up all night working on Guiseppe's phone. He burst into the office in his usual harassed state, apologising for the commotion he caused. Then to everyone's surprise, even the chief's, he was followed by the deputy chief constable in a more decorous demeanour. The deputy had known Walter had been in his lab all night and had given him a lift in his official car. He sat down next to the chief.

Then Groves walked in. He'd been in his office considering his next moves. Not much had sprung to mind. The team had instantly risen from their seats. They knew they were struggling and wanted to show their support. 'Thanks everyone. Please take your seats. This is likely to be a long meeting. I'm going to ask Walter to let us know what he's gleaned from Guiseppe's phone as he's been working all night and needs to get home for some kip. Walter. The floor's all yours.'

Walter was too tired to stand. But he knew what he was going to say would enliven the meeting. As he had arrived late, he'd not had time to update Groves or anyone else on the team. His manner gave nothing away. The deputy was the only other person who knew the bombshell that Walter was about to unleash.

Walter seemed to be talking to himself. 'I can't believe people don't use passwords on their phones. It makes my job so much easier. Please remember that.' He scrutinised all the faces staring at him. Now he wanted to explain in simple terms what he'd learnt. It shouldn't be a problem. They weren't stupid. The corners of his mouth turned up into a wry smile. His eyes were sparkling. He was really going to enjoy this. Those who knew him well realised he had something of importance to say. They seemed to move to the edge of their seats.

'Guiseppe's phone has nearly three hundred names and addresses in it. In total, eighty-seven are British numbers, then there are numbers for people all around the world. European countries being predominant. Some, but not many, appear to be family members.' Then he remembered he needed to clarify why he thought that. 'That's all the Russo family, including their known close relatives.' He looked around the office. They were still following his narrative. No problem so far.

'Now comes the really important bit. Guiseppe had highlighted various names. A hundred and twenty-four to be precise. I didn't understand at first. Then I noticed that those names that were highlighted had notes attached. But they were definitely password protected. I thought it rather strange.' Pausing more to consider his next commentary, he looked around the office again. They were hanging on his every word.

'Then I checked the unhighlighted phone book entries. Ladies and gentlemen, you'll all be amazed to learn that they also had notes attached. But they weren't password protected.'

Now Groves was sitting on the edge of his seat as were most of the officers. Walter was in his element.

'I have looked at all the notes that were not password protected. They all followed the same pattern. They just named various artists. Some had up to ten recorded. Some also had them numbered in a seeming order of preference. Most had a figure of currency next to each one.'

Several officers were way ahead of him. Groves looked at the chief and couldn't resist saying, 'Another little thing that needs clearing up.' The chief laughed.

Walter hadn't finished. His smile appeared to be infectious. 'I have broken the password that Guiseppe used. It was Gustav, as Gustav Klimt the artist which was the name of his recently departed dog. As I keep saying, always use a password but don't make it too easy to crack.' A pause, 'I looked at Metcalf Buchanan first.'

Someone couldn't wait and called out, 'Come on Walter. Tell us. What did his note tell you?'

Walter couldn't stop smiling, 'You've probably all guessed correctly. It showed the Turner and an amount in English pounds. It showed all his other paintings that you have recovered with amounts next to them. I know it's totally unprofessional, but I'm willing to bet no one gets close to the actual amount that is recorded next to the Turner.'

Several started to call out figures. The highest was called out by Roland. A million. Groves called for calm and then hypocritically added his own guess at half a million.

Walter couldn't contain himself. He burst out laughing. All his inhibitions a thing of the past. 'No one is close. Six and a half million.'

They could have heard a pin drop.

Six and a half million for a stolen painting. Then the silence was broken by an officer from the Arts and Antiques squad. 'When you consider, if this painting was put up for sale it would probably fetch at least six hundred million or even more, it's a bargain.'

Officers and civilian staff started to talk amongst themselves. They all understood exactly what Walter was saying. Groves was ecstatic. He called for quiet. 'Walter. I believe we all understand what you're saying. Those with highlighted details and password protected notes have obtained paintings unlawfully.'

Walter scrabbled in his old briefcase and pulled out a couple of clear plastic folders, each holding several sheets of paper. He handed the first one to Groves. 'Everyone whose name and address in Britain is highlighted, is on these sheets. Also the paintings that they have acquired illegally and how much they have likely paid.'

He passed the second folder to Groves. 'These are the names, addresses and details of what paintings people around the world have. They are all from the highlighted list.'

A wit called out, 'I hope they are all in alphabetical order?'

Walter was sluggish with humour. Indignantly, he responded, 'Naturally. On the last name.' All those present burst out laughing.

As the office returned to a semblance of order, the chief stood up. 'Ladies and gentlemen, this might be the finale in relation to the stolen artwork. We are going to need a lot of help re manpower. Mr Groves, I shall see what I can arrange. The logistics are going to take some working out. Today is

Thursday, can we provisionally look to take action early on Monday?'

Groves was agreeable. He looked at Alison who nodded and then to Murray who also nodded. 'Seems like Monday is going to be a good day.'

CHAPTER
FIFTY FIVE

The meeting drew to a close. Everyone had a lot to talk about. Outstanding enquiries were put on hold. The chief spoke to his deputy. 'I'll speak to Walter later. He has excelled all the way through this enquiry and at times kept it going. I will make sure he is well recognised for all his hard work.'

The deputy was a little concerned. He'd been a detective for most of his service and had noted what he considered an overlooked crime. Wistfully he replied, 'I'm sure Walter would be grateful. Going back to what he discovered in the unhighlighted names etc. Technically, one could consider that those people were seeking to buy art when it became available. Illegally. The amount shown by the actual artist they were seeking could be the amount they were willing to pay or go up to.'

The chief saw where his deputy was going. 'Jesus. Are you suggesting we should go after them all for a conspiracy charge? How many did Walter say there were? Well over a hundred.'

The deputy looked hard at his chief. 'The problem arises. Say the press get hold of it. They would have a field day whatever works of art are recovered. They are never satisfied. They'd crucify us.'

The chief thought for a few seconds. 'I see your point. We could go to the DPP and get their authority to drop it. Then they'll worry that they would be castigated for preventing very rich punters from being charged. And they would have to be very rich to purchase the stolen art. I'm sure some would also be prominent people. Then the press have another go at us. One law for them and one for the rest of us. At the moment, I think we may have our hands bound.'

The deputy added, 'The Home Secretary would be in the same boat if we approached her. I can't see a way around this.'

Pausing as thoughts whistled in and out of his head. The chief could not see any way he could ignore the crime. He would have to go after them all.

He called to Groves who was chatting to a group of scientists, 'Mr Groves. A word please. Your office.'

Groves broke away from the group and went to his office. The chief was already in his chair behind his desk. His elbows rested on the chair arms and his extended, steepled fingers were touching his bottom lip. Groves read the sign. A problem. He sat in one of his spare chairs. 'Problem sir?'

'Yes. Rather a big one.' He went on to explain about the unhighlighted people and the offence of conspiracy. 'The question I have is what do we do?'

Groves only saw a minor problem. He didn't want to sound flippant, but it was hard not to. 'I believe that we should crack on with all the British addresses that are highlighted on Monday. As to the unhighlighted people, I believe we should hold that in abeyance. I don't foresee a problem with that. They don't actually have any art, so we won't lose anything by leaving it for a while. We could even send them letters at a later date telling them to report to a certain police station with their lawyers to be interviewed and charged. If they don't, we send someone to go and get them. Then tell the press.'

The chief was elated. A way out. 'Brilliant. That's the way we'll proceed.' Then he remembered something that he'd overheard. 'Mr Groves. I heard that Guiseppe's phone was hidden in a cavity under his dog bowl. One of the searchers apparently took a phone call from you suggesting he look there. Is that correct?'

Groves hesitated a little too long. The chief noted it. 'Yes. I made the call.'

'And may I ask, why?'

'It was something that occurred to me.'

The chief laughed. 'I suspect your epiphany may have come from the same apparition that helped to locate Brendan Slack's mobile.'

Groves couldn't help himself. He burst out laughing himself, 'Very likely sir. Very likely.'

'When you next see the apparition, please pass on my thanks,' and with that, he rose and strode from the room. He had an appointment to arrange with the PCC.

Groves went round to his seat and chuckled to himself. He sat reading the lists from Walter for nearly a quarter of an hour before going into the main office. Some of the British names were well known people. Even a couple of politicians. It was really going to bring the pains on. But the end of the art trail was in sight. Calling Alison and Murray, they assembled around Doreen's computer.

Groves knew what they had to do. 'I think it would be prudent to ask the CPS for a named liaison officer we could work with. I'll sort that out. Then we need to know the location of each address and which constabulary covers them. Murray, can you sort that out with Nathan?' Murray nodded as he wrote in his notebook.

'We need to establish who has what art and where it actually should be. Alison, can you team up with Roland and sort that out?'

Alison was writing in her pocketbook and replied without looking up, 'Good as done.'

Groves knew he'd have to work with the CPS, but he wanted to keep ahead of the game. 'Alison. How do you think we should proceed? Should we apply for all the search warrants and dish them out at the briefing? Or, let the constabularies apply for search warrants for the addresses on their manors?'

Alison looked up. She pondered the question. Groves waited. Slowly she came to what she considered was the best solution. 'I think as a matter of security, I should apply for all of them in conjunction with the CPS and dish them out at the briefing.'

Groves reflected upon it. If the addresses became known before Monday and there was a leak, it could jeopardise the whole operation. 'I'd like the briefing to be held on Sunday evening for all the team leaders when the warrants would be allocated. The problems arise when they brief their teams on Monday morning. It only takes one bad apple to blow the whole operation apart. I don't know how we can prevent it.'

Murray had already considered the prospect previously of a bad apple destroying a case. He had a sort of answer. 'I thought about this once before. I don't think it's illegal. What I said to the team leaders was that some of the addresses were under surveillance and phones were being tapped. It sort of answers the question. Anyone thinking of making a call would quickly realise they would be identified and arrested, and anyone making a quick visit wouldn't know if they were seen by a surveillance team and again get themselves arrested.'

Alison stared at him. Laughingly she uttered, 'You devious, sly, old bastard. I never thought you would come up with something like that.'

Groves loved it. Then he thought about it before proclaiming, 'I like that. Just to cover ourselves, we could put a surveillance team on one of the addresses. We could even listen to one of the phones we have. Good thought Murray. I consider that problem solved.'

Murray smiled as he rounded on Alison, 'Please, sly, devious, and bastard I accept, but old. No way.' All three chuckled.

Groves conceded that another problem was if there were a lot more secret rooms. 'We'd need architects to check measurements at each address. I don't see that happening. Murray. Any thoughts there?'

Murray was quick with his answer, 'Sorry boss. That one's got me.'

Groves moved on. 'I don't see the point of an art expert. We know what each of these thieves has got. Any other paintings should be seized and sorted out at the local nicks.'

Alison wanted to know more logistics, 'How many officers should attend each venue?'

Groves sat back in his chair. He put his hands behind his head. He hadn't got a good answer. 'That's a damn good question. If they live in big houses or stately homes like Hawthorne and Buchanan, we'll need a fair number of officers at each. I think we'll have to work out how many attend each individual premises.'

Murray was resolute, 'That shouldn't take too long boss. We can see how big each house is on the internet. If we wanted, we could get land registry plans. Put a couple of detectives on it. Shouldn't take too long.'

'Good idea Murray. Can I leave that with you?'

Murray had no qualms, 'Good as done. Well, by tomorrow afternoon.'

Groves felt contented. Just two questions had him stumped. How many officers would the chief come up with and where could he hold his briefing?

CHAPTER
FIFTY SIX

By late Friday afternoon, a lot had been achieved. A folder had been created for each address. There were copies of documents obtained from the internet. An aerial image and a floor plan of the property. More importantly, there was an image of the stolen painting and where it actually should be. Copies of PNC printouts of people known to the police. Lastly, there was a search warrant. Eighty-seven folders in total.

Some of the houses were as large as Hawthorne's and a total of twelve officers were deemed necessary for a search. The size of the house would dictate how many officers would be needed. Groves' team were going to be responsible for several of the larger premises which may have concealed rooms. Nearly everything was ready.

Friday evening at 7pm found Alison, Groves and Murray in Rustington's Establo Lounge restaurant waiting for John. He walked in, not actually wobbling but cautiously taking each stride carefully. Sitting down gingerly, he felt better and relaxed. All acknowledge him. Even Alison stated it was good to see him without his cast.

The waiter was at their table and quickly took their orders. Food and drinks were delivered hurriedly. The restaurant's food was basic but good. Still not a patch on Carluccio's or Blanc's. The idea was serve people quickly, see them leave and then get someone else at the vacated table. That suited the four police officers. They all wanted a quick meal, discussion and away.

Groves wasn't going to hang around. 'Oscar. First things first. From the chief and all of us on the team, thanks a million for the phone under the dog bowl. I'm told the bowl was absolutely disgusting to pick up or hold. It's unlikely the searchers would have found it.' He bit into a cheeseburger. Then while still chewing, he added, 'Giuseppe was definitely the broker.'

Fishing in a pocket, he pulled out a creased wodge of folded papers and slid them across the table to John. Those on the outside now bore Groves' greasy finger-marks. 'These are copies of the papers I promised you. The highlighted ones have stolen paintings and the others wanted to buy some.' John tucked the bundle into his own pocket. He'd scan it later at his leisure.

Alison was not happy with Groves talking with his mouth full. She took over. She wasn't aware the phone information came from John. It didn't actually surprise her. 'We know the inside agent was Jake and now, that the broker was Giuseppe. His killer appears to be his wife Francesca who managed to disappear from the scene effortlessly. She's no shrinking violet. She didn't try to rescue him, just kill him. He apparently expected to die. We are still not sure where she is in the pecking order of the organisation. Have you any idea?'

John emptied his mouth. He took a mouthful of warm beer. 'I have been trying to work that out. My informant has also disappeared.' He considered his options. Should he name Catherine? He knew that Groves would eventually work out she was the forger. Would he work out that she was also a violent and devious woman? Unlikely. John actually liked her. He remembered her remarking that she may also become a victim.

Something was trying to force its way into his brain. He couldn't quite get it clear enough. It would come to him; he was sure of it. The whole Russo family were criminals one way or another. He made his decision. He laid his knife and fork down. 'I think I should let you know that I believe Catherine Russo is, without a doubt, the forger. She is also a woman not to be underestimated. She knows where Campbell and the laird are hiding.'

Before he could utter another word, Alison blurted out, 'Where are they John. Has she told you?'

John didn't want to lie. 'She has definitely not told me where they are.' Looking at Alison, 'Please believe me.'

Alison was fuming. 'Don't lie to me John. This is important.'

'I'm not. You've obviously worked out she was my informant. I pushed her on it. She said she'd deal with them but didn't tell me where they are.'

Alison dropped into a major sulk.

John wanted to continue. What was it he was trying to get into his brain? 'There's something that is bothering me, but at the moment, I can't fathom out what it is. Catherine seemed confident that she could deal with Campbell and the laird. If so, she's got to be rather tough.'

The thought kept coming back. Then it was there. A throwaway line that Catherine had said. Perhaps she didn't realise she'd said it? Or had she said it deliberately? As a clue? 'Give me a second. I'm nearly there.'

They ate and drank in relative silence for nearly two minutes. John was far away. His brain was trawling through the conversation he'd had with Catherine. The others whispered to each other so as not to disturb his notions. Alison casually looked at her watch. Then turned her wrist so Murray could see it. John noticed out of the corner of his half closed eyes. That's it. Got it.

'Brilliant Alison. Thank you,' and he swallowed the remainder of his beer. All three looked at him expectantly. 'Francesca. She is the main person.' He picked up his burger and took a large bite.

No one spoke. They waited. John wiped his mouth and sat back in his seat. 'When I spoke to Catherine and asked what her real name was, she said Catherine Russo but carried on to extol her mother's virtues and antecedents. The fact that she was the matriarchal figurehead and the person with all the ideas. Plus she was the killer of the son of a mafioso many years ago. And how she got away with it.' He cogitated further about the conversation and the murder of Guiseppe.

'When she killed Guiseppe, she must have hoped it would stop you finding out who had what. Did she know he kept a phone with everyone's details on it? Unlikely.' He considered what he'd said. It wasn't right.

As though hypnotised, he drifted slowly as he interrogated himself, 'Mind you, She must have known. Someone had to keep details of who wanted what. It was unlikely to be her. It had to have been Guiseppe. Yes. She knew. But she still killed him. Why? Stop him going to prison? What if it had gone wrong and she'd been caught? The whole thing looks like a family affair.' He snapped out of his slight trance and looked at the others.

'I think that's it. A complete family affair. Francesca set the whole thing up. The only outsider they actually needed was Jake.'

Alison was closely following every word. 'There's only one thing I would like to know. How did they find all the punters?'

'I don't know... yet.

Another thing I learnt, there were three others in the group with Hawthorne and Buchanan. Trouble is, I don't know who they are. I'm sure a study of their phones will probably divulge their names.'

Groves was more than happy. No one had to go back and trawl through the museum's paperwork. Everything seemed to be clicking into place. Walter could sort the phones out. Monday was as good as ready. But he had his own question for John, 'Why kill her husband?'

Murray had thought that himself. He believed he had the definitive answer. 'He was an old man. He would soon die if sent to prison. Not the best place to end your days. I bet his wife would have killed herself if she was about to be caught.'

John was pensive. 'I agree, Murray. As she got away, it leaves her and her two children at large. They must have a bolt hole somewhere. The money they must have made over the years will be astronomical. If they got six and a half million for one painting, what would the total be for over a hundred? They could afford to buy a place anywhere in the world. Their house in Italy and those in the UK are too dangerous for them to use.' He looked up at the ceiling and asked rhetorically, 'Where the hell is it?'

No one had any idea.

Murray idly queried of John, 'Would the members of Hawthorne's group know?'

Groves answered for him. 'No. They have no need to

know. They just buy the paintings.' He paused as what he said had stirred a thought. 'I wonder how they pay? Cash surely has to be out of the question. Cheque, unlikely, but possible. Bankers draft or transfer? I doubt they'd do it in instalments?'

Alison came out of her sulk when she seemed to spot an angle. She challenged Groves, 'How did Guiseppe pay Jake? It had to be a reasonable amount as without him, the whole caboodle would come crashing down. I reckon we need someone who is good with figures and knows banking procedures. The whole lot of them have made blatant mistakes in the past. If we could find one more mistake, we might find their bolt hole.'

Groves agreed. We'll have a look at this over the weekend. I'm sure Jake wasn't paid by money from NSL Delivery Services. Guiseppe may have used another account. More likely cash for Jake. But he'd have to acquire it from a bank. He surely wouldn't have kept large amounts of cash about. We would have found it by now if he had. If we can find a payment to the Russo family from one of the punters, it might lead us to their bank and then their address. It's a possibility.'

John looked at his mobile and sent a short text. There was a ping as a reply was received.

Simon knew what he needed. He searched a drawer he hadn't looked in for a couple of years. Right at the bottom, he found it. It was so big, it defeated the object. You couldn't drive and look at it: you just needed a good memory once you decided which way you wanted to go.

He slipped the atlas under his arm as he went to his car. Throwing it onto the back seat, he set off for Carluccio's.

CHAPTER
FIFTY SEVEN

John was already there when Simon arrived. They were seated at a corner table with a good view of the door. Both ordered beer. John gave him a resume of the main problem. How to get Campbell and Buchanan to return to the UK?

Simon was fully aware of what Campbell had done in Tenerife and the Cotswolds. Alison had spared nothing when she had relayed the events. It didn't take an expert to work out that Campbell had killed before. There had been no hesitation. The first kill was always the hardest. Simon knew that the more you did it, the more hardened and proficient you became, and the less you worried about it. Beginners always seemed to hesitate. Even just a little could be one's downfall.

John continued with his narrative, 'I know they are somewhere near a small Swiss village called Ormont-Dessus. It's en route to Gstaad. I would estimate that they are within a quarter of an hour's drive from the village. On those roads, it can't be much more than five miles. Now the problem arises who do we get to go there and locate them?'

Simon found Ormont-Dessus in his atlas. He looked at the terrain. 'That would be a bit of a problem. The first is where does one stay and the second is how does one locate them? Whoever goes will stick out like a sore thumb if it all goes pear-shaped.' He knew what was needed. 'We need a local who speaks the language.'

John's phone rang. 'I think we need to meet. I know someone who meets all the requirements.'

'When and where?'

'Can you get to Ashford tomorrow for eight?'

'Usual place?'

'Yeah,' and Rocky hung up.

John snorted, 'Looks like Rocky might have someone lined up. Fancy a trip to Ashford tomorrow morning?'

Simon was still engrossed with the map and said, 'Show me warned. I suppose you want me to drive?'

'That would be great. Can you pick me up about sixish?'

'I'll be in the parking area outside your place. Don't be late.'

They went their separate ways.

* * *

John liked Simon's Lexus. It drove well even over the majority of potholes. The seat was so comfortable, it was hard not to nod off. Simon knew John wasn't interested in early morning conversations. Within less than ten minutes, John was fast asleep.

Rocky was already in the café with Zena, having a healthy breakfast when they arrived. Zena was introduced to John and Simon. She had been at the Kent facility for a couple of years but had met neither of them face to face. She had quickly teamed up with Rocky and they'd become a formidable partnership. He was always dressed smartly in a suit, she tended to prefer military fatigues and boots.

Zena favoured short spiky hair with blue and pink tints.

Rocky's hair was always short and neat, tinged with a bit of grey. They both had hazel eyes and unremarkable features. It had served them well during their military careers. Now they could practically read each other's thoughts and were able to anticipate the other's actions. Their joint address book was the dream of many a security officer and those who were in it were often glad of the fact.

John said between mouthfuls of fried food, 'You all know the problem. We have to be careful as Campbell is a violent killer. I don't want anyone coming unstuck if he gets the slightest whiff that we're looking for him. I don't want anyone using a satnav on a phone or in a car. Maps only, which can easily be disposed of securely. I'm sure any cameras in Europe would not be a problem to you two?' He loaded his fork with egg and sausage.

Zena watched him in astonishment. No wonder he was the size of a brick out-house. She nodded. It was her contact that they were putting forward. An intelligence officer in the Swiss Army who she had lived with on and off for a few years when she was a lot younger. Someone she knew well. Now a ski instructor in Gstaad and a member of the mountain rescue team. She gave a resume of his antecedents. Completely trustworthy, a trained burglar and killer.

John questioned how he could scour the area without drawing attention to himself. Zena had all the answers. He would supposedly be looking to start up a ski school in the area. Simple. He spoke the language and had a traceable background in Gstaad. What more was needed?

Rocky, Simon and John looked at each other. The perfect person for the task. Now all they had to do was offer him the role. How were they to approach him? A telephone call or email could always be traced. It didn't matter how good you were at covering your tracks, there was always the off chance something might be missed. And sure as eggs are eggs, the police would stumble across it.

To travel there would leave a clue somewhere. Rocky and Zena would find something so why couldn't anyone else with the right skill set do the same? Not worth the risk. A conundrum.

Rocky had a solution. Similar to something he'd done once before. It was complicated. And needed perfect timing.

* * *

Catherine was considering her options. She was based in the best hotel in Ormont-Dessus, less than eight miles from Buchanan's chalet. She was using her passport in the name of Catherine Russo and she was speaking fluently in Italian. She had no qualms about anyone taking an image of her from the hotel CCTV. She would be long gone before the police started any enquiries.

Francesca wanted them dealt with. Why? Neither knew of anyone except Jake or Guiseppe. They may have seen the delivery men but not darling little Leo. He always kept out of view. It was not a risk worth taking. The money the family had made from the sale of paintings was astronomical. They could all end their days by the lake in prodigious luxury. What is she up to? Have I missed something?'

Then it hit her. Shit! She's worked out that I could have been the only one who grassed up Guiseppe. Is she setting me a test? Is Campbell expecting me? Does she expect me to be killed? Punishment for Guiseppe, her beloved husband and bastard of a father? She stared out of the window. Has she told Campbell where I am? Will he come for me? What do I do?

Do I tell the British police where they are? Not much they can do. Start extradition proceedings with the Swiss? Good luck with that. What is John Whiles planning? He knows where they are. He could tell the police. Will he? Why hasn't he already? Will he send someone? Catherine smiled. Then she started to snigger and then it turned to a full blown laugh. He was going to send someone. She knew what she'd do. Calling to the barman, she downed the vodka he brought her in one.

CHAPTER
FIFTY EIGHT

John looked at Simon. 'What do you think?'

Simon said slowly and thoughtfully, 'If Rocky says it's doable, it's doable. Military grade gear would attract a lot of attention. A toy wouldn't.'

Rocky butted in, 'It's definitely not a toy.'

John turned to Zena, 'It's your show. How do you feel?'

Zena was happy. 'It'll work. He'll be so intrigued. He won't be able to decline.' She had her fingers crossed.

John said, 'Ok. Let's do it.'

Rocky took all the pieces out of the workshop one at a time and laid them delicately on the grass. Zena began to assemble them. First the thin fuselage in two pieces. Then she unfolded the wings and locked them into position before clipping them into the slots in the fuselage. Then it was the tail section. There were plastic bolts that held everything securely.

Both Rocky and Zena fiddled with the plastic camera eventually fixing it in position. Although they weren't going to use it, it had to be there to balance the fuselage. Then they slipped the nosecone and propeller over it. Everything was plastic except for a few small electrical contacts and some batteries.

It was a project the two of them had been working on for some time and was nearing completion. They just couldn't solve the problem of the metal in the batteries. There was no such thing as a plastic battery, yet. Their guidance system was cobbled together from a young child's plastic, handheld tablet and a small hook was visible beneath the fuselage.

As the sun began to heat up the array of miniature solar panels on the wings, the propeller started to twitch. The batteries were already fully charged and would last for at least twelve hours without an additional charge from the panels. The theory they were working on was keeping the drone airborne for several weeks. They believed it could fly at an altitude of about twelve thousand feet and recharge the batteries daily. Lower than airliners but higher than smaller pleasure aircraft.

The last thing Rocky rolled out of the workshop was a set of pram wheels welded to a frame. Both he and Zena lifted the drone carefully onto them. When it was ready to be launched, the wheels and frame stayed firmly on the ground.

Zena put a miniature plastic canister onto the hook and checked it was secure. Then both checked their work. They were satisfied. They needed at least fifty yards to take off. Rocky pushed a switch on the top of the fuselage and stood back. The propeller started spinning and the drone shot forward. It was airborne within forty yards. They recovered the wheels and frame.

The drone soon worked out where it was and set off. At a sedate thirty miles an hour! Too slow to attract any attention and unlikely to make even the smallest of blips on a radar screen. It was able to navigate over mountains and along valleys. It could accumulate enough battery power during the day to keep it airborne during night-time when it just circled.

Zena knew where Hans was going to be at 9am on any given day. He would walk out of the hotel and meet the small group he was to lead that morning on two black runs. He lived by the hotel clock chiming nine. He had never once been late. The drone was circling above the group at about one thousand feet. They were all watching it with varying degrees of amusement.

As Hans strode out of the hotel, the drone sank considerably lower to about a hundred feet and the canister dropped from the underbelly of the fuselage swaying on a tiny red and white parachute. It landed less than three feet from him. Written in bold red paint were the words, Hans Weber. He picked it up and looked at it as the drone stopped circling and started on its leisurely return journey. The canister had a three wheel plastic security code system. Laughing to himself, he put it in his anorak pocket. He'd open it later by just breaking the plastic. He knew who had sent it and that there was a small burner mobile phone inside it.

The burner phone rang in the workshop and Zena answered it. Hans didn't identify himself but said in perfect English, 'I'm in my apartment. Completely secure. Because it's a burner phone, I presume you want something that is not strictly ethical?'

Zena told him the story of Campbell and Buchanan. Who had been killed and the fact that they had evaded the British police by hiding somewhere in Switzerland near Ormont-Dessus. She asked him if he could visit the area and see if he could locate them. Hans agreed to see what he could do. He hated killers of security officials whatever nationality they were. Then the conversation became more personal.

On Sunday afternoon, Catherine was in the bar reading a book. As people entered the hotel she just raised her eyes, checked them over and then returned to her book. Now she saw him. Casual but alert. Fit with large muscles concealed beneath a slightly too tight shirt. Hands moving freely by his side. Hair short that won't drop across his eyes. Footwear that wasn't the normal trainers but something slightly more solid. Trousers that were well fitting but allowing freedom of movement. A face that seemed to have a permanent smile etched across it. Tanned from Switzerland's summer sun. Eyes that seemed to skip easily from one person to the next. Seeing everything he was looking for.

Catherine shut her book. The wait was over. She knew a killer when she saw one.

Hans went to the bar and waved to the older barman. Then he leaned forward and spoke quietly. A low denomination Swiss franc note crossed the bar. Hans turned to walk away and bumped straight into Catherine who spilt her drink. He knew she hadn't been there seconds earlier. She'd been reading a book when he entered the bar. He was no slouch. She'd deliberately put herself in his way. He knew it. Why?

Speaking fluently in Italian, Hans apologised. Catherine was impressed. She apologised in Italian for being clumsy by getting in the way. Hans knew she wanted to speak to him and had gone about it in a classic way. He reciprocated in the classic way of offering to buy her a fresh drink.

They adjourned to her table. Each trying to way up the other. Hans knew the woman had obviously been there sometime. Was she waiting for him? Had Zena leaked some information? He was looking for two men, not a woman. He'd quickly assessed that she was a professional in his field of expertise and not a prostitute. She wasn't showing any sign that she fancied him. She'd quickly sussed him. Was she after them as well?

Catherine considered what to say. She didn't want to be too obvious in case she'd made a mistake. They danced around a conversation where each was trying to give a signal to the other. Then Catherine saw her opportunity. They'd somehow got onto travel. Oh, how long had it been since she'd visited Tenerife? Just before she'd gone to Scotland. Brig O'Turk in the Trossachs. Hans took the bait.

'Without wishing to insult your intelligence, you have obviously worked out who I am and what I am doing here. I have also come to the assumption that you may also be here for the same reason.'

Catherine was warming to Hans. She chuckled, 'I had to be sure. Campbell is a vicious killer. I had been considering dealing with him myself, but he is taking no chances.'

Hans understood. 'I'm here just to locate their exact position. Not kill them. I believe the people who have tasked me will make efforts to get them back to Spain or England.'

Catherine leant forward, 'Look. Pass my name, Catherine Russo, to the people who tasked you. They know who I am. I'll show you exactly where Campbell is. Have you a map?'

Hans flipped open a small paper map of the area. Catherine regarded it and with a pen put a small cross on it. 'That's where they are.'

Hans thanked her before enquiring, 'Why do you want them dead?'

'Personal.'

Hans was enjoying her company. His sparkling blue eyes danced. 'Good enough reason for me.' Then, 'My name is

Hans Weber. I am a ski instructor. I would like to visit the place tomorrow and see what it's like.'

Catherine looked at him enquiringly, 'You haven't always been a ski instructor?'

'No,' was all he said.

* * *

Groves was getting ready for Sunday evening's briefing. Officers were going to be attending from nearly every force in the UK. The chief was liaising with some of his counterparts. Security of the information was to be paramount. All of the premises had been photographed from the air by the Sussex and Surrey police helicopter who were apparently on training flights around the UK. That was the reason given if anyone asked. It was better than relying on the internet.

The Ageas Ballroom at Hampshire's cricket ground had been secured for the briefing due to its size. It would easily accommodate the eighty-seven team leaders and various chief constables or their deputies. The Sussex officers from the murder teams were already there, setting up seating and overhead projection equipment.

Cars began to arrive and were shown where to park. Their occupants were greeted by the chief constables of Sussex and Hampshire and then escorted to a side room where they could get refreshments. There were large amounts of braid on display. Every chief constable was aware of the artwork already recovered by Sussex Constabulary and wanted to know how much was within their beats. Groves soon had the meeting under way.

CHAPTER
FIFTY NINE

Throughout the UK on Monday morning at 5am, various police officers assembled at pre-determined locations. Team leaders briefed them as to why they were there, where they were going and what they were looking for. The majority of the officers had no idea about art except what they liked or disliked. They would seize every painting and sort it out later with an expert.

All had either read articles or seen TV reports about the artwork already recovered by Sussex police. They were told their searches were as a result of this. Some knew the people they were going to be visiting and their standing within society. When told their subjects were to be arrested, some looked at one another in bemused amazement. Each team leader finished their briefing by explaining that their people may be under surveillance or having their phones monitored.

A lot of chief constables hadn't been up so early for a long time. They were not going to miss an opportunity to see a successful raid conducted by their officers.

At 5am, rather a lot of rich people had rude awakenings. Doors were knocked on and some were broken down. From eighty-seven searches, eighty-three people were arrested and artwork recovered. There was no one at home in just four houses although paintings were recovered from each.

Two parliamentarians from different political persuasions tried shouting the odds but got nowhere. Bankers and chief executives from various establishments and even charities were introduced to an early morning call from their local police. Rich people whose source of wealth was from dubious means were also visited. All were arrested.

Lawyers were beckoned from their beds to attend police custody suites as their rich clients demanded their immediate presence. There would be no excuse for a tardy attendance.

When their lawyers demanded their clients be immediately released, the majority of prisoners were dumbfounded when the police refused. Hadn't the police heard of them? Didn't they know who they were? What did the police mean when they said they wanted to interview them? Their lawyers broke it to them gently. Most said nothing until they were charged. Then all hell broke loose when some were placed in cells. The sheer audacity.

Groves and some of his staff were recording the details supplied to them by the team leaders. Chief constables and other senior officers from around the country were celebrating their own officers' achievements. Press officers from constabularies and the Met were being summoned and told what had happened. Numerous media outlets were briefed. Several news reporters in large vans with roof-top antennas descended on the Hampshire County Cricket Ground.

Paintings were being removed from gallery walls and seized by the police with assorted paperwork. Curators were shocked to find out that some of the art hanging on their walls had been forgeries. Extremely good fakes, but fakes nevertheless.

Artwork recovered was valued by experts who were contacted by the press. All hoping for a bit of publicity as they tried to outvie each other's estimate. The early morning news channels were dominated by the raids and seizures. Many hours work was going to be required by designated officers and the CPS to prepare each case for court.

Groves broke away for a few minutes and updated John.

*　*　*

At 9am, Hans and Catherine left her room and went to his car. Catherine could not contain herself and burst out laughing when she saw it. An old, battered Renault with skis and poles strapped to the roof. 'Well, it's certainly inconspicuous around here. How does it get up and down the mountains?'

Hans laughed with her, 'Please don't insult Karl. He might sulk and break down.'

Amusingly, she claimed, 'You name your car? You are a very sad man.' Both got into the old car and she directed him. Within twenty minutes Catherine told him to pull in at a viewpoint. The vista in front of them was mainly of the mountains across a forested valley. She pointed to a large chalet lodge that was just visible amongst the trees. 'There. That's it. They are both there.'

Hans took out a specialist monocular and set it to record video before he scanned the area. It appeared there was just a track from the road that led up a slight incline to the chalet. He asked, 'How do they get supplies?'

Catherine knew. 'Delivery every Monday and Thursday. Same man in same van. Post is once a week on a Saturday.'

Hans looked cautiously at Catherine. 'If I were to do it, I'd get a lot closer with a good rifle. They can't stay indoors for ever.'

She agreed. 'Trouble is, there are various items scattered about that would give advance notice of anyone approaching the chalet. If Campbell got wind of someone, he would likely be out and deal with them.'

Hans gazed back at the chalet. Knowledge of the area would give Campbell the advantage. His mind was racing. You could never be sure of finding all the devices. Miss one and you might end up dead. He looked up at the mountains. There was no way that anyone could get to a reasonable position without being visible to the chalet. If Campbell was as good as everyone implied, it appeared that to get anywhere near him would be fatal.

Catherine watched him warily and could see what he was thinking. She had considered it all as well. 'What do you think?'

Hans was thoughtful. 'Some of those in England are very good. They would probably spend a few days in the forest clearing any devices they may find. They are not all nice and friendly,' and he winked at her, 'like me.' She smiled. 'How they would deal with Campbell would be down to them.'

He looked back through the monocular. He caught a glimpse of light reflecting from the side of the chalet. It was from the Rolls. A door had been opened and closed. Someone had got into it. He focused on the track. He might just be able to see into the vehicle. As the car travelled down the track towards the road he focused hard on one small section.

The car passed through his field of vision in a second. He was lucky to see even the car. He had no chance to see who was in it.

They got back into the Renault. Catherine confided, 'I can't get too close in case he recognises me. It's not that he's ever seen me but he may have a picture of me.'

Hans said, 'That's a serious problem for you.'

She already knew roughly what she was going to do.

CHAPTER
SIXTY

John was at home. He knew what had been planned. If it all went smoothly, the country would have an awfully large amount of genuine art restored to the correct gallery. There would be a lot of irate, rich prisoners shouting the odds via very expensive lawyers. Then they would all end up facing the same court.

The phone rang. No number in the display. Rocky or Zena. John answered. It wasn't a long call. What were they to do? No one from England could go anywhere near Campbell and the laird. John had the answer. 'Leave it to me.'

He sat still with a glass in his hand. Carol walked into the room and recognised the signs. She retreated quickly to the kitchen. He knew how to engineer a meeting. Would it be held against him? Possibly. Not if he explained it fully first. No time like the present. He picked up his phone.

'Hello. How may I help you?' A female voice and not who he expected. He hadn't misdialled.

'Would His Grace the Duke be there? My name is John Whiles and I'd like to come and see him.'

The woman was the duke's personal secretary. 'Hello Mr Whiles. I've heard a lot about you. Unfortunately, His Grace is not available today due to prior commitments. Would 10am tomorrow be suitable? He has a luncheon appointment at 1pm and can't afford to miss it. That should allow you sufficient time.'

John was agreeable. There was a lot to discuss. He drained his glass. What would the minister say? He dialled the number he had for her.

* * *

Catherine and Hans went skiing. They scanned the chalet from the mountain. If anyone saw them, they'd assume they were highly competent skiers. There were only black runs and no average skier would dare to take them on.

* * *

John was suited and booted with neatly pressed shirt and brand new tie from Hansfords men's outfitters of Chichester. He'd even polished his shoes and tried to comb his hair. Carol insisted he look his best. Now he was driving himself to the duke's personal entrance to the castle.

As he parked next to a government Range Rover, Watson sauntered out to meet him. John stepped out of the car and Watson beamed. He made no effort to conceal his enjoyment. 'A remarkable transformation Mr Whiles. Please follow me,' and he turned and strode off. Now John could keep up.

When they reached the lounge, the duke stood up and proffered a hand that John took. Watson, in a loud voice without shouting introduced, 'Mr Whiles,' and then much quieter but audible added, 'I think.'

A lady about thirty years of age and immaculately dressed was seated opposite the duke and had some book work on a side table. The duke introduced her as Susan, his private secretary. John walked to her and shook her hand. The Home

Secretary smiled and said, 'I heard the news yesterday and this morning. I was intrigued. Anything to do with you?'

John paused before settling in the chair he'd used when he had his pot-leg. 'Possibly,' he answered defensively. The duke waited as he sat down.

'Now Mr Whiles. To what do we owe this pleasure?'

'Something has occurred and I would like both your opinions as to what should be done. It is a longish story which started with the brutal murder of Brendan Slack. I am aware that the chief constable has kept Your Grace informed about a lot of the enquiries undertaken by the police. If I overlap with some, I apologise. I have information that the police are not yet aware of and therefore would ask that you please treat what I say as confidential.'

The duke looked at the Home Secretary, Susan and then back to John. 'Having been aware of what you have achieved in the past, I agree. I'm sure that you will inform the police at the relevant time.'

'I certainly will.' John looked at Susan and the Home Secretary.

Susan was desperate to hear what this man had to say. From what the duke had told her previously, she knew he could probably have information that would stir up a whole lot of trouble for a lot of people. She agreed readily to his confidentiality request. The Home Secretary nodded.

John started the story from the beginning. Everything. Why Brendan was murdered by Mike Calder and how it all revolved around a painting by Turner. How Lynne came to be murdered by Campbell and how the Spanish identified him so quickly. The discovery of Clifford Samsun and the murder of Hawthorne. The death of Mike Calder. All the stolen art and how it was acquired with the assistance of Jake. How Buchanan was found to have the Turner. The murders of NSL Delivery Service employees by Leonardo. The arrest, detention and murder of Guiseppe by his wife.

All three listened spellbound. The duke had believed he was aware of everything. The chief had kept him informed but only regarding basic details of Brendan's murder. The rest was a complete revelation to him. To Susan, it was what stories are made of. The Home Secretary was smiling. She knew John had been instructed not to involve himself in the police's enquiries. Reading between the lines, she saw his fingerprints all over it. She held her counsel.

John didn't make any reference to Rocky and various other of his associates. He mentioned Catherine as a source of information and flippantly revealed that she may try to kill Campbell. He glossed over how he came by certain facts. Then concluded his narrative by disclosing exactly where Campbell and Buchanan were in Switzerland and the problem it would cause the police in trying to extradite them.

Then he came to why he was seeking advice. He made reference to how many famous paintings the police had already recovered. The value of which was so high it was unimaginable. The embarrassment for certain establishments would be immense. People of standing would be hauled before the courts. And all the time, two men responsible were languishing in a large, beautiful, Swiss chalet.

John pronounced, 'I have always upheld the law. Some say with a cavalier attitude. I know that we will never see either Campbell or the laird face justice. They could be in

Switzerland for the rest of their lives. Extradition would be no problem for them. Even if the police got close to it, they'd be up and away somewhere else.'

He looked at the Home Secretary addressing his comment primarily to her. 'I cannot see how these two men can be lawfully returned to face justice,' and he paused for a second. 'But there might be a way.'

The Home Secretary started to chuckle as she replied, 'Oh. I wondered why I had been asked to come down to the country. I'm all ears, but I promise nothing.'

Susan was on the edge of her seat as the duke said, 'Get on with it man. Don't keep us in suspense.'

CHAPTER
SIXTY ONE

The Home Secretary considered it. There was nothing illegal in what he suggested. Theoretically, she supposed it could be classed as a case for the Foreign Secretary. But the artwork had been stolen in the UK. And then, what a feather it would be in her cap. She knew the right woman in Switzerland to speak to. They were both members of a small group of female politicians in Europe.

The duke was thoughtful. Rhetorically, he enquired quietly to himself, 'So, pictures in Sandringham and Balmoral can be privately owned and if they so pleased, they could be placed on display, or not. But the Royal Collection is held for the nation by the monarch. Yes. I knew all that.'

Susan was engrossed with a tablet computer. She'd found what she wanted. 'He's right. I like the fact about the Rolls Royce. I'm sure if the right person is approached, they'd have to be extradited. For a minor thing like that. So simple if one thinks outside the box.'

John sat passively looking around the room, wondering how it would all turn out. Watson entered and reminded the duke of his luncheon appointment. The duke was miles away, thinking of those he knew who could make a very discrete enquiry. Absently he asked for a coffee. Watson knew immediately to postpone lunch. He asked what the others wanted to drink before strolling from the room. Fifteen minutes later, he was back with a tray of cups and a couple of cafetières. John was still admiring the room. He'd not had time to do so before.

They had come to their respective decisions. The duke made a phone call before summoning Watson. 'Can you get the car. I need to go to Sandringham.'

The Home Secretary checked her phone's address book and pressed to dial a number. She spoke fluent French to her friend in Switzerland. The President of the Swiss Confederation. A post conferred yearly on one of the seven members of the Federation. Actually, although known as President, she was more commonly known by her true title, First Among Equals. The call lasted fifteen minutes.

At the conclusion of the call, she looked into the middle distance as she sipped her lukewarm coffee. Then she looked at John. 'That's going to cause a member of the Swiss Confederation some serious problems. Action is being taken immediately by their Federal Office of Police regarding the stolen painting and the Border Guard Corp are going to be visiting the chalet to arrest the two criminals.'

John wasn't sure what to say. 'I think the English police and others will be thankful.' He wanted to be clear on one point, 'You did warn her about Campbell being a skilful killer?'

She smiled ruefully as she affirmed, 'I did not mention my source of information and it wasn't asked for. The Swiss Federal Police will be acting on her information alone. Should the painting be discovered, it will be handed to our ambassador for restoration to its rightful owner.'

The members of this small group went their separate ways; Watson driving the duke and Susan to Sandringham; the minister was driven back to her London office and John drove home. He only had one more week off sick before returning to full time work at Scotland Yard. He considered what he should tell Groves. He had to update him. A quick phone call and John was off again.

* * *

No one paid them any attention. They sat nursing their second cups of coffee and nibbling pieces of cake in the Cube at the Edge café in Ford. Proper coffee with great taste. John had grown to dislike a lot of the varieties available elsewhere. He needed a proper fix of a decent brew to get his mind working. Furthermore, he needed some roasted coffee beans from the shop; Carol had ground so many recently and he'd drunk so much at home, he'd run out.

Groves had listened. Questions were gathering pace. 'Blimey Oscar. How the hell did you find them in the middle of a Swiss forest?'

John was reticent. 'I don't think you would really like the full answer. I didn't do anything illegal but suggested to some friends that I'd like to know where they might be. They managed to locate them and also noticed that the index plates on the Rolls had been changed from English to Swiss.'

Groves was a little worried. 'I can't write that down. I'd be crucified.'

John was confident. 'Don't write anything down. I'm led to believe the top person in the Swiss administration has also found this out. She has sent members of the Border Guard Corp to arrest them and deport them. To enter Switzerland in a vehicle bearing false index plates is illegal. No right of appeal.

Straight out. Either back here or to France who will also refuse them entry.'

Groves glared at John. 'If she is ever asked where the information came from, will she name you?'

John smiled. 'No of course not. She's never heard of me, and furthermore, who is going to question the top woman in Switzerland?'

Groves knew somehow that John had got the information to the woman. How he'd done it would have to remain a mystery. But then who cares. Campbell and Buchanan would soon be back to face justice.

* * *

In Switzerland, Campbell and Buchanan heard several loud bleeps and looked at the monitor in the lounge. Travelling along the track from the road was a blue people carrier with four persons inside. He checked his Russian made MP443 Grach semi-automatic pistol. He was ready. He told Buchanan to keep out of sight. The vehicle hove into view and stopped within a few yards of the front door. All four passengers got out. They were all wearing the same smart blue uniforms. And torso body armour! It meant nothing. Anyone could buy a disguise.

Campbell watched through the window as a woman took out a phone and photographed the Rolls Royce. Then there was a knock on the front door. He slipped the gun into a pocket and stuck his hand in and around the grip. He wasn't going to let go. In English he called out, 'Who is it?'

In a heavy accent he got an answer. 'Border Guard.

Campbell MacIntyre and Metcalf Buchanan. You are to be detained and deported to England for entering Switzerland illegally in a vehicle incorrectly marked.'

Campbell had noticed they were all wearing full holsters and each had a Taser that they kept their hands on. One actually had the Taser in his hand. They could be anyone. What should he do? If they were there to kill him, opening the door would be a mistake. If they were genuine, not opening the door might be a mistake. He needed to have an advantage. He ran through the chalet and out of the back door. Then following a short path, he ducked down and came out behind the four officers.

Campbell had his advantage. 'May I see some identification.'

They all began to turn around and one let a hand drop towards his sidearm. Campbell determined they weren't who they claimed to be. He pulled out his gun. All four watched him in horror. The person with the Taser was just slightly too far away to use it. The man with his hand close to his holster made a move to grab his own gun. He had no chance. Campbell fired before the gun had left its holster and the guard dropped to the floor. The others could do nothing. They couldn't see if he was alive or dead.

'Who sent you?'

The man who appeared to be in charge replied, 'We are Swiss Border Guards. You were to be deported,' and he looked at his fallen comrade. Then back at Campbell, 'Not now. You are a murderer. You face our court.'

'What's to stop me killing you?' There was a sudden sound from the undergrowth. Like a gentle whisper of wind. The bolt from the crossbow hit Campbell square in the back between his shoulder blades. The impact pushed him slightly off balance. His body shook and his hands dropped. The Border Guards saw their opportunity. They weren't taking chances with their Tasers anymore. All drew their firearms and fired. Bullets flew the few yards and slammed into Campbell's chest. He couldn't do anything. His arms were flailing and his body was dancing to a macabre tune. He finally fell.

Buchanan crept out of the back door. He was alone now. No one to look after him. Self-preservation was kicking in. Why the guards hadn't put someone round the back never occurred to him. Slowly he made his way to the Rolls. The guards were looking outwards towards Campbell, away from the house and the vehicle.

The engine started as he knew it would, well-nigh as the key turned. He was already in gear and floored the accelerator. The car hurtled forward. He was halfway along the drive before any of the guards could call for help. At the junction with the road, he turned left virtually on two wheels. He wasn't stopping for anyone. The road started to descend and he saw the speedometer was showing nearly a hundred. Way too fast. He knew there were bends coming up. He eased his foot gently down onto the brake. Nothing happened. Buchanan started to panic. He stamped on the brake. The car was going faster and faster as it gathered more pace downhill. He was struggling to keep it on the road.

The first two slight bends were negotiated, just. The third was nearly a thirty degree bend. The signs warned him. Slow Down! He couldn't. He saw the black and white chevrons giving him another warning. Buchanan knew the road. He kept stamping on the brake. He knew there was a long drop if he didn't make the bend. Why weren't the brakes working? What could he do?

The car smashed through the chevrons at a ludicrous speed. His life didn't pass before him because he was too busy screaming as the wheels of the Rolls left terra firma. Buchanan was only airborne for six seconds and then became part of a massive fireball as the car exploded on the jagged rocks in the ravine below.

The guards were concerned for their colleague and making sure that Campbell was no longer a threat. An ambulance and assistance were called for. None thought to check the undergrowth for their saviour. She'd already gone. Her trip through the forest to her firing position was easy. The cameras were exactly where she'd have placed them. Easily dodged.

As the Swiss authorities descended on the carnage at the chalet and the crash site, Catherine returned to her hotel. She was ready to leave and paid her bill. The noise of sirens was echoing and rolling around the mountains. Her car, a Mercedes was parked several streets away. She'd left the crossbow in the forest. She had no further use for it.

She needed a quick drink before she left. The barman saw her enter the bar and knew what she really liked. Vodka Russian. He poured a double and handed it to her as she sat on a bar stool. It was downed in one. She rose to leave but was handed another double. What the heck, she downed it. Then it was off to her car and she would disappear.

Hans returned to Gstaad and his work as a ski instructor. He'd been at the viewpoint and witnessed the arrival of the guards. He hadn't seen everything but enough. He'd caught a glimpse of Campbell and heard the reverberation of the first gunshot as it rolled around the area. Then he watched enthralled as Campbell seemed to be dancing as a volley of shots rang out. The noise of the gunfire died down and there was no further sign of Campbell.

Then, as Hans was about to leave, he saw the Rolls tearing along the track towards the road. He watched it swing violently onto the road and hurtle out of sight. No one was following it. He put his monocular away and got back into Karl. Slowly, he drove away. It wasn't long before he heard an explosion. He glanced towards the mountains and watched in horror as freshly fallen snow on one of them broke free and gathered pace as it slid down towards the forest in the valley. It was from the mountain where he and Catherine had skied.

Catherine drove off. She wasn't interested in joining her mother and little Leo at Lake Como. She had millions in her own bank accounts. She could go anywhere in the world she pleased. Zurich airport was her first point of call. She'd dump the car and catch a plane. Where to? Somewhere exotic. She'd never been to Rio. That'll do.

CHAPTER
SIXTY TWO

The president had called a member of the Swiss Federal Assembly. Yes of course he'd pop over and see her. As he arrived he was met by the police. He never got any further. He was arrested. In the vehicle he queried politely, 'What's it all about? I've stolen nothing.' They drove past the main police station.

'Where are you taking me?'

'To your house first. We need to collect a painting that doesn't belong to you.'

He didn't say anything else. He couldn't stop asking himself, how did she know? She'd never been to his house.

* * *

The Duke of Norfolk arrived at Sandringham and was met by the housekeeper. As refreshments were served the Surveyor of the Queen's Pictures arrived. He was flustered. He acknowledged the duke and was introduced to Susan. It was the first time the duke had ever spoken to him and he wasn't sure why. But why at Sandringham? He rarely came here. The duke briefed him as to why he'd requested his presence. He became even more flustered. They were soon being led to the dining room by the housekeeper.

The painting was hanging high up on the wall. It had been there, according to the housekeeper, for the last three years to her knowledge. It was cleaned once a year whilst in situ. They needed a stepladder. The housekeeper disappeared and soon returned with the maintenance man carrying a large wooden stepladder with handrails either side.

The surveyor had never seen or examined the painting previously. How did the duke get to hear about it? He wasn't going to question him. He climbed the ladder. He looked at the brush strokes. As they should be. He shone his little torch at the signature. Not sure. It didn't look quite right. It wasn't. Shit.

He climbed down the ladder. The first thing the duke said as his feet touched the floor, 'Well?'

'I need it off the wall to be sure. I need to have a really good look.'

Susan demanded, 'You must have formed an opinion?'

The surveyor didn't know what to say. Sit on the fence? Surely the best option. 'It could be a fake.'

The duke came to his rescue. 'I'm sure it's a fake. I hope within a couple of hours to be able to say so definitely. The genuine painting is being sought as we stand here. Once I know it's been recovered, our ambassador to Switzerland will let me know. Then we shall organise its repatriation to its rightful owner.'

Susan was a lot more stringent. 'Please arrange for that forgery to be taken off the wall.'

The duke and Susan went out to the car as Watson ran out after them. They needed to be back in Arundel tout de suite.

*　*　*

In Switzerland, the president listened to the report by the head of the Border Guard Corp. She cared little about Campbell or Buchanan. She was more concerned for the injured guard. He'd recover. All she needed now was a report from the head of the Federal Police. She didn't have to wait long. They'd recovered the picture from the man's lounge. It was on its way to her office. She made a phone call to the British Home Secretary.

*   *   *

The duke was updated. He informed the Surveyor of the Queen's Pictures. The fake was soon removed from the dining room wall. It left a clear outline of where it had been. It didn't really matter. It was the exact same size as the original which would soon be in its place. Catherine was too good to make a silly mistake like the wrong size.

Susan called John. He took the call. She practically concluded with "all's well that ends well." He didn't agree. Relations between the Swiss and the British were on a high but there was more to it. How did a painting that had been purchased privately get forged?

John called Groves and brought him up to speed. Groves updated his officers. He didn't disclose his source. Most didn't give two hoots about Campbell and Buchanan and what had befallen them. Alison privately hoped they both suffered. Groves updated the chief.

When it came to the painting, several officers began to wonder how it came to be forged. It had been purchased by an anonymous bidder at an English auction house. The ultimate owner was obvious when the forgery was discovered in Sandringham House. How did the original come to be in Switzerland?

Groves was only on the phone for twenty minutes. It all seemed to fit into place. The auction house took possession of the painting and then informed potential clients that the picture was to be auctioned. Then a month later, a catalogue was prepared with the painting's details including a thumbnail image. The picture was made available to be viewed by potential bidders prior to the actual auction. A lot of them took measurements and photographs.

The auction house had similar insurance cover to the museums. Sure enough, they had photographic evidence confirming the licence plates of the vehicle that collected it. NSL Delivery Services. As it was the responsibility of the purchaser to arrange transport and pay all fees, everything was concluded to the satisfaction of the auction house.

John listened as Groves told him the system of buying a painting from an auction house. He stayed silent. Groves waited for a response. Then it came. 'Does the auction house keep records of who viewed the painting and when?'

Groves was slightly indignant, 'I don't know. I didn't ask.'

'The forger had to be one of them. Catherine Russo perhaps?'

'All right, I'll ask. Anything else?'

'The anonymous bidder intrigues me. We know on whose behalf they were bidding. Jake would never have had such authority to bid at an auction. It would have to be someone quite high up. Maybe from the Palace or the museum.'

If Guiseppe had arranged for a forged copy of the painting

to be made, he must have known who was going to bid and how much for the original. So the bidder who represented the buyer must have also known about NSL Delivery Service. They would have arranged the transport and paid all the bills. Braithwaites would have been called into action. We need to know who the bidder is.'

Groves couldn't help himself, 'Every time I speak to you, you throw a spanner in the works. I'll see what I can do.' Then he asked mockingly, 'Anything else?'

John laughed as he said, 'If I think of anything, I'll let you know.' But something was still troubling him. How did Guiseppe find so many rich people willing to become thieves? How did he approach them? Or was it someone else who made the initial approach? No millionaire would entertain a person like Jake? John had both his feet up and a large glass of red wine on an occasional table. Who was the mystery bidder?

Groves spoke to Murray and Alison. 'We need to find out who the person was who did the bidding. Any ideas?' Alison believed she had an answer.

'Nearly every time a well-known piece of art goes for auction, there is a camera present. So if there is a record price bid, the auction house gives a copy to the press. It's good publicity for them. Perhaps there was a camera present the day it was sold.'

Groves cocked his head. 'You thought of it. Can you please see what you can find out?'

John knew who he was going to ask. The duke could ask the Palace. He agreed to do it. They were already aware that he had discovered the forgery. How, didn't concern them. Anything to help him restore the original to its correct owner was their goal. The Surveyor of the Queen's Pictures was asked. He didn't know. His predecessor had been in post at the time of its purchase.

The duke's contact at the Palace considered the question. How could he find out who was the bidder? The Palace archives. Details of all purchases were recorded. The man said, 'I'll call you back,' and the line went dead. He ran to the archives. A few minutes later he was back on the phone.

'Hello Your Grace. For the last twelve years, should any painting be sought as a private acquisition, the same person is called upon. Firstly to confirm the painting's provenance and estimated value. Secondly to bid for it anonymously on behalf of which ever member of the household requests it. His name is shown as Nicholas Gulstrum. A chief curator of the British Museum.' The duke thanked him profusely. Then they discussed a couple of other matters unrelated to paintings.

John called Groves. 'Got a name for you. Nicholas Gulstrum. A curator at the British Museum. He is the anonymous bidder. Jake's boss. Looks like they could be in it together.'

'Cheers Oscar. Alison has recovered some CCTV from the auction house. I'm sure when it's viewed, it'll show him. When it does, I'll get him nicked asap. We have interviewed him already and it looks like he pulled the wool over the officer's eyes. I don't suppose you'll tell me how you found out?'

'A lucky guess?'

Groves chuckled, 'I hope the information is better than that!'

CHAPTER
SIXTY THREE

Gulstrum was in his snug office. He took the call from the security officer housed at the entrance to the museum. Should he make a run for it? Where would he go? He had a bank account tucked away in the Cayman Islands with just short of three million pounds. Not much really nowadays. His wife didn't know. The police would never find it. All the details were in his head. Nothing written down.

He was too old. Sixty-nine. He knew he looked much older. He'd face the music. What would he get? A few years if he was lucky at his age. The judge might take pity on him. When he'd spoken to that copper with the stupid cravat, he was telling the truth most of the time. Brendan Slack was a good friend. Why the hell did they have to kill him? He'd never done anything bad in his whole life.

Someone rapped on the door. Reluctantly he called out, 'Come in.'

A security officer from the museum and three detectives walked in. The lead officer, DC Copeland said, 'Nicholas Gulstrum. I am arresting you for Conspiracy to Steal, Theft and Handling Stolen Goods.' Then he cautioned him. Gulstrum answered, 'I shall answer any questions. I am guilty. Would someone please pass me my coat. I feel the cold terribly.' He was escorted back to Chichester Custody Suite in a warm police car.

Gulstrum declined a lawyer, declaring that he was going

to tell the truth and admit his guilt. His interview was to be videotaped, and again he didn't object. He had decided to hold nothing back. He was going to be candid in answering every question. Naming names, places and paintings but he'd keep quiet about his bank account in the Caymans. It was to have been his little nest egg for when he eventually retired. Now he considered it as his prison release fund.

The interview began with the customary caution, and identification of those present. Then the officers began their questions. They started at the beginning and listened carefully to every answer. Breaks were taken at regular intervals. As the interview progressed, details were relayed to Groves. Some of the answers given were revelatory. At the interview's conclusion, Gulstrum was asked if he wished to add any additional information. He considered his answer.

'No thank you. I think I have explained everything. If anything else occurs to me, I shall let you know.'

Nicholas Gulstrum was taken to a cell. He was feeling buoyant and slightly lightheaded. His pulse was racing. He could feel it. He knew it would settle down. It always did. The interview had been tiring and stressful. He considered what he had said. Lying down on the thin blue mattress, he felt satisfied. He needed a nap. Wrapping his thick coat around himself and pulling the thin blanket up, he drifted off to sleep. He wasn't going to wake up ever again.

An hour passed before the gaoler opened the cell door to offer him a drink. He summoned a doctor but knew it was way too late. The murder team's office was contacted and Groves informed. He told his officers at the evening's briefing. The only comment passed was, 'at least he wasn't murdered.'

Everyone was grateful for that.

* * *

Lunchtime the following day found John enjoying the sun in the courtyard of The Edge café in Ford. He had already finished his cup of coffee and was considering a second. Leaning back in his chair he contemplated the remnants of his cake. To get up and order another coffee and cake would be much too strenuous an activity. He'd only intended to buy more roasted coffee beans. He closed his eyes. Would they wake him if he dozed off?

His phone rang and vibrated in his pocket. Pulling it out he answered. Groves was on way to update him. John knew he'd get another coffee when he arrived. Closing his eyes again didn't help. The phone call had seen to that.

John listened intently as Groves briefed him as to what Gulstrum had said. 'He was originally approached by Giuseppe Russo who put a proposition to him. Russo had somehow found out that rich patrons, who donated money to the museums, were often given private access to the galleries. For each rich patron that Gulstrum told him about, Giuseppe paid him two thousand pounds.'

John whistled. 'Wow. Not bad.'

Groves continued, 'Yeah but even better, Gulstrum reckoned over the years he'd given Giuseppe several hundred names in total. The majority were not even rich donors, but just people who had come to Gulstrum's attention from his work in the museums.'

John jumped in with a thought, 'Was Jake doing the same?'

'Gulstrum was adamant. He claimed he didn't know about Jake's involvement.'

John considered the numbers, 'Several hundred names. The vast majority were obviously not interested in stolen paintings or becoming criminals. I wonder how Giuseppe approached them. How did he distinguish which people were likely to take a gamble and become thieves. What if he approached one who was honest and they took umbrage and reported the fact. Well, Giuseppe would likely have been caught years ago. We'll never know unless one of your prisoners spills the beans.'

Groves concurred and added contemplatively, 'Another thing. Gulstrum claimed that occasionally rich acquaintances or patrons of the museums would ask him to give an estimate of a painting's worth. They would request that their details remain confidential. Because he was trusted, they would ask that he represent them in any auction by bidding on their behalf.' Groves took a mouthful of coffee.

'John. Gulstrum told the interviewing officers that Giuseppe would give him five thousand if he named who he was representing. If he could tell Giuseppe what figure he could bid up to, he'd get another thousand. He claimed that had happened no more than twenty times.' Groves paused. 'Now it gets a lot more complicated.' He paused again and took a mouthful of coffee.

'The officers from the Arts and Antiques Squad believe that an accomplice of Giuseppe would approach other likely bidders and coerce, or blatantly threaten them into dropping out of bidding. Then Giuseppe, or his accomplice would approach the buyer Gulstrum was representing and point out they'd face no competition during the auction and get the painting for a lot less than they were expecting to bid up to. Then he would try to either recoup his outlay or just recruit them as corrupt buyers in the future. More an investment as it were.'

John followed the logic but was struggling with the maths. He quickly gave up, accepting that it would amount to a lot of money. Then a thought occurred to him, 'How did he get to deal with NSL Delivery Services?'

Groves chortled. 'So simple really. When he was the winning bidder, it fell upon him to arrange the full payment to the auction house from a secure bank account, and then arrange the painting's insurance and transport to the new owner. Guiseppe told him to use Braithwaites to transport the paintings. Out of those twenty odd paintings he bid for, he claimed to have won sixteen. He gave all the buyers details and what pictures they bought. He had a remarkable memory.'

John understood but one slight problem intrigued him. 'Any idea what Guiseppe did with the forgeries he had made for the four losing bids?'

'Gulstrum wasn't privy to that. The interviewing officer asked but Gulstrum didn't know. I think he was mainly commissioned to work for foreign buyers. People who might have attracted unwelcome attention if it became common knowledge that artwork would be moving abroad.'

There was a pause in the conversation. Groves expected a further comment from John and waited for it. 'What did he do with all the money he made?'

'We didn't find much at his house. Just a normal joint bank account with his wife. I've got a couple of financial investigators looking into where it might have gone. He couldn't have spent it all without some outward sign, but there's nothing out of the ordinary. He probably stashed it all away somewhere.' He paused as though ready to change the subject.

'Our lip reader was of minimal help. She saw Brendan tell the assistant curator that the Turner was a forgery and he would inform the museum at the earliest opportunity. We can't confirm either way if he did or didn't. The phone records don't show us.' He drained his mug and continued, 'Talking of phone records, Gwendoline and the laird had Guiseppe's phone number in their contacts lists on their phones.'

John considered everything. He didn't have any more questions. He stood up and asked, 'Coffee for the road?' Groves nodded.

As John returned with yet two more coffees, Groves was happy. 'Well Oscar. It looks like we've come to the end of the enquiry. Now it's just topping and tailing all the prisoners. We are sorting out the paperwork and maintaining a watching brief at each of the court appearances. Galleries and various museums are getting their genuine pictures and we are collecting the forgeries. It looks like the majority of those charged will lose their exalted positions in society and have to pay astronomical fines and some will no doubt end up in prison. Another week and we'll be going after those that wanted paintings but never actually got one. There's a lot of them.'

John thought of one last question that he considered important. 'Have you any idea where Francesca, Leonardo and Catherine might be?'

'None. Francesca and Leonardo were both traced back to Italy where they have just disappeared. They could be anywhere. Probably using false names. There are international arrest warrants for them but I doubt if they'll ever be executed. Catherine just disappeared after she told you she would. We believe she was the forger but can't really prove it. She's got away with whatever she's done as nothing can be proved against her.'

John smiled. He knew she had to have been the forger. Whatever else she'd done would remain a mystery.

All he could think of saying was, 'Interesting.'

Groves pulled a folded piece of paper from his jacket pocket and handed it to John. 'Something on a different vein. The chief has had a letter from the Palace thanking us for assisting the duke and Home Secretary in recovering a picture in Switzerland. I noticed the details were on the list I gave you. We had no part in that. Do you know anything about it?'

John laughed, 'Are you kidding? I don't know anyone in Switzerland. Seems like a good result though.'

Groves smiled. He knew John would never give him a straight answer if he had any involvement. He had one other question he had to ask. Would he get a straight answer? Unlikely. But he had to ask. 'The chief was summoned to London to see the Home Secretary who briefed him on the circumstances of the deaths of Campbell MacIntyre and Metcalf Buchanan. Again, in Switzerland. She never told the chief how the Swiss became aware of their location. Any ideas where that information might have come from?'

John laughed raucously, 'I can honestly say, I didn't tell

them,' and he laughed again.

Groves knew. He read between the lines. John probably didn't tell them. Somehow, he got someone else to tell them. Campbell and Buchanan had not faced a court of law. Groves didn't really care. Their fate had been sealed in Switzerland. Serves the bastards right!

Groves believed he had the answer to the last piece of the puzzle. He drank his coffee and launched into the details. 'Something that was worrying the Arts and Antiques Squad has finally been solved. Some of the prisoners have talked, probably hoping for a more lenient sentence as a result. They've answered the question: how come this never came to light before. For instance, when a painting was lent out by the museum for an art exhibition, Jake arranged the transport. Well, we both know that he was likely to use Braithwaites.'

Then he continued his narrative. 'Most of the main art exhibitions are for a reasonable amount of time. Normally twelve months or so. Some are a lot longer. At the exhibition's conclusion, the art work has to be returned to the museum. If it had been swapped for a forgery when it had been delivered, the experts at the museum would likely as not notice it wasn't the original on its return.' He slurped his latte.

'Now we know they were given back the original ,' and he burst out laughing.

John wasn't surprised. It was something that had occurred to him. 'Now that is very interesting.'

Groves added with a large smile, 'They just reversed the procedure using the security vehicle from Braithwaites. When the original painting had been purchased from Giuseppe that was due back at the museum, Braithwaites transported it and replaced the forgery with the original. Giuseppe actually gave the criminal who had bought it from him a discount. It was as if that person was renting it for a set time period.' Groves started to laugh.'

John saw the funny side and laughed with him.

Groves could hardly hide his enjoyment of the revelation. Still sniggering with tears in his eyes, he added, 'If the painting was to be lent out by the museum in the future, the buyer that Giuseppe had originally sold it to was offered it at a third of what they paid originally.' He couldn't contain his amusement. 'What a bloody shrewd business man he was.' He wiped away the tears of mirth that rolled down his cheeks.

John smiled as Groves composed himself. Then a rhetorical question that John had asked himself before slid to the front of his mind. 'Giuseppe must have had somewhere secure where he kept all the forgeries. Can't see any of those in custody having any idea where that would be.'

Groves didn't really care. As far as he was concerned, no one could answer John's question. Maybe one day someone would stumble across them. Probably a dog walker. They seemed to find everything.

John was sanguine. 'When you think of what your team has discovered over the last couple of months, it's a great epitaph for Brendan Slack. Without his death, one wonders how long they would have kept going in their criminal endeavours?'

Both sat in the afternoon sunshine nursing their coffees deep in their own thoughts.

CHAPTER
SIXTY FOUR

Jimmy was speaking without a lisp. He'd been given the all clear by the doctors after a month. His cheek had virtually healed. Two months had passed and he'd practically said nothing in all that time. Just to make sure. No chance of titanium rods now and definitely no scars. Amber was looking after him when she wasn't working and he looked forward each day to her return from work. They'd lived together in his terraced house in the centre of Chichester from the first week they'd met.

He only had eyes for her. She only had eyes for him. Besides nursing him, she ran his house more efficiently than he did and turned out to be a really good cook. They were in love. They'd even met each other's parents. Something he had declined with any of his previous girlfriends. In fact, Amber was the only girlfriend who had survived for more than a fortnight! He'd even introduced her to Damien and Roland. They could see it was a serious relationship.

Jimmy was back at work. He had all the exhibits to sort out relating to the murder of Brendan Slack and subsequent incidents. It would keep him busy for the best part of a fortnight. Groves and the team had moved on to another enquiry and Jimmy wouldn't have to say much as he'd be working alone mainly. His facial exercises were conducted rigorously every hour as he contorted his face into strange shapes. Amber was his driving force. He loved her.

* * *

Matteo had been a member of the Italian Carabinieri for most of his working life. But he had become old and slow due to a recurring knee complaint. Because he only had a year and a few months left before he drew his pension, the hierarchy let him move to a judicial office in Como. He rode an old, police Moto Guzzi motorcycle and delivered summonses to transgressors of road signs. His uniform was that of a police traffic officer. And like all, he carried a sidearm. It had never once left its holster in anger.

On Monday morning, he was handed his week's work. Over sixty summonses to be served. He knew it wasn't going to be taxing. If it rained, he'd seek shelter in a café until it stopped. He'd never once got wet. Like a true policeman. Then when the sun shone, he rode the roads of Italy around Lake Lugano and Lake Como. He loved his job.

He headed to the western side of Lake Como where the driver of a red Alfa Romeo was to be served with a summons for failing to stop at a junction. He needed to ascertain the driver's name and examine his licence. The person could then either pay a small fine, if they accepted responsibility, or elect to go before a court. Nothing serious. Most people paid up straight away. The vehicle was registered to a Leonardo Rossello.

Matteo pootled along the side of the lake. The view was breathtaking. He kept glancing across the still water at a couple of ferries that were plying their trade, crossing back and forth disgorging passengers and collecting new ones. He'd have to cross the lake later and would use one of the ferries.

He arrived at the registered address of the Alfa Romeo's owner. A pleasant villa with a boathouse to one side and a twin garage to the other. He judged it to have at least seven bedrooms. The Alfa was next to a silver Mercedes on the hard standing in front of the garages. Yes. They'll obviously pay up straight away. He put the motorcycle on its stand and opened a pannier. Fishing about in it, he found his receipt book.

Returning towards Como along the coast road were a couple of marked Carabinieri people carriers. They'd been on a training exercise at the north end of Lake Como with the marine unit. The driver of the lead vehicle saw Matteo and recognised him. He put all his emergency lights on and set the siren off. Matteo looked up, waved cheerfully, and laughed. Inside the villa Leonardo heard the noise and looked out through a window. He was shocked. Two Carabinieri carriers and a police motorcyclist waving at them apparently to go around the house.

He yelled to his mother in a panic, 'The police are surrounding the place. They've found us. There's vehicles outside. What shall we do?'

Francesca had thought that one day they would be found. Today's the day. The longer they had been there the safer she had felt. She would easily delay them. She knew what she had to do. She had to save her son. He had a lot of his life left. Her's was nearing an end.

'You know what we agreed. Don't panic. Get to the boat. You know where the car is hidden. Get in it and disappear.' Leonardo didn't really care much for his mother, or anyone else for that matter. Making an effort, he ran to her, kissed her on the cheek and ran to a side door leading to the boat house. There was just the one speedboat in it. He jumped in and sat behind the steering wheel. As he turned the ignition key the twin engines fired up.

Matteo heard the noise and started to stroll towards the boat house. Then he heard the unmistakeable sound of a gunshot from inside the villa. A window broke beside the front door as the bullet whizzed through it and disappeared harmlessly into the undergrowth at the side of the road. Nowhere near him. What the hell is happening? The boat hurtled out of the boat house onto the lake. Matteo ran back to his motorcycle. He'd never used the radio and now he was yelling down it for backup.

Another gunshot. Matteo automatically ducked down. This time a picture window broke. The bullet flew off harmlessly like the first. They were nowhere near him.

Several more bullets were fired aimlessly through the picture window. Then there was the sound of yet another gunshot. But no bullet left the villa. No more bullets. Quiet.

Matteo crept forward. It didn't occur to him to draw his own weapon. He looked cautiously through the broken window next to the front door. Nothing visible. Then he moved to the broken picture window to what appeared to be a reception room. Francesca was lying on the floor. He saw the gun next to her and an ever increasing, red pool of blood. He ran back to his motorcycle and updated the control room who were trying to work out who he was. They'd not heard his call sign before.

His old colleagues had heard his call and were rushing back to help him. They knew who he was.

Leonardo looked back at the villa as the speedboat was swiftly skimming across the lake. He'd soon be the other side and away. He couldn't see the Carabinieri carriers. Where the hell were they? His mother was going to kill herself to divert their attention. He couldn't see any police personnel. They'd probably all gone inside the house. She must be dead by now.

As he turned to see how much further he had to go, the boat clipped a mooring buoy. The speedboat took off and did a slow half barrel roll and landed upside down. It pinned Leonardo under the water. His legs were trapped under the steering wheel. He struggled frantically to free himself. Then he tried to force his head above the water around the side of the boat but couldn't. He needed air. He wasn't going to drown. He was too young. Too rich.

He felt hands pulling at him. Someone was trying to save him. Thank God. If only they would hurry up. He couldn't hold his breath much longer. Several hands were pulling at him. They managed to get his head above the water into the fresh air. He took a large gulp of the precious oxygen as he looked at his rescuers.

They were in a large powerful boat. It was full of Carabinieri. They'd finished their weekly exercise and were returning to their base in Como itself. He didn't care. One of the officers dived, fully clothed, into the lake's still water. He carried a set of bolt cutters which he used to cut off the steering wheel. Leonardo could move his legs. The hands were still holding his head above the water.

Leonardo wriggled free and was unceremoniously yanked aboard the large boat. His mind was working overtime although he'd nearly drowned. How do I get out of this mess? The officer on the Carabinieri's boat contacted the control room and they married it up with Matteo's report. They wondered what it was all about? Why did he try to escape from Matteo? He was only going to serve a summons.

Detectives were soon swarming all over the villa. They

were trying to make sense of what had happened. Matteo couldn't help. Leonardo was taken to Como and arrested. They weren't sure why but he wasn't going to be released until it was all sorted out.

It took them two days. Leonardo screamed for a lawyer. He had to be free. Then he could disappear. But they wouldn't let him out. Why did they want photographs and fingerprints?

The Italian police circulated them. They soon discovered the international arrest warrant. Discussions were had between the British and Italians. Art experts flocked to the villa. Paintings were delicately removed from walls. Galleries and private collectors were contacted. It soon became a media circus.

Three months later, Leonardo's knuckles were turning white as he gripped the rail of the dock with both hands in number one court at the Old Bailey. His expensive English lawyer had told him to plead guilty to the two murders of the Braithwaites' employees. He told him the judge would look favourably on him if he did. Leonardo knew better. 'Not guilty, My Lord!'

The trial didn't last long. He didn't have much of a defence. The jury didn't believe a word of his arguments. They were out for less than three hours before returning their unanimous verdict of guilty on both counts of murder. The judge definitely didn't look on him favourably. Life imprisonment with a minimum of thirty years.

Leonardo collapsed to the dock's floor. His brain in overdrive. He wouldn't get out until he was in his seventies at the earliest. About as old as his parents were when they both died. Shit!

* * *

Amber got home from work and found Jimmy dressed immaculately. He told her of a really good result at court and he wanted to celebrate with her. She dressed smartly and they walked arm in arm to Blanc's restaurant. No expense spared. Jimmy was happier than ever. He could talk freely and eat whatever he wanted as long as it wasn't too chewy. No point in pushing his luck.

When they arrived at the restaurant, Maurice led them to a large, round table beautifully laid and decorated. A long table stretched away from it. All laid for a group of twenty people. They were already seated. Amber recognised her friends and Jimmy saw his. He'd spent nearly a week organising the event.

Amber looked at him enquiringly. Before she could ask what was happening, he slid from his chair and dropped to one knee and asked her the question.

The applause of their friends was taken up by the staff and other diners.

THE END

GLOSSARY

POLICE RANKS

PC	Police Constable
DC	Detective Constable
PS	Police Sergeant
DS	Detective Sergeant
Insp.	Inspector
DCI	Detective Chief Inspector
Supt.	Superintendent
Chief Supt.	Chief Superintendent
Commander (Metropolitan)	Commander
DCC (Constabulary)	Deputy Chief Constable
ACC (Constabulary)	Assistant Chief Constable
DAC (Metropolitan)	Deputy Assistant Commissioner
CC (Constabulary)	Chief Constable
Commissioner (Metropolitan)	Commissioner

ABBREVIATIONS

Airwave	Police Radio System
ANPR	Automatic Number Plate Reader
Asp	Modern Extendable Baton
Black Rat	Traffic Officer

Box 500	MI5
C	Head of MI6
CO	Commissioner's Office: aka New Scotland Yard
CO19	Firearms Unit
CODEC	Computer Programme
Church	Customs and Excise
CPS	Crown Prosecution Service
CRO	Criminal Records Office
Door Bosher	Hand Held Battering Ram
FME	Force Medical Examiner
GCHQ	Government Communications Headquarters
HA	Home Address
HOLMES	Home Office Large Major Enquiry System
India '9 9'	Call sign of Police Helicopter
IPCC	Independent Police Complaints Commission
IR	Information Room at New Scotland Yard
JTAC	Joint Terrorism Analysis Centre
MIT	Major Investigation Team
MOD	Ministry of Defence
MP	Member of Parliament
Plasticuffs	Thin Plastic Handcuffs
PM	Post Mortem
PNC	Police National Computer
PoLSA	Police Search Advisor

PPS	Parliamentary Private Secretary
RO	Registered Owner
SAS	Special Air Service
SB	Special Branch
SBS	Special Boat Service
SIO	Senior Investigating Officer
SIS	Secret Intelligence Service (MI6)
SOCO	Scenes of Crimes Officer
The Job	Metropolitan Police Publication
The Met	Metropolitan Police
The Yard	New Scotland Yard
Trojan	Specialist Firearms Officers
TSG	Tactical Support Group
USB	Universal Serial Bus (Storage Device)
'4 2'	Surveillance Motorcyclist
5	MI5
6	MI6